RAVIK'S MERCY

Braxians - Book 2

REGINE ABEL

CONTENTS

READING ORDER

The Braxians series is part of the Veredian Chronicles universe. While this book can be read as standalone with a complete romance arc and no cliffhanger, to fully enjoy the overarching story, it is recommended to read both series in the following order:

1. Escaping Fate, Veredian Chronicles 1
2. Blind Fate, Veredian Chronicles 2
3. Raising Amalia, Veredian Chronicles 3
4. Anton's Grace, Braxians 1
5. Twist of Fate, Veredian Chronicles 4
6. Ravik's Mercy, Braxians 2
7. Hands of Fate, Veredian Chronicles 5
8. Krygor's Hope, Braxians 3
9. Defying Fate, Veredian Chronicles 6
10. Keran's Dawn, Braxians 4

RAVIK'S MERCY

For Braxia. For the future. For revenge.

As the rarest hybrid in the galaxy, Mercy has been forced to hide in plain sight for fear slavers and collectors would hunt her down. Quite ironic, considering her late father had been the greatest slaver of the Guldan Empire. Determined to make amends for some of the wrongs he has done, she goes on a mission to Braxia. But those plans are quickly derailed when she encounters Ravik; a mountain of a man with a fearsome face, and a planet in turmoil...

As the new ruler of Braxia, Ravik is surrounded by enemies. His planet is teetering on the brink of bankruptcy and stuck in ancient, bigoted ways. When an exotic, sassy, and strong female reluctantly accepts his protection during her stay on Braxia, she becomes both his strength and his greatest weakness. As his detractors plot and scheme against him, Ravik fears the horrors of his past will destroy the fragile happiness and glimmer of hope this woman has brought him and his people...

In this brutal, unforgiving world, greed, hatred, and twisted obsessions will clash in a bid for power, for the future, and for revenge!

This dark romance is not for the faint of heart. It contains explicit scenes of violence. Sensitive readers please abstain.

DEDICATION

To Nero. This book wouldn't have seen the light of day without you. Thanks for always being there for me whenever my Muse keeps flipping me the bird and takes one of her countless leaves of absence. You're not only an awesome friend and a great inspiration, you possess the best shoulder to cry on, and know just how to kick me out of my wallowing in self-pity.

To all the fans who clamored for Ravik's and Mercy's story. You lit the fire under me that kept me going. I hope this novel will live up to your expectations.

Much love.

WARNING

Ravik's Mercy is a dark romance intended for readers over the age of 18. This book uses mature language and contains explicit sexual content, dubious permission and graphic violence that may be disturbing to some people. If you are a sensitive reader then this book isn't for you.

Otherwise, welcome to Braxia!

~Regine Abel

PROLOGUE
RAVIK

My fingers itched to crush Hagan Soluk's skull. If he knew the depth of the hatred I still bore him and the seven survivors among the Fifteen, he wouldn't be stoking my ire any further with his endless sniveling.

"Enough!" I shouted, slamming my fist on the arm of my throne while seething with anger. The slapping sound against the white stone and polished bones of my seat echoed through the large hall. "This isn't open for debate. I have no patience for your whining and complaining."

My gaze roamed over the Council; twelve men, four of whom I would kill in the worst possible way at the first opportunity. Each one of them, leaders of their respective clans, would appear intimidatingly powerful to a non-Braxian. To me, most of them were no more than worms I would gladly crush underfoot. They shifted in their white stone seats laid out in a half circle before me. Behind them, their firstborn sons and respective Clan Elders sat in attendance. My own two sons, Keran and Ganek, sat on each side of my throne.

"You've had three years for the transition. Why the fuck are you not ready?" I demanded.

"Demand has been steadily declining for most of our exports,"

Hagan argued, "and the prices of imports have soared. With slave labor, we could still manage. But since the abolition, we've been drowning."

Four of the twelve councilmen nodded with mumbled words of approval.

"You're drowning because you didn't adapt," said Krygor Aldriss, dismissively. "My son gave you and the others plenty of advice on how to diversify your business and provided you with potential fields to grow into. You *chose* to ignore his recommendations. Now, you pay the price."

Hagan's dark-brown eyes burned with anger and resentment as they turned towards Krygor. "I will not have my clan beholden to your half-breed!" Hagan said, spitefully. "All of his so-called *suggestions* would put us and our fates under his thumb. I would see my clan starve rather than bow before one such as him."

Krygor leaned back against his chair, a lock of his long, salt-and-pepper hair dropping in front of his pitch-black eye. "Well then, it looks like you're in the process of getting your wish."

Smug bastard...

I fought to repress a smirk. Krygor, leader of Clan Aldriss, was one of only three men I fully trusted on my Council—with my life.

"Half-breed or not, Anton Aldriss has brought great prosperity to all of us who followed his advice or entered into business agreements with him," intervened Elder Pattel Veelan, another trusted friend. "Times aren't changing, Hagan. They have *already* changed, and Braxia is being left behind."

"Then Braxia needs to retake its leadership role rather than kneel to off-worlder rules," Hagan snapped, earning himself more nods and whispers of approval.

"And how will we do that, you fool?" I asked, fed up with having the same, pointless arguments for months. "Every civilized planet in the Eastern Quadrant has joined the Galactic Council. Their rules for membership are clear. Why are we still talking about this? The Great Wars have ended. Non-contractual slavery is over. Science and trade are the future. I will not have you further waste my time rehashing these tired, old complaints. Braxia *will* evolve into modern times, even if I have to beat it into our people."

"Not all planets have joined the Galactic Council," Clan Leader Raylor Caldes said in a measured tone. "The Sarenians refused."

"Pariahs," I countered, waving a dismissive hand. "Their predatory nature violates countless edicts of the Galactic Council."

"Maybe so, but they would make powerful allies. Between them and the few rogue planets in our Quadrant, we would have a formidable alliance," Caldes continued. "The Western Quadrant also has a number of planets that haven't joined the Council. Among them, one that is quite keen to form an alliance with us."

"Oh?" asked Hagan, his eyes sparkling with interest.

Raylor Caldes nodded. "Yes. The Guldans are also seeking allies to oppose the Galactic Council's tyranny. They are extremely wealthy, highly technologically advanced, and possess an impressive network of mercenaries."

"And have made enemies of the Tuureans," said Elder Fenton, my best friend. "The Guldans are almost completely isolated in the Western Quadrant. They are under more embargos and retaliatory measures than you have hair on your head. Whatever benefits we might reap from such an alliance would pale in comparison to the massive losses we would sustain in a war against the Galactic Council."

"If we are to make alliances," Krygor said, "the Tuureans are the ones we should pursue. In fact, my son Anton happens to be friends with their leader, Admiral Lee."

"Again with that fucking half-breed," Hagan muttered so low I barely heard him.

"Is there something you would like to share with the rest of us, Clan Leader Soluk?" Krygor asked Hagan. "If you wish to issue a challenge, I will eagerly accept."

Krygor waved at the empty, circular space between their seats and my throne, where innumerable duels had taken place. The stone tiles covering the floor of my Hall had taken an even darker tone over the years from the countless times blood had been spilled over them.

Hagan stirred uncomfortably in his chair and rolled his broad shoulders. His flat nose twitched as he shook his head. Like all Braxians, he was massive and muscular, a giant by galactic standards. Yet, he looked scrawny in comparison to Krygor, who was only slightly smaller than me. Unlike Krygor, Pattel, and myself, Hagan didn't come from a warrior clan. All of those in his bloodline were smaller than ours. Unless he appointed a champion to fight in his stead, Hagan would get crushed by someone like Krygor. As much as I would enjoy my friend breaking a few of his limbs, Hagan would die by my hand.

Raylor cleared his throat, stirring the attention away from Hagan who failed to hide his relief.

"The Tuureans do not share any of our interests," Raylor said with disdain. "Quite the opposite. They've destroyed one of the Guldans' largest slave breeding empires, and they make it nearly impossible for anyone to pursue any type of flesh trade in the Western Quadrant. The Guldans are looking to establish a new network here, in the Eastern Quadrant, to trade both slaves and technology. Magnar Ravik, they could be the perfect partners to take us into that new era you speak of, while allowing us to maintain our way of life."

"The topic of slavery is closed and will not be reopened," I said in a tone that brooked no argument. "Indentured servants are the only type of slaves that will be allowed on Braxia, and their contracts of servitude will be registered in the Hall of Records with a start date, end date, and detailed terms. Remember that this rule becomes effective next week. You are all responsible for ensuring it is enforced within your own clans, or you'll be fined along with the offenders."

From the bitter and resentful looks aimed at me, I already knew which clans would be paying heavy fines.

"Will you not at least speak with the Guldans?" Raylor insisted.

I sighed in irritation. "I will speak with them about potential technology trade agreements, but that is all."

Raylor pursed his lips in displeasure but gave me a sharp nod.

"Change is hard, but the sooner you stop fighting the inevitable, the better off we will all be," I said in a conciliatory tone. "You are the leaders of the Elder Clans and those who must set the example. However painful this process may be for all of you, personally and otherwise, remember what dark times we've emerged from. Braxia was on the verge of bankruptcy. Without these changes, and yes, Hagan," I said, staring at him, "without the help of a half-breed, it is far more than our slaves we would lose. Now, I will hear no more of this. You have your marching orders."

I rose from my seat, indicating the meeting was at an end. The clan leaders and their clansmen rose as well. After striking their chests with a fist and bowing their heads in a reluctant show of respect from some of them, they walked out of my Hall. Krygor, Pattel, and Fenton lingered. My sons, Keran and Ganek, eyed me questioningly. I gestured with my head that they were free to leave.

"If that son of a krillik won't challenge me, I will," Krygor muttered, eyeing Hagan as he exited my Hall.

"You will do no such thing, Krygor Aldriss. That worm's blood is mine to spill," I said.

"Careful, Ravik, my friend. The walls have ears," Fenton said, a reproving expression on his face.

Despite his prominent Braxian forehead, strong brow, broad, flat nose, and square, jutting jaw, Fenton's face held an odd softness that testified to his gentle nature. Although one would be foolish to interpret his kind disposition as a sign of weakness.

"Eavesdroppers are the least of the Magnar's concerns," Krygor said, with a grim look. "I fear a rebellion is brewing."

Pattel recoiled. "Hagan wouldn't dare!"

"He wouldn't lead or organize it unless he felt confident he could get away with it," I said, running my fingers through my long, black hair. "He's a coward, but overly proud and greedy. He would join a rebellion, but I'd expect Clan Caldes or Clan Zotan to lead it."

"You really think we're on the verge of civil war?" Pattel asked, his brow creasing.

I shook my head. "No. Not a war, but definitely a coup or an assassination attempt."

My gaze roamed over the light beige walls of my Hearing Hall, covered with the banners of the various clans populating Braxia—the Elder Clans' banners at the top with their vassal clans beneath them. A few of them would fall before everything was said and done. The question was whose banners would fall, my enemies' or mine?

"My clan has ruled Braxia for seven generations," I said, my eyes boring into Pattel's. "My father and his sire almost ran this planet into the ground, but I will mend it. Braxia *will* change. The clan leaders can plot all they want. I do not intend to fall. But should that happen, my sons will rise and see me avenged."

"And so will we," Krygor said.

"And so will we," Pattel and Fenton echoed.

CHAPTER 1
MERCY

The heavy stares of the Guldans weighed on me. Ignoring them, I forced myself to walk at a casual pace through the busy streets of the financial district of Kenzenia, Guldar's Capital City. High-tech prosthetics camouflaged the cheetah-like spots that graced my neck, arms, and legs in an elegant line. And yet, I felt as if the passersby could see right through them. If those markings—my Veredian heritage —became exposed, they would descend on me like vultures. Those who didn't seek to sell me outright for insane profits would try to breed me to produce more like me.

To my knowledge, only two Veredian-Guldan hybrids existed throughout the known universe: my youngest sister's adopted daughter Lenora and myself. Collectors would pay obscene amounts of credits for a rare being such as I. Should they further discover that, like all Veredians, I also possessed a unique psi ability, they would be even more rabid in their desire to possess me.

But they couldn't see through my prosthetics. It was the absence of a male by my side to claim ownership over me that drew their stares. My collarless neck stated that I wasn't a house-slave. As a Free Woman, I should have been escorted by my father, a brother, or a male relative if I wanted to go out on a stroll, or by a slave to carry whatever goods I was off to purchase, usually groceries.

While still very backwards in their ways, Guldans had started to evolve with some slight overtures towards female emancipation. Free Women could now legally walk the streets without a chaperon, but it still drew the unwanted type of attention. I had foolishly thought that, with Kenzenia being the most international sector of the planet, mentalities would have been more forward thinking.

Wrong.

I should have taken a hovercab instead of yielding to the sentimental urge to tread through the streets of my second home world: my father's birth planet. He'd taken me to Guldar only three times, forced to hide me because of my mixed blood. This planet was as beautiful as its social values were ugly. Despite the many hostile male stares aimed at me, I reveled in the warmth of the sun on my face, the golden sky overhead shimmering while wispy clouds hung almost still around the fat, ghostly shape of our giant moon, Khora.

Tall, cigar-like buildings lined the eerily spotless streets of Kenzenia. Beige, black, and gold in color, their metal and glass surfaces reflected the dancing lights of the sky, giving the entire city the impression of heaving under shallow breaths.

A wealthy-looking male, maybe in his late thirties, placed himself directly in my path and tried to make eye-contact. Under different circumstances, I'd hold his gaze and give him a proper tongue-lashing. It took all of my willpower to cast my eyes down demurely and circle around him, giving him a wide-berth. Staring him down would have been deemed a challenge and opened the door for him to make further inquiries about my identity and whereabouts, or even to demand reparation for that *disrespect*. But being a Free Woman, he couldn't accost me without cause or be accused of harassing another man's property.

Property... Fuck that shit. No man would ever own me.

The silhouette of Master Belduk's office building loomed ahead. Realizing that my steps had accelerated as I neared my destination, I forced myself to slow down. The notary had been charged with handling my father's succession. After his death and, more recently, my half-brother Varrek's demise, I had become his only remaining child and sole heiress.

The tall, glass doors of the fifty-story high building parted upon my approach. Straight ahead, smack in the center, an imposing security guard manned the reception desk. The trickling sound of water from the elaborate water-fountain behind him filled the hall. Its long basin ran from the left side of the wall almost to the middle of the room. A few females sat on long, cushioned benches before the basin. Their mates—or guardians—stood nearby, engaged in hushed conversations with other males.

On the right side of the reception, a giant statue of the god Menuk, the Hand of Justice, watched over the path to the elevators. As soon as I headed for them, the guard hailed me. Repressing a sigh of annoyance, I schooled my feature to the proper level of demureness.

"You've called me, Sen?" I asked, clasping my hands before me and looking at his nose.

Tilting his head to the side, his green eyes slowly undressed me.

I'd made sure to wear the traditional Free Woman outfit. The flowy, white dress had a plunging neckline that hinted at the curve of my breasts, cinched at the waist by a golden cord. Sleeveless, bare back, and split on both sides up to my thighs, it was designed to flaunt a woman's assets with each step while hiding the naughty bits. I'd tied my knee-length, black hair into a heavy bun. Normally, it would have covered my back, but its unusual length—although traditional for a Veredian Warrior—would have drawn too much attention. Guldan females usually kept theirs to the middle of their backs.

"Are you lost, Sana?" he asked.

My heart seized in my chest, realizing how much he had in common with my late brother Varrek. The same silvery white hair parted by black horns recurving over his head, their tips pointing back up. The main differences lay in the color of his skin, a creamy brown a few shades darker than mine, where my brother's had been silvery grey —a gift from his Xelixian mother. Like most Guldan males, tribal tattoos adorned the right half of his cleanly-shaven face. Their burnished gold color complemented his complexion.

"No, Sen, I am not lost," I said in a soft voice. "I am here to see Master Belduk."

"The notary? On your own?" he asked, narrowing his eyes.

"I am expected," I answered, noncommittally. "With your permission, I should make haste not to be late. It would be improper to have the man wait."

I'd hoped my wording would mislead him into thinking I meant men plural, as in Master Belduk and my 'male guardian.'

"Indeed," he said, pursing his lips, his gaze lingering on my breasts. "You may proceed to the twenty-seventh floor."

"Thank you, Sen," I said, with a slight bow of the head.

The weight of his stare burned holes in my back as I made my way to the elevator. Once more, I had to silence the paranoid fear that the prosthetics between my shoulder blades, which hid my Veredian markings at that location, could have been damaged.

As the elevator flew upwards, I cast a brief glance at myself in the mirrored wall on the left side of the cabin. Reassured that the markings on my exposed arms and the sides of my legs didn't show, I fixed the lock of hair that had gotten tangled in my left horn.

The elevator opened on the reception area of the legal firm, which also housed Master Belduk's practice. A pretty hybrid slave greeted me as I entered. By her dusty blue skin, I could only surmise she was half-Avean, but I couldn't figure out which other species she was mixed with. She escorted me to Master Belduk's office, knocked, then opened when he bid us enter. She held the door, gestured for me to proceed, and then made a discreet exit once I walked in.

Master Belduk was well past his prime. Although I knew him to be in his early eighties, he looked closer to one-hundred. With an average lifespan of 140 years, Guldans usually looked more fit at that age. He rose to greet me, but didn't move from behind his desk.

"Welcome, Sana Vrok," Belduk said, waving at the chair in front of his desk.

"Master Belduk," I said in greeting while settling on the chair.

It instantly adjusted to my size and height, the nanites in the leather-like material shifting slightly beneath me. Chic and sleek, the notary's office boasted nothing but shades of black, grey, chrome, and white. Guldans took great pride in their technological and scientific advancements. They never missed an opportunity to flaunt both as signs of wealth and status.

"It is unfortunate that we should finally meet under such circumstances," Belduk said, the intensity in his light grey eyes made all the more unnerving by the way they strangely blended with his uncommonly pale skin for a Guldan.

"Indeed. But that is the way of life," I said with the proper level of calm acceptance.

By most cultures' standards, neither my father nor my brother had been good men. But I had loved my dad. Even six years later, his death still broke my heart. My half-brother, though… That was far more complicated. Still, his recent passing haunted me. My heart knew that I had done the right thing by capturing him for the countless crimes he committed against Veredians, which ultimately led to his downfall.

Belduk harrumphed his assent, then summoned a holographic screen. Each side displayed the text in the right direction for us to read. I silently thanked my father for teaching me the Guldanese alphabet and language, even though I'd been raised according to Veredian beliefs.

The notary launched into an endless enumeration of all the assets that my father had bequeathed to my brother, as well as those personally owned by Varrek that now belonged to me. Despite his monotone delivery, Belduk failed to put me to sleep. My mind was reeling from the sheer magnitude of the wealth I had come into. But my self-preservation instincts also screamed in warning. The glimmer in the old man's eyes, the way he licked his lips as he listed the mind-boggling sums held in various accounts, entire fleets of top-of-the-line spaceships, tech and medical patents—to name a few—clearly indicated he wanted a piece of it, if not all of it.

As he neared the end of the list, his eyes flicked to my neck and left wrist on multiple occasions, as if to re-confirm something he'd already verified many times. As per the law, unmated Free Women had to dress in white to broadcast their single status. A collar indicated she was promised to her future mate, while a bracelet indicated courtship with the sire's blessing.

After what felt like an hour, Belduk finally stated the last item. Shutting off the holographic monitor, he leaned forward and clasped his hands on the desk before him.

"An impressive inheritance, Sana Vrok," Belduk said.

"Indeed," I said. "My father and brother were wise businessmen."

He nodded slowly. "I imagine you have plans for all this wealth?"

"Of course," I said.

I held his gaze for a few seconds, making it clear I had no intention of elaborating any further, then lowered my eyes to avoid the challenge. He would be too pleased to seize the opportunity.

Belduk pursed his lips, a heavy silence hanging between us.

"So where do I sign?" I asked at last when the silence stretched too long.

"Well, it's not that simple, Sana Vrok," Belduk said with false sympathy. "As a Free Woman, you may only receive, withdraw, or inherit sums below one hundred thousand credits without the oversight of a guardian. Yours ranks in the billions."

Are you fucking kidding me?

My nails dug into my palms while I struggled to maintain a neutral face.

"I wish you would have made me aware of that fact beforehand so that I would have been prepared, which would have avoided wasting both our times," I said.

The slight narrowing of his eyes confirmed that my voice had not quite succeeded at hiding my seething anger.

"Oh, no time is wasted, Sana Vrok," Belduk said with a somewhat malicious smile. "I took the liberty of calling your guardian, as appointed by your father before his passing."

My blood froze in my veins. Belduk's thin lips stretched as his smile broadened. He knew this wasn't good news for me.

"How thoughtful of you," I said with a thin voice.

My mind raced as I tried to figure out who my father could have given me to and what his intentions might be. For the first time, I genuinely regretted not accepting my sister's offer to send a small Tuurean fleet with me to Guldar to collect my inheritance. But that would have created a whole other set of problems.

Belduk reached for his com and informed his assistant to bring in their guest. I schooled my features to remain neutral. Whoever this man was, my father wouldn't have appointed him if he didn't genuinely believe that he would do right by me. I just hated walking in blind.

The door opened, and the same hybrid slave walked in followed by a striking Guldan man. Broad and muscular, his curly, shoulder-length, brown hair framed a handsome face with full lips, deep, green eyes, and thick, dark-brown horns. Our eyes met. The glimmer of shock on his face, triggered by the sight of me, quickly hidden. Recovering promptly, he narrowed his eyes, and his sensuous lips stretched in a smile laced with malice.

Oh Goddess! Doruk!

As the assistant made a quiet exit, a slight frown marred Doruk's forehead, making me realize I had not risen to my feet upon his entrance, as expected of females as a sign of respect.

"Doruk," I said, standing up with my head bowed.

"Ravena Vrok," he said, his deep voice sending shivers down my spine.

A million questions raced through my mind. Why in the Goddess' name would my father appoint his twisted, former right-hand man as my guardian? My father had operated the largest slave empire in the Western Quadrant. My mother had been his property. Despite that, an unlikely love had blossomed between them. Doruk, one of his crewmates, had always hated the privileged treatment my mother and sisters had received. Although we had never met in person, Father had shown me plenty of pictures of him. Had he shown Doruk pictures of me? How much of my existence did he know?

"Master Belduk," Doruk said, stopping a couple of steps in front of me, "I would like a private moment with my ward before we finalize our business."

"Of course," Belduk promptly said. He pointed to a motion sensor embedded on his desk. "Simply wave your hand above it when you are ready for me to return."

Without another word, he walked out of his office, and closed the door behind him. Doruk's eyes never strayed from me as he retrieved a small device from the pocket of his black dress pants. I recognized the military grade, high-tech scrambler. He placed it on top of the notary's desk and activated the device. That he'd want to disable any microphone or cameras that might eavesdrop on our conversation gave me hope. But knowing the depth of his hatred towards my mother and sisters, and the depravity with which he'd abused the slaves on board my father's ship dampened it.

Once more, Doruk undressed me with his eyes, this time burning with lust. He slowly licked his lips.

"I've got to give it to your mother. She played a masterful game."

"My mother didn't play any game," I said, lifting my chin defiantly.

"Oh, but she did," Doruk said, advancing towards me, invading my space. "She played your father all the way into his grave."

I took a step back, but he continued his advance. The edge of the desk pressing against the back of my thighs prevented me from retreating further. He stopped in front of me, his pelvis pressing against my stomach. I leaned backwards and turned my face away from his.

"She loved him," I said, looking at the right wall covered with abstract, monochromatic art.

"She made him *weak*," Doruk hissed in a surge of anger.

Guldans respected strength and success. Among the many things considered a weakness, love ranked the highest. Emotions made people act irrationally. A Guldan would sell his own child or mother without hesitation if it made financial sense.

Doruk rested a hand on top of the desk, leaning further into me, his muscular chest squishing my breasts. I wanted to lean farther back but it would press my nether region even more against his.

"Maheva's genes were always strong," he said. Bending his head, he inhaled my scent. His lips almost brushed the side of my neck. "She's stamped her features on each of her girls, except that deliciously submissive Sevina. Too bad that one keeled over."

My face snapped towards his as I glared at him, my hands gripping the edge of the desk to refrain from clawing at his face. The malevolent glimmer in his eyes confirmed he was taunting me, daring me to act. I never got to meet my younger sister, Sevina. As a hybrid Veredian-Guldan, my father had hidden me right after my birth, even from my own mother. He'd let her believe I had been stillborn so that he wouldn't be forced to sell me to a collector. Forty-nine years had gone by before I finally got to meet my mother for the first time, and that had only been a few weeks ago. Because of her powerful kinetic abilities, my father had sent Sevina on a mission to retrieve what he had believed to be a large shipment of celesium, a rare metal worth a fortune. Instead, she'd found kaledium, a highly radioactive metal. Sevina had died from radiation poisoning soon after.

I held Doruk's gaze, this time refusing to be intimidated or to bow to those backwards Guldan protocols.

His smile widened. "You have the same fire as your mother and Sevina's daughter. Those arrogant little bitches. As much as I hated them, I would have given anything for a chance to fuck them into oblivion. Especially the tight cunt of that niece of yours, Amalia."

I stared back at him, silently, refusing to let him rile me up.

"Maybe I'll just fuck you," Doruk said.

His hand slipped under my plunging neckline to cup one of my breasts. I pinched my lips but continued to stare at him in silence. Doruk flicked his thumb back and forth over my nipple, and then gave it a brutal tweak, making me hiss, before letting it go. His gaze followed the movement of his fingertips as he traced a line from my neck, around the curve of my shoulder, and down the length of my arm.

"I bet this soft skin of yours is a graft hiding some lovely Veredian markings," Doruk said before locking eyes with me again, daring me to deny it.

I had enough.

"What do you want, Doruk?" I asked. "You want to fuck? Is that it? Is that your price to put an end to this farce so that we can finalize this business, and I can get my ass off this rock?"

His eyes widened at my unexpected outburst and crude language. As my guardian, by Guldan laws, he could discipline me for behavior that would no doubt be considered disrespectful. But I was done playing his game. If he intended to expose me, nothing I did or said would change a thing. However, my father wouldn't have put me in this situation if he didn't believe Doruk would do the right thing. And my father didn't gamble, especially not when it came to his only daughter.

"Want to know what a hybrid pussy feels like?" I asked, placing both my hands on his ass and thrusting forward against him. "I don't think Belduk will approve, but I'm sure there's a surface around here we can use."

Doruk painfully grabbed a fistful of my hair at the back of my head and pulled my face inches from his.

"You think I won't call your bluff, little girl?" he asked, his breath fanning against my lips. "You think I'd have any qualms plowing that tight cunt of yours on that old bastard's fancy furniture?"

He crushed my lips in a brutal kiss, his hand releasing my hair to close around one of my horns in a gesture of control, of dominance. His tongue forced its way into my mouth. I didn't fight it, but I didn't respond to its coaxing. Despite Doruk's cock hardening against my stomach, my initial fear upon seeing him enter the room continued to wane.

He broke the kiss and locked eyes with mine. His smoldered. Under different circumstances, I might have consented to a horizontal dance with him. I didn't care much for pretty men; I liked them big and brawny. Judging by the kiss, unwelcome though it was, Doruk clearly had some skill. But he was a monster who had raped and abused countless slaves, and threatened every female in my family.

"To answer your question, *Guardian*, I think you came here to honor my father's wishes."

Although he tried to hide it, I didn't miss his slight flinch. As expected, I'd struck a nerve. Doruk was a bully. He enjoyed exercising his dominance over others just for the pleasure of watching their distress. But for all his faults, Doruk had been my father's most loyal crew member.

"Your father was a fool," Doruk grumbled. "He had the world at his feet and threw it all away for a female. Any Guldan would drag you home, fuck you senseless until the interest fades, and then sell you for the fortune we both know you're worth." His gaze roamed over me. "Like all Veredians, you're hot as fuck."

"But you won't," I said, matter-of-fact.

Shoving away my horn he'd been holding, he tossed my head back and finally moved away from me.

"Don't get cocky with me, little girl. Your father saved my life twice and gave me a far better future than I could have ever hoped for. I would sell you in a heartbeat, but I have always known the day would come when he would collect. And so, I shall comply. But make no mistake, that debt of honor is now fully repaid. Once all this is signed, see that you leave Guldar before sunrise. As Gharah is my witness, if we cross paths again, I will make you my whore."

Leaning forward, he picked up his scrambling device, deactivated it, and then shoved it in his pockets. He checked that his clothes weren't a mess, then waved his hand over the motion sensor. I smoothed my fingers over my hair to fix it after the way Doruk had roughly handled me and glanced at my cleavage to make sure my breast wasn't hanging out.

Belduk's speculative eyes flicked between Doruk and me as he entered. I waited for both men to be seated before settling back in my chair next to my guardian.

"It is good to have you here to sort out this considerable inheritance, Sen Sidik," Belkduk said.

I bristled but reined in my flaring temper.

"There is nothing to sort out," Doruk said in a clipped tone. "Gruuk Vrok has bequeathed his entire estate to his daughter, Ravena Vrok, my ward, who I duly recognize in the female sitting beside me."

"But... but..." Belduk said, his grey eyes bulging in his long face. "She's unmated! That's far too much wealth to be left in the hands of a female. According to the records, Sana Vrok is days away from her fiftieth birthday. Her birthing years are fleeting. She must be mated and bred in all haste to ensure an heir to this substantial inheritance. Until then, this estate should be kept safe under the jurisdiction of a capable male."

"And what male would that be?" Doruk asked. "You?"

Belduk licked his thin lips, greed flashing through his eyes. "Well, I'm not asking for the honor, but I most certainly am highly qualified for the role."

"And next you'll ask to court her, too, so that her birthing years don't go to waste?"

Doruk's voice oozed with sarcasm. In a different setting, that would have been my kind of response.

The notary's face heated to be so brutally called out on his obvious plans.

Belduk sputtered. "I... I didn't—"

"I have no time for this," Doruk interrupted. "Give Sana Vrok the acceptance form to sign. Then proceed to transfer all the assets to her name and funds to her accounts. I want confirmation before we walk out of this office."

My heart leapt in my chest. I'd feared an uphill battle and for Belduk to throw countless administrative loopholes devised specifically to delay or thwart my ability to take ownership of my inheritance. With Doruk's demand, I would be free and clear to leave, especially considering his 24-hour ultimatum.

"Before you leave?" Belduk exclaimed, then shook his head. "That is not possible, Sen Sidik. Transactions of this magnitude take days to make sure they are put in the right accounts. There are tax considerations and—"

"Do not take me for an imbecile, Master Belduk," Doruk spat in a menacing tone. "I've been the right hand to Gruuk Vrok—who ran the biggest slave empire in this Quadrant, if not in the entire known universe. I know how quickly large transactions are completed when processed through legal channels. We've bought entire fortresses and fleets of interstellar vessels with full ownership transferred within minutes. So, don't fuck with me. Now bring up that blasted form."

Despite biting my cheeks, I miserably failed at hiding my smirk. Belduk glared at both of us in turn and mumbled something under his breath. He tapped a few instructions on his datapad before placing it on the desk in front of me. Doruk reached for the tablet at the same time I did, and snagged it while giving me the 'hands off' look. I clasped my hands on my lap, reminding myself to calm down. This would all be over soon enough.

Doruk flipped through the pages of the acceptance form, then demanded to have the appendices it referred to also made available for his review. A smart request, considering the appendices contained the exhaustive list of the assets. Belduk could have kept some items off the list. However, everything turned out to be in order. Despite his greed, the notary had a successful practice that he would be foolish to jeopardize over an attempted con job.

Doruk extended the datapad to me, and I pressed my thumb on the signature box. In spite of his obvious displeasure, Belduk took it from me and proceeded to execute the transfer. It turned out to be the longest hour of my life, where I simply sat in silence, utterly ignored by the two males. However much of a sick bastard Doruk happened to be, my father had chosen well by appointing him as my guardian. He triple-checked every single transaction completed, ensuring I had full ownership, free and clear of any type of hold or claim. No further action would be required on my part to access the assets. Thanks to my father's foresight, aside from our family's estate on Guldar, his entire holdings had been placed in intergalactic banks and, therefore, outside of Guldan jurisdiction. Once under my name, Belduk couldn't revert anything without filing a case with the Financial Court of the Galactic Council.

By the time it was finally over, Belduk no longer made any effort to hide his displeasure. He was as happy to see the back of us as we were to leave his office. On our way to the elevator, Doruk commed the valet to have his hovercar brought out front. It pulled up at the same time we reached the entrance. My guardian's firm grip on my upper-arm made it clear he wasn't ready for us to part ways just yet.

The passenger door of the bullet-shaped, silver-colored vehicle slid open. Still holding my arm, Doruk led me to it and, for a second, a sliver of fear coursed through me. Had he been so thorough ensuring I had full ownership of the estate so that he could coerce me into yielding it to him? As my guardian, he fell under the unwritten rule that he couldn't take me as his mate to prevent abusive appropriation of the ward's assets. But that rule had been broken a few times before. With him being barely a little over fifteen years my elder, and with significant wealth of his own, he would be deemed a suitable husband.

I entered the vehicle, the door closing almost instantly behind me, and waited for Doruk to get in behind the driver's seat.

"Destination Vrok Estate," Doruk said to the vehicle's artificial intelligence as soon as his door closed.

I breathed a sigh of relief; he wasn't abducting me to some forsaken place.

"Acknowledged," the A.I. said.

Our seatbelts automatically wrapped around us and the vehicle lifted off, ascending about fifty meters vertically before flying towards my father's home on autopilot.

The silence hung heavy between us. I didn't mind it, not wanting to form any kind of bond with this man. He stared ahead, brooding. My own mind sorted through all that I had to handle before my departure.

The hovercar slowed down as it pulled up to the landing pad of the estate, drawing me out of my musings. I turned to Doruk, who continued to stare ahead. What I wouldn't give to know what thoughts occupied his mind right now.

"Thank you for everything," I said, the words somewhat scorching my tongue.

"I didn't do it for you," he snarled with a sideways glance.

Oh well, I tried.

I shrugged. "Thanks, anyway."

The hovercar stopped, and this time, Doruk fully turned towards me, his green eyes boring into me with a cold, hard glint.

"Be gone from my planet by sunrise. And heed my warning well, Ravena Vrok. See that our paths never cross again, for it is not your father's friend you will meet."

He waved his hand in front of the control panel of the vehicle and my door slid open.

"Noted, Sen Sidik," I said. "Just so we're clear, know that the same applies to you."

His chuckle resonated behind me as I stepped out of the vehicle.

"I hope we do meet again, little Veredian," Doruk said. "I will enjoy you."

Looking over my shoulder, I smirked at him. "No, Sen Sidik. *I* will enjoy *you* on your knees, like a good boy, receiving the punishment you more than deserve."

Doruk burst out laughing, an undefinable glimmer in his eyes.

"Arrogant, just like your mother," he said, shaking his head. The passenger door closed and, without sparing me another look, he turned the vehicle around and left.

A heavy weight lifted off my shoulders as he faded from view. I walked up the stairs to the two-story mansion, surrounded by a landscaped garden. I'd never quite understood why my father had acquired this specific house. Isolated on a large parcel of land, built in all metal and glass, it looked as cold as it was sleek with curved angles and wall-to-ceiling windows. Inside felt just as clinical with an overabundance of white and light grey. At least it made the rooms appear even more bright and spacious than they already were. I had visited this house once as a child. My father had explained that an interior decorator had taken care of furnishing it. I had realized then that he only owned it to have a place to stay during his rare visits to Guldar, but he didn't consider this place his home. Thank the Goddess, as I wouldn't shed a tear if—when—it got seized once I left.

With the clock ticking, I hurried out of my ridiculous, traditional, Guldan dress. I loved dressing sexy and showing a bit of skin, but not when my body was exposed due to the laws of men.

The amount of work that awaited me was daunting. But thankfully, I had arrived a few days ago and had started sorting through my brother's files in my father's former office. Varrek had made it his own since our father's passing.

After packing all the items and mementos I intended to bring with me, I settled down at Varrek's desk and began downloading and transferring every single file on record.

CHAPTER 2
MERCY

The chiming sound of the perimeter alarm going off on my armband startled me. I muttered a curse word at the unwelcomed intrusion and secured the crate I'd been placing inside my personal shuttle's hold. Turning on the surveillance monitors inside the shuttle bay, I quickly scanned the various camera feeds. To my relief, there only appeared to be two men headed for one of the side entrances of the house. By the flickering of the images, they had activated a scrambler that hadn't yet managed to break through Varrek's rotating frequencies. Despite the house's isolation and the added bonus of the cover of night, it made sense for the intruders to seek the most inconspicuous location to hack the locks and break into the house.

Had they delayed ten more minutes, they'd be staring at the fading lights of my shuttle taking off. I pondered for a minute whether or not to confront them. They wore civilian clothes and didn't appear armed, although they probably had a concealed weapon of some kind. If Doruk had sent them, he'd know beyond the shadow of a doubt that I was alone in the house. Since he didn't know the extent of my combat skills, he'd likely assume me to be easy prey. Yet, I doubted he was behind it. He'd given me until morning, and I trusted he'd keep his word.

That left Belduk.

Seeing me come alone to his office this morning likely tipped him that I had no protector in residence. I believed him greedy enough to have me abducted. He had the means to make my wealth disappear into his own coffers without a trace, and me along with it. While confident in my ability to take down those two men, fighting them struck me as an unnecessary risk. They could have backup beyond my detectors' range. Worse, they could have some crazy new Guldan tech that I couldn't fend off, even with all the Tuurean enhancements my ship could boast, courtesy of my baby sister.

Between Doruk molesting me and Belduk's nonsense, I would have welcomed the opportunity to vent today's frustration. But it would have to wait for another day. I cursed again, remembering the bag I hadn't brought down yet from my bedroom. A quick glance at the monitor indicated the men closing in on one of the side doors. In the time it would take them to hack through the lock, I could run up to fetch the bag, get back down, and take off. But that also felt like too great a risk. The bag contained nothing of sentimental value; just some clothes, toiletries, and a few womanly comforts.

Hopping inside the shuttle, I fired up the engine and opened the shuttle bay door. The short runway outside, and flood lights alongside it, lit up. Although the intruders wouldn't have heard the door opening, the lights would be a dead giveaway. By now, they were likely racing to the entrance to see what was going on.

I shot out of the shuttle bay and launched a wide range scan. Through the window, I watched the two men running to the entrance of the house, looking at me. Even though they couldn't see me, I waved mockingly at them. They raced towards their personal shuttle hidden behind the tall bushes a short distance from the estate. To my relief, the scanner didn't pick up any other vessels nearby. That didn't mean they wouldn't be coming.

As I raced upwards to clear Guldar's atmosphere, my radar displayed up the two men's shuttle in pursuit. Like me, they were flying right below the speed limit that would trigger an inquiry from ground control. I couldn't afford to draw their attention. A single female, Free Woman or not, had no business leaving the planet without supervision. Once I left Guldar's atmosphere, I'd be free to push my shuttle to its highest speed. With my current head start, those bastards would never catch me.

And then a second vessel showed up on my radar, this one moving on an intercept course. Calculating our trajectories, by the time I cleared Guldar's restricted speed zone, they'd be right on top of me. They'd likely use a tractor beam to immobilize me, which would make my job of dispatching them easier. But I needed to prepare in case they tried to hit me with an EMP blast to fry my ship's systems and leave me dead in the water.

I diverted all non-essential power to my shields and maintained a steady course. The ship's com beeped with an incoming hail from the intruders' shuttle. I ignored it. Minutes later, Guldar's shimmering night sky gave way to the infinite, starry darkness of space. No sooner did we clear the restricted zone than the second ship fired its tractor beam at me. My shuttle jerked under the pull which forced it into a quick stop.

I smiled.

"Time for you bastards to discover why you shouldn't mess with a Veredian."

As much as I wanted to play with those sons of a krillik, I needed to disable this second ship before the would-be-intruders' shuttle caught up to us. I fired my own tractor beam at them, not to pull their ship, but because mine would release a series of nanobots specially encoded with a single command: shutdown any non-vital system. As expected, within seconds of their vessel getting hit by my tractor beam, its lights began to flicker as its systems all became disabled.

That was how I had disabled my brother's ship when I'd captured him a few weeks ago.

The intruders' ship finally caught up to us. They didn't use their beam on me. When I tried to use mine on them, their shield prevented my nanobots from reaching their systems. Instead of the EMP blast I'd expected, they fired photon torpedoes at me.

What the fuck?

Were they actually trying to kill me? Despite getting brutally rocked by the impact, my shields absorbed the damage. But I wouldn't wait to see how much they'd be willing to throw at me. While charging my EMP, I executed some evasive maneuvers to dodge their other shots. I had no problem killing. Under different circumstances, I would have blown up their asses after the first shot. However, taking a Guldan life in Guldan space would trigger an investigation I didn't need. The less they knew about me, the better.

My EMP chimed, indicating a full charge. Taking aim, I fired a first shot to take out their shield, and then immediately fired a second one to fry their systems. Their distress beacon launching was all the confirmation I needed that they couldn't pursue. Selecting the preset course to the Belevar space station, I initiated the warp jump to get out of here.

I needed to reclaim my battleship, the Falcon, that I had left there. Although it was a Guldan ship, its size would have required me to dock at one of Guldar's spaceports. That, in turn, would have meant going through customs and border patrol. I sent a message to my small crew to prepare for imminent departure; I wanted the ship restocked and refueled upon my arrival.

After completing the jump and following a half-hour flight, the massive silhouette of the Belevar space station showed up on screen. My father had all but owned that station, having greased many palms and funded multiple businesses that operated there. Even their law enforcement had been on his payroll.

After our father's death, Varrek had made sure to uphold those relationships. And so did I, now. Thankfully, Belevar was an intergalactic space station. The locals didn't give two shits about gender, race, or cultural beliefs. Here, as long as you had credits, they'd happily work with you. While appreciative of the relative safety I enjoyed on Belevar, pressing business awaited me halfway across the galaxy in the Eastern Quadrant.

I landed in the shuttle bay of my battleship, still docked at the Belevar station. My First Officer, Sarah, greeted me upon my arrival. She had nothing major to report, except to warn me of the unusually heavy Guldan presence on the station. My presence no longer raised eyebrows on Belevar. Most people here knew I was Gruuk's daughter. They also knew better than to mess with me. They simply had no idea I was half Veredian. Even here, I wore my prosthetics.

As soon as Sarah completed her report, I ordered her to set a course for the Venus Hive pleasure barge located in the Eastern Quadrant. She raised an inquisitive eyebrow, but I merely smiled, leaving her curiosity unsated. Sarah didn't belong to my very limited inner circle. As my current mission would take me into many hazardous places, I didn't want to risk bringing my usual crew with me, mainly constituted of Veredian females. She, and the rest of my current crew, belonged to a trustworthy circle of Terran and Dantorian mercenaries I often did business with. While the Galactic Council had declared Veredians an endangered species, and therefore under its protection, we still needed to be careful; which meant remaining cooped up in safe places.

And I'm sick of it.

Sick of hiding and of being hidden. In a few weeks, I'd celebrate my fiftieth birthday. A third of my lifespan had been thrown away living in secret, for fear of being sold to collectors. But worse, to avoid the Guldans forcing my mother to be bred by as many Guldans as possible in the hope she would birth another like me.

Guldan hybrids were extremely rare as the females weren't normally allowed to mate outside of our race, and females from other species couldn't survive the pregnancy. Guldan babies came into the world fully horned. The viciously sharp tips shredded alien mothers from the inside out. But Guldan females had developed an inner shell that protected us. My mother had only survived birthing me because of her Veredian psi ability. She was a powerful healer. With a touch, she could mend any cut, wound, fractured bones, and even old scars.

I'd finally met her for the first time a few weeks ago. I missed her terribly. Part of me wanted to return to Xelix Prime where she now lived with my sister, my niece, and their mates before heading to the Eastern Quadrant. Mother hadn't known of my existence. While she'd rejoiced at having me back, the rest of our family had reacted with mixed feelings at discovering she had actually loved my father. After all, he had built his wealth enslaving and force breeding Veredians. My youngest sister, Aleina, had taken it the hardest. She had eventually made her peace with it, but it had left a scar on her relationship with Mother.

Although it wasn't my burden to bear, I felt a great deal of guilt about my father's actions. And yet, I loved him. He'd been good to me and made so many sacrifices to protect my mother and her other children. Still, in spite of his efforts to treat his slaves with kindness, the pain and suffering his *business* caused could never be denied or overlooked.

My family had embraced me with open arms, but I knew that every time they gazed upon my face, eerily similar to my mother's, they also saw the black hair, black eyes, and black horns I'd inherited from my father. Retrieving my inheritance had only been one of my goals when I'd set out on this mission. While financially comfortable on my own, the tremendous wealth inherited from my father would go a long way to helping finance the construction of the new home world for the liberated Veredians. But more importantly, I was hoping to recover my brother's clients list. With it, I could track down all the Veredian slaves that had been sold over the years; among them, Galicia and Gerana, the twin daughters my mother had given birth to from her third pregnancy.

I couldn't undo the harm my father had done, but giving my mother her children back and helping to free all my other Veredian sisters was the least I could do. Based on what I'd found so far in Varrek's files, he had been in the process of establishing a new base on Braxia. With the Galactic Council cracking down on slavery in the Western Quadrant, moving his business to the East had made sense. I didn't know much about Braxia except that their males were scrumptiously massive and brutish looking. Sadly, by all accounts, they treated females even worse than Guldans.

Thankfully, my old Terran friend William worked as the right hand to Anton Aldriss, the powerful Braxian hybrid who owned the Hive Network: the largest and most luxurious chain of pleasure barges in the Eastern Quadrant. He had previously put his resources at our disposal to track down my brother. I hoped he would assist me again as he had strong connections on Braxia.

I looked forward to visiting Venus Hive again. Aside from Tuur—the new Veredian home world—and Xelix Prime, where our strongest allies lived, that pleasure barge was one of the few places I could fully be myself; no mask, no disguise. Just me. Ravena Mercy Vrok.

Settling down at my desk inside my personal quarters, I sent a video message to William to warn him of my impending arrival and request an audience with Anton. The journey to Venus Hive would take three weeks. With such a great distance, the message wouldn't reach him for at least a couple of hours. That task done, I sent a brief message to my mother and sister to let them know of my successful trip to Guldar and to inform them of my current destination. I felt guilty being so cryptic. I'd waited my whole life to be reunited with them, and now I didn't know how to handle it. I didn't know how to belong.

Turning on my computer, I uploaded all of my brother's files retrieved on Guldar. I had three weeks to plow through them. By the time I reached Venus Hive, he'd have no more secrets from me.

Venus Hive never ceased to amaze me. The space station had grown again since the last time I'd visited it. The word on the street claimed it could now accommodate close to eight million people. Divided into two sections—the Commons and the VIP Area—Venus Hive catered to every form of entertainment; from music concerts to dance shows, casinos to gladiator arenas, fashion and gastronomy, and of course, every possible shade of adult entertainment.

William greeted me at the docking bay. We were the same age, yet where my hair retained its shiny raven color, silver strands had already begun streaking his light brown locks. Tall and muscular, the former mercenary had maintained his formidable shape. Although the humans' lifespan now averaged 120 years, they still greyed early in comparison to other species. Smile lines crinkled around

William's deep blue eyes as I approached him. He extended a hand in greeting, a Terran salutation protocol I usually disliked, but not with him; he didn't suffer from sweaty, clammy palms. He took my hand in his firm grip, then leaned forward to place a friendly kiss on my cheek. His five o'clock shadow pricked my skin, but it wasn't unpleasant.

"Hello, Mercy," William said, gesturing towards the hovercar waiting for us.

I smiled. "Hello, Will. Thank you, once again, for answering my call. I'm starting to pile up the I.O.U.s as you Terrans like to say."

William chuckled. "You certainly are. Maybe I should cash in now," he said as I entered the vehicle.

The door closed, and I waited for him to circle around the other side to enter.

"Oh, and what type of payment do you have in mind?" I asked after he settled in and closed his door.

"HQ," William told the car's A.I. before turning to me as the vehicle started moving. "I haven't decided yet, but I wouldn't mind being introduced to one of your Veredian sisters. They're all stunning. A healer or a mind-reader would be a very nice added bonus."

I snorted. "Good luck with that. The Admiral is very protective of the Veredians. He'll likely demand you move to Tuur if you want to mate one of the Sisters."

"Ugh," William said, wrinkling his nose. "Pretty as you all are, I'm not butting heads with the Tuurean leader."

"Wise man," I said, teasingly. "So then, what will it be?"

"You know, I'm not doing this for any kind of repayment. We're friends. And I happen to support your actions. This slavery business needs to end. You'll always have my help on that front."

"Thank you," I said with genuine gratitude. "It means a lot."

His answer hadn't surprised me. Still, it warmed my heart to know decency still existed out there. Especially from someone I considered a friend.

"Anton will help you, but Braxia is a krillik's nest. I fear for your safety."

"You know I can take care of myself," I said, both touched by his concern and annoyed by his overprotectiveness.

"Yes, Mercy, I know you can fight," he said in a conciliatory tone, "but even Anton wouldn't face off against a pureblood."

"He's a hybrid, I'm a Veredian Warrior," I countered. "I'm faster."

"That, you may be, but a Braxian Warrior can also kill you in one blow. One mistake is all it would take."

I pursed my lips. "Fair enough. I'm not going there to fight, anyway. I just want to shutdown whatever operation my brother may have had running there and find the clients list. The Goddess willing, I'll be in and out of there in a handful of days."

"Good," William said as the vehicle pulled up alongside the busy walkways in front of the Venus Hive HQ.

William got out and circled around the car to help me out, but I'd already exited. He gave me an annoyed look that made me chuckle. Human males had this endearing thing about being *chivalrous*, an archaic set of behavioral rules towards females meant to denote respect and courtesy. It personally struck me as often inconvenient for the male, but sweet nonetheless to be on the receiving end.

A handsome, young security guard approached, nodded at us, then entered the car, no doubt to go park it somewhere. We headed inside the gleaming white building.

"I cannot free myself right now to accompany you to Braxia," William said, "but I'd like you to let me assign one of my guards to your security detail so…"

"Fuck no!" I exclaimed as we entered the sleek building that both housed the Venus Hive HQ and Anton's private penthouse. "I've had enough of the whole chaperon bit on Guldar."

"I knew you'd say that," William said, rolling his eyes.

"Then why did you offer?" I deadpanned.

"So that, when you get spanked and finally put aside that ridiculous pride of yours to ask for help, I'll be able to say I told you so."

I caught myself almost making a face at him. In the few weeks spent on Xelix Prime with my niece and her children, her mischievous ways had already started rubbing off on me.

As we headed toward the elevators, my gaze lingered on the sexy but tasteful paintings that graced the white walls of HQ. They differed from the ones I'd seen the last time I came here but remained in the same spirit; sexy couples of all pairings locked in steamy embraces and various BDSM scenes artistically posed with no naughty bits on full display, just heavily hinted at.

The receptionist, a pretty redhead named Dana, nodded at us before opening her com, probably to inform Anton of our arrival. We headed for the elevator at the back of the gleaming white and chrome hallway beside the reception desk. Five numbered elevators stood on each side of the corridor. The door of Elevator One, located at the end of the corridor, opened at our approach, the luminescent tribal patterns framing and lighting it up.

"With that said, your timing couldn't be better," William said as the elevator flew upwards to the penthouse. "The Magnar will arrive shortly. He normally wouldn't have visited Anton before next week, but the Gladiator Annual Championship ends tomorrow night and, of course, Braxians are dominating."

I snorted. With their average height looming over seven-and-a-half feet and average weight of 330 pounds of pure muscle, the mere sight of those giants sufficed to make most opponents freeze in fear. Despite my earlier bravado, William was right to warn me off from engaging in battle with them.

"Well, I cannot wait to see what the purest bloodline of Braxia looks like," I said in a teasing tone.

William chuckled and shook his head. The elevator door opened on the large entrance hall of the penthouse overlooking a luxurious living area. We didn't go down the three steps into it but instead followed the same hallway, left of the elevator, that William had taken me through the last time I had visited.

"I will never understand you," William said, teasingly. "Beautiful women like you usually go for the most handsome men."

I shrugged. "I like my pets to be pretty. I like my men beastly and ferocious."

"So I've learned," he mused with a wink.

I affectionately bumped shoulders with him as he knocked on the door to Anton's office.

We'd met a couple of decades ago during a business deal. He'd been interested, but while I greatly enjoyed his personality, he hadn't attracted me that way. Being a good sport, he hadn't turned into a jerk as men often did after getting rejected and hadn't tried to mess up the deal to screw me over out of spite. From there, a slow friendship had blossomed. I could go months, even years, without speaking to him. Yet the moment we met, it always felt like we'd last talked the day before.

William opened the door when Anton's muffled voice bid us enter.

"Your guest has arrived," William said to Anton as he waved me in.

"Ms. Vrok," Anton said in greeting, rising from the chair behind his massive, dark wood desk.

"Mr. Aldriss," I responded after a thank you nod at William.

My old friend made a discreet exit as Anton walked around his desk to approach me. He gestured toward the comfortable leather chair in the sitting area across from his desk. My eyes flicked towards the red Empire chair in front of his desk. I'd actually looked forward to sitting in it, considering the first time I'd visited this office, my sister had occupied that Terran antique.

I almost felt guilty walking with my knee high, black leather boots on the shaggy beige carpet. I settled down on the brown, leather couch and crossed my legs. Anton's dark eyes flicked to the side of my exposed thighs, taking in my Veredian markings there, his gaze moving up to the ones along my exposed arms and neck before locking eyes with me. An amused smile stretched his sensual lips.

My cheeks heated slightly. I'd always been a bit of a flirt, especially when faced with a man attractive by my standards. However, this time, I hadn't meant to make a move or flaunt my assets. Anton was happily mated, and I respected such vows. The absence of lust in his stare should have stung my pride. Instead, it further increased my respect for him. From all accounts, he and his wife had had a tumultuous start to their relationship, one that would have irrevocably broken most couples. Yet, after five years of marriage, their devotion to each other was a thing of legend.

"May I offer you something to drink?" Anton asked.

I shook my head. "No, thank you. I'd rather keep my head clear and endeavor to make a good impression."

Anton chuckled and took a seat in the chair across from me, his massive frame filling it. Although a half-breed, he had inherited the prominent forehead, strong brow line, and broad, flat nose of his Braxian father. His human mother had given him softer, less brutish features, and a smaller size than a pureblood, although imposing by non-Braxian standards.

There was something about beastly men that turned me on. Too bad most Braxians turned into complete bastards when it came to relationships.

"Thank you for making time in your busy schedule to see me, Mr. Aldriss," I said with a smile.

"Anton," he said with his rumbling voice.

"Only if you call me Ravena," I said.

"Certainly, Ravena," he answered.

I didn't miss the slight narrowing of his eyes. William had probably referred to me as Mercy. It was my middle name, neither Guldan nor Veredian, but one that I only allowed those in my inner circle to use.

"I understand you have business on Braxia?" he asked, although he didn't state it as a question.

"Indeed," I said. "I'm embarrassed to ask for your help again so soon, but you are the only Braxian I know."

Anton smiled. It softened his otherwise fearsome face.

"Think nothing of it," he said, waving a dismissive hand. "According to your niece's daughter, Zharina, you and I will become family when she marries my son in who only knows how many years from now."

I snorted and shook my head. On top of her impressive healing powers, my niece's young three-year-old daughter appeared to have inherited a form of foresight. To our collective shock, she'd claimed

Anton's son as her future husband, even though they had never met physically.

"That little brat is trouble," I said affectionately. "Still, I appreciate it."

"That said, is there any way I can discourage you from going?" Anton asked.

I frowned. "Why?"

Anton heaved a sigh. "Braxia is not a very nice place. Hybrids do not fare well over there. I should know," he said, his tone hardening. "And females have it just as bad. You are both. Worse still, you are unique." He cast a meaningful glance at my horns and then at my Veredian markings. "Many clans struggle financially since the end of the Great Wars. Selling you would completely turn their fate around."

I pinched my lips at that same argument again which had forever been the bane of my existence.

"I thought the Magnar had forbidden the hunting of hybrids?" I asked.

"He has, but male half-breeds continue to turn up dead in ditches and dark alleys. It takes more than an edict to erase centuries of fanaticism. Braxians love the purity of their bloodlines."

The barely veiled bitterness in his tone spoke volumes of the abuse he'd endured growing up. I couldn't begin to imagine what it must have felt like living every day of your life wondering if it would be your last, simply because your blood happened to be mixed with a non-Braxian.

"Female hybrids are always welcomed to be used as clan whores to entertain both the clansmen and their guests."

"Surely, they don't assault any female that visits your home world?" I asked, slowly rocking my crossed leg back and forth.

"Women don't visit Braxia," he said, a serious look in his eyes. "And those who go there are accompanied by their mate or some kind of male protector in case anyone got funny ideas."

I sighed heavily, hiding none of my annoyance.

"I know it is difficult for independent women to deal with such a backward thinking culture, but for your sake, I would ask that you place yourself under the protection of my father's clan."

I brushed at non-existent lint on the short skirt of my skin-tight, leather dress. Funnily enough, one might have thought Anton and I had consulted with each other for our outfits; he wore black leather pants and a form-fitting dark grey t-shirt.

"What does that entail?" I asked.

"You would cover your markings, stay at the clan's compound, and be escorted wherever you need to go."

"Fuck. That."

"Which part? Your markings, the escort, or the compound?" Anton asked.

"All of the above?"

"Ravena…" Anton said with a stern look in his eyes and a 'be reasonable' tone of voice.

In that instant, I could almost see my father addressing me in a similar fashion. My chest tightened with the familiar pain of loss. Even after nearly six years, I still mourned my father.

"I refuse to hide my nature anymore. I've been hidden my whole life. Enough is enough. Regarding the compound, I have to stay at my brother's place on Braxia. It will be faster if I can work around the clock. As for an escort, I'm not there on a sightseeing tour." I clasped my hands in front of me and lifted my chin somewhat defiantly. "If I need to move, my butt gets on a hoverbike. Good luck to anyone trying to keep up with me."

I loved speed and had even done a bit of racing, to my father's great displeasure. But more importantly, I'd had enough of being shackled and 'protected' from everyone and everything.

Anton pursed his lips, pondering.

"Listen, I don't mean to be difficult. I know you're trying to help, but isn't there some way I can be afforded some wiggle room?" I asked, almost pleadingly. He was doing me a huge favor simply by listening to me. I didn't want to come across as ungrateful or precious. "Would it help if we made it publicly known that I am under the protection of the Tuureans?"

"Everyone is aware that Tuureans will hunt down anyone who threatens a Veredian, but that threat would hold more weight if you had a Tuurean with you. It's a long ride from the Western Quadrant for them to get here to rescue you. By the time they arrive, your buyer will be long gone."

It was my turn to purse my lips. I had Tuurean armor, courtesy of my sister, but that didn't solve my 'you need a chaperon' problem.

"In other words, I'm fucked."

Anton gave me a commiserating smile. "If you allow my father to introduce you in the Magnar's Great Hall as his guest and agree to have one of the clansmen accompany you when you move around the city, I believe it will be enough."

"But I get to stay in my brother's residence?"

Although reluctant, Anton nodded.

"As long as you allow the clansmen to verify the security of his house."

"Fine," I said, scrunching my face.

Anton chuckled. "Good. Then it is settled." He rose to his feet, and I followed suit. "You must stay with us. We've already had one of the guest rooms prepared for you. My Grace has been looking forward to your arrival. She would love some company and to hear news of the Western Quadrant."

"You honor me," I said, surprised by the unexpected invitation.

"The Magnar is scheduled to arrive in a few hours. If you're up for it, Grace and I will take you both out to sample some of the wonders of Venus Hive."

Now, *that* sounded like a plan.

"You're on," I said with a grin.

CHAPTER 3
RAVIK

"Their expectations are unrealistic," Anton said with a frown.

"And yet, they expect me to have answers for them," I said with a discouraged sigh.

I stepped up to the tall window of Anton's living area. It overlooked the main walkway of the VIP section of Venus Hive. The clever layout of the buildings and the décor gave the impression of looking at a landscaped plaza with muted colors and unobstrusive business signs barely visible from this viewpoint.

"The lesser clans don't have the means to invest in new ventures. Even if they did, they don't have any plans," I said, running my fingers through my hair. "We have nothing to export that other planets want. Without wars, no one needs to hire our clansmen as warriors. Hagan is chanting to revert to the old ways that got us into this situation to begin with, and now fucking Caldes wants to ally with the Guldans."

Anton's sharp breath intake had me looking at him over my shoulder. He had no love for clan Caldes after Raylor's son had nearly murdered Anton's wife and their unborn child.

"You want to steer clear of the Guldans. They are trouble," Anton said.

"I'm well aware. But Hagan and Raylor are right in that Braxia needs new allies, and the Western Quadrant might be a solution. If I don't find a way to turn around our failing economy, I *will* have a civil war on my hands."

"Hmmm," Anton said, rubbing his square chin pensively. "Have you considered—"

The chime of the elevator interrupted him. Its door opened with a swish, quickly buried by Grace's peals of laughter and the throatier one of the female accompanying her. Their hands were laden with bags from whatever shopping spree they'd just been on.

"You're back," Anton said, heading towards the newcomers.

My breath caught in my throat, and my brain ceased to function when the head of Grace's companion suddenly jerked towards me. The finely carved motifs on her black horns shone under the overhead lights. Stomach in knots, skin heating, I stared at the embodiment of pure perfection. Tall and statuesque in her skin-tight leather dress and draped in her knee-length, dark hair, she looked like a vengeful goddess come to pass judgment upon mortals. Her stunning, almond-shaped eyes, black as sin, widened as they stared straight into the depths of my soul. High cheekbones framed a dainty, slightly upturned nose in a delicately sculpted, heart-shaped face. Her plump, sensuous, pink lips parted in shock. The bag in her right hand slipped from her grasp and fell to the ground with a soft thump. She ignored it and rubbed the back of her neck as if something had stung it.

"No fucking way…" she whispered, bewildered.

The swear word snapped me out of my stupor.

"Ravena?" Grace asked, confused. "Is everything okay?"

Ravena. Beautiful name for a goddess.

She looked at Grace, disbelieving, before turning back towards me. She shook her head as if to snap out of whatever daze had overtaken her.

Having somewhat recovered from the shock of her beauty—barely—I realized my brutish appearance must have frightened her. That females cowered before me no longer came as a surprise, but from her, it stung.

"Do not be afraid, Madam," I said, attempting to keep my voice and demeanor non-threatening. "I am not as savage as my appearance may suggest."

She shivered, and her skin erupted in goosebumps. I couldn't tell if my words or the sound of my rumbling voice had caused it. But the appreciative way her gaze glided over my massive body had me involuntarily puffing out my chest and flexing my bulging muscles.

"I'm not," she whispered in a throaty, sensual voice.

Her pink tongue peeked between her luscious lips to wet them. Blood rushed to my groin in response. I had seen many beautiful females in my lifetime and never thought one could rival Grace's beauty. But this Ravena was depriving my brain of its ability to function.

"Ravena," Anton said, "please meet our guest, the ruler of Braxia, Magnar Ravik Xeldar. Magnar, please meet our friend, Ravena."

I bowed my head and slapped my fist to my chest in the traditional Braxian greeting. A strange smile stretched her lips as she delicately pressed her palm over her heart and then waved her hand towards me in an offering gesture. I'd never seen this form of greeting before and didn't know what species she belonged to. The markings on her neck, along the side of her arms and legs clearly appeared Veredian. Her light brown skin also matched that species. But the horns threw away that assumption. Could she be a hybrid?

Ravena picked up the bag she had dropped and walked down the three steps into the living area. Despite Grace's height of 5'10" and her ridiculously high heels, she appeared dwarfed next to her guest who wore flat, knee-high boots. At a glance, I estimated Ravena to be around 6'4. Still short in comparison to my 7'6" but nice nonetheless.

Anton approached Ravena and relieved her of her bags. She turned grateful eyes towards him, a most beautiful smile stretching her lips. I barely managed to silence the growl that rose in my throat. Even though her gaze held no covetous glint as she looked upon him, *I* was the alpha—the apex alpha—in the room. In my presence, the attention of the prime female should be solely focused on me. I blinked at the violence of the primal response she stirred within me.

"It is a pleasure to meet you, Magnar," she said, taking a couple more steps towards me.

"Please call me Ravik," I said, hungry to hear the sound of my name on her lips.

"Ravik," she said with a smile. "It almost sounds like my own name, Ravena."

"Indeed," I said, stepping away from the window to approach her. "Odd, isn't it?"

She shrugged. "More like fated. The Goddess has a strange sense of humor."

The way she said it implied an underlying meaning I didn't get. Behind her, Anton leaned forward to kiss his mate and free Grace of her own bags.

"I'll be right back," Anton said, preventing me from asking Ravena what she meant by fated.

"Come have a seat," Grace said, gesturing towards the living area.

She flicked her waist-length, reddish-brown hair over her shoulder, a speculative glimmer in her amber eyes as Ravena and I complied. Just like in Anton's office, dark-brown leather couches occupied the large sitting area with a dark wood coffee table in the middle. A large family portrait of Anton, Grace, and their three children occupied the center of the off-white wall facing us. Pictures of the children in various settings hung on each side of the portrait. Although heartwarming, it was an odd sight. According to Anton, posting family pictures was a common tradition among Terrans and many other species in the Western Quadrant. With Grace being human, she naturally observed that culture.

Ravena took a seat slightly off the center of the three-cushion couch, then leveled her obsidian eyes on me. Her position guaranteed I'd have no choice but to sit right next to her. Usually, males and females alike sought to put as much distance as possible between themselves and Braxians. Her boldness further fanned the burning attraction I felt towards her.

I settled by her side as she crossed her legs, the tip of her foot brushing against my calf. Grace perched herself on the arm of the chair across from us where her husband usually sat whenever he entertained me here. She, too, crossed her long, shapely legs made infinite by the short length of her red sarong draped in a halter dress style. Where Grace had pale, creamy skin like freshly fallen snow, Ravena's was sun-kissed, like golden honey.

"I hope you're both hungry," Grace said, her amber eyes flicking between Ravena and me. "We're taking you to Risqué, the fanciest restaurant on Venus Hive. I'd have taken you to Sade instead, but I wouldn't want to shock the Magnar's sensibilities. He's a bit of a prude," Grace added teasingly.

I frowned at her, and she grinned two rows of perfect, white teeth at me. The heavy weight of Ravena's stare drew me. I faced her, and she held my gaze, unwaveringly.

"Are you?" she asked, daringly.

"I am not," I said with a bit of a growl.

She raised a perfectly drawn brow with an expression halfway between dubious and mocking. "Are you sure? There's no shame in being prim and proper."

I leaned forward. "Do I look prim to you?"

She bit her bottom lip and gave me the most shameless once over. My shaft jerked in response, the blossoming scent of her arousal driving me to distraction. Despite her delicate bone structure, this female held an undeniable inner-strength that I found oddly appealing. Braxian women were *trained* from birth to be submissive—correction, to be subservient. I didn't like the latter, but there was something undeniably erotic when a female, especially a strong-willed one, voluntarily yielded control and power to her man.

Ravena opened her mouth to answer, but her eye flicked towards Anton returning to the room. I groaned inwardly and straightened under Anton's overly perceptive stare.

"What did I miss?" he asked, sitting in his usual chair.

He wrapped his muscular arm around Grace's waist who was still seated on the arm of the chair. She leaned against him and kissed his forehead. The love between them always felt bittersweet to me. Grace reminded me of my Lissy, whose blood still stained my hands and ate away at my conscience. Had I been a stronger man, I'd have a hybrid son the same age as Anton. In many ways, Anton now filled that void in my heart.

"Ravik was trying to convince us that he wasn't too prudish to go to Sade instead of Risqué," Ravena said with false innocence.

Anton's lips parted in shock as I turned to frown at Ravena. She batted her eyelashes at me. I couldn't decide whether I wanted to lay her across my lap and spank that delicious behind of hers or kiss her senseless. We'd only known each other a few minutes, and yet, she seemed perfectly at ease with me, and I with her. Aside from Grace and her infant daughter, I couldn't remember the last female that had been playful with me. Besides Lissy…

I chased away the painful thought.

"We are *not* taking you or the Magnar to Sade," Anton said to me before casting a suspicious look at his wife.

Grace blushed prettily and fiddled with the hem of her dress.

"Why?" Ravena asked. "Is that place so terrible?"

Anton shook his head. "Not terrible at all, quite the contrary. But as implied by its name, it is a fetish club. The most luxurious you'll ever get to set foot in and guaranteed to satisfy any kink or fantasy one may entertain. But it's not exactly the type of place one brings distinguished guests such as yourselves. It would get… awkward, especially with my mate being an exhibitionist."

"I see," Ravena said, her eyes widening, although the spark within them seemed to say she wished to see even more.

"*Anton,*" Grace said reprovingly, her cheeks taking on a scarlet tinge.

He stared at her, unrepentant. "You shouldn't have brought up Sade if you didn't want to be outed."

"I don't think I like you very much right now," Grace said, frowning at Anton.

Anton chuckled. "You don't like me. You *love* me."

They stared at each other, and Grace's features softened. She leaned forward and kissed him. My chest tightened again, and I averted my eyes. Thankfully, they kept it brief. Grace hopped off the arm of the chair and affectionately ruffled Anton's long, black hair.

"Come on, Ravena," Grace said, "Let's go get primped up. I'm getting hungry!"

Ravena unfolded her legs and rose to her feet, giving me a magnificent view of her perfect behind, tightly hugged by her black, leather dress. The light smirk on her lips when I looked up indicated she knew I'd been admiring her rear. My eyes remained glued to her as she strutted away, her hips swaying. Gorgeous though it was, I wished her long hair had been tied up to give me an unobstructed view of her delicious curves.

The minute she turned the corner, my eyes snapped towards Anton who was staring at me with intensity.

"Who the fuck is she?" I demanded.

"Family," Anton said, with a dead serious look in his eyes.

"What?"

"She's the aunt of that child, Zharina, who communicates telepathically with my son Gavin, and claims they are to be wed when they come of age."

"So she *is* Veredian? But those horns—"

"She's a hybrid Guldan-Veredian."

My heart skipped a beat. "How is that even possible?"

"That's a story for her to tell," Anton said. "I am sending her to my father on Braxia."

My blood froze, and an irrational rage I barely managed to repress had my spine stiffening nearly to the breaking point.

"What do you mean 'sending her to your father'?" I asked, my voice dangerously low.

Anton narrowed his eyes at me. "She has business on Braxia. He will offer her his protection during her stay."

"*I* will protect her," I said a tone that brooked no argument.

I had the utmost respect for his father, Krygor Aldriss, but I didn't want him anywhere near my woman. She became mine the moment she entered the room, and her eyes undressed me with a glimmer of approval. If any man could prove a rival, it was Anton's father.

"Ravik, she's a breathtaking female and one who, oddly enough, likes brutish looking men like you and me—even more so like you. Braxia is on the verge of a civil war. You becoming involved with a half-breed female, not even half-Braxian, will further fan the flames." Anton leaned forward, his stance somewhat pleading as he tried to reason with me. "Guldans are knocking at your door. Once they realize what she is, they will hunt her down with a vengeance. She's worth a fortune."

"If the war comes, it will do so with or without her. As for the Guldans, I will personally deal with them. They will not dictate what happens on my home world."

"Ravik…"

"Would you have given up Grace over possible threats from your clan?" I asked, interrupting him.

Anton's eyes widened. "Grace is my soulmate. Are you saying—?"

"I'm saying that the last time a female stirred me this strongly dates back thirty-eight years ago with my Lissy. However rotten the timing, the Fates will decide its outcome, not any pressure Braxia would impose on me. I didn't help you get rid of Braxia's shackles only to don them myself."

Anton cringed then nodded in concession.

"If anything happens to her, Braxia will have an even greater problem on its hands."

"The Tuureans," I said on a hunch.

"Yes. But not just because they are protective of the Veredians. The Tuurean leader cares deeply for Ravena. If she comes to harm, the Ancestors help Braxia."

My temper flared again. "Admiral Lee?" I asked, my voice taking on a sharp edge. "What does he want with her?"

Anton smirked, and I clenched my jaw, embarrassed by my primitive display of jealousy.

"The Admiral is already mated and harbors no romantic interest towards Ravena. But he does love her and will bring down the entire Tuurean fleet on Braxia if she's not returned safely."

I narrowed my eyes, reading between the lines. "You think Guldans might orchestrate a confrontation to force us into an alliance with them."

Anton nodded. "Braxia cannot defeat the Tuureans on its own, especially not if their fiercest allies, the Xelixians, join the fray. You'd need the Guldans, and probably the Sarenians as well, for a chance to survive."

"Which is exactly where the Guldans want us," I said, nodding slowly.

"Yes."

I gazed at him affectionately. "For a businessman, you would have made quite the military advisor."

Anton chuckled and averted his eyes, looking somewhat embarrassed. "To be successful in business, one needs to recognize what people truly want and what motivates them. And then you either cater to it or thwart it." He paused, his lips parting and eyes widening as if suddenly struck by an idea. "You know, the Tuureans could become your greatest allies. They are settling a whole new planet for the Veredians since their home world has been destroyed by a solar storm. This could open the door to many trade opportunities for Braxia. You should take advantage of Ravena's stay to broach the subject with her."

I shifted on my seat, perking up at that possibility. Although I'd never admit it, I was growing desperate to find a solution for Braxia. A civil war would end us. If I believed for one minute one of my rivals could turn the tide for us and bring my home world back to its former glory, I'd abdicate in a heartbeat. For all its flaws and backward ways, I loved Braxia and would see her rise again.

"Would she welcome such conversations? You who gauge people so well, what are her motivations? What does she want?" I asked.

Anton stared me straight in the eyes. "Her motivation is redemption and making amends for the wrongs her father and brother have wrought on the Veredians. But what she truly wants... is you."

CHAPTER 4
MERCY

The Goddess had one messed up sense of humor. After forty-nine years of existence, she finally puts my soulmate in my path, and he turned out to be the fucking Magnar of Braxia. What was she thinking? Of all the species to mate into, his was worse than Guldans. But the tingle of the Tuning couldn't be denied. The minute I'd entered the room, needles had pricked my nape, the sensation only growing in strength as I approached Ravik. Too many of my Veredian Sisters had described the phenomenon for me not to recognize it for what it was. This psychic trait manifested whenever one was in the presence of the one other being in the entire universe that had been created for them.

And the Magnar was the most magnificent beast I had ever laid eyes upon.

My beast.

Just thinking of that mountain of a man and his fearsome face had me weak in the knees, and throbbing with need. Despite my height, the top of my head barely reached his shoulders. His biceps were bigger than my head, and his large, callused hands could crush my spine without effort. And yet, it had taken all of my willpower not to throw myself on him and lick, one-by-one, every single bulging vein that criss-crossed his muscular arms.

Why the fuck did he have to be the Magnar? With my irreverent nature, I was bound to create some kind of diplomatic incident. Thankfully, he hadn't taken offense to my earlier banter. I couldn't help my flirty and taunting ways. Sure, I could try to curb those tendencies, but if anything were to work out between us, he needed to know the real me; impertinent, sarcastic, unrepentant, and cocky.

The question was, did I actually want this to work? I wasn't, and never would be, the submissive type. No man would ever—could ever—control me. No society would ever enchain me. At forty-nine, I was too old to change; not that I'd want to. From my reading about Braxia, the Magnar would be one year older than I, raised by the most intolerant, backwards thinking man in the Eastern Quadrant. How could we ever possibly have a harmonious relationship? And Braxia? I'd just found my family who lived on the other side of the galaxy. I didn't want to part from them again.

Why couldn't he have been a hybrid? From the first time I'd laid eyes on Anton, I'd known my mate would likely have Braxian blood. After I'd sorted things out with my father's inheritance, Varrek's clients list, and freed my younger sisters, I'd planned on taking a trip to this Quadrant's Haven. The sanctuary planet was home to various species, including many half-breed Braxians who had fled the persecution against them on their home world. I'd hoped to find myself a nice male, who shared the human values of the local population, which promoted acceptance and gender equality.

The clip-clop of Grace's insanely high heels drew me out of my musing. After a quick shower in the guest bedroom that had been assigned to me, I'd put on one of the dresses I'd bought during our little shopping spree. Like me, Ravik had black hair, obsidian eyes, and seemed to like dressing in dark colors. I'd initially planned on wearing a black dress again, but Grace had insisted on me wearing a short, backless, white dress that flattered my coppery complexion. While comfortable with heels, I'd refused to wear the sky-high stilettos she'd suggested. Nevertheless, the silver sandals I settled on had respectably high heels.

At Grace's request, once dressed, I went to her room so she could fix my hair. She made an elaborate bun that wouldn't hide my exposed back. Next, she wanted me to wear one of her pairs of earrings.

Sitting at the elegant vanity in the left corner of the room, I watched her reflection through the mirror as she made her way to an imposing dark wood dresser. It occupied a large section of the wall at the right of the massive bed, also built with dark wood. Grace rummaged through the top drawer, which contained a large collection of jewelry. I shifted on a cushioned stool while glancing around the room. Elegant and sparingly decorated, the light grey walls made it look even more spacious. But the walls, which also served as giant screens, held my attention. Currently, they'd been set to resemble windows looking out into luxuriant gardens from the exotic planet Kigamot Sek.

"These are just perfect!" Grace said, returning to me with the precious baubles cradled in her palm.

Each earring consisted of a large, tear-shaped Pleusian pearl, artistically wrapped in a silver coil which spiraled around it. She hooked them in my pierced earlobes, then took a step back to admire her work.

"Up, up," she said, waving her hands for me to rise from my seat.

I complied, my heels making me tower over her even more. She bit her plump, bottom lip, painted in the same blood red as her nails, and gave me an appreciative once over.

"Ravik is going to swallow his tongue when he sees you," she said with a mischievous glint in her eyes. "You're smoking hot even without makeup!"

My face heated. I was aware of my own beauty and never cared much for makeup aside from the occasional lipstick or lip gloss. And tonight I wanted Ravik to see me, not artifices to enhance me.

Coming from one as stunning as she was, the compliment felt even more flattering. She had not been at all what I'd expected. Beautiful females marrying wealthy, unattractive men—by 'normal' standards— were often social climbers or cold-hearted bitches. Grace was sweet, always eager to help—and to please—and genuinely appreciative of any act of kindness or display of friendship. She was easy to love.

She lured me in front of the mirror to admire her handiwork. The white dress was deceptively demure, tying around my neck in the back like a halter dress. The nude back cut so low it could have been taken straight from the Guldan traditional Free Woman dress. Despite the mid-thigh length of the skirt, it still had slits on each side, almost up to my hips. My exposed arms and legs flaunted my Veredian markings. Grace had twisted some strands of my hair, wrapping them around my head like a crown and knotting the rest into a bun.

"How in the world did you manage to make my hair hold like that with only two long pins?" I asked, amazed by her masterful work.

"When you are married to a man who wants quick and easy access to everything, you learn some tricks. Anton loves my hair down," she said, twirling a reddish-brown lock of it. "He only agrees to me having buns because he can undo them by pulling out a single pin. But yours is way too long to get away with just one."

Grace turned around, the flowy skirt of her red Grecian dress swirling around her. The long slit on her right side gave a glimpse of her shapely leg with each step. Cinched at the waist, the chest consisted of two straps of luxurious fabric covering each breast in a plunging neckline.

"Let's go mess with the men's heads," Grace said with a giggle, leading the way to the living room.

I followed in her wake, my heart fluttering in anticipation of Ravik's reaction. The men rose to their feet upon our entrance. Anton purred, a smoldering look descending upon his features as he gazed upon his mate. Grace blossomed under his approving gaze and walked up to him, her hips swaying. Anton wrapped an arm around her, his hand resting on her behind as he pressed her against him and captured her lips in a searing kiss.

Ravik's onyx eyes burned right through me, his thick lips twisting in a half-snarl. The naked hunger on his face had my inner walls clenching and my skin heating. He prowled towards me, his tight shirt hugging his bulging chest muscles that rippled with each movement.

My mouth went dry as he stopped a couple of steps in front of me. Even with the heels on, he still dwarfed me.

"You look stunning, Ravena," he said, his gravelly voice making me shiver.

I loved the way he said my name, as if he tasted and savored every syllable while picturing it was me rolling over his tongue. Although I didn't sleep around, I wasn't prudish and had no qualms taking my pleasure when and with whom I saw fit when the fancy struck me. But until today, never had I burned so fiercely for a man. Had Anton and Grace not been present, I'd already have torn Ravik's clothes off.

"Thank you," I said with a teasing smile. "I'm glad you approve."

He snorted. "I most certainly do."

"Let us be on our way," Anton said, leading his wife to the elevator, his hand resting on her hip.

Ravik gestured for me to proceed before shadowing me. The lift chimed seconds before the door opened. We entered, Ravik filling up the space, the top of his head almost touching the elevator's ceiling. He stood close enough for me to feel the warmth of his body. I wanted to lean against him and feel his hands on my bare skin. The elevator came to a stop, its door opening. As if he'd heard my unspoken wish, Ravik placed his callused palm on the naked small of my back to give me a gentle nudge to exit the cabin. A bolt of lust exploded in the pit of my stomach, and my nipples pebbled.

His thumb gently caressed my skin before he removed his hand, leaving me feeling bereft and needy. Exiting after us, Anton and Grace quickly took the lead. Two massive Braxians awaited us at the entrance; Ravik's security detail. I couldn't imagine why in the world someone as fearsome and powerful as he would need them, but then again, he was the ruler of his planet.

It took us ten minutes to walk from the penthouse to Risqué. The walkways bustled with activity; many of the patrons making their way to their place of choice to have their meal—some casually strolling, while others hurried through the crowd. Despite a dominant number of humans, no doubt due to the large number of Terran colonies nearby, a wide variety of alien species commingled. While the dress code in public areas was fairly strict, masters were allowed to have their *pets* on a leash. So far, all of the ones we'd encountered—but one—had been human pets.

Where patrons nodded respectfully in greeting upon seeing Anton, most of them cowered and made way for Ravik. My man was a behemoth. When one patron almost bumped into me, Ravik placed his hand on my hip to pull me to him.

To my delight, he didn't remove it, even after the 'danger' had passed.

By the time we reached Risqué, his hand no longer rested on my hip but on the bare skin of my back. A bit of a hush fell over the crowded place upon our entrance. Many eyes widened and mouths slightly parted in shock as the patrons took in the giant by my side. Unlike Grace, I wasn't an exhibitionist. Yet, the bewildered stares of the crowd lingering on Ravik's possessive hand on my back did weirdly delicious things to me. I loved knowing that the mere sight of my man set such fear in them. That *I* would be the one to tame that fearsome beast.

We reached Anton's private booth, located on an elevated dais against the back wall in the center of the dining room. Circular in shape, it offered a perfect view of the stage and of the dance floor before it. There, a handful of couples swayed to the soft ballads played by a small orchestra. Grace and I slipped onto the seat covered in dark red leather, her from the left and me from the right, before our men took their places at our sides. I let my gaze roam over the room. The beige walls made it look immense, the color sharply contrasting with the shiny, dark brown, wooden floor. Wall lamps, propped at the top of pillars strategically placed so as not to obstruct the view of the stage, provided a soft, ambient light.

Considering the chic décor and refined clientele, the presence of more pets kneeling at their masters' feet surprised me. The one closest to our table appeared to be a human male. However, a set of straight lines on his skin, above his collar, reminded me of gills. From a distance, I couldn't tell whether he possessed webbed hands and feet to confirm my assumptions he was a human-Jalunian hybrid.

A pretty, blonde waitress in a second-skin of a white leather dress with matching blood red lipstick and high heels, came to ask what we wanted to drink. Her green eyes flicked a few times towards Ravik. I had to bite the inside of my cheeks as her expression alternated between fear and awe of his brutish face and massive, muscular arms. I realized then that Ravik's guards had made themselves scarce, although I didn't doubt for a minute that they lurked well within intervention range.

After the waitress left to fetch our drinks, we consulted the menu and finally settled for The Train, a degustation option with wine pairings in which we would receive samplers of every single item on the special menu until we begged for mercy. It offered well over one hundred specialty dishes from twenty-three different planets, and an extra forty dessert choices.

The evening proved quite delightful with the food being as exquisite as the company. Learning about Grace's singing career, and all the work that goes on behind the scenes, fascinated me. Discovering more about Anton's immense pleasure barge empire had my head spinning. Running Venus Hive alone seemed like an impossible undertaking. And yet, he had six more stations scattered throughout the Eastern Quadrant.

However, Ravik turned out to be the most pleasant surprise. Having witnessed the wonderful relationship of many couples who had experienced the Tuning, I hadn't questioned Ravik being the perfect match for me, being my soulmate. But behind his rough, barbaric exterior, the Magnar hid a keen intelligence, an impressive breadth of knowledge in art, culture, and obviously politics, but best of all, an irreverent sense of humor like me. Except, in his case, he liked fucking with your mind and making you wonder if he was serious or not.

Grace gave up somewhere around dish sample number twenty-one. I plowed through an additional seven before yielding as well. The men chowed down on at least double that. Anton conceded first. Although Ravik stopped at the same time he did, I suspected he could have gone on much longer.

Nevertheless, appearing sated, he leaned back against the leather seat, and spread his right arm on the backrest behind me. While he didn't touch me, the heat of his skin had me tingling and craving for greater contact.

Anton gently brushed Grace's hair from her face before caressing it with his fingers. She turned her luminous, amber eyes towards him and smiled. He leaned forward and kissed her softly.

"Let's dance," he whispered to his mate.

She nodded. They excused themselves and slipped off the couch, Anton leading Grace by the hand. I envied the easy love and obvious devotion between them. Without going into details while she'd done my hair earlier, Grace had given me a glimpse of some of the hardships she and Anton had faced before finally finding happiness together. The haunted look on her face that I'd caught in her reflection in the mirror hinted at far more terrible times than she'd let on. While she clearly wanted Ravik to find the same kind of happiness, and also appeared to like the idea it might be with me, Grace had given me a clear warning that a difficult road awaited us ahead.

Anton pulled his wife into his embrace. She buried her face in the crook of his neck as they began to move to the music. His movements, incredibly fluid for someone so big and muscular, impressed me. I turned to face Ravik and raised an inquisitive eyebrow.

"Aren't you going to invite me to dance as well?" I asked.

"No," Ravik said, his voice devoid of any emotion.

My brows shot up. "Seriously?"

He nodded.

"Why? Are you afraid to step on my toes?" I asked, taken aback.

Seeing how he appeared to want to devour me for dessert, I had expected him to jump at the opportunity to hold me close.

"As a matter of fact, I am," he said, his deep voice rolling over me like a rumbling purr.

My lips parted in shock. I'd meant to tease and taunt him. This brutal honesty left me speechless.

His smile broadened at my stunned expression. "Braxians do not dance as couples. Females perform erotic dances to entertain the males.

And the males perform tribal dances, usually as part of ceremonial rituals or as a challenge before a battle. The latter hasn't happened in decades."

My eyes flicked towards Anton and Grace tightly wrapped around each other as they danced amidst half a dozen other couples.

I pointed at them with my chin. "As you can see, it's not that complicated, even if you don't have any sense of rhythm."

Ravik tilted his head to the side, a lock of his black hair falling over his left eye. "I never said I didn't have rhythm."

"Then you have no excuse," I replied. "As you won't invite me, I'm asking you to dance and will take any refusal as a personal rejection."

Ravik snorted, and his lips stretched further. Unlike Anton, smiling didn't soften his features but made him look even more feral, like a hungry beast baring its teeth at its prey.

"Are you so eager to find yourself in my arms, little raven?" he asked, his eyes smoldering.

"What if I said yes?" I asked.

His gaze roamed over me with a possessiveness that made my stomach clench.

"Then it would be rude of me to deny your desires. Come on, then, little bird."

His massive hand swallowed mine as he led me to the dance floor. His grip, gentle yet firm, reminded me how easily he could crush my bones just by squeezing a bit. My stomach fluttered, and my breath quickened with anticipation. I didn't know him well enough to have any actual emotional attachment towards him, but the purely animal attraction between us overwhelmed me. I'd never responded so strongly to any male.

He stopped near the left edge of the dance floor and drew me to him. His right arm wrapped around my bare back, his hand slipping under the fabric on the side of my dress, his fingers resting on the naked flesh above my waist. His other hand rested on the small of my back, holding me tightly against him. Rough and callused, they felt like burning irons on my skin. I nearly moaned when my breasts, and then my pelvis, pressed against his hard body. My palms found their way to his shoulders and trailed over the rippling ridges of his muscles to rest on each side of his thick neck. The top of my forehead brushed against the side of his chin as I leaned in to inhale his earthy, male scent.

Ravik began to sway to the music, and I followed his lead. His movements didn't have the fluidity that Anton had displayed, but he clearly had rhythm. I shivered as his thumbs began to draw slow circles on my skin. His chest vibrated against mine with a low chuckle. He knew very well the power he held over me. That should have irritated me, but it didn't.

I lifted my head, and our eyes locked. Goddess, he was ridiculously tall and broad. Unless he bent forward or I got up on my tippy toes, my arms couldn't reach far enough to clasp my hands behind his neck.

Ravik lowered his head towards me. "You are playing a dangerous game, little bird," he whispered.

"I can be reckless and bold, but some things you don't play with."

He held my gaze as if attempting to read my mind, then his eyes dipped to my lips. They parted in response, inviting. A muscle ticked on the side of his square, jutting jaw, and he clenched his teeth. I couldn't decide if I felt more frustrated by his restraint or elated by his obvious struggle to resist his attraction to me.

"I hear you are coming to my home world," Ravik said. "Why?"

I stiffened at the sudden change of topic. His hand on my side moved up. If he'd stretch his fingers further they would brush against the side of my right breast.

"Personal business," I said noncommittally.

He narrowed his eyes at me, and I barely resisted the urge to squirm. That response shocked me. Aside from my father's stern stare, no one had ever made me feel like this before.

"I have reason to believe my brother was trying to set up a slave ring on Braxia," I continued. "I'm going there to shut down whatever he's started and hopefully retrieve something that will help me find my younger twin sisters, who were sold over thirty years ago to a bounty hunter."

Ravik frowned, then nodded slowly. "What proof do you have of this slave ring?"

"In our family home on Guldar, I found documentation on equipment he ordered and construction work he had commissioned on Braxia," I said, my thumbs tracing the rock hard curve of his sizeable trapezius muscles on each side of his neck. "I believe he also planned on setting up a lab to refine and distribute Bliss."

Ravik bared his teeth in sudden anger. "He was behind that wretched drug?" he hissed.

I lifted my chin, trying to silence the inevitable shame I always felt when reminded of the terrible things my family had done. The highly addictive drug had caused ravages in the short time Varrek had managed to distribute it before his demise. No cure existed for that addiction, and withdrawal always led to death.

"Yes," I said, my tone slightly clipped. "So you understand why I must go."

He nodded again. "Braxia is going through troubled times. It isn't a safe place for a female, especially one as exotic as you."

I shrugged. "Anton already warned me of it. His father will ensure my safety."

"He will do no such thing," Ravik snarled, his grip tightening around me.

My eyes widened, and my heart sank.

"You would deny me entry to your world?" I asked, my eyes flicking between his.

"While wisdom dictates that I should forbid you access for your own safety, I will not. However, no other man but me will give you his protection. It will be my shield over you; no one else's."

My stomach flip-flopped at his commanding tone—and the almost vicious look in his eyes—as he dared me to challenge his statement.

"Someone is possessive," I whispered.

Ravik's hand under the edge of my dress caressed me from the side of my breast to the curve of my bum, this time with zero effort at subtlety.

"I also do not play," he said, his voice between a promise and a threat.

The music ended, and I almost whimpered when he released me, wishing to remain in his embrace a while longer. I hated feeling so needy and chose not to throw myself further at him by asking for a second dance. I shivered. My skin, where his burning hands had held me, suddenly felt cold. Ravik's palm found its way to my hip as he guided me back to Anton's private booth. Although I appreciated the feel of his hand on me again, it was on my bare skin that I wanted it.

We resumed our seats, joined shortly thereafter by Anton and Grace. As soon as he settled next to me, Ravik placed a possessive hand on my thigh left exposed by my short skirt. Although tanned, his skin almost looked white against mine which was quite a few shades darker. I stared at it before looking up at him. He held my gaze, daring me to challenge his claim. Without missing a beat, I responded by placing my own on his thigh. He snorted, then inclined his head in agreement.

Sensing our hosts watching us, I peered at them. Grace stared with undisguised curiosity and excitement. Anton observed us with a somewhat troubled expression. It didn't take a genius to guess he felt uncertain of the wisdom regarding any involvement between the Magnar and me. I shared those concerns. And yet…

"I never knew you were such a good dancer, Ravik," Grace said, leaning against her husband. "I'll have to tell Naya. She'll demand a dance with her 'Maga Ravi' before you leave."

"You will do no such thing," Ravik said with a falsely threatening expression.

Anton chuckled, his fingers fiddling with his wife's hair. "Our daughter is quite looking forward to seeing you in the morning. She says you and my father give the best pony rides."

Picturing Grace's and Anton's three-year old daughter hanging on to Ravik's forehead as he horsed around the living room under her peals of laughter had me chuckling as well. He glared at Anton and then at me. That made me chuckle even more. I could totally hear Naya with her baby voice calling him Maga Ravi. The three children were spending the night at their Uncle Marcus' place to give their parents the freedom to entertain us and would return in the morning.

Ravik opened his mouth to respond but abruptly stopped as one of his bodyguards seemed to appear out of thin air. He obviously hadn't, but I'd been too intent on the Magnar to notice his approach.

"A word, if you please," the bodyguard said.

Ravik excused himself and followed his guard to a room at the back of the restaurant. My gaze followed them until they fell out of sight. Turning back to my hosts, I gave them a curious look. Grace's shoulders sagged, and her lips pursed into the loveliest pout.

"I bet he's leaving," she said.

"Leaving?" I asked.

"For Tagar to interrupt Ravik's leisure time, something serious must be happening on Braxia."

I frowned and cast a worried glance towards the still closed door.

"Ravena," Anton said, making me turn back to him. "You should know that Ravik has demanded the privilege of ensuring your protection."

I nodded. "Yes. He told me as much in no uncertain terms," I said in a teasing tone.

Anton's serious expression sobered me.

"Then I would request you do the same for him," he said, making me recoil in surprise. "The attraction between you two is plain to see. They will try to use you to hurt him. I respect your wish for independence, but please do not make yourself a target."

I wanted to bristle at the comment, but something in his demeanor made me realize he genuinely feared for Ravik... and for me.

"Are things that bad?" I asked.

"Yes. Worse, even, than anything I could describe," Anton said, running a hand through his hair. "A third of the population is unemployed and starving. Braxians are proud. Most refuse the relief efforts Ravik has set up to support them until their clans can bounce back. Aside from battle, too large a proportion of Braxians have no trade or technical skills. They have little to no resources worth trading, and among the few who do, many have lost everything because of stupid vendettas over bruised honor."

He cast a side-glance at his wife. The remorse burning in his eyes confused me. Grace smiled affectionately and caressed his cheek. He closed his eyes and leaned into the touch before turning his face and kissing her palm.

What could she have possibly done to him to deserve his vengeance, one that has remorse still haunting him today?

"Braxia has alienated a lot of former allied planets because of excessive revenge over stupid incidents. They're not facing embargos, but they might as well be. The Braxians fucked up, yet they expect Ravik to clean up their mess. Those who want to go back to the old ways are fueling the brewing discontent in an effort to overthrow him."

Anton's eyes flicked to the right. I followed his gaze and saw Ravik exit the room with his guard.

"So I beseech you. During your stay on Braxia, tread carefully."

"Your words have not fallen on deaf ears," I said, in a pledging tone.

We quieted as Ravik approached, a grim expression on his face. His guard stopped at a respectful distance to grant us privacy.

"I must return at once to Braxia." The nerve ticking on his temple and the stiffness of his stance expressed the extent of his aggravation. "It appears everything that could go wrong decided to do so in my absence."

"What's going on?" Grace said, her voice laced with concern.

"Packs of joarkals have been rampaging through the countryside, and now, it appears a large pack is moving towards the capital."

"That's too early," Anton argued, his prominent forehead wrinkling in a frown.

"Exactly," Ravik hissed. "Something, or *someone*, has spurred them into hunting a month early. And Caldes' Guldan guests conveniently happen to have arrived hours after my departure. Pattel just informed me that they are already doing the rounds, trying to garner support from the clans for a potential alliance between our peoples."

"That son of a krillik," Anton said between his teeth.

"They're trying to push you into a corner," Grace whispered.

"Yes. But I will not allow it. Come," Ravik said, extending a hand towards me. "We must depart."

I instinctively took his hand. Anton signaled the waitress and told her to put everything on his tab before following us with Grace. The guards awaited us outside next to a stretched hovercar, big enough for six passengers. That we would ride instead of taking the ten-minute walk back to the penthouse expressed the extent of his eagerness to return to Braxia.

One of the guards remained in the vehicle while Tagar escorted us to the elevator, but he didn't follow us up. As the door of the elevator opened on to the penthouse, I silenced the pang of sorrow that made my chest tighten. This wasn't how I had pictured ending the evening. I didn't want to see him go just yet.

But he said you're under his protection…

Still holding my hand, Ravik pulled me after him as he headed toward the sleeping quarters. He stopped in front of my bedroom.

"Pack your things. Be quick," he said.

"My things? But… I have a ship and crew…"

His massive hand wrapped about my nape, his hold firm but gentle. He leaned forward, his lips inches from mine. "They can follow after. You travel with me and enter Braxia at my side."

My stomach clenched under the heat of his body so close to mine and the domineering intensity in his eyes. I realized he'd been closing the distance between our faces when the firm cushion of his lips pressed against mine. I leaned into him, my palms splayed on his chest. His tongue invaded my mouth like a conqueror, leaving no doubt about who was in command. The taste of the Dantorian wine we had drunk with our meal lingered on his breath. Too soon, he lifted his head, his obsidian eyes boring into mine.

"Be quick," he whispered.

His thumb caressed my bottom lip before he dropped his hand. Turning around, he marched with determination to his own room a few feet down the hallway, on the opposite side from mine. My knees wobbled as I entered my bedroom and hailed my First Officer Sarah on the com.

"Sarah," she answered.

"I'm leaving immediately for Braxia aboard the Magnar's ship. Please have my Falcon ready and on standby," I said while packing my few toiletries in the bathroom. "I'm hoping there's room in his shuttle bay for it to fit. Otherwise, I will need Tommen to bring it to me on Braxia. I will give you confirmation shortly."

"Understood," Sarah said.

"Ravena out," I said before ending the com.

I quickly changed into black leggings and a long-sleeved, dark-grey sweater. While it irked me to continue to hide my genetics, Anton's warnings still resonated loud and clear in my ears. Until I had a better understanding of the situation with Ravik's crew, and on Braxia, discretion sounded like a wise approach.

It took me minutes to gather my things. I hadn't really unpacked anything, since I'd only planned on spending a single night on Venus Hive. A soft knock on my door startled me.

"Come in," I said, closing my bag.

The door partially opened, and Grace's heart-shaped face peeked in. She carefully looked around the room, as if to confirm I was alone. I laughed and waved her in.

"You're not interrupting anything naughty."

Her gorgeous face heated, and she entered, clutching a small bag in her hand. The door closed behind her with a soft click. The way she chewed her bottom lip and approached with hesitant steps made me wonder at the contents of the bag.

She cleared her throat. "I... Listen, I hope you're not going to find this out of line. So... I apologize in advance if you find any of this offensive."

Now she had me really curious.

I shrugged. "It takes a lot to offend me, but your disclaimer is duly noted."

She licked her lips nervously and extended the bag towards me. My jaw dropped after I opened it. I looked back at her with disbelieving eyes. Grace appeared on the verge of running out of the room for cover as she awaited my reaction.

I burst out laughing. The tension bled from her shoulders, relief settling on her beautiful features.

"Denax?" I asked, waving the bottle containing a clear liquid. It served as lubricant and powerful dilator.

Grace's face heated again. I almost felt sorry for her. That milky-white complexion of hers hid nothing of her embarrassment.

"Trust me. Braxians cannot mate with humans without Denax, or they will kill them. They're too big."

I smiled, unable to hide my amusement. "I'm not human, Grace. Despite our similarities, we are anatomically different."

Her brows shot up in surprise and curiosity.

"Guldan females never tear." I tapped the side of one of my horns, being careful not to stab myself on its sharp tip. "Our offspring are born fully horned. They would shred us to pieces if our inner walls weren't reinforced and flexible enough to adjust as needed."

Grace's lips parted in shock. She stared at my groin like she could see right through clothes and skin at what I'd just described.

Shaking her head, she looked at me in awe. "You really are made for him."

That sobered me.

"More than you know, Grace."

A troubled look descended on her face.

"What is it?" I asked.

She hesitated then gestured at the bed, inviting me to take a seat as she herself settled on the edge.

"I have known Ravik for nearly six years now. He has never reacted towards any woman the way he has with you. I barely know you, but I know you could grow to be very important to him. He's like a father to Anton and me. In many ways, he made it possible for us and our children to have a safe future together." Her eyes flicked between mine, pleadingly. "Please, don't hurt him."

"I assure you, Grace, it is not my intention."

"I believe you, but..." She hesitated, appearing to look for the proper way to word her thoughts. "Braxia is a terrible place with a dreadful culture. People sometimes do horrible things that haunt them forever. But no amount of remorse can ever erase the damage and the guilt they bear."

By the haunted look in her eyes, I realized that she was no longer just talking about Ravik, but Anton as well.

"Do not let his outward appearance fool you. Ravik is a good man who carries a great deal of pain inside. He deserves to be happy. I hope it can be with you."

My throat tightened. I didn't know what Ravik had done for her to give me such a veiled warning, but I understood guilt all too well.

"We've all done things in the past that we regret. What matters isn't what we did, but what we're doing now to be better," I said.

"I'm glad he met you. Please be safe," Grace said before hugging me.

I returned her embrace. At that moment, I realized that my instant affection for Grace had been partially caused by how similar her personality was to my late sister, Sevina. Like her, she had been a submissive, gentle soul with her heart on her hand. She had only ever wanted to live in peace with others and be loved for who she was.

A firm knock on the door startled us. I didn't need to ask to know who it was. Grace released me, and we both rose to our feet.

"Oh!" Grace said. "I almost forgot. Just so you know, if you are using contraception, it probably won't work with a Braxian."

A second, more forceful knock on the door kept me from answering.

"Come in!" I said, shoving the dilator bottle back into the bag and slipping it inside my luggage.

The door opened on Ravik, looking even more imposing than I remembered. His eyes narrowed suspiciously at Grace, who smiled at him with a semi-guilty expression on her face. I grabbed my bags and stepped in front of her, breaking his line of sight.

He refocused on me as I marched up to him. "Ready when you are, big boy."

He snorted. "I assure you, little bird, I am no boy."

Grace's chuckle joined mine as Ravik took my bags from me, and we headed for the elevators. My farewells to Anton and Grace were bittersweet. However odd this couple appeared to be at first glance, they were seriously growing on me. I regretted not having a chance to see their children and missing the gladiator finale that would take place the next day. But destiny awaited me ahead.

CHAPTER 5
RAVIK

Distracted by my woman supervising the transfer of her vessel to my shuttle bay, I half listened to Baldur, my ship's captain, as he gave me his report. I wanted him to go away, his voice like so many gnats buzzing in my ears. Ravena fascinated me and stirred emotions within me that I'd never thought to experience again.

It frightened me.

Even before that too brief taste of her, I'd known she would become an obsession and a weakness. I couldn't understand her obvious attraction to me. By intergalactic standards, nothing about my face would ever qualify as handsome. On Braxia, beauty was not a common trait for males, nor was it sought after. The more feral and bestial the features, the purer the bloodline, and the more fearsome the warrior. Beauty was only required for females. Stunning, smart, and with an irresistible sass that bordered on insolence, Ravena could have any man she wanted. Yet, the scent of my woman's arousal lingered in my nose, and her heated response at my touch still had my blood boiling with the need to conquer her.

But what does she want?

In this liberal era, most prosperous and technologically advanced planets enforced strict rules of gender equality in all aspects of life. A large number of single females came on pleasure barges such as those in Anton's Hive Network on a quest for exotic entertainment. The many dominatrices and mistresses leading their pets around on a leash were further testimony of how the world had changed, and how we'd been left behind.

No, we've been refusing to change with it.

On Braxia, a female caught seeking sexual fulfilment would be cast down as a whore and declared a clan toy to be used by any male, at any time—however he wished—for his pleasure. But here in the rest of the world, females were encouraged and empowered to explore their sexuality like males had for millennia. Was I entertainment to her? A fleeting, exotic affair to scratch an itch during her short, planned stay on Braxia?

While that very probable prospect triggered a dull ache in my chest and ignited an irrational anger deep within, reason dictated it would be the best possible outcome for all concerned. Having such a gorgeous female as my concubine for a short while would gain me praise and admiration. Anything more serious would trigger some major outcry. But even if I wanted to weather that storm, what did I have to offer her? She was the outrageously wealthy heiress of the once, most successful slaver in the galaxy. I was the ruler of a backwater planet on the verge of bankruptcy, if not war.

Looking around the shuttle bay at my four dozen shuttles and fighters, Ravena's small vessel sitting amongst them further highlighted the gap between us. Sleek, elegant, and at the height of technological excellence, it put my own battleship to shame. Clearly of Guldan design with its sharp, angular edges, it also possessed some other influences, dominantly Tuurean.

"Has everyone returned to the ship?" I asked.

"Everyone except some of our guests, Magnar," Baldur replied. "The non-warriors stated that, as they would be of no use in the hunt, they would remain to honor the Braxian gladiators in the championship."

Ravena's soft but determined steps resonated on the dark metal plating covering the floor as she approached us.

"Pattel returned as well?"

"Yes, Magnar."

As much as I wanted him with me on Braxia, this wouldn't do. I resisted the urge to place a possessive hand around Ravena's waist when she stopped by my side. Baldur's eyes flicked towards her before he quickly averted them.

"Have him come to my quarters and prepare for immediate departure."

"Yes, Magnar," Baldur said.

He slightly bowed his head and struck his chest with his fist as a salute before leaving.

"Come," I said to Ravena. "Let me show you to your quarters."

The thick, reinforced metal doors parted before us as we exited the shuttle bay under the curious eyes of the crew. Females very rarely got to travel onboard a Braxian ship, unless they were sex slaves to see to the needs of the crew. And those were only allowed on long missions, not short trips like this one. The other rare cases were if a foreign guest traveled with us, accompanied by a spouse or daughter. But they usually preferred to fly alongside us in their own vessel. I couldn't blame them. Ravena's stunning beauty drew even more stares. In many ways, Caldes was right in making a parallel between Guldans and Braxians as perfect allies. Like us, they jealously kept their females tucked away on their planet. With both our cultures treating women as mere breeders and fuck toys, they had no reason to travel.

That shameful realization only further highlighted the steep hill I needed to climb to drag Braxia out of its antiquated ways.

Ravena's eyes flicked this way and that as she evaluated my ship on our way to the sleeping quarters. Technologically, it paled in comparison to her shuttle. Nonetheless, it was a beautiful battleship, equipped with the most advanced Braxian technology, weaponry, and top of the line amenities and comforts.

"Burnt-red flooring," Ravena mused out loud. "Interesting color."

I smiled. There was indeed something ominous about it and its dark grey edges, although the pale grey walls helped lighten the overall mood.

"You will find that Braxians are particularly fond of black, dark grey, and maroon."

She nodded. "I had indeed noticed that Anton wore a lot of black and so do you," she said, giving me a quick once over.

I liked the way she looked at me; especially the way her gaze lingered on my muscles. Whatever Braxians lacked in facial beauty, and despite our massive sizes, our bodies were considered works of art. With our high metabolism, we'd yet to see a single overweight Braxian. The slightest effort, and ample nutrition, sufficed for us to gain muscle mass.

"And you as well, little bird," I countered as we crossed the guests' and officers' sleeping quarters.

"I like black or white. White because it looks great with my skin complexion," Ravena said, looking at her wrist. "And black because it makes me feel sexy and naughty."

I chuckled. "There's no question you are both, with or without black."

Her lips stretched in a smirk. The memory of her taste, the softness of her tongue against mine, had me aching for seconds.

"Truth!" she said, an unrepentant glimmer in her eyes.

I stopped in front of the secured door at the end of the corridor; which led to my private suite. Unlike most other sections, whose doors possessed windows you could see through, these were completely occluded and bomb-proof. I placed my hand on the scanner embedded on the wall. The red light at the top turned white, and the door automatically opened with a soft hiss. I didn't go in.

"New access," I said.

"New access requested by Magnar Ravik," said the synthetic voice of Hana, the ship's artificial intelligence. "New guest, please place your hand on the scanner."

Ravena complied without asking any questions. A white light scanned her from head to toe, while another beneath her palm archived a copy of her digital print.

"New guest, please state your full name, loud and clear," Hana said when the scanning lights faded.

Ravena appeared to hesitate for a split second before she spoke. "Ravena Mercy Vrok."

My brows shot up.

Mercy?

"Ravena Mercy Vrok, successfully registered," Hana said. "Magnar Ravik, please state Ravena Mercy Vrok's security clearance level."

"Security clearance level three," I said.

"Security level three now activated for Ravena Mercy Vrok. Registration complete."

Under the current circumstances, it was a little foolish on my part to give her level three when only level one was usually granted. It merely allowed the guest to come and go as they pleased, as well as lock their private room against anyone with clearance level three or lower. William vouching for her certainly helped. But still… for some irrational reason, giving her less than three felt disrespectful.

My suite had four other individual quarters, two of which were reserved for my sons, Keran and Ganek. The adjoining room to my private quarters had never been occupied, as it was reserved for the female I would claim as wife, concubine, or bedroom slave.

I led her to it.

"These are your quarters," I said, showing her in.

Just like in the hallway, dark and light greys and paler shades of maroon dominated. Darker reds would not be used in a female room as it spoke of strength, power, and fury. A massive bed stood in front of a large window, which looked out into the void of space. The dresser, vanity, and breakfast table constituted the only other pieces of furniture within the room, all of which were bolted to the floor.

"This is your dressing room," I said, pressing an inconspicuous pattern on what appeared to be a normal wall panel.

Multiple light-grey shelves and magnetic clothes hangers lay empty. A long bench covered with a red-striped, grey cushion occupied the center of the small rectangular room. The crew had laid Ravena's bag on top of it.

I closed the door and opened the one next to it. "This is the hygiene room, although I believe you call it a fresher in the Western Quadrant."

She nodded and gave the room a cursory glance. Her slight frown at the sight of the particle shower didn't go unnoticed.

"If you wish to bathe with real water, you may use my private bath," I said with a smirk. She raised a curious eyebrow. "This way, little bird."

Ravena's eyes widened when I pressed against a third wall panel that didn't have the hidden symbol. It opened on a small corridor which led to my bath area, although it could almost qualify as a *small*, ten-square-meter pool. As in her room, the back wall was one large window into space. The room was completely bare aside from some dim, recessed lights on the side walls, and a shelf with towels and bathing products. Ravena whistled, her eyes sparkling.

"I'm so all over this one," she whispered and glanced at the front wall, accurately guessing that the central panel hid a door. "And where does that lead?"

"My bedroom, of course," I deadpanned.

"Connecting rooms? How convenient."

"Is it?" I asked, stepping closer to her.

I didn't know what I'd expected but not that she'd step even closer, her breasts brushing against my stomach. Despite her respectable height, Ravena had to crane her neck to look up at me.

"Very," she said.

Her boldness did strange things to me. I'd never been with a non-submissive female before, let alone one as forward as her. Leaning down, I placed my hands on her behind and lifted her up. A soft gasp escaped her lips, but she went along, wrapping her legs around my waist and her arms around my neck.

"That 'nothing' dress you wore earlier was better," I growled, frustrated by her leggings and long-sleeved sweater that denied me the feel of her bare skin.

The memory of its softness beneath my palms had blood rushing to my groin. Not giving her time to respond, I crushed her lips while pressing her body closer to mine. Her lips parted, welcoming my tongue. I explored and plundered, savoring her sweet taste and wanting more. Although she followed my lead, she didn't yield full control to me. Ravena's hands fisted my hair, and she tilted her head to the side to deepen the kiss. Our tongues danced together before I sucked on hers. The sexy moan that rose from her throat almost drowned the chime of my door.

My brain froze for a moment, wondering who the fuck would dare disturb me at such a time. And then I remembered.

Pattel.

Fuck.

Breaking the kiss, I gazed upon my woman's face. The smoldering look in her eyes almost had me ignore Pattel and carry her straight to my bed.

Soon.

I put her back down on her feet and straightened. Her confused look made me smile. She'd been so lost in the moment she hadn't heard the chime.

"I have a guest."

"What?" she asked, further confused.

The chime ringing again startled her, answering her question.

"Seriously?" she asked.

I chuckled. "Hold that thought. It will be brief."

Ravena's gaze burned in my back as I opened the hidden door into my bedroom and closed it behind me.

I ran my fingers through my hair to fix it and brushed a hand over my shirt.

"Open door," I said, standing a few feet in front of it.

Obeying the vocal command, it slid open revealing my Councilman. His eyes flicked around the room, no doubt looking for the source of the delay.

"Come in, old friend." I smirked as he approached me, feeling like a naughty teenager. "Baldur tells me you are returning to Braxia with us."

"Indeed. It is troubling news that joarkals should be on the hunt at this time." His deep green eyes filled with concern.

"It is. But one we will face without you."

Pattel recoiled, his eyes widening in shock. "What do you mean?"

I moved a couple of steps closer to him and put a hand on one of his broad shoulders, giving it a friendly squeeze.

"Your clan has greatly distinguished itself in the championship, in the tournament it also had set up. It angers me that I will not be able to give you proper tribute in person. But you will not be cheated of your rightful moment of glory."

Pattel blinked, then appeared torn between pride and the need to argue.

"You flatter me, Magnar. But Braxia…"

"Braxia can wait an extra day for your arrival," I interrupted. "By all accounts, it will be days before we're done killing them or chasing them away." Raising my second hand to his other shoulder, my eyes bore into his. "I've always been honest with you, and that will not change now. As a friend, I want you to enjoy this win. But as the Magnar, I *need* you to do so. Your clan's victory is also Braxia's. Our people need to see us prevail and receive intergalactic accolades. Your success will be celebrated throughout the home land; the success of a clan who has embraced change."

Pattel's eyes widened in understanding, and he slowly nodded in agreement. "Smart call. I will make sure to give all Braxian participants as much media exposure as possible."

"Good man," I said, releasing him.

"See you in two days," Pattel said. He struck his chest with his fist and left my quarters.

"Com to the bridge," I said once the door closed behind my friend.

"Baldur listening," the captain answered over the intercom.

"As soon as Elder Pattel and his men have left the ship, set a course for Braxia."

"Acknowledged."

"Unless an emergency arises, I am not to be disturbed."

"Yes, Magnar."

"Ravik out," I said, ending the communication.

My eyes flicked to the hidden room leading to the bath, and the fire reignited in the pit of my stomach at the thought of my woman. I cursed my negligence for not procuring some Denax before boarding the ship. Then again, it might be a good thing. As much as I ached to bury myself inside of her, even with the dilator, I doubted she would be able to take one of my girth without tearing. I wanted her screaming my name with pleasure, not in agony. There were other ways to bring each other to completion.

As I approached the door, the sound of splashing water made my heart skip a beat. I had hoped she would make use of it while waiting for me, and not change her mind by taking refuge in her room. I kicked off my boots and stripped out of my clothes, which I casually discarded on the chair near the door.

Naked as a newborn child, I opened the door and stepped onto the soft, heated, anti-slip floor surrounding the pool. Ravena, fully naked as well, floated on her back in the center of the pool, her long, obsidian hair splayed around her like a dark halo. Blood rushed to my groin at the breathtaking view of her beauty. She didn't move, didn't try to hide, allowing instead her gaze to roam over me. My shaft hardened, rising until it stood erect before my stomach. The fear I expected its sight would elicit in my woman never came.

"Tell me to leave," I said, giving her one final chance to retreat.

She straightened, an indecipherable expression on her serious face, and extended an inviting hand towards me. I lowered myself into the warm water and closed the short distance between us. Ravena's hands reached for my chest, caressed their way up to my shoulders and around my neck before her fingers buried themselves in my hair. I drew her into my embrace, and her legs closed around me. A feral growl rose from my throat at the searing heat of her naked flesh against mine.

Propping her up, I captured her lips, devouring her mouth while my hands freely roamed over her body. She tightened her hold around me, her core pressing against the tip of my cock. It jerked in response, eager to bury itself within her. Fisting her hair gently, I tilted her head back to cover her jawline with kisses, and then traced with my tongue the Veredian markings along the soft curve of her neck. Ravena shuddered in my arms, a strangled moan escaping her throat. The divine sound sent another jolt of desire straight to my groin. I licked her markings again, eliciting the same strong reaction. As their light-brown color darkened to almost black with each caress, their sensitivity to my touch seemed to increase.

With a gentle tug on her hair, I forced her to lean farther back, exposing her perky breasts to my eager mouth. I licked around the areola, a darker shade of brown than her golden skin, and then nipped at the little button before sucking on it. It hardened under my ministrations as the sound of Ravena's breaths came in short, quick successions. After giving her other breast a bit of attention, I straightened her and reclaimed her mouth. I would never tire of the silken feel of her tongue against mine.

Holding herself up with one arm around my neck, Ravena sneaked a hand between us to close it around my shaft. My hips thrust upwards in an involuntary reflex. Liquid fire poured into my loins, and I growled with unsated hunger. Although my cock was too big for her fingers to close around it, she still managed to stroke me, stirring a slow-building inferno within me. With my arm around her waist, my other hand caressed the rounded curve of her ass, dipping down and around until my fingers found her burning core.

Ravena threw her head back and moaned as I began to massage her little nub. My mouth latched onto her exposed neck, licking and nipping at her markings.

"Ravik," she whispered in a throaty voice when I slipped one of my fingers inside of her.

The sound of my name on her lips nearly drove me insane. With my finger still dipping in and out of her, I waded through the water to the edge of the pool. I sat her at the edge, forcing her to let go of my cock. The need to taste her superseded the terrible sense of loss. Lifting her legs over my shoulders, which forced her to lie down, I buried my face between her thighs. She cried out, her back arching off the floor. The most exquisite taste exploded in my mouth as I lapped at her with ravenous hunger and dipped my tongue in and out of her opening.

Ravena writhed under my touch, one hand fisted in my hair while the other kneaded her own breast. My abdominal muscles contracted painfully from the throbbing ache in my cock. Knowing that I couldn't fuck her, I wanted to wrap my hand around it and stroke it with wild abandon until I found the release it demanded. But my woman's pleasure had to come first.

With my lips sucking on her clit, I inserted two fingers inside her, dipping them in and out with growing intensity. Her tight walls gripped them, contracting in the precursor spasms of her imminent climax. There was something unusual about the texture of her inner walls, not unpleasant, but not as soft as other females. They also seemed to have some rippling ridges within. When my free hand brushed against the Veredian markings on the left side of her leg, Ravena detonated with a guttural cry, her pelvis lifting off the edge of the pool.

I continued my sensual assault on her until she came down from her high. Pulling myself out of the water, I drew her away from the edge of the pool. I lay down next to her, the rubbery surface of the floor soft beneath us.

Still a little dazed, Ravena nonetheless turned to kiss me. This time, her tongue demanded control. It threw me at first, unused to females trying to take charge. But I allowed it, too distracted by her hands caressing my chest. She rose to her knees. Water dripping from her long hair sticking in dark swirls to her skin. She resembled a dark water fairy come to seduce an unsuspecting mortal. She straddled me while pursuing her exploration of my body. Her silken palms and divine lips left a blazing trail of pleasure in their wake.

A deep moan rumbled in my chest when her delicate hands wrapped around my cock. She rubbed her face on it—with something akin to reverence—and began to stroke me with both hands. I hissed in incommensurable bliss when the searing heat of her mouth closed around the head of my shaft. I was too big for her to take much more than that, but between the eager movements of her hands along my length, the hot wetness of her mouth, and the skillful caress of her tongue drawing circles around the tip of my cock, a raging volcano was building up inside me. One hand fisted on my side, the other rubbing her horn and hair, I gave myself over to my woman.

Eyes closed, my head arched back, I began cresting. Ravena suddenly stopping had my eyes jerk open in disbelief. She climbed on top of me and rubbed her sex on mine. When she reached for my cock to align it with her opening, a wave of panic surged through me.

"NO!" I exclaimed, trying to gently buck her off.

She latched on to me and gave me a threatening look. "Stay!" she hissed.

I held her hips to prevent her from lowering herself onto my shaft.

"I'm too big, Ravena. You will find no pleasure in this, only injury."

"I am Guldan. We do not tear. We adjust."

"But…"

"Enough!" she snapped. "You are mine, Ravik. You will not deny me. I will not be harmed. The Goddess made me for you, and you for me."

The certainty in her voice made me waver. Heart pounding in both fear and anticipation, I kept my hands on her waist as she lowered herself onto my cock, ready to lift her up at the first sign of distress. Eyes locked with mine, her palms resting on my chest for support, she rocked her hips up and down over me, taking more and more of me with each downward movement.

"Ancestors," I whispered, disbelieving.

Ravena smiled smugly as her warm sheath gradually adjusted to my girth until I was fully buried inside of her. She was extremely tight around me but didn't seem in pain or feeling any type of discomfort. The rippling ridges I had felt alongside her inner walls while I finger-fucked her earlier, were now giving me the most exquisite torment.

"Don't you ever fucking deny me again, Ravik Xeldar," Ravena hissed in a threatening tone as she slowly began to ride me. "Your cock, your body, and your pleasure are mine."

"Ravena," I choked out, my blood having turned to liquid fire.

My palms found their way to her breasts as she accelerated her movements. Head thrown back in ecstasy, Ravena's hands covered mine as I fondled her. But I needed more. I started thrusting up into her. She cried out in approval.

But that still wasn't enough.

Flipping us around, I lifted up her legs and plowed into her.

"Yes! Ravik, yes! Harder. Fuck me harder. Stop holding back. I won't break."

When I continued to control my pace, she viciously clawed at my side, drawing blood. I growled threateningly at the challenge. She brutally fisted my hair. My scalp stung as she drew my face closer to hers.

"Either fuck me like a real man or get off me!" she hissed.

Anger flared in equal measure to my wounded pride. My hand closed around her long, slender neck and tightened its hold as I growled into her face. Lips parted, pupils dilated, Ravena's bronze skin flushed from the onset of air deprivation. Fearless, she smiled, her eyes smoldering.

"Challenge accepted," I hissed back, releasing my hold on her neck. "Remember, you asked for this."

I rammed myself home. She gasped, her back arching off the floor. Pulling back to the tip I slammed my cock back in, the head hitting her cervix.

"Yes," Ravena moaned. "My beast…"

The desperate need in her voice undid me.

"I'm going to wreck you," I whispered before giving free rein to my passion.

With complete abandon, I pounded into her, spurred on by her rapturous moans, her hands feverishly pawing at me, and the rabid hunger she'd awakened in me. Most females would have broken under such an unbridled assault. Not her. Not my Ravena. She took everything I gave with a feral voracity. The echoic nature of the bathroom amplified and multiplied the sound of our labored breaths, the slapping of flesh meeting flesh, and our voluptuous sighs.

Ravena's body suddenly seized as she toppled over the edge. Her inner walls clamped down on me, the undulation of their rippling ridges wresting my own climax from me. Slamming my pelvis against hers, holding her tightly, my cock buried deep, I roared my release as my seed shot out inside of her. My entire body felt on the verge of combusting as liquid ecstasy poured out of me. I pumped in and out of her a few more times until the last of my essence was spent, then rolled us around so that I wouldn't crush her.

Destroyed by the violence of my orgasm, I lay still, Ravena lying on top of me, my cock still buried inside of her. The room spun and blood rushed in my ears. Ravena's labored breath fanned on my chest, her horns pressing against the side of my neck.

My arms tightened around her as the room settled around us and our heartbeats slowed to a normal pace.

"My beast," Ravena whispered, her arms holding me possessively. "I'm never letting you go."

I smiled.

CHAPTER 6
MERCY

My body thrummed with the most exquisite soreness. I rubbed my face against the soft skin of Ravik's muscular, hard chest, careful not to cut him with the sharp tips of my horns. One leg propped over his, my thumb circling one of his nipples, I reveled in the heat of his body and the tender post-coital intimacy. Ravik's hand rested possessively on my behind.

I'd always enjoyed sex on the rougher side, but I'd never expected to want it so wild and savage. Yet, it had been the most mind-blowing experience I'd ever had. Despite my bravado, taking him had not been easy. Ravik's cock was beyond massive. I thanked the Goddess for my Guldan heritage. While we naturally did stretch to accommodate any size—within reason—I'd never been with someone this big. In my impatience, I'd pushed my body to adjust too fast. It had hurt a bit, but it was the right kind of pain. Even now, I craved more of him. After the first round by the pool, he'd taken me against the wall, and once more in his bed. Considering the late hour, we should both be sleeping, but the sexual tension between us continued to sizzle too fiercely.

As a determinedly independent woman, and a bit of a control freak, it was a strange dichotomy that I craved the more dominant side of my man to come into play between us. I loved how his strength and power made me feel fragile and vulnerable, yet safe. I didn't want to submit, but for him to take charge and unleash his beast.

However, amazing sex and power exchange in the bedroom constituted the least of our problems. Grace's words replayed in my head. In the past few hours with Ravik, whenever his gaze rested upon me, if it didn't burn with lust, it would either be troubled or filled with what I could only interpret as a deep-rooted pain. In the upcoming weeks, I would need to get him to open up.

His hand roaming on my back told me we'd be going into round four. My fingers traced the sharply defined lines of his abs while my tongue teased his nipple. Ravik's chest vibrated under a deep purr. That instantly got me wet. I loved having such power over this mountain of a man.

A strident sound resonated through the room, snapping me out of the lustful mood that had been blossoming within me. Immediately on alert, I sat up and gave Ravik an inquisitive look, as he straightened and rolled off the bed.

"Urgent communication incoming from the bridge," said Hana, the ship's A.I., over the intercom.

"Open channel," Ravik said, reaching for his clothes.

Jumping to my feet, I hurried to fetch my own, which I had thankfully brought into his room between two rounds of wild sex.

"Magnar," Captain Baldur said over the com, his voice filled with tension. "Sorry for the interruption, but we have a serious situation on our hands."

"Report," Ravik said while slipping into his pants, not bothering with any underwear.

"The ship is experiencing a cascade of systems failures. We only noticed them a few minutes ago but we have reason to believe they began shortly after our departure. They are occurring at an exponential rate and are starting to target critical systems. We may need to abandon ship."

Ravik's brutish face took on a savage expression as anger suffused his features. He shoved his feet into his boots as he pulled on his shirt.

"On my way."

"I'm coming as well," I said while finishing dressing. "Give me a second to get some tools."

Ravik glowered at me. "I do not have time for this. You will stay here and—"

My temper flared.

"Don't start," I said, pointing a menacing finger at him. "I know more about technology and hacking than your entire crew combined. I'm not going to sit here because I don't have a cock while less competent people than I make decisions that might result in my ass getting blown up or landing on a slaver's block. So you fucking wait while I get my shit."

Ravik marched up to me, snarling. I could tell he wanted to put me across his knees, but I wouldn't back down.

"Tread carefully, female. Sharing my bed does not give you control over me or my ship."

Holding his stare, I raised my chin defiantly.

"Do not make me regret this. Move your ass," he said, gesturing with his head for me to get going.

I didn't wait for him to say it twice. The slapping sound of my bare feet pounding the floor bounced off the walls as I raced to my room, through the pool room and the secret passage connecting to it. I grabbed my portable computer, barely bigger than a datapad, and a data stick containing most of my tracer programs and hacking subroutines, then shoved my feet into my boots. My bedroom door opened, startling me. Ravik stood in the doorway, looking more somber than ever.

"Come on," he growled, his voice laced with impatience.

Without waiting for my acknowledgement, he turned around and left. I closed the magnetic clasp of my boots then chased after him. Red lights blinked in the hallways while the crew raced to different sections of the ship to deal with the various malfunctions. I had to skip-run to keep up with Ravik's long strides.

He marched onto the bridge, the captain jumping to his feet upon our entrance.

"Magnar, we—"

Baldur's voice cut off, his eyes widening upon noticing my presence in Ravik's wake. He frowned, his gaze flicking to the computer in my hand before turning back to his ruler.

"Report," Ravik said, almost angrily.

Baldur snapped out of his distraction, although still clearly confused.

"Forgive me, Magnar. We believe our systems have been targeted by some kind of virus, but we can't pinpoint it. It's moving too fast."

He displayed a map of the ship on the giant screen above the navigation board. Multiple sections of the vessel blinked red, many turning yellow or orange as the captain spoke. I immediately recognized the pattern.

"At this rate," Baldur said, "we'll be completely dead in space within an hour. Our propulsion systems have already begun showing some distress. We need to abandon ship before the emergency launch pads also get shut down."

"That's exactly what they want you to do," I countered.

The captain and the four other officers on deck all frowned at me, shocked that I would intervene in what they clearly considered an inappropriate intrusion. One of them, with light-brown hair and striking light-green eyes opened his mouth, probably to put me back in my place, but appeared to change his mind after casting a wary glance towards Ravik.

"What makes you say that?" Ravik asked.

"This virus—and I believe it is indeed a virus—has been running for hours," I said, approaching the screen. "If they wanted to kill you, they would have already blown up the ship. This hack is insidious, progressing in a calculated manner." I pointed on the map at the different systems that had already been shut down. "All secondary systems, nothing vital but enough to start setting a panic and the narrative that the ship is dying. If I wanted to trap you aboard the ship, I'd disable your escape route. They've taken out the shuttle bay so the fighters can't go out, but they haven't touched the escape pods."

Baldur blinked, his frown deepening. "But there's nothing of value on this ship aside from the Magnar himself. Even if the whole plot was to take the ship, the damage this virus is causing will not be worth the repair cost. This makes no sense."

"It does if they want to capture us without a battle," Ravik said. "Escape pods are weaponless. Whoever sabotaged the ship must know the landing coordinates pre-programmed in the pods. They'll be lying in wait to scoop us up while we sit there helpless."

My lips parted in shock. I had not thought of that possibility. I eyed Ravik with even greater respect.

"What are you doing to counter this?" he asked his captain.

Baldur ran a nervous hand through his hair. "Our best minds are trying to track down the virus and isolate it, but so far, without success. We can't even trust our ship's self-diagnostics. Tagar has taken a few men to the shuttle bay to attempt to regain control so that we could possibly take off in the shuttles."

"Captain, I need to connect to your ship's mainframe," I said, staring at Ravik for approval before my eyes flicked back to Baldur.

He recoiled, as if I'd grown a second head. "What?"

"Proceed," Ravik said.

Baldur stared at Ravik in disbelief.

"Do not make me repeat myself," Ravik growled, looking on the verge of snapping his captain's neck.

Baldur stiffened, then blanched. Turning around, he tapped on the control panel of the navigational board. A hidden panel slid open revealing various connection slots. Refusing to let my temper flare at this nonsensical drama, I hooked in my computer and activated the holographic screen.

"Aren't you going to get infected as well?" Baldur asked in a dubious tone, which barely hid his resentment and disdain.

"Nope," I said absentmindedly.

I could feel the Braxians closing around me to look over my shoulder at my screen. It didn't bother me as they couldn't read the Guldan text it displayed. A quick diagnostic confirmed my suspicion. I knew this Guldan pattern well. For a second, I wondered if they'd done this to capture me, but that seemed pretty excessive. Appropriating my inherited wealth and selling me to collectors didn't justify starting an interplanetary war. Plus, they hadn't known I'd travel onboard the ship, as it had been too much of a last-minute thing.

"I can stop the virus," I said, plugging my data key into the ship's mainframe and tapping some instructions to release the antivirus. "And I can restore most of the systems affected, but some will require manual repair."

"Good girl," Ravik said. The glimmer of pride in his eyes filled my chest with a pleasant warmth. "Can you make us battle worthy?"

I bit my lip while pondering how to answer the question. "First, I need the antivirus to finish deploying and to initiate the system restore. And then we can see what we're working with."

"How did you find the cure so quickly?" Baldur asked, making no effort to hide his suspicion.

Ravik narrowed his eyes at his captain but didn't intervene, which pleased me. I was a big girl, able to fight my own battles.

"I know it because technology is my job and because there isn't a single piece of Guldan hardware or software that I don't know."

"Excuse me?" intervened a Braxian with pretty, pale-green eyes. Despite his rough traits and severe expression, there was an odd softness to his features, like that usually found in good-natured people.

"You heard me correctly. This virus is clearly of Guldan signature." My hip leaning against the side of the console and my palm resting flat next to the control panel, I stared at him with my usual sassy attitude. "Now, no need to get those brawny muscles of yours all twisted in knots; I had nothing to do with it. Your captain here," I added, pointing at him with a gesture of my head, "should be able to confirm the virus was first planted before the Magnar and I boarded this vessel. Not to mention that I wasn't even supposed to be here. So, can we drop the suspicions and work on solutions?"

He scrunched his brutish face, his thick brows bunching to form a single continuous line. I raised a questioning eyebrow at him. He pursed his generous lips, and then grunted his assent.

"Good," I said, before turning back to check on my holographic monitor. "As I was saying before this interruption, with the virus being of Guldan origin, and assuming the Magnar's speculation is accurate—

which I believe is likely the case—even repaired, this ship may not be able to face off against Guldan forces. Our technology is far too advanced."

"We have tremendous firepower," Baldur argued, his pride visibly stung.

It was so cute, I wanted to pet him.

"You do," I conceded. "But it's completely useless against ships you can't see. After the Tuureans, the Guldans possess the best stealth technology. At the same time they decloak, they'll be shooting you full of holes. You'll never have time to evade."

"But you told Fenton you know Guldan technology well," Ravik said, referring to the pale-green-eyed Braxian. "How do I get past their cloak? I would see the face of my enemy."

"That would be telling," I said.

Ravik frowned, his expression darkening.

"Relax, big boy. One thing at a time."

Ravik stiffened, and his officers gasped, giving me an outraged look.

Fuck.

Me and that damn irreverent mouth.

"Sorry. I mean Magnar," I mumbled.

The chime of the antivirus finishing to deploy gave me an excuse to focus on my computer. Within seconds, the map of the ship's systems confirmed the progress of the virus had stopped. I typed a few more commands on my computer. It ran a series of empty functions that would resemble a complex subroutine to the laymen, especially ones who couldn't read Guldan. I needed that distraction to cover the real method by which I would revert the damage.

Placing my palm on the navigation board of the ship, as if for support, I stared unseeing at the holographic screen of my computer, pretending to be observing the program running on it. Extending my psionic senses, I used my touch activated Veredian power to seek out a ship-wide subroutine in which to implant my command. In my mind's eye, every program running the ship appeared like a ghostly tree diagram, spreading its branches in every direction, each connection instinctively recognized and catalogued.

I understood viruses well because *I* was the greatest of them all.

While nanites remained my favorite method of propagation for their versatility, software also worked well, especially in this instance. I targeted the life support systems, which connected to every subsystem of the ship in one form or another before implanting a revert command. Unlike my niece Amalia, who could take control of entire systems and perform complex reprogramming, I could only issue a simple command that would spread and replicate until it met its end condition or it had saturated the host. In this case, my command would reset every system to yesterday morning—hours before the virus was implanted—and then self-destruct.

I never left behind any traces of my viral presence.

In my head, I could see it spreading over the ghostly tendrils of the tree. Refocusing on the room around me, I furtively looked at the Braxians surrounding me. To my relief, none had noticed me using my psi ability. I gazed up at the screen, and a smile stretched my lips when many of the red sections on the ship's map reverted to orange, then yellow, then white.

"Fuck me," Baldur muttered, his eyes glued to the screen.

Unlike the Guldan virus which had targeted systems in a specific sequence, mine just spread in every direction at once.

"It will take about fifteen minutes to complete its work," I said, facing Ravik. "Add to that however long it will take some systems to reboot after the reversal."

"Well done, little bird," Ravik said, his eyes gleaming with pride.

"Indeed," Fenton said with an unreadable expression in his gentle eyes.

Baldur grunted, which I once more found endearing. I almost wanted to adopt him as a pet. I had a thing for big and grumpy.

I preened under Ravik's approval and the stunned admiration of his officers, and then curtsied in a sign of thank you. Moments later, the blinking red lights on the ceiling turned off, signaling the end of the alert.

"As soon as the reset is complete, I want ship-wide diagnostics of all systems, especially engineering," Baldur said to one of the crew.

"Yes, Captain."

Ravik crossed his arms over his chest, his eyes boring into mine. I loved how that pose made his bulging biceps appear even bigger. And those veins… My mouth watered reminiscing how they had felt under my tongue.

"And about facing off those who did this?" Ravik asked, his tone making it clear he wouldn't welcome an answer that said no.

I shifted uncomfortably, not sure how to tackle this sensitive topic.

"Whatever your thoughts, you may speak freely," Ravik said, having sensed my discomfort.

"Before speaking of pursuit," I said cautiously, "maybe we should figure out who planted this in the first place."

"We're already working on that," Fenton said.

"On my honor, I am ready to vouch for every single man in this crew," Baldur said, forcefully. "I have personally chosen or trained them. They are completely loyal to the Magnar."

"I second that," Fenton said.

"And I," Ravik said. "These men have been with me for years. I trust them with my life. Not so much some of the guests who traveled with us and remained on Venus Hive after our departure."

"It is my assumption as well," Fenton said. "I have already reached out to Pattel to have him keep discreet tabs on them."

"William is your man if you want to find out about anything shady happening on the space station," I said. "When Anton hears what has transpired here, he will put all of his resources at your disposal to track down the culprit."

"I'm sure Pattel will think of that," Ravik said. "But it doesn't hurt to make sure he does."

Fenton nodded in response to Ravik's pointed look.

"All right then," I said, still concerned we might have a double-agent onboard. "I'll be brutally honest. I think going after them might be suicidal."

Baldur snorted, his condescending look stating loudly he thought fear dictated that reaction. Although it irritated me, I didn't take the bait.

Leaning against the edge of the navigation board, I crossed my arms over my chest, like Ravik had previously done. "If they are indeed waiting to ambush the pods, we don't know how many ships are waiting for us, what types, or what kind of firepower they pack. By the time we're close enough to reveal them, we may not be able to escape if we're outnumbered."

Ravik nodded slowly. He pursed his lips while he reflected on my words. "How do you intend to disable their cloak?"

"With a virus that could be embedded in a tractor beam or photon torpedo," I said with a shrug.

"Tractor beam?" Ravik asked. "Does it have to be outgoing or can it be incoming?"

I blinked, unsure what he meant.

"Your concerns are valid," Ravik said in light of my obvious confusion. "But I'm thinking that if they are waiting to tow in our escape pods en route to a safe destination, we should give them what they want."

My eyes widened in understanding, and an impressed smile blossomed on my lips. "You're a fucking genius!" I exclaimed. Uncrossing my arms, I rested my palms on the edge of the console, my eyes going out of focus as I performed a quick mental analysis of his implied tactic. "Yes. That would totally work."

Fenton, Baldur, and the other two officers' lost expressions made me grin.

"It will take me some time to prepare, but yes, it can be done," I said, exchanging a conspiratorial grin with Ravik. "Let's get to work, then."

～

An hour later, we launched rigged escape pods en route to the human colony of Gielyn, the closest, safe planet to the original location of Ravik's battleship, Drakkar. Applying a bit of a convoluted method, we managed to hook the cloaking shield of my Falcon to the Drakkar's systems, using their engine to boost its strength. My vessel used Tuurean cloaking technology which, to this day, had not been breached by any other species.

After less than thirty minutes of following the pods, a Guldan battlecruiser decloaked, four of its tractor beams latching on to the first few pods in range. Still cloaked, the Drakkar stopped out of weapons and detection range. Too small to see, the egg-shaped delivery containers attached to the pods, five on each, flew off the surface of the escape vessel and burst open, spilling their contents into space; viral nanites specially programmed by yours truly.

As more of the pods approached, two destroyers decloaked, each firing their tractor beams at the incoming escape capsules. Although the Drakkar was a bigger, more powerful vessel, the Guldan ships were of a far more advanced design. Their combined firepower could seriously jeopardize the Braxian ship's integrity.

The destroyers had only drawn in a couple of the pods, the battlecruiser having captured at least a dozen, when the nanites' magic began to manifest itself. Four frigates surrounding the other three ships blinked in and out of existence, their cloaks disintegrating. The crew of the battlecruiser was the first to realize we'd turned their trap on them. They released the new set of pods they'd been reeling in and opened their hatch, no doubt intent on dumping their previous catch.

"Blow them up," Ravik said, a feral expression on his face.

"Acknowledged," Baldur said, setting off the charges that had been loaded in the pods.

The battlecruiser shook from the violence of the multiple detonations, its hull breaching in various locations. The destroyers were obliterated within seconds, the first explosion nearly splitting them in half before chain explosions finished them off. Three of the frigates managed to warp out of there, the fourth sustaining severe damage from flying debris.

"Let's go finish them," said a blonde-haired officer with light-brown eyes.

"No," Ravik said. "As much as I want to crush their bones with my bare hands, the three who jumped might return with friends. Baldur, get us as far away from here as possible. I have some Guldans to meet back home."

"Yes, Magnar," Baldur said, hitting his chest with his fist.

Ravik extended a hand towards me. Without a word, I took it and let him lead me off the bridge.

CHAPTER 7
RAVIK

We landed on Braxia a little after nightfall. Despite her eagerness to go to her brother's home, Ravena agreed to stay the night at my fortress. Beyond my selfish need to have her with me—and in my bed—I didn't want her entering that place without having it secured first. Having her by my side before my subjects, my scent all over her, my claim clearly stated, would give any Braxian pause before they considered messing with her in any way.

Krygor Aldriss and Raylor Caldes greeted us at the landing pad. To my surprise, Caldes seemed genuinely pleased by our early arrival. I had expected him to be fuming about the failed abduction attempt. But he only appeared impatient to have me meet his Guldan guests. Although he would have had time to regain control of his emotions, Raylor had never been much of an actor, his feelings always plain to see. I wondered then if he truly had no clue what had transpired. This, in turn, raised the question as to whether the Guldans were merely using him as a puppet in a more nefarious scheme.

As we entered my hall, the female servants got on their knees, their heads bent in submission. Their male counterparts stood in a tight row behind them, heads also bowed and hands clasped behind their backs. My guards, guests, and clansmen held a fist to their chests. Ravena bristled at this sight. Her disapproval stung. Yet, she would have been far more offended six years ago before I had begun implementing changes in the treatment of women.

I waved a hand for them to rise, which signaled the males to be at ease. All eyes openly spied my woman with a mix of curiosity, hostility, and awe at her beauty. My chest swelled with pride, not only to have such a female on my arm, but at the poised, regal way in which she carried herself, unfazed by the open scrutiny she'd fallen under.

My sons approached us, their gazes lingering on Ravena before shifting back to me.

"Father," they said, pressing their fists to their chests.

"My sons," I said, placing a hand on one shoulder each and giving them an affectionate squeeze. Turning towards my woman, I gestured at my sons. "Ravena, this is Keran, my oldest, and Ganek my youngest. Sons, this is Ravena."

I placed a possessive hand on her hip for all to see the nature of our relationship. The need to call her my concubine burned my tongue, but she hadn't given her formal consent… nor had I asked.

My sons' eyes widened in an almost imperceptible manner. I knew them too well for it to escape my notice. Still, they saluted her the same way they had me. She responded with the traditional Veredian greeting, placing her palm on her heart before waving her hand towards them in an offering gesture.

"A pleasure to meet you…" Ravena hesitated, uncertain what to call them.

"Jakar would be the title used for my sons," I said, gently.

She gave me a grateful smile. "A pleasure to meet you, Jakar Keran, and you Jakar Ganek."

"The pleasure is ours, Madam," Keran said, an indecipherable look on his face. "I hope you are both hungry as we awaited your return for evening meal."

"We are indeed," I said, gesturing for Keran to lead the way.

He nodded his full head of hair, as black as mine and his youngest brother's. Turning on his heels, he marched towards the dining hall where the Elder Clan Leaders would joins us. My gaze roamed proudly over my sons and the rippling muscles of their strong backs. Born to me from different long-ago concubines—now returned to their respective clans—their height and size nearly matched mine, and their features left no doubt as to the identity of their sire. However, both sons had inherited their mothers' eyes with Keran's being grey and Ganek's being brown.

The dining hall's dark grey walls and maroon stone floors would have been somber if not for the tall windows through which Braxia's sun bathed the room with a soft light. In the center of the room, a large table shaped as a U could accommodate twenty-five people. My sons usually sat next to me at the head. The elders would divide equally along the sides with whatever distinguished guest might be in attendance. The cushioned, high-back chairs lined the outer side of the tables, the center area remaining unencumbered so that servants could easily serve us and performers—usually erotic dancers—could entertain us.

Across the room, in front of the main table, twelve ten-person tables were reserved for senior or honored members of each of the Elder Clans. On the left and right sides of the main table, long but narrow tables were set for wives and concubines. The females quietly filed in. Like the males, they stood in front of their chairs, waiting for my sons and me to be seated first.

A single glance sufficed for Ravena to understand that, as a female, she'd be expected to sit with the other women. The look on her face made no mystery I'd have a fight on my hands if I sent her there. How could I have forgotten to discuss the Braxian protocols with her in the 24 hours it took us to get here?

Without a word on my part, my youngest son, Ganek, gestured for one of the male servants to bring a fourth chair to the head of the table. A hush fell over the room. Only the Dagna, the Magnar's wife, would sit at the head of the table. A distinguished guest such as a female ambassador, which technically Ravena could pass for, would have the honor of sitting at the main table, but on the sides, not at the head.

Grateful for my son's initiative that let me off the hook, I led

Ravena by the hip to the chair next to mine. Keran stood before the chair at her right and Ganek at my left.

I sat down, my sons followed suit, and then so did Ravena. I smiled, pleased that she had so well understood the protocol even without explanation. The rest of the attendants took their seats, aside from Caldes who remained standing. The servants immediately started buzzing around us, bringing dishes and drink.

"Magnar," Raylor Caldes said, "the Guldans I have told you about are here. With your permission, I would like to invite them to your table."

I narrowed my eyes at him, still finding no deceit, only excessive eagerness. Fenton and Krygor stared at him, their gaze assessing. I'd contacted Krygor and my sons as soon as we'd set in motion the plan to turn the Guldans' trap on them. If they had sought to abduct me on my way home, chances were they'd seek to neutralize my sons as well. I leaned back against my seat, pondering.

Ravena's eyes flicked between Raylor and me. Despite her neutral expression, I could sense the tension within her. To my relief, as much as I knew she hated it, and of her own volition, my woman had once more covered her markings with a long-sleeved, ankle-length, black sheath dress. Until we got rid of these Guldans, I preferred to keep her genetics a secret.

"You may," I said.

Raylor responded with a triumphant smile, having no idea about the tongue lashing I had in store for his guests. He nodded to Siltar, his second-born son, who ran to get the Guldans. Minutes later, he returned with two males; one with black horns and silver-white hair, the other with brown horns and dark brown hair. Their polite smiles faltered as they approached the table and noted Ravena's presence. They looked around the room, as if seeking someone or something before their gazes returned to my woman, a frown marring their foreheads. The silver-haired Guldan appeared the most troubled.

"Magnar," Raylor said, "I am pleased to introduce you to the Honorable Hartuk Tellin and Lorik Zorak, Guldan Ambassadors, here to hopefully negotiate a mutually beneficial alliance."

"Magnar," both men said, slightly bowing their heads.

I stared at them without returning the salutation. Raylor's lips tightened ever so slightly. With a stiff smile, he invited the Guldans to take a seat, while three servants poured wine for my sons and me. When they turned to leave, Ravena tsked and raised her glass.

"Forgetting something, sweetheart?" she asked.

Amidst the gasps and shocked faces of the males around the table, Krygor lifted an amused eyebrow while Fenton made no effort to repress a snort. The servant, the hybrid daughter of a former slave, cast a wary glance towards me. I gave Ravena's glass a meaningful look, indicating for her to proceed. Lips parted in shock and eyes bulging, the girl complied, her hands slightly shaking as she served my woman wine. Conversation resumed as the servants moved to other guests.

Once everyone was served, I raised my glass and silence once more fell over the audience.

"To new friendships," I said, looking at Ravena who winked at me. "To new alliances," which had Caldes perking up, "and to thwarted kidnapping attempts," I concluded, my eyes boring into Harturk's, the silver-haired Guldan who seemed to be in charge.

Both he and his companion stiffened while shocked gasps and outraged cries erupted all around the room.

Holding the Guldan's gaze, unflinching, I downed the contents of my glass and held it up for a servant to refill.

"Hear!" said Fenton, Krygor, and my two sons, while raising their glasses as well.

They emptied their glasses, Ravena emulating them.

"What is the meaning of this?" Raylor asked, torn between shock, outrage, and something akin to fear.

I related a short version of the incident, keeping Ravena's part a secret, as per her prior request. Raylor grew paler with each word, his incredulous eyes flicking between his guests and me.

"A most unfortunate occurrence. I'm glad to see you've escaped unharmed," Hartuk said with false sympathy. "Are you certain they were Guldan ships? Such a scandalous act would jeopardize the alliance efforts between our peoples. I can assure you that forming a bond between our two peoples is a high priority for our Emperor."

With a head gesture, I indicated for Captain Baldur to proceed. Rising from his clan's table, he approached the central area of the main table and displayed a holographic replay of the Guldan ships de-cloaking, capturing the escape pods, and then exploding.

Angry cries filled the room as the clans shouted for vengeance. I let them run for a moment longer before raising a hand to demand calm.

"And yet," I said, "on the same day the Guldan Ambassadors arrive on Braxia and begin campaigning without my consent, your people attempt to assassinate me."

"An upsetting coincidence," Hartuk said, waving a dismissive hand. "We certainly didn't mean any disrespect by sharing information with your people about the technological and financial benefits for Braxians in the case of an alliance between our peoples." His gaze rested on Ravena, speculating, before returning to me.

I narrowed my eyes at him.

"That said, it appears we've underestimated Braxian technology," Hartuk continued, rubbing a hand over his right horn. "Aside from the Tuureans, no other species have managed to break through our cloaking shields. Are you already trading technology with Guldans?"

Hartuk pointedly stared at Ravena. I bristled at the insolence of his gaze upon my woman.

"Guldan females are normally not allowed off planet, let alone without a guardian. I do not see him anywhere, Sana…?" Hartuk asked Ravena.

Anger flared inside of me that he would dare address my female without asking permission first. It was grounds to issue a challenge. I barely held back. Officially, Ravena was a distinguished guest at my table, not my concubine or my property. He, therefore, could speak to her like he would any other guest. However, he had to know it to be an implied rule, similar to those observed on Guldar.

Ravena leaned back against her chair, crossed her legs, and clasped her hands on her lap, an impertinent look on her face. "Ravena Vrok, not that it's any of your business, Sen Tellin."

More shocked gasps rose around the room that a female should address a male in such a fashion. Hartuk's pale skin reddened in outrage. He opened his mouth, as if to snap at her—which would have given me leave to fuck him up—but stopped, his eyes widening as if in sudden realization as his gaze roamed over her black horns.

"Vrok?" he asked. "As in—"

"Yes. As in the daughter of Gruuk Vrok."

"You are orphaned and unmated! Where's your guardian?" he snarled.

I straightened in my chair, my muscles tensing as I prepared to challenge him. Ravena's soft hand caressing my arm stopped me. I turned to face her, but her eyes remained locked on the white-haired Guldan.

"His ass is where it needs to be; back on Guldar where it belongs."

"You are violating our laws!" he shouted, jumping to his feet. "This female must be returned to our home world," Hartuk said, looking at me.

"*This female* is a free woman and under my protection. Guldan rules do *not* apply here. This is Braxia," I snarled.

Despite their displeasure at Ravena's lack of submission, Braxia patriotism prevailed as the men within the room all grunted or shouted their agreement with my statement.

Hartuk's jaw worked as he pondered on an appropriate response. Then his lips stretched in a borderline malicious smirk.

"I didn't mean to imply otherwise, Magnar," Hartuk said, his tone obsequious. "But this female just inherited the greatest wealth on Guldar, with some of the most advanced technologies and scientific discoveries known to our people."

Despite the shock of that revelation, I forced my features to remain neutral, while Ravena's hardened.

"It strikes me as an odd coincidence that the first ever Guldan attack against you should occur the same day this female traveled on your ship," Hartuk said, his tone growing in confidence. "Her guardian is duty-bound to bring her back home to be mated and to breed a suitable heir for that wealth. Could it be that in his effort to uphold his word to her sire, as honor demands, he has attacked your ship not realizing who she was traveling with? After all, they didn't shoot the pods but carefully retrieved them."

The wind changed as the Braxian males muttered their approval. Hartuk was proving to be a skilled ambassador, playing to our obsession with honor, and to the dominant and controlling nature of my people. They could relate to that line of thinking where females were nothing more than property and broodmares.

Ravena opened her mouth to answer, but my ship's captain spoke first.

"A fair assumption," Baldur said in a conciliatory tone, "except for the fact that the virus which sought to force us off the ship and into the escape pods had been planted well-before she was even invited to travel with us. So no, Ambassador, *she* was not the target; the Magnar was."

Hartuk pinched his lips and cast a glance towards Raylor who gave him a troubled look.

"So you see, Ambassador Tellin," I said, with a smug expression, "unless you can bring us those behind that attack, you will not find me overly receptive to your alliance overtures."

"Your people *need* our technology to catch up with modern times," Hartuk said forcefully.

"As you said, *Ambassador*, I've just inherited some of the most advanced technologies and scientific discoveries known to our people," Ravena said with a taunting glint in her obsidian eyes.

Krygor's deep chuckle echoed mine.

"Sit," I said to Hartuk, "my people hunger."

With a wave of my hand, I gestured for the servants to resume bringing food. His face constricted as if he'd bitten into something sour, but the Ambassador complied. However, it was his silent companion who gave me a sense of unease, his green eyes filled with a hard edge, weighing heavy on Ravena.

Once all the plates were served, three human females in skimpy leather outfits walked to the center area of the main table. The one in front wore a black bustier and thong set, knee high boots with sky-high, needle-heels, and a flogger hanging on her hips. She led the other two females by a leash in each hand. They wore similar outfits to their mistress, but theirs were blood red.

I glanced at Ravena, who observed the females with undisguised curiosity. Sensual music began playing through the hall's sound system. The submissives stood still while their Mistress circled around them, her hands caressing their luscious bodies, lingering on their breasts, their asses, and slipping under their thongs to finger their pussies.

Ravena cut a piece from her rhomak steak, the red meat traditionally cooked medium-rare, and brought it to her lips, her eyes never wandering from the females. The Mistress directed her subs to kiss and grope each other while she executed a sexy dance around them, stripping some of her clothes, and theirs as well, in the process.

The Mistress suddenly pulled out her flogger and used it on her subs, hard enough to leave some nice red stripes on their backs and their behinds. Although the females hissed under the sting, they clearly enjoyed the careful abuse of their Domme. By the time they finished their show, all three were naked but for their boots. The scent of their arousal didn't stir me like it used to. A single musk could now have my cock stiffen, and it belonged to the female sitting by my side. Seeing the small patch of trimmed, dark hair on the Mistress' pussy reminded me of Ravena's cleanly shaven one.

No, not shaven. Hairless.

Like all Veredians, Ravena's only body hair could be found on her head, her eyebrows and her eyelashes. The thought of her taste on my tongue as I licked her up and down had my pants tightening. The feel of her riding my cock had my blood boiling with the urge to drag her back to my quarters. But I endured nearly a dozen more performances before the meal ended and I could finally take my woman back to my room.

~

"Interesting female," Krygor said, taking a seat across the meeting table in my private chamber.

The sun would rise in another hour, at which point we'd be ready to ride out to hunt the roaming joarkals. Nothing had ever been so hard as parting from Ravena's delectably warm, naked body, sleeping in my bed.

Fenton sat next to him, and both my sons framed me.

"Indeed," I said, noncommittally.

"It appears I should visit my son more often, seeing the type of females he forms friendships with," Krygor said.

"And I," said Fenton and my sons in turn.

I chuckled. "You'd only end up returning to that concubine you keep going back and forth to," I said teasingly to Fenton.

He shrugged dismissively. I never quite understood why he hadn't simply taken her as his wife. Thala came from a good bloodline. Graceful, submissive, adept at running a household, she also clearly had affection for him. Yet, he seemed indecisive.

"Ravena is as beautiful as she's smart," I said, making no effort to hide my pride.

"And cocky," Krygor said. "I would never have expected to find that sexy on a female."

"It is disconcerting," said Ganek, my youngest son.

"And yet, oddly appealing," Keran said.

I nodded, baffled myself by how much her strength and confidence turned me on.

"Will she truly share technology with us, or was she merely placating the Guldan?" Keran asked.

That sobered us. My oldest son, ever the practical one, always went straight to the point.

I sighed. "Honestly, I don't know. In truth, I had no idea of the extent of her wealth until that Guldan revealed it." My eyes flicked towards Krygor. "Your son had mentioned her close friendship with the Tuureans, and that we should seek an alliance with them instead."

"That would be phenomenal!" Fenton exclaimed. "The Xelixians are the only ones who managed to get through the cold exterior of those cyborgs."

"Yes, but we have nothing to offer them in exchange… for now," I said pensively. "I have to tread carefully so that Ravena doesn't think I'm using her for her connections or inheritance."

Fenton nodded. "She's an invaluable asset right now. One that you cannot afford to alienate if the Guldans are going to launch other attacks against you."

I glared at him.

"Spare me the angry looks, old friend," Fenton said. "We're all well aware that your interest in her is genuine, but you remain the Magnar. The needs of your people come first. And if that means using her, then so you must. However, she appears to have genuine affection for you. The Ancestors willing, she will volunteer her assistance so you do not have to manipulate her into it."

I clenched my jaw, my hands fisted on my lap. This felt wrong and yet, his arguments remained valid. Krygor gave me a sympathetic look. Yet he, too, shared Fenton's opinion.

"She wishes to go to her brother's house when she wakes," I said, changing the unpleasant topic.

"My clansmen have already secured the perimeter," Krygor said. "My youngest son, Gorav, has offered to escort her inside to make sure it is safe there as well while we go for the hunt."

I shook my head. "That second Guldan, Ambassador Zorak, is up to something. The way he looked at her last night, I don't want Ravena this isolated while all of our warriors are off in the woods hunting."

Krygor bristled.

"Relax, Krygor," I said, in a conciliatory tone. "I do not question your son's combat abilities. He is a Berserker after all. But no amount of combat skill will keep him safe against Guldan technology."

"So what do you propose?" Keran asked.

"She comes with us."

"To the hunt?" Ganek exclaimed, disbelieving.

"She'll refuse to stay here, and I cannot imprison her," I said, irritated. "Our best warriors will be present. Ravena isn't unreasonable. She'll stay at the back."

"Very well," Krygor said. "Just beware of Caldes. Even though they're not warriors, his clan insisted on joining the hunt."

"What the fuck for?" I asked.

"Respect," Fenton said. "Despite his clan's elder status, their lack of prowess on the battlefield and systematic absence in the large hunts make them look inferior. They have still not recovered from the shame Gerwin brought upon them, while Krygor's clan keeps climbing in fame and power."

"And he sure hates me," Krygor said, with a sadistic smile.

As much as I admired Anton's father, sometimes he creeped me out. After Gerwin—Raylor Caldes' firstborn son—had nearly murdered Grace, Krygor had carried out Gerwin's execution. He'd taken a sick pleasure skinning him alive, making it as slow and excruciating as possible. That punishment had served as revenge against all those who had abused his son for years for merely being a half-breed.

"Should we fear foul play from him then?"

"I highly doubt it, although we shouldn't dismiss any possibility," Fenton said, shaking his head. "For all his faults, Raylor isn't stupid, and he is fiercely patriotic. Only a fool wouldn't see the danger of allowing a foreign force to take out or control our ruler. Raylor wants to return to our old ways, not to be under the thumb of the Guldans."

"Agreed," Keran said, "But I still want increased protection for my father."

Seriously?

I turned to look disbelievingly at his face, so like my own.

He held my gaze and shrugged. "Whoever attacked your ship will want to finish the job. Regardless of technology, the Magnar cannot be allowed to fall to an alien force on his home world while surrounded by his men. Braxia would not recover."

I harrumphed but nodded my consent. Although he had a point, I hated being babied. In my fifty-one years of existence, I'd never been defeated in single combat. It irritated me to no end that my sons and counsel would feel duty-bound to protect me when I was Braxia's protector.

"Any word from Pattel?"

"He will arrive within the next three hours," Krygor said. "He did a few of the media tours you requested but cut it all short to return promptly. Too many of our fiercest warriors are with him. The old man will gladly face your wrath for his disobedience, but he will not let you fight without him."

Shaking my head, I snorted. "Pattel is just eager to spill blood and not let us catch up to him with our hunt trophies."

"As if that were even possible. That old bastard had thirty-year head start on me," Krygor grumbled.

"And yet, he'll remain in the lead for at least another thirty years," Fenton said.

"More like fifty," I said with a chuckle. "Remember how his father continued to crack skulls in battle and hunt large predators well past his 130th birthday?"

My companions nodded with respectful smiles at the thought of the late Dolgir, former leader of Clan Veelan.

"You have a couple more hours to rest," I said. "Then gather the men and meet outside the stables. I want us ready to depart as soon as Pattel lands."

The men acknowledged my order and nodded before taking their leave. Keran stayed behind, an unreadable expression on his face.

"Has any servant provided Ravena with moon juice?" Keran asked, as soon as we were alone.

I stiffened and gave my son a disbelieving look. He held my stare, unflinching. I clenched my jaw, controlling my flaring temper. Although his question felt out of line, it remained valid.

"You are my heir," I said, hoping to placate him.

"That's not the point, and you know it, Father," Keran said in a tone that brooked no argument.

While my annoyance grew, I couldn't help the sliver of pride and respect that blossomed in my heart. My son would be a great ruler after me.

"You have made a lot of changes already that the people are struggling to adjust to," Keran said in a reasonable tone. "No one can challenge you taking such a beauty to your bed, but her boldness and independence adds salt to the wound. If she births you a hybrid…"

"Veredians are technically barren," I snapped. "Only mating with Xelixians and Korletheans yields a minute chance of a successful pregnancy. So there's nothing to worry about."

"That stopped being true a month ago," my son countered. "They've recently found the cure for their reproductive issues and inability to birth sons. Multiple Veredian pregnancies have been confirmed in the past few weeks."

I turned away from him, my gaze roaming blindly over the hunting trophies hanging on my walls; horns, bones, and skulls of Braxia's fiercest predators. I barely knew Ravena, and yet, I knew beyond any doubt that she was meant to be by my side. The mere thought of letting her go had my blood boiling with rage. But to imagine a Braxian infant with her golden skin and black horns suckling at her teat had my chest tightening with longing—a feeling soon replaced by the searing pain of Lissy's memory.

Keran's hand rested on my shoulder in a comforting gesture. "I can see the chemistry between you, and I *do* want your happiness, Father. None deserve it more than you. But now is not the time."

"I will *not* send her away," I said, daring him to challenge me.

"I certainly hope not," Keran said, his smirk widening at my surprise. "She saved you once, holds the patents to some of the best technology available in the galaxy, and has powerful allies. Keep her close, bind her to you, but do not impregnate her… yet."

"Yet?" I asked, confused.

"Stabilize Braxia, get rid of the Guldans, and settle your score with the remaining Fifteen."

I stiffened, shocked that he would bring them up before me. Of course, everyone, even my own sons, knew of my shame, of my crime. Still, I found no condemnation in my son's eyes.

"And then?"

Keran smiled. "And then, follow in Krygor's footsteps. Once

Braxia is back under control, lead by example with your reformed laws on hybrids."

With one last squeeze of my shoulder, my son turned around to leave.

"You make me proud, Son," I called out as he reached the door's threshold.

Keran stopped and looked at me over his shoulder. "As do you, Father."

CHAPTER 8
MERCY

Warm, callused hands roaming over my skin stirred me from my slumber. My eyes still closed, I smiled and purred as Ravik's hands traced my Veredian markings on the side of my calves. The heat of his breath fanned along them before his lips peppered them with soft kisses, trailing a path up my inner thigh. His broad shoulders forced my legs opened as he settled between them. My stomach fluttered and my pulse picked up in anticipation.

He blew hot air over my pussy, making me shiver, and then covered it, too, with light kisses and gentle nips. I squirmed, wanting more.

"Stay," he grumbled in a commanding tone.

I fisted the—predictably—maroon bed cover, grinding my teeth with impatience. His tongue teased me, systematically avoiding the seam of my pussy. His fingers continued to caress my markings, sending a steady stream of pleasure straight to my groin. Ravik had quickly discovered that my markings darkened when aroused, which also made them erogenous. He could literally make me climax just by touching them. The ones at the base of my neck that tapered off between my shoulder blades were the most sensitive.

His finger, long and thick, teased my slit in a slow motion before dipping inside me. Shallow at first, it sank in further with each stroke. It was just enough for the nerve endings of my inner wall's ridges to awaken and throb with need. The ridges not only enhanced a Guldan female's pleasure during penetration, they gave their partner's cock rippling caresses and an extra squeeze as it moved in and out of her. Unlike most other female species, we didn't have a G-spot, but multiple ones; each of the ridges along our inner walls acted as such. There was no missing our sweet spot.

I whimpered, needing more. Ravik chuckled and inserted a second finger. At long last, the burning heat of his mouth wrapped around my clit while his fingers continued to work me over. Fiery tendrils twisted and coiled inside my stomach, my nipples hardening painfully as pleasure built up within. I pinched my nipples hard, the sting sending another jolt of bliss straight to my pussy. I wasn't a masochist, but a bit of pain and a good spanking always excited me. The memory of Ravik's massive hand choking me for challenging his virility while he rammed his cock inside me had moisture pooling between my legs.

Ravik grunted in approval, the movement of his hands inside me and of his tongue on my clit accelerating. My breath grew labored and my skin tingled as I neared the edge. Letting go of one of my breasts, I took a fistful of my man's hair, my pelvis rising. With his free hand, Ravik raked his nails over my markings, strongly enough for a nice burn.

I exploded with a throaty shout, my back arching off the bed. A white haze descended before my eyes, my body seizing in spasms of ecstasy. Before I could regain my senses, Ravik flipped me onto my stomach. His large hand smacked my right butt cheek with a meaty sound, sending another bolt of pleasure straight to my pussy. While his hand soothed the sting, his teeth sank into the fleshy part of my left butt cheek. My legs jerked in response, and a strangled moan escaped my throat. He kissed the flesh he had bitten and gave my right butt cheek a second solid slap.

Dripping wet and aching with need, I didn't resist when Ravik grabbed my ankles and dragged me to the edge of the bed.

"On your knees," Ravik growled, his hands pulling my hips up towards him.

I'd barely done so when I felt the tip of his cock pressing against my opening. Although careful not to harm me, Ravik wasn't gentle. And I fucking loved it. Thick and long within me, I'd never felt so full, so utterly possessed. One hand holding on to my hip, the rough palm of the other caressed my back as he pumped in and out of me. When his fingers brushed over the markings between my shoulder blades, it felt as if lightning had struck my clit and spread electric tendrils along my legs and up my spine. I cried out and nearly collapsed.

Ravik held me up and slapped my ass twice in lieu of punishment, each strike resonating blissfully in my pussy. Letting go of my hip, both his hands wrapped around my horns, forcing my head to tilt back as he pounded into me. I screamed his name and begged for more.

Guldans loved having their lovers grab their horns while we fucked. The nerve endings at their base became erogenous when aroused, just like my Veredian markings. Pulling or applying pressure on our horns sent sparks of pleasure down our spines.

I came undone again, shouting his name. Ravik cried out, no doubt fighting the urge to climax as well from my inner walls clenching spasmodically around him. Boneless, overwhelmed by sensations, I would have collapsed face first into the mattress if not for him holding me up by the horns. No doubt realizing the danger of hurting me, he let go of my horns, one arm wrapping around my waist and one hand closing around my neck as he forced me to arch back into him.

"You're so fucking tight, little bird," Ravik grunted, his face inches from mine. "You feel so damn good around my cock. My woman…"

Between strings of naughty words, Ravik's hot breath came in short bursts in my ear as he continued to fuck me hard. His movements became erratic as he neared his own orgasm. Without relenting on his punishing pace, he tightened his hold around my neck, partially constricting my airways while his fingers found their way to my clit, rubbing it feverishly.

A blinding white light exploded before my eyes as I crested again, liquid fire coursing through my veins, setting my skin ablaze. My ears rang from the roar of his release. His seed shot out inside me in hot, powerful bursts as my inner walls rippled and squeezed him from all sides. Holding me impaled on his cock, Ravik got us down on the bed, spooning me while we both caught out breath. I trembled, cocooned in his embrace, having never been so thoroughly fucked.

"My goddess. You were made for me," Ravik whispered, his strong arms holding me with a care that sharply contrasted with the unbridled way he had taken me.

I interlaced my fingers with his and pressed my back against his hard, burning chest, feeling safe, sheltered, and revered. Feeling home.

An hour later, Ravik and I bathed—or rather he washed me—in his huge bath, similar to the one aboard his ship but a couple of square meters bigger. Here, however, the white walls made the room look even more spacious. Vertical strips of intricate tribal symbols were carved in evenly spaced intervals on the wall, with sconces placed in the flat sections. The maroon edges of the pool offered the only splash of color, surrounded by the dark grey rubbery floor.

When a mostly naked Braxian servant walked in, asking my man if he needed assistance for his morning ablutions, I nearly lost my shit. Ravik promptly sent her away, stating her bathing services would not be required in the foreseeable future. When the door closed behind her, I glared at him, itching to claw his brutish face as my blood boiled with an irrational jealousy. Warm water lapped at our naked bodies as we stood near the edge of the pool.

"You have a fucking slave coming to bathe you?" I hissed.

He held my furious stare, expressing no guilt whatsoever. "Muna is not a slave, but a servant," Ravik said impassively. "I abolished slavery on Braxia three years ago. All my servants are paid and here of their own free will."

He took a step towards me. Still upset, I backed away until the edge of the bath prevented any further retreat. Ravik placed his hands on top of it, on each side of me, cornering me.

"It is custom on Braxia for males to have bedroom slaves—now servants. It doesn't necessarily mean sex is involved, although it commonly is," he said. I bristled at that comment, but Ravik ignored me and continued. "Wives and honored female guests may also have a female servant assist them in bathing. Maybe I should get you one and watch while she lathers that delectable body of yours in soap."

When his attempt at lightening the mood failed, Ravik allowed his irritation to show through.

"I am fifty-one years old, Ravena, a third of my potential lifespan, with two adult sons. Where do you think they came from? Did you expect me to have been celibate this whole time while waiting for you to enter my life?"

That stung, all the more because I'd known my jealousy to be stupid in the first place. I had not minded the strippers last night because their performance had not involved them planning on touching my man. But this female—this Muna—had come here with that specific intent. The thought of her writhing beneath his body had me seeing red. He was *mine*! Annoyed and embarrassed, I tried to push him away, but he might as well have been a mountain.

"The past is irrelevant. Only now matters," Ravik said, pressing himself against me. "My body is yours. My cock is yours. As long as you will have either, no other female shall lay hands on me."

Although I'd never admit it, his words made me feel warm and fuzzy inside. Yet, for some irrational reason, I wanted to remain grumpy a while longer.

"Yeah well, I don't do pledges," I grumbled.

"I didn't ask for it, nor do I need one," Ravik said, a hard glint in his eyes. Releasing the edge of the bath, he placed his hands under my bum and lifted me high enough for him to rub his erect cock against my slit. "I will slowly and painfully kill any man who touches what's mine. And if you allow it, the Ancestors help you."

I opened my mouth to deliver some snarky remark but a strangled cry came out instead as Ravik impaled me with his cock. The burning sensation quickly abated as my body, having grown familiar with his, quickly adjusted to his girth.

"You are mine, Ravena Mercy Vrok. All of you belongs to me. And I don't fucking share what's mine," he said before starting to pump in and out of me, his mouth swallowing my moans.

Water splashed around us as he quickly had me singing his name in ecstasy, before joining his voice to mine in a powerful release. After catching our breath, we hurried through our bath and then to his bedroom to get dressed. A hearty first meal with cold and hot meats, breads, and other foods I didn't recognize, had been laid on the breakfast table of the bedroom. Located on the third floor of the Magnar's Hall, it had a large patio carved directly into the mountain face that rose in the back of the building. The right side of the terrace overlooked one of the main plazas of the Xeldar Clan's compound— Ravik's ruling clan.

From what little I'd been able to see, a Braxian clan essentially lived within a compound reminiscent of ancient fortified cities. The Clan Leader, the Elders, and the elite of each clan lived inside the walls, while the rest of the clansmen lived in small clusters of homes right outside the walls; except for the farmers who were far more spread out.

As we ate our meal, Ravik informed me of his wish for me to join them in the hunt. I had mixed feelings about his honesty as to the motive behind the invitation. Part of me felt aggravated at yet another male thinking I needed protection, even though his concerns had merit. The other part looked forward to it. I'd heard of joarkals and the kind of havoc they could wreak if allowed to rampage unchecked. The thought of hunting one had my adrenalin flowing. Although he didn't come out and say it, the lineup of men who would accompany us clearly indicated the Braxians feared another assassination or kidnapping attempt.

Not wanting to take risks in case things turned sour, I equipped my Tuurean belt and bracers. Their clever design made them resemble fashion accessories. But once activated, the nanites would unravel to shield me into the most resistant body armor in the known universe. To my belt, I attached a pouch of seeker nodes. The small metal balls used the planet's magnetic field to travel a straight line in any given direction and deliver whatever had been encoded in the nanites it carried. I plaited my hair in a long braid, weaving a broad, silver ribbon through it. A large tassel-like decoration hung at one end; one of my latest inventions.

While early morning air on Braxia hovered on the cooler side, daytime temperatures required lighter clothes. I couldn't justify wearing another long-sleeved turtleneck to hide my Veredian markings. Anyway, it would have interfered with my Tuurean armor should the need arise to wear it. To my utter displeasure, I applied my arm prosthetics so that I could wear a sleeveless crop-top. As I would wear another pair of leggings to hide my legs, no prosthetics were needed there.

So much for no longer living in hiding.

I tried not to let the thought depress me, but it was taking its toll. After my father's death, I had promised myself to start living at last since revealing myself would no longer put either of them in danger. Yet, here I was, repeating the same old routine. Beyond concerns for my own safety, there always seemed to be someone important to me who required my genetics to remain secret for their own welfare. Maybe I should have just gone to the planet Haven in the Eastern Quadrant to find myself a Braxian hybrid and dragged his ass back home to the Veredian city of Haven on the planet Tuur, or to Xelix Prime where I could stop hiding and live without fear.

A surreptitious side-glance at my beast of a mate as we made our way to the stables, where the men were gathering, erased all thoughts of any kind of hybrid. Beyond the Tuning that dictated I would eventually fall in love with him more than I ever could any other, Ravik was genuinely growing on me. While our still fairly short relationship had been heavily sexual, we'd also been doing a significant amount of talking during our trip here from Venus Hive and between bouts of feral sex.

One would never suspect such a rough, brutish exterior to host as brilliant a mind as Ravik's. While swift to flare, my man's temper didn't control him. Even when murder shone in his eyes, he remained rational in his decision-making and in his actions. His dedication to the welfare of his people, even those who showed open hostility, commanded respect. Ravik carried the weight of the Braxian world on his shoulders. The near impossible feat of reversing the decline of his people could literally be the death of him. And yet, he didn't complain, plowing forward with single-minded determination.

I understood well the emotional and mental strain that Ravik faced, fighting against the culture of the society he grew up in while juggling his own internal conflicts. I'd witnessed my father being torn apart between his love for my mother and his deep-rooted Guldan beliefs that demanded he enslave her and the rest of the Veredians.

In spite of that, Ravik had earned the undivided loyalty of fierce warriors. The incident on the ship had been an eye opener. But even now, as we walked through the dark stone streets of the compound, all eyes—males, females, and servants alike—shone with respect as they rested upon him. It made my chest swell with pride.

My beast of a man.

Despite being as hard and harsh as its people, the Braxian countryside held an undeniable beauty. The buildings within the compound, although simple in their mostly square and rectangular design, stood proud and elegant under the shimmering silver sky. Once again, the similarities between our worlds struck me; with Guldan's own sky also shimmering but in hues of gold. Built in different shades of grey stones, white, maroon, or silver accents decorated their facades. Most of them had the same kind of ornate carvings in evenly spaced vertical stripes as I'd seen on the walls of Ravik's bathroom.

My jaw dropped as we approached the stables. Outside, many Braxians stood next to nightmarish creatures. The six-legged beasts vaguely resembled horses in their shape. Thick scales covered their bodies, including their draconic heads. Razor sharp, dagger teeth filled their massive jaws. Horns of various sizes rode from the middle of their snouts up their foreheads. Fan-like appendages sat folded on each side of their faces. I suspected bad news followed if they ever opened. A long, scorpion tail and massive, sharp claws at their hoofed feet completed the tableau. Despite my height of 6'4, my chin barely reached the back of the beasts.

Although not afraid, I gave the creatures the proper respect—and space—they deserved.

"They are karvelis," Ravik said, "the distant cousins of the Xelixian cavas."

My eyes widened, the similarities now visible to me, although the cavas only had scales around the face, neck, and underbelly. A soft, leathery skin covered their backs.

"Are they as smart?" I asked, intrigued.

"As much as I'd like to say smarter than the cavas, equally would be the honest answer," Ravik said, gazing upon the creatures with pride. "My clan breeds them. In times past, they were the greatest battle steeds a warrior could have. Now, they make formidable hunters to regulate predator population near vulnerable cities and villages. Some of our clients use them for search and rescue missions. More recently, we've been raising a new breed that is proving quite phenomenal in animal racing."

I perked up. "Oh Goddess, I love racing! Can they be mounted?"

Ravik frowned. "Well… yes. But it's dangerous."

My back stiffened. The look on my face must have said it all, as he took on an uneasy expression.

He sighed. "I do not challenge that, given the opportunity, females can perform as well as males on many fronts—better, even, in some."

"But?" I asked, crossing my arms over my chest.

"But, karvelis are scaled to Braxians dimensions. They do not tolerate saddles or reins that would give the rider something to hang on to. With their size and phenomenal speed, few species can safely ride them while racing," Ravik said, in a reasonable tone. "Once the hunt is over and you've had a chance to look into your brother's business, I'll take you to see the new breed. Whether you get to mount one, let alone race with it, is still to be determined."

Although aggravated by the finality in his tone, he'd made a strong case. Being raised according to Veredian values, while also learning about my Guldan heritage, made me extra sensitive to any male behavior that even remotely hinted at male superiority. I'd done stupid things in the past in response to that, deliberately putting myself in harm's way to prove a point, that having tits and a pussy didn't make me inferior or incompetent. I still struggled with that knee jerk reaction but had greatly improved since, forcing myself to pause and assess arguments against what I wanted.

The heavy stare of Clan Leader Caldes drew my attention. He didn't avert his eyes when mine connected with his. His disapproving expression made no mystery of how he felt about my participating in the hunt. But his buddy, Hagan Lorvis, reeked with aggression. He and a few others had expressed open hostility towards me from the moment I'd set foot on Braxia and throughout last night's meal. That they showed the same level of animosity towards Ravik and his close friends provided little comfort.

Keran walked out of the stables, followed by two massive karvelis —one slightly darker than the stones that paved the street and the other a striking shade of dark blue.

"Let me introduce you to Voltar," Ravik said, raising his palm towards the midnight-colored beast.

The creature approached us, stopping right in front of him, and tilted his head down to press the flat front of his snout against Ravik's hand. Ravik rubbed it in a gentle caress then held his hand up while the karvelis opened his mouth and closed his dagger-teeth around it. I gasped and placed my hand on Ravik's forearm, ready to pull him free. He chuckled, his free arm wrapping around my waist.

"Do not fear, little bird," Ravik said. "It is the common greeting. Voltar reminds me of how lethal he is. And I am stating that I acknowledge his strength and trust him to never use it for ill against me. Voltar," Ravik said when the creature released his arm, "this is my female, Ravena. She is mine. She is pack."

I stared at the beast in awe. The vertical slit of his pupil widened as his yellow, reptilian eye examined me. I instantly realized that Voltar was assessing me. The cavas also needed to accept you into their pack to allow you to mount them. Once they did, they would go to any lengths to keep you safe, even at the cost of their own life. I assumed the karvelis behaved in a similar fashion.

Moving his face away from Ravik, Voltar pressed his snout against my crotch and sniffed audibly.

I recoiled and cast a disbelieving look at my man. "Is he for real?"

Ravik's arm tightened its hold around me, keeping me in place while his 'pet' sniffed away. "Relax," he said, visibly amused with my discomfort. "He's memorizing your scent."

Scrunching my face, I let the creature have at it under the mocking stares of the other Braxian hunters, gathered outside the stables. Once done 'memorizing' the odor of my privates, Voltar raised his head to stare me in the eyes. He emitted a threatening growl and bared his teeth, sending a shiver down my spine.

Ravik held even more firmly. "Do not run," he whispered. "It's okay."

"Do I look like I want to run to you?" I asked, my voice heavily laced with sass.

I instinctively knew that Voltar was testing me, evaluating my worth as his friend's mate. If he were anything like the Xelixian cavas —and my gut said they were even more evolved than that—then his intelligence shouldn't be underestimated. Although he couldn't speak himself, he could understand and react upon most basic conversations, analyze day-to-day situations, and take actions accordingly.

Holding his stare unflinchingly, I removed the bracer on my right arm and raised my hand before Voltar's mouth. From the corner of my eye, I saw Ravik's lips part in shock. A hush descended over the men assembled around us. My gut had told me to respond to Voltar's challenge with one of my own, but I now wondered if I'd been too bold. Guldans valued strength and despised weakness. Ravik hadn't needed to tell me not to run; I wouldn't have. But, with this gesture, I was forcing Voltar's hand into accepting me and pledging not to harm me. Would he view this as a show of trust—which it was meant to be —or as arrogance and a misplaced sense of entitlement?

To make sure he wouldn't assume the latter, while I didn't break eye-contact with him—which could have been construed as a show of submission—I slightly bowed my head as a display of deference to his superior strength. The threatening growl turned into a rumbling purr, indicating his approval. His mouth opened and closed over my limb, his front teeth stopping just shy of my elbow. The pointy edges of his teeth pricked my skin like so many needles, but didn't draw blood.

He released me after a few seconds, his snake-like, split tongue shooting out to give the back of my hand a quick lick. Straightening, he turned to the side as if waiting for us to mount him.

"My goddess," Ravik whispered with possessive pride, "you were made for me."

Surprised, I looked up at him. I couldn't define the expression on his face, but before I could ask any question, he drew my face to his and crushed my lips with a hunger that left me reeling and weak in the knees. When he released me, his eyes clearly said that, if not for the hunt, he would be dragging me back to his bedroom right now and keeping me there for the foreseeable future.

I slipped my armband back on. Under the heavy stares of his men, Ravik helped me up onto Voltar's back and then climbed behind me. Something more than the karvelis accepting me had just happened, but I couldn't figure out what. The animal's broad back forced me to spread my legs wider than any other mount I'd ever ridden. The lack of reins or saddle unsettled me. The rider needed to learn to move in harmony with the creature to keep his balance. The only means to stabilize oneself was to lean forward and hang on to some of the horns on the side of his neck. It further drove home what Ravik had been saying about the dangers of riding the racing breed for non-Braxians. My overall shorter height and arm-length meant stretching further to get a grip on them, which would destabilize my seat on the beast.

The rest of the men mounted their karvelis, and we set off. Wonder and a sense of surrealism washed over me. Here I was, light-years away from my home world, surrounded by feral-looking giants, and riding on the back of a fearsome beast while snugly held against the Braxian ruler's strong body. The men looked awe-inspiring clad in their black, form-fitting, combat uniforms. Each of them had a blaster hooked to their hip, but the spears, swords, battle axes, and bows strapped to their back made me tingle with anticipation. The Braxians' reputation on the battlefield remained unrivaled.

A massive, older Braxian with greying brown hair and green eyes rode up to us, followed closely by approximately twenty men. He nodded respectfully at Ravik before slightly falling back, although remaining in close range. I assumed him to be Elder Pattel, whose arrival we'd been awaiting before setting off. I noticed then that all of their uniforms had a colored patch on their shoulder with some kind of symbol matching the banners I'd seen hanging on the walls of Ravik's Hall; their clan sigils.

Due to our large numbers and the size of the karvelis, we moved at a fairly slow trot and would only speed up once we'd cleared the sprawling village outside of the city walls so that the riders could spread out and avoid unfortunate accidents. That gave us a few minutes to talk before the thundering sound of our mounts' clawed hooves— and the need to hang on for dear life—would make it impossible.

"So what was that about back there, with Voltar?" I asked. "Why did everyone look at me funny? Did I do something wrong?"

Although I'd read plenty about the Braxian culture before my arrival, and even more so after discovering through the Tuning that Ravik was my soulmate, many subtleties of the dos and don'ts escaped me.

"No, little bird," Ravik said. "You did nothing wrong, quite the opposite. It was bold of you to present your hand to Voltar. Worst case scenario, he would have rejected you, like he has many others in the past."

My stupid jealousy instantly reared its ugly head. I didn't know what was up with me. I'd never been so ridiculously territorial. Then again, I'd never met my soulmate before.

"Other females?" I blurted out, kicking myself immediately for it.

Ravik chuckled smugly. "No, silly girl. That was the other part of why what you did turned out to be such a good thing."

I cast a questioning look at him over my shoulder.

"Females do not present their hands to karvelis," Ravik explained. "They're too scared. The rare few who have attempted to do so over the past century were all rejected. And I mean females who tried with karvelis other than mine," he specified with a mocking tone.

That earned him a playful elbow jab in the ribs, which made him chuckle further.

"Like all those of his kind, Voltar respects strength. He would not pledge his life to one he feels wouldn't do the same for him. He deemed you an equal, a hunter, and a protector." The seriousness of his tone made me realize this was far more important to him—maybe even *for* him—than I thought. "My people obsess with purity of blood. To have an alien female by my side, one of mixed blood herself, is ruffling feathers."

I stiffened. It didn't surprise me, seeing how they treated half-breeds like Anton. Still, it stung. Obstacles just seemed to keep piling up against us.

"Tell me, Ravena, what are your intentions?" Ravik asked, the tension in his voice subtle, yet unmistakable.

My heart skipped a beat, uncertain how to answer. I'd always been the one avoiding commitment. A Seer had warned me that I wouldn't meet my soulmate until after my brother's death, so I didn't see the point in getting attached to someone I would eventually end up leaving. The occasional affair, no strings attached, no complications, had suited me perfectly. With his current situation, strong sense of duty, and the burden of the Braxian culture, I feared he might reject anything beyond a temporary fling.

For a second, I considered playing dumb, pretending to have no idea what he was referring to. But we were both grown adults, and I wasn't a coward.

"I thought you said that I belonged to you, and that you'd kill any other man who touched me?" I said, testing the waters.

"I know my own stance and made it clear," Ravik said, his tone hardening. "I asked for yours."

His stance implied keeping me, in spite of all the adversity he'd face—I hoped. Licking my lips I braced myself and took the plunge.

"How much do you know about Korletheans?" I asked, hoping he'd play along until I got to the point.

He narrowed his eyes at me. "As much as everyone else; mainly that they're powerful psychics, Seers, and Oracles."

I nodded in response. "They have something they call the Tuning."

Ravik recoiled, his eyes widening.

He knows what it is.

I licked my lips again, my eyes flicking between his, trying to assess how much of it he understood.

"Veredians can feel it, too?" he asked, his gaze shifting ahead for a second to see how far Voltar had taken us.

Looking ahead, I saw that we would soon reach the open field. I turned back to him to answer his question.

"Most of us can, but not all," I said, my pulse picking up.

"You felt it?" he asked, although his question came out more like a statement.

My throat too constricted to answer, I nodded.

"When you first met me?" he insisted.

I swallowed hard and then nodded again.

A slow smile stretched on Ravik's lips, his eyes filled with a proud and possessive gleam. Tension bled from my shoulders, and I relaxed against him. Careful not to stab himself on my left horn, he placed a kiss on my temple.

He pressed his palm on my stomach, his fingers splayed, and his thumb moving up and down in a slow caress.

"My closest and most trusted advisors recommend that you drink moon juice for the time being," Ravik said cautiously.

My stomach knotted, and my chest constricted. After nearly 150 years of living on the brink of extinction, Veredians had finally found a cure to our fertility problems. For my people, every birth was a blessing, regardless of the sire, or the conditions under which the child had been conceived. Contraception didn't belong in our vocabulary. In a few weeks, I'd turn fifty. That left me another twenty-five years of fertility.

"Is that what you wish?" I asked, failing to hide the tension in my voice.

"No, it is not," Ravik said, without hesitation. My heart soared. "But it's not about what I want. Ultimately, it is your body. I cannot—

will not—force you to drink moon juice. However, there are… things you should know before you make a decision."

"Things about Braxia?" I asked, feeling both confused and relieved.

"About Braxia. About me." The flash of pain and shame that crossed his eyes told me this would be a difficult talk. "But it will have to wait. For now, my *mate*, we hunt."

My stomach flip-flopped at thus being claimed. Ravik kissed the top of my head, then nodded at one of the hunters near us. The man lifted to his lips a whistle-like object. When he blew in it, instead of the shrill sound I expected, it came out as the deep rumble of a foghorn. Ravik leaned forward, forcing me to follow suit. His hands reached for two of Voltar's horns.

"*Fargleh*," Ravik said in Braxian.

I didn't need a translation device to guess its meaning. Voltar surged forward. It was a rough ride. Without Ravik's weight holding me down, I would have bounced right off the mount. And yet, it was fucking exhilarating. The wind whipped past us, my long braid waving like a flag. The scenery quickly changed with the forest looming ahead.

Braxia wasn't called the dark planet for nothing. Not only did it look black from space, but bright colors didn't naturally occur in that world, whether it was in the flora, fauna, or minerals. While all basic colors could be found, they usually leaned towards the darker shades. In spite of that, it didn't feel oppressive, giving off instead a sense of strength, power, and solemnity.

Giant, ash-colored trees with massive trunks spread their long limbs towards the sky. Dark colored green, blue, and red leaves adorned their branches. The scent of fresh dirt and wet leaves greeted us with an underlying sweeter scent, which probably came from wildflowers or wild fruits hanging from the trees or berry bushes nearby. Small critters scurried into hiding as we stampeded through their habitat.

After thirty minutes of hard riding, a signal went off on Ravik's armband. Until its screen lit up, I had assumed it to merely be a decorative element of his armor. But based on the dots appearing on it,

I recognized it as a scanning device, tracking the predators they intended to make their prey. A quick glance at the other riders indicated they, too, had detected the roaming joarkals. The number of dots and the fact that the pack was so close to the ruling clan's compound made me uneasy.

Ravik raised a hand, and all the men slowed down. His trusted friends closed ranks around us. In the distance, we could hear the howling of the beasts. Having returned to a slow trot, Ravik released the horns and straightened, allowing me to do the same. Some of the hunters dismounted and pulled out their bows. The incredibly thick string clearly required tremendous strength to pull, more than I had without the enhancement of my Tuurean armor. They nocked their arrows, advancing at the ready.

According to Ravik, the first wave of arrows was meant to knock out some of the pack with a powerful paralytic. When I asked him why not simply shoot them with dart guns loaded with tranquilizers, he explained that the darts couldn't pierce through the hard carapace of the creatures, unlike arrows. The arrow also made it harder for the joarkal to keep moving, giving the drug more time to take effect as they were fairly resistant to anything.

Voltar stopped, the folded leathery skin alongside his neck fanning. I stretched my neck to look above it in an attempt to see what threat he had detected. The forest stood still, even the birds having gone quiet. Besides the trees and small berry bushes, a number of long, rough-edged, light grey rocks littered the forest. Dark-red, spiky flowers grew on top, although they were probably mushrooms. Nothing else stood out. Even the foliage of the trees seemed cowed from bristling in the slight breeze.

It took me a moment, thinking at first my vision was playing tricks on me. Then, one of what I'd initially believed to be rocks, prowled with feline grace towards us. The four-legged creature seemed to be covered in stone with a broad, flat head. The maroon flowers turned out to be spikes running from its forehead, along its spine, and down its scorpion-like tail. Vicious talons protruded from its paws.

No wonder dart guns wouldn't work.

However badass the Braxian arrows looked, even those didn't seem able to pierce the joarkal's outer shell. As more of the rocks started moving, the men made a protective wall between them and us.

That annoyed me.

Ravik jumped off Voltar. From the look on his face, he'd clearly intended on ordering me to remain mounted, but it was obvious that without him to keep me stabilized, I'd likely topple off at the first step Voltar made. To be fair, I deliberately exaggerated my discomfort to force the issue. It would likely come back to bite me in the ass when we'd look at the racing breed, but I'd deal with that situation then. Reluctantly extending a hand towards me, Ravik helped me down. At the same time, the whistling sound of arrows being loosed sounded off ahead, soon followed by the pained and angry roars of the targeted beasts. With a battle cry, a first group of Braxians charged the joarkals rushing towards us.

Ravik armed his battle axe and, fisting my braid close to my scalp, he drew my face to his and gave me a hard kiss. He released me, his eyes sparkling with excitement and the anticipation of battle. Turning to face Voltar, he pressed his palm to the flat part of the karveli's snout.

"I entrust you with the safety of my mate," Ravik said.

Voltar snorted, jerking his head in a way that eerily reminded me of a nod. With one last glance towards me, Ravik smiled then rushed towards the others to join the fray.

Four men stayed back, close to me, all from Krygor's and Pattel's clans. Among them, I recognized Gorav, Anton's youngest, pureblood brother. He would escort me to Varrek's home to secure it before I entered. It upset me at first that these men couldn't partake in the hunt in order to babysit me. But I quickly realized that I was only an extra task for them to keep an eye on. They were actually tracking the movements of the predators on the terrain and directing the men towards the hot spots.

Even from the relatively short distance, the battle looked like a well-choreographed ballet. In spite of their massive size, Braxians didn't lumber about, their speed akin to that of the Xelixians, but slightly slower than Veredian Warriors. But their strength left me reeling. They didn't only strike the creatures with their weapons, but also with their fists. Their blows knocked back the beasts or rattled them. Each joarkal easily measured three meters long—not counting their also very long tails—and a little less than two meters high. Between their impressive muscle mass and stony carapace, shoving them around had to require tremendous strength.

Ravik took my breath away. As the beast charged him, he swung his battle axe, striking the joarkal on the side of its face with the flat back side of the weapon. He obviously intended to stun, not kill. The creature's head jerked far to the right, and it stumbled, losing its momentum. Still, halfway through regaining its balance, the beast swiped a massive paw at Ravik, the blade-like claws aiming for his face. He blocked it with the staff of his battle axe, holding it with both hands, and then parried a second, and a third swipe. On the fourth, the joarkal pressed with all its weight, probably trying to break the staff. Ravik's muscles bulged under the effort as he shoved back the predator just in time to dodge out of the path of its scorpion tail stabbing into the location Ravik had just been standing in. Spinning on himself, he swiped his battle axe around, giving it greater velocity, and struck right under the pit of the joarkal's front leg, cutting deep through the leathery skin and muscles of the underbelly.

The creature reared its head up, roaring in pain. Without missing a beat, Ravik spun in the other direction and slammed the blade of his axe into the softer underside of its neck. A dark-blue liquid gushed from the critical wound. The beast attempted to back away, but my mate rammed into its wounded side with all his strength and weight. Toppling to its side, the joarkal tried to get back on all fours to protect its vulnerable underside, but Ravik backhanded it and then punched its bleeding neck wound. The beast toppled on its side, clawing feebly at empty air as its lifeblood poured out of him. Another swing of Ravik's battle axe put an end to the creature's agony.

Watching my mate battle proved quite the humbling experience. As a Veredian of the Warrior breed, I possessed excellent combat skill. It had significantly fueled my already cocky and self-confident personality. But I could clearly see that without the assistance of the advanced technology developed by my Veredian Sisters and the Tuureans, I couldn't have defeated that creature in single combat. I didn't even know that I could win against a Braxian. A single blow from them would crush me. One mistake would suffice to ensure my demise.

It was a sobering thought.

As Ravik turned to aid one of his men trying to finish off its target and with a second joarkal charging him, my armor suddenly went active. The black nanites unraveled the celesium shell from my belt and armbands, covering my body in the most impenetrable armor in the known universe. Startled, I looked around me, seeking what threat could have triggered its auto-defense. The four Braxians by my side all gaped at my transformation, their expressions going from shock to wariness. Aside from my horns, clad in my armor, I looked exactly like a Tuurean female. With good reasons, too, but ones that I couldn't share with them.

However, I couldn't focus on their worries right now. Voltar tensed next to me, the slit of his reptilian eyes widening as he suspiciously looked around, but he, too, didn't seem to see anything.

As with the Tuureans, the armor automatically covered my face with a dark visor and my braid with an intelligent armor. The nanites in the braid's armor synchronized to my neural waves so that they would respond to mental commands. Added to my natural combat skills, this priceless gift from Admiral Lee, the military leader of the Tuurean army, turned me into a lethal war machine. Within seconds, the celesium completely formed around me, its systems going online.

The graphic display turned on inside my visor, the scan indicating the presence of multiple people surrounding us. As the enhanced vision of my visor kicked in, it revealed the blurry silhouettes of a dozen Guldans. Weapons drawn, they were stealthily closing on us, camouflaged by a cloaking shield.

"INTRUDERS!" I shouted.

The Braxians closed protectively around me, looking this way and that for their invisible foe. The fools didn't realize *they* were the ones in danger right now, not me. I raised my fist in front of my chest. The air shimmered around it, then an energy shield formed in front of me.

"Shields up!" I shouted, squeezing past Gorav just as a few of the Guldan took aim at us.

Unable to see them, and therefore unaware, he tried to stop me until the sparks of a few blaster shots bounced off of my energy shield. One of my four companions collapsed, hit by a couple of shots directly to his chest. The remaining three raised their own shields and armed their blasters.

"Fall back," I ordered.

The Braxians complied. I doubted it was so much out of obedience than in response to the blaster shots raining on us. They closed ranks, their shields touching each other to make a single protective wall before us. While blindly shooting at our invisible attackers, we slowly backed away.

Reaching into my pouch, I retrieved a few seeker nodes, which I held in my palm. I pushed a 'disrupt Guldan shield' command at the nanites contained within them, using my Veredian power. Over the years, I'd learn the hard way to be precise in the simple commands I could give to avoid disaster. Had I not specified the specs of a Guldan shield, the nanites would immediately have begun attacking my own shield and that of my companions. I flicked the seeker nodes individually in the direction of the closest Guldans. Once in motion, they would use the planet's magnetic fields to travel up to 300 meters —or before that if one hit a target—and then deliver its payload.

Within seconds, the targeted Guldans' cloaking shields collapsed, making them visible at last. Angry roars arose from my companions, echoed by Voltar who took on a menacing stance, hovering protectively next to me. The revealed Guldans rushed us. Voltar and the other karvelis belonging to my four companions, charged our attackers in response. Thankfully, they provided the necessary distraction for me to repeat the process with the seekers and reveal the remaining Guldans.

"That's all of them," I shouted.

The words no sooner left my lips than two of the three Braxians still standing, jumped into the melee, Gorav staying by my side.

I tapped my braid, its armor parting at the base to eject the wide, silver ribbon I'd woven into my hair. Pushing my Veredian power into the ribbon, the 'tassel' stiffened into a pommel while the rest of the ribbon turned into a blade. It didn't come anywhere near the quality of my celesium sword—another gift from the Admiral—but it would cut any bastard who got in my way.

Gorav stared at it with disbelieving eyes.

"Let's go kick some ass," I said with a broad grin.

"Ravena, no!" Gorav exclaimed.

Ignoring him, I dashed towards two of the Guldans on our flank who were pointlessly firing their blasters at the karvelis. Their thick scales appeared to deflect the shots, but not the pain caused by the impact. The first one, with short, brown hair aimed his blaster at me while his companion armed himself with his sword. My shield absorbing the shots convinced him to switch to his sword as well. I didn't slow down as I barreled towards him. His eyes widened, and he braced himself, no doubt ready to use my momentum to toss me to the ground.

Just as he raised his sword to swipe at me, I slid to the ground, my speed carrying me forward. Startled, he didn't have time to jump out of the way before I knocked him off his feet, my raised sword taking a good bite into his thigh. He screamed and rolled to his side, raising his shield just in time to avoid being bludgeoned by Gorav.

Without missing a beat, I jumped from the slide back onto my feet and whipped my head around at the second Guldan rushing towards me. Obeying my neural command, the tip of my braid extended, wrapping around his neck. Before his hands could even reach for the armored braid, sharp blades protruded from it, severing his head. His face took on a surprised expression before the braid released him, the tip shrinking back to its normal length. The Guldan's head fell off, his beheaded body advancing a few more steps before collapsing to the ground.

I turned around just in time to see Gorav kick the shield out of the hand of the Guldan, still on the ground, unable to get up from the blows my companion rained down on him. The Guldan tried to swipe his sword at Gorav who just dodged it before catching his opponent's wrist, squeezing it hard enough to break his hand and make him let go of his weapon with a scream. Still holding the Guldan's wrist, Gorav brought down his fist on his victim's thigh. With a cracking sound, the Guldan's leg jerked, folding in the wrong direction as he bellowed in agony, his eyes rolling in his head. Gorav grabbed the wounded man's horn, lifting him up with one hand, like a weightless ragdoll, then slammed his head on the ground. The back of his skull exploded like an overripe fruit, spilling blood and gore. The Guldan's body twitched violently, then went still.

I looked up at Gorav with horrified awe. There was something utterly sexy about the bloodlust on his face.

"Nice work," I said, before glancing at our other two companions.

With his teeth, Voltar was tearing off the leg of a Guldan who appeared already dead or dying, considering the guts spilling out of his belly from what looked like claw wounds. One of the other karvalis stabbed his target twice with his scorpion tail. Within seconds, the Guldan's face turned red, foam pouring out of his mouth. He fell to the ground, face first, convulsing. The karveli stepped on his back, breaking his spine, on its way to another prey. The other two Braxians were busy breaking limbs and crushing skulls of their own.

"They've got this. Let's go to Ravik," I said, running towards the forest.

"It's too dangerous for you there!" Gorav shouted.

"Yes, but there might be more cloaked Guldans there," I countered without slowing down. "The Braxians will be defenseless."

That convinced him despite his obvious reluctance. "They know," Gorav said, following me. "We warned them."

Of course they would have. They'd been in communication with them coordinating the attack to begin with. Why they hadn't joined us was quickly answered as I took in the mayhem reigning within the forest. An angry roar behind us had me looking over my shoulder.

Voltar chased after us. His presence reassured me. As we ran forward, Gorav warned Ravik of our approach over his com.

This wasn't a battle; it was carnage. A fresh wave of joarkals had descended upon the Braxians still dealing with the first pack. Surrounding them, another two dozen cloaked Guldans gleefully fired away at the Braxians. To my horror, I quickly realized they were choosing their targets. Not so much sparing as avoiding some of the Braxians, even aiding them by firing at the joarkals that threatened them. In the confusion, I couldn't recognize the Braxian faces but tried to do so with their sigils on their shoulders.

I found Ravik surrounded by his closest allies, battling the group of joarkals. As we approached, an unexplainable wave of energy swept through me, with an irrepressible urge to kill. I blinked and shook my head, trying to fight the feral state that wanted to take me over. Gorav seemed to feel it as well, but it didn't faze him.

A few of Ravik's men had erected a protective shield around them, shooting blindly, mostly in the completely wrong direction. They were under heavy fire. At this rate, their shields would soon be depleted, leaving them defenseless. There were too many Guldans for me to reveal them the same way I had done with my seekers. Even if I tried, with the number of people and creatures running around, they'd likely end up in the path of the seekers, causing them to go off before reaching their intended targets.

No doubt considering me safe, Voltar jumped into the battle alongside his master. Clearly itching to join the fray, Gorav nevertheless remained by my side, shooting in the general direction of the forest. For once, I actually welcomed this protection, which allowed me to analyze the situation, looking for a solution. The Guldan's blasters didn't flash when fired, making it impossible to know their location. Even the impact on the shields gave no sense of the direction from which they'd originated.

And then it hit me. The Braxians didn't actually need to see the Guldans, only to know exactly where they were.

"Gorav, what's your com's channel frequency?" I asked.

He frowned, taken aback by the question. After a brief hesitation, he communicated it to me. I plugged it into the interface of my armband, and queried the subroutine that allowed my suit to detect the Guldans before sending it through the com channel to all Braxians. It upset me that the likely traitors would receive it as well, but the needs of the many outweighed those concerns. I normally wouldn't share this type of technology, but the Tuurean cloaking shields remained more advanced and undetectable with this subroutine.

"You're a fucking genius, female," Gorav grunted.

I grinned.

With this software upgrade, the Braxians armband scanner showed them the exact position of every Guldan within a three-hundred meters radius. While they still couldn't see their targets before them, the Braxians fired the bows and blasters with deadly precision, most of them hitting their mark. The tide turned as a number of the Guldans attempted to beat a hasty retreat. No longer under heavy fire, the men holding the shields turned to the beasts.

"Pattel, your command," Ravik said to the elder warrior in a barely understandable growl. "Krygor, Keran, with me."

I expected Ravik to tell me to stay back but, to my surprise, he glanced at me, a savage look on his face. His chest vibrated with a growl. I lowered my visor, realizing he couldn't see my face through the dark material. A glimmer of recognition flashed through his eyes.

I understood then that Ravik had entered battle rage; a rare genetic trait passed down within warrior clans. Those who achieved it were called Berserkers, revered by their clans. On the field of battle, once a Berserker entered battle rage, he could enhance the strength, speed, and endurance of his clan mates, turning them into Furies. That bloodlust and extra strength that buzzed through me stemmed from him.

He grunted again, then turned around and took off chasing after the Guldans. I followed, feeling stronger and faster than ever before.

CHAPTER 9
RAVIK

My blood boiled with rage, a red haze filling my vision at the cowardly attack. They had targeted my mate, forcing her into battle and kept me from going to her using swarms of joarkals. They reeked of forxis, a hallucinogen known to cause extreme bouts of aggression. This had been a well-coordinated effort with the assistance of Braxians.

I raced through the forest, already knowing the Guldans ahead would escape. As soon as Ravena made their location visible on our radar, Clan Lorvis, Clan Sedrak, and Clan Arthol broke rank to chase after the Guldans. All three conveniently happened to be led by one of those who remained of the Fifteen. They'd been fighting at the edge of the battle, close to the Guldans, and yet remained unscathed while members of other clans fell to blaster shots.

As we approached a clearing ahead, the dots of the Guldans disappeared from the radar. The angry roars that rose behind me echoed mine. I realized then that a few more men—mine and some from other clans—had followed us.

Good. More witnesses to his execution.

The trees parted to reveal Clan Leader Torvin Sedrak, surrounded by four of his men. He started advancing towards me with a falsely disappointed expression. But mine must have revealed that I wasn't fooled. Chin lifting in defiance, his eyes narrowed and his face hardened.

I raised a hand, indicating that my men not advance any further as I marched closer to Torvin, my breathing still slightly labored from the run. The men who'd accompanied me fanned around us. Thankfully, Ravena stood back with Krygor and his youngest son, Gorav.

"The Guldans have escaped you," I said, the battle rage haze making my words come out slurred and growly. "How convenient when you were so close to them and can move faster than them."

Torvin's eyes flicked this way and that, taking in which clansmen were in attendance, no doubt gauging how much support he might garner. When they settled on Ravena, hatred flared, and his mask dropped.

"This has nothing to do with the Guldans, does it, *Magnar*?" Torvin asked, putting as much contempt as he could in my title. "This is about that human cunt and that abomination she gave you. You're pining over that filthy slave, and rather than taking a proper Braxian mate, you're still chasing after alien pussy," he spat, casting a meaningful—and contemptuous—glance at Ravena over my shoulder. "You've learned nothing. No wonder Braxia is on the verge of bankruptcy. You're running it into the ground, turning us into pathetic farmers, taking orders from Krygor's half-breed."

Looking at the men around us and at the others trickling in from the woods, he pointed at me, taking them as witnesses.

"This is your ruler," Torvin shouted so all would hear him. "An alien lover, who bows to a half-breed. Probably sucks his cock while he's at it. He has rejected every alliance that could bring us back to our glorious warrior ways; starves our clans by taking away our slaves; charges cutthroat fines to those who won't follow his rules; spits on our customs; forbids retaliation against trampled honor; and now brings a fucking female to the battlefield. He is unworthy of the title Magnar."

An odd sense of peace settled over me as mutterings from the men rose around me. In a few minutes, I would kill this man, painfully. For

Lissy, for my son, for his disrespect to my Ravena, and to me, and above all, for betraying Braxia.

"Whatever your grievances with the way I rule Braxia, you forfeited your life the day you brought foreigners to attack and kill Braxians on their home world to further your own agenda," I said, in a voice devoid of emotion.

Torvin flinched, a glint of panic settling in his eyes. "You've been slaughtering the Fifteen. THAT's what this is all about."

I ignored his desperate attempt at diversion.

"The joarkal reek of forxis, which drove them to madness. Hundreds of innocent Braxians have died during their rampage instigated by your Guldan friends," I continued, inexorably. Angry head nods and murmurs of agreements welcomed my words. "The joarkal population will take years to recover from the massacre we were forced into. Countless of our brothers lay dead or injured in that forest because those cowards you allied yourself with shot them while hidden. Yes, *my woman*, the alien, for the second time is the reason we stand victorious. So no, Torvin Sedrak, this isn't about any of the things you've claimed, but about your treason against Braxia. Lissy is merely more fuel to my rage."

"I've committed no treason! You are the traitor!" Torvin yelled, taking a step back.

"For your crime, Torvin Sedrak, you will face execution by my hand through single combat. For assisting you in this crime, your four companions will be flayed and spiked in front of your compound as a reminder of what awaits traitors. As for what remains of your clan, they will stand trial or face banishment."

"Judgment heard and seconded," Krygor's voice said behind me.

"Judgment heard and seconded," Keran said.

I planted my battle axe in the ground like a flag, as it would do too quick a job of killing my opponent, and extended a hand towards Krygor. He approached me and handed me his sword.

"NO! This is a farce!" Torvin shouted, looking for support that didn't come as more and more voices rose in support of my ruling.

"You can die fighting with what little honor you have left, or you can try to run like the cowards you've aligned yourself with."

Realizing at last that there would be no escape for him, Torvin raised his sword and charged me with a war cry. The dying embers of my battle rage reignited, and I embraced it, letting the bloodlust wash over me. Sword in hand, I met his attack head on, easily parrying the blow. Adrenalin coursed through me, putting me in a strange state of feral euphoria. I laughed as Torvin swung his blade at me with all the strength he could muster. Each clash of our blades sent tremors along my arms, but I welcomed the slight discomfort.

Despite his combat skills, my opponent always tended to be a fool in battle, allowing his emotions to get the better of him. He was tiring himself without causing any damage or gaining any advantage.

Intent on toying with him, I blocked a few more blows and waited for him to raise his weapon. Timing my counterattack, I backhanded him savagely. Blood exploded from his mouth as he stumbled backwards, under the approving cheers of the assembled crowd. Recovering quickly, Torvin came at me again with his sword. I deflected the blow and backhanded him again, hitting the same side of his mouth. This time, he spit out a couple of teeth. The back of my hand pleasantly stung from the force with which I'd struck him.

Enraged, Torvin slashed at me in a frenzy. I was humiliating him by slapping his face like a little bitch instead of punching him like a worthy opponent. I parried and deflected his attacks, inflicting shallow to deep cuts in-between each of his flurries, circling around him like a predator. But as much as I enjoyed canvassing his body with weeping wounds, I soon tired of the game.

Hungry for the sound of his bones breaking, I turned the tables on him, this time, being the one to press the attack. He backed away from the fury of my assault, feebly parrying what he could, enduring the pain of what he couldn't. Rushing him, I grabbed a hold of his weapon hand, immobilizing it, and slammed the pommel of my sword on the same side of his jaw I had been backhanding. Part of the bones caved in with a satisfying crunch.

Torvin's scream of pain gurgled as blood flooded his mouth. His left fist connected solidly with the side of my face. Although it should have rattled me, battle rage dimmed the feeling of pain. Still holding his wrist, I brought down the pommel of my sword on the back of his elbow, busting his arm. He roared in agony as his sword fell from his now-limp hand. Despite his pain, Torvin brought his knee up, aiming for my groin or my gut. I barely managed to turn slightly, his knee slamming into my side with bruising force. For all the contempt he inspired in me, I gave him a begrudging respect as a warrior for fighting through the pain and not begging for mercy.

I backhanded his broken jaw again, feeling more bones giving way under the impact. Torvin wobbled on his feet. Releasing the wrist of his broken arm, I wrapped my hand around his neck and pummeled the other side of his face with a series of hard punches under the encouraging shouts of the crowd. Although still conscious, Torvin went limp. With a savage cry, and in an animal display of strength, I lifted my opponent by the neck with one hand before slamming him down on the ground. The crowd roared its approval while the air rushed out of Torvin.

I gazed upon my rival's bloodied, broken face, his body lacerated with cuts, his arm lying at an odd angle, my bloodlust far from sated. He twitched, fighting to remain conscious. I hoped he would succeed for a while longer. His punition would not only serve to assuage part of my need for vengeance for Lissy, my son, the innocent Braxians killed by the joarkals, and for his betrayal against Braxia, but it would also serve as an example for any other who would even consider pursuing such a foolish course of action.

Marching up to my battle axe still planted in the ground, I picked it up and extended the bloodied sword back to Krygor. He swiftly approached to relieve me of it. My eyes connected with Ravena's. She stood regal in her celesium armor, her visor down, her beautiful face fierce and devoid of any condemnation. My woman held my gaze, unflinching, the barely perceptible nod of her head confirming her support.

My goddess.

A hush fell over the men as I stomped back towards Torvin, who was struggling to get back on his feet. I kicked his shoulder with the sole of my foot, knocking him once more on his back.

"This is for bringing dishonor to your Ancestor's clan," I said, bringing down the flat back of my battle axe on his left calf. He screeched as the bones shattered, his body shaken with spasms. "This is for betraying Braxia," I said, crushing the bone of his other calf. "And this is for the innocents who fell because of your treachery."

His eyes rolled to be the back of his head as I smashed the elbow of his remaining good arm. That wouldn't do. I wanted him conscious for the final blow. I prowled around his broken body, eyeing him with contempt. Lifting my head, I gazed upon my people surrounding me. They eyed me warily.

"I am your Magnar," I shouted to them, my voice defiant. "Many of you balk at change and yet, twice in less than three days, we've almost been defeated because we're living in the past without proper technology. The world is leaving us behind, and those who would ally with Braxia seek to control us."

The men nodded, grave expressions on their faces. Even Raylor nodded, a troubled look straining his features. My gaze turned to my woman, and I pointed a hand towards her.

"You demand that females be kept as slaves to your pleasures, as broodmares because you think them inferior creatures. And yet, we all stand here because my female allowed us to see our foe when we'd been sitting blind, taking fire from cowards. Her blade still drips with the blood of the one she has slain. Do you see weakness in this female?"

The men eyed her with a disconcerted admiration and a confused form of respect. She was challenging everything we'd come to expect from females. But how could it be otherwise when we indoctrinated our own females from birth that they were inferior beings, only living to serve men's needs? How could they show their true worth when any independent thinking on their part, or display of autonomy, would be severely punished?

"Braxia WILL change," I continued, pivoting on myself to look at every single one of my men. "I will *not* let us fall into darkness and become vulnerable to external threats. And yes, major changes come with pain. But as the Ancestors are my witnesses, if I have to beat change into you, then I will. And those of you who oppose my ruling, I am here," I said, spreading my arms wide. "Any and all challenges will be accepted."

"For Braxia," Krygor shouted. "Long may be your reign!"

"For Braxia," the voices of the men shouted back.

I walked back to Torvin who had regained consciousness. Breath shallow and eyes filled with pain, he watched me with a glimmer of resignation.

"For your crimes, you will not receive a warrior's funeral, but will rot here, feeding carrion eaters. May your fate serve as an example. Any and all who would betray me and Braxia will face the Magnar's mercy… and find none." Raising my battle axe again, my gaze bore into Torvin. "Your punishment was for your crimes. But this is for my Lissy."

The back of my battle axe shattered his groin. Torvin's strangled cry died as soon as it began. His body shuddered, and his eyes turned glassy. Lifting my head in the deadly silence around us, I made eye contact with three of the remaining Fifteen present in the clearing. Two averted their eyes, fear and resentment burning within. The third held my gaze with a strange air of acceptance.

Turning back towards Ravena, I took her hand. "Let's go take care of our fallen," I said to my men, and led my woman back into the forest.

The trip back home had been quiet and solemn, the successful hunt bittersweet. To my relief, we had sustained far fewer casualties than we'd first believed. Guldans had not been shooting to kill but to stun. I could speculate a number of reasons why they would have done so. Without Ravena's intervention, we would have fallen, stunned by invisible enemies, laying helpless while being trampled and devoured by the joarkals, leaving no evidence of the Guldan's treachery. In one fell swoop, they would have eliminated the heads of all the clans that opposed an alliance, leaving room for a puppet Magnar they could manipulate at will.

I still seethed that we'd failed to capture a single Guldan alive. Nevertheless, their corpses constituted irrefutable proof of their meddling and of their attack on Braxia. In light of the magnitude of the evidence, the two Guldan Ambassadors had no leg to stand on when I expelled them from Braxia. Where Ambassador Tellin made a last ditch effort, asking me not to condemn all of Guldar for the failings of the few, Ambassador Zorak didn't argue, graciously accepting their dismissal.

Too graciously.

Even Raylor Caldes showed eagerness to escort the Guldans back to their ship. This incident had been yet another severe blow to Clan Caldes. After the disgrace his first-born son Gerwin had brought upon them, being indirectly responsible for the death of many Braxians was the last thing he'd needed or wanted.

But the Guldans and Caldes' woes ranked pretty low in my list of concerns right now. Although she hadn't spoken them out loud, Ravena's mind overflowed with unanswered questions. They were sensitive topics I hadn't planned on raising with her until we'd had a chance to see where this relationship was headed. I didn't want to talk about Lissy, didn't want to tell her about the shameful things I had allowed, and the horrible crime I had committed. But Ravena was my soulmate.

Aside from battle rage, Braxians possessed no psi abilities. However, even though I couldn't feel the Tuning like she did, every fiber of my being screamed to me that she was the one. I wasn't in love with her—yet—nor was she with me, which made having this conversation now all the scarier. Through the eyes of love, she might be more inclined to forgiveness and acceptance. Regardless of my reluctance—and yes, my fears—I needed to be the one to tell her. The longer I delayed, the more likely she'd discover it on her own, maybe in an even darker light.

Ravena followed me quietly as I led her by the hand to my private quarters. My pulse picked up as we walked to the patio at the back of the bedroom. I often had meals on the smaller, dark stone table by the railing overlooking the plaza. This time, however, probably sensing the need for privacy, Muna had laid a snack for us by the larger table near the water fountain, directly carved into the mountain face that blocked off the front and right side of the patio. A long dark-grey stone bench ran along each side of the table, covered with a comfortable dark-red, water-resistant cushion.

I invited Ravena to take a seat. For a moment, I considered sitting next to her but then decided to sit across from her. Not knowing how she would react to my confession, I wanted to give her some space.

She pulled her long braid in front of her, slowly stroking it while staring at me with a serious, expectant look. I cleared my throat, my stomach knotting with rising anxiety.

"It appears you are meant to forever be my savior," I said, in a pathetic effort to lighten the mood.

Ravena smiled and then nodded in acknowledgement.

"You not only saved many lives, but you are helping my people open their eyes about the worth of females, just like Anton did about the worth of hybrids. For this, I can never thank you enough," I said, with genuine gratitude.

"It will be a slow process," she said. "I wish Guldar's Emperor would be as open-minded as you. I know what great challenges you face with these changes, and I respect you all the more for it. You're a good man."

I snorted, wondering how much of that respect would remain in a few minutes.

"No, Ravena. I'm a lot of things, but not a good man. I have allowed and done terrible things. The kind of things that haunt you forever and can never be undone." I rubbed my face with both hands, wishing I could draw Ravena into my arms and bury my face in her hair instead, in search of comfort. "Yes, I am making much needed changes. Sadly, they come way too late for far too many innocents," I said, the familiar pain of Lissy's death crushing my heart.

"Innocents like Lissy?" Ravena asked in a soft voice.

My heart skipped a beat, and my stomach dropped. Did she already know? My eyes flicked between hers, trying to assess what she knew.

"You dedicated your final blow to her," Ravena explained. "Who was she? And who are the Fifteen?"

Sorrow, shame, and fear of the contempt I would undoubtedly read in her eyes once I'd confessed, twisted me inside. Taking in a deep breath, I took the plunge.

"Thirty-eight years ago, for my twelfth birthday, my father gave me a human slave. She was a beautiful wisp of a girl, a fourteen-year-old named Lissy." Even after all these years, her delicate face still appeared clearly in my mind's eyes with her pointy chin, high cheekbones, heart-shaped lips and big, blue, doll eyes. "I had become sexually active a few months prior, and Father considered it a rite of passage to deflower a human female."

It was more than a rite of passage. Virgins were hard to come by. Beautiful human virgins even harder. Wealthy clans paid high prices to get willing young females for their sons to bed. It became a sign of status. Between the ages of eleven and fourteen, a Braxian male's girth was still small enough for a human woman to handle with reasonable ease. By fifteen, coupling with a human usually resulted in serious tearing without Denax. However, frequent and excessive use of the dilator endangered the woman's health.

"Within a year, I committed the unforgivable. Not content to fall in love with a slave, I also impregnated her with a male." My chest ached reminiscing about the way she'd fearfully revealed her pregnancy to me. I'd been both excited and terrified of what that would mean for us. "As you may have found out from Anton, under my father's rule, Braxian law decreed that half-breeds were abominations to be eradicated lest they taint Braxian bloodlines. An exception was made for females who would then be used as clan whores. But, in defiance of that law, I allowed my son to live and kept him a secret for fifteen months."

Ravena's hands tightened around her braid, her gaze penetrating, and her shoulders tensing.

"Your father discovered his existence," she said, when the silence stretched.

"Yes," I said, swallowing past the lump in my throat. "While he lived, my father, Magnar Sigmer, had been a zealot and a bigot. For his own son, the future ruler of Braxia, to taint our bloodline, the purest on our home world, and with a slave no less…"

"He must have completely lost it," Ravena said, her eyes filling with compassion.

I snorted. "That's quite the understatement. It had been foolish of us—of me—to think this could go on forever. A human snitched on us. The Narinda colony's ambassador came to discuss possible trade agreements." My lips stretched in a sneer, my hatred for the human still burning bright. "He knew Braxian protocols. When Lissy refused him, he complained to my father who had guards escort him to her quarters. If she refused him again, they would hold her down for him and then punish her. Apparently, she was breastfeeding our son when they barged in."

Ravena shifted in her seat, no doubt imagining the barely seventeen-year-old girl that my Lissy had been at the time, watching in horror as the guards dragged our child away. Variations of that image still haunted me.

"That bastard never got to fuck her. The guards finding her with a hybrid superseded any courtesy to a foreign guest," I said bitterly. "After realizing the consequences of his lust, the coward left Braxia behind him along with the irreparable damage of his actions. He must have known I would come after him because he broke all contact between our peoples."

The Ancestors knew I had sought opportunities to cross paths with him, but he'd always managed to avoid any place where I might show up. He eventually met his untimely demise thanks to a misfired arrow during a hunting trip, courtesy of a mercenary hired by yours truly.

"My father recalled me early from the training camp where I'd been. I naively thought he had summoned me as a reward for the distinctions I'd earned during combat training." A sad chuckle escaped my lips thinking back on the foolish boy I'd been. "The guards directed me to the courtyard where he awaited me. When I saw over a dozen juveniles from Elder Clans gathered there, I thought they came to celebrate me."

Ravena shuddered, her obsidian eyes riveted on me as she listened with morbid fascination. I gazed upon her beautiful face as if to memorize the way she looked before contempt for me filled her eyes. I didn't want to speak anymore, but I'd already gone too far. If we were to have any chance of a future together, this truth, however horrible, needed to come out.

"The moment I stepped into the courtyard, their malicious smirks and condemning expressions told me something was wrong. That's when I saw my Lissy, naked and shackled on an altar. Our son, Goliath, wailed for his mother, trapped in a cage like an animal."

I remembered hesitating when she'd chosen that name for our son. Although pleasant sounding and appropriate in that the boy would grow to be a giant by human standards, the story of his demise at the hand of a smaller man had struck me as an ill omen.

"My father made me watch as the juveniles took turns—fifteen in total, one for each month I'd kept my son's life a secret. He chose them because their age made them the perfect size to fuck a human without killing her in minutes."

Ravena's hand covered her mouth, muffling her horrified gasp. That moment was forever burnt in my memory, and not just the dreadful sight of those men violating my female as I stood there, helpless. The sounds were the worst as they panted and groaned with pleasure under the cheers of the others; Lissy's desperate cries as she begged me for help; the heart-wrenching screams of my son who had been old enough to understand they were hurting his mother while I, his father, stood there not coming to her aid.

I closed my eyes and exhaled loudly, my hand rubbing the stabbing pain in my chest.

"By the fifth one, Lissy stopped calling out for me. When the last was done, my father held the cage up for me. That's when she finally understood that the punishment wasn't for her alone. She begged and pleaded for me to spare Goliath. She even offered to send him away or ask that we sell him as a slave, as long as we spared his life. But that would never have happened. Not with my father. Not after he'd setup this whole circus."

I ran a shaky hand through my hair, shame and guilt burning like acid in my gut.

"You see, the altar usually has a wall at its head. Once the female has been punished, the sire is expected to bash the child's head on it so the blood and gore can rain down on the mother's face. When the deed is done, he is to place the corpse on her chest, there to remain through the night."

Ravena's hand slipped to her chest, gripping her heart as if to contain it. Head slowly shaking from side to side in denial, her eyes pleaded for me to say I hadn't done it. My throat constricted painfully while my blood seemed to turn to acid in my veins. I lowered my head in shame, unable to withstand the condemnation and the disgust that would follow.

"I couldn't bash his head on that wall, but I couldn't let him live either. I'd known it all along but wanted to live the illusion of a happy family. When I delayed to act, my father threatened to do it himself. He would have made a spectacle of it, so I broke our son's neck and placed his dead body on her chest. And thus they remained until the next morning." My voice choked on those words. I inhaled deeply to get the strength to continue. "Lissy took her own life the following day. From the doctor's account, she would have died anyway from internal injuries."

Ravena abruptly rose from her seat and walked away, stopping in front of the waterfall, arms wrapped around her waist. The sense of rejection struck me like so many daggers in my chest. I fisted my hands on my lap, trying to contain the vivid pain that had been my companion for decades, made even more acute at the thought of losing the one female that had reawakened my heart in all those years and given me the desire to wish for more.

"I could have saved her," I whispered, the same regret gnawing at me. "I could have saved them both by simply renouncing my clan. Instead, I spent the next thirty-eight years with their deaths on my conscience."

"No, you couldn't have," Ravena said over her shoulder in a voice hard as steel, laced with barely repressed anger. "Your father wouldn't have allowed tainted blood to sully his bloodline. With or without your cooperation, they would have been made examples of."

I wished she'd turn around so that I could see the expression on her face.

"You're right," I conceded, realizing that I'd never looked at it from that angle, too swallowed-up by self-hatred. "He would have destroyed them, and probably killed me as well or tortured me until I recognized the error of my ways. But that doesn't change what I've done. The Fates have made it a point to remind me of my sins" I said, laughing sadly in self-derision. "Six of those juveniles—well, make that four now—sit on my council. Every day, I eat and drink with them, work with them, socialize with them. And all I see, are those bastards rutting over my Lissy while she begs me to save her."

"Those remaining of the Fifteen?" Ravena asked, turning around to face me.

Her hard stare bored into me. I hated being unable to read her emotions right now, aside from sensing her underlying anger. Where condemnation and contempt would have crushed me, anger I could deal with.

"Yes," I said, holding her gaze.

"You've been killing them, one by one."

"Yes."

She nodded slowly, then crossed her arms over her chest, eyes narrowing at me. I braced for whatever would come next.

"Is that why you asked me about moon juice this morning?" Ravena asked, her voice cold enough to freeze an erupting volcano. "As a warning you will have to kill any male offspring we might conceive?"

"NO!" I shouted, jumping to my feet, seething with anger. "No one will ever again harm my woman or child because of genetics." My hands fisted spasmodically with fury and the urge to break something. "Thirty-eight years ago, I failed to show the same courage that Krygor had when he allowed Anton to live. He faced contempt and challenges to his leadership of the clan for standing by his convictions. He and Lissy opened my eyes. I have devoted my life to abolishing those barbaric laws. But that only goes so far. No matter how severe the punishment, people will still break laws. It is mentalities that must change, and that takes time."

She studied my face as if hoping to find there the answer to some question. I withstood her examination stoically, not daring to let hope blossom that she might forgive my crime.

"Do you still love her?" Ravena asked, with a neutral tone.

"Yes," I said, matter-of-factly. "I will always love her. Some say it was nothing but puppy love, that the tragic events and my guilt have made me embellish what had only been a childhood fling. Others, like my father, claim she'd been using me, ensnaring the future ruler of Braxia with her wiles in the hopes I'd elevate her station from slave to concubine." I shrugged. "Either could be true, or both could be false. It doesn't matter to me. Growing up under my father was a never-ending nightmare. Lissy gave me the rare moments of happiness I ever experienced back then. For that alone, she will always hold a special place in my heart."

Ravena pulled her long braid before her again, fingers fiddling with it as she began pacing. Lost in thoughts.

"You never married. Why?" Ravena asked, observing me from the corner of her eyes as she slowly strolled back and forth.

"Marriage is optional on Braxia. Most males do not take a mate but will take any number of concubines over the years. There is no concept of legitimacy for offspring here," I said, walking around the table to reduce the distance between us. "Most unions only seek to form lasting alliances between houses and clans." I paused and took in a deep breath, getting to the heart of her underlying question. "After Lissy, no female made me want more than mere sexual release, or a good bloodline for my heirs. Until you."

Ravena stopped her pacing to look at me, a strange expression crossing her features.

"What of you?" I asked. "Why is such a beautiful, smart, and independent female unwed and childless?"

She shrugged. "Until recently, conceiving was impossible with any species other than Korletheans. Considering Guldan's enslaved them to breed with Veredians, they weren't really eager to hang out with me or any of my kind," she said, with sarcasm dripping with an undisguised contempt for the Korletheans. "But I didn't mate and avoided serious relationships because an Oracle had told me early on that I would meet my soulmate shortly after my brother's death and being reunited with my mother. So I waited."

My heart leapt. She'd claimed me as her soulmate during our ride to the forest. In light of my confession, did she regret the wait?

"Veredians are barely coming back from the brink of extinction," Ravena said, resuming her pacing. "Contraception is anathema to us. You and I have been pretty active. What if I'm already pregnant?"

I didn't try to hide from my face the pleasure such a prospect gave me. Yes, there would be challenges, but whatever the future held for us, I wanted a child with this woman… and more.

"Then I will happily fight for both of you, to keep you safe and ensure no one ever threatens you." I marched up to her, forcing her to stop her pacing. "But what of you, Ravena? If you are pregnant, would you want a child sired by me?"

She recoiled. "Of course," she said, as if I'd asked a ridiculously obvious question. "You're my soulmate."

My stomach knotted, and my heart leapt.

I swallowed hard, my eyes flicking between hers. "Even now? Even after what I've done?" I whispered.

Ravena's expression softened as her gaze roamed over my features. She closed the distance between us and pressed her palms to my chest. I shivered, my hands covering her much smaller ones, hope taking root again deep within.

"I cannot deny that your tale is deeply troubling," Ravena said in a soft voice. "But you were a boy under the tyrannical rule of a fanatic. We've all done terrible things in our past. Believe me, mine is far from pristine."

The haunted glimmer in her eyes made me wonder what dark secrets tormented her. She cupped my face in her hands, her thumbs caressing my cheeks. I closed my eyes and leaned into her touch, my heart melting with affection for my mate.

"What matters is what we do about it today," Ravena continued. "In the short few days I've known you, I've seen the relentless battle you're leading to bring about change and to prevent such horrors from ever happening again. I know what you've done for Anton to help ensure his safety and that of his family. They've never given me any details, but I can see that Anton is still haunted by things he has done to Grace in the past. The guilt and remorse he continues to feel was impossible to miss during one of our conversations at Risqué. Whatever happened, I am glad Grace forgave him because that man worships her."

"They are soulmates," I said, carefully drawing her into my arms. "He has sacrificed much and more to be with her, and to make her happy. Whatever the future holds, on my honor, I will fight for us."

"That is all I can ask," Ravena said.

Rising on to the tip of her toes, she pulled my face towards her to give me a short, but tender kiss before resting her head on my chest. My arm closed around her slender waist, my free hand slipping through the silky length of her long hair to hold her nape.

Joy, fear, gratitude, and uncertainty all battled for dominance within me. She hadn't rejected me for the horror I'd committed; her whose people cherished every new life as they fought for the survival of their species. It further cemented the improbable emotions she'd awakened in me. I barely knew Ravena, but every fiber of my being screamed to me that she belonged by my side, that no other would ever complete me like she could.

But so many wanted my downfall. It was selfish of me to keep her and, worse still, to consider having a child with her. I should help Ravena get whatever she came to Braxia for and then send her away. If she ever came to harm because of my enemies, it would destroy me. And yet, I couldn't let her go. The Ancestors forgive me, but I needed her.

My arms tightened around my mate as I begged the ancient spirits to help me protect her.

CHAPTER 10

MERCY

In the two days that followed the savage hunt, word of my combat skills, and what I had done to turn the tide in favor of the Braxians, spread like wildfire. The way people stole weird glances at me, you'd think I'd grown a second head. I was growing restless and increasingly fed up with acting reasonable.

I'd fought for so long to be freed of the overprotective cage in which my father had held me captive to hide me from those who would hunt me, only to shove myself right into another one. Not only did the damn prosthetics still hide my Veredian markings, but I'd also remained cooped up in Ravik's fortress since the hunt. He wanted to make sure all Guldans had departed the planet before he 'allowed' me to spend time at my brother's house.

Allowed… Seriously?

I'd had it and intended to confront him about it. When I'd awakened this morning, Ravik had already left. He always rose early for some secret meetings with his close council or to go spar. As per usual, he would come back and have breakfast with me on the patio before the actual start of his 'normal' day.

Ravik walked in to find me dressed, my computer and tech kit

149

ready to go. His smile faded, his eyes narrowing into a speculative stare. "Going somewhere?" he asked.

I lifted my chin. "You know where I'm going, Ravik. The question is: will your men accompany me, or should I call Krygor?"

He grimaced in exasperation and unshouldered his sparring staff before marching to his armory on the opposite side of the bedroom. He tapped on the discreet symbol on the wall which parted to reveal a walk-in sized room containing a variety of staff weapons on a stand, wall-mounted racks of blasters, and display shelves laden with bladed weapons from daggers to broadswords. Ravik put away his staff and started removing his sweaty shirt as he exited the room, en route to the bath.

"I asked you a question," I snapped, angered to be ignored.

"One to which you already know the answer," he snarled, balling his shirt before tossing it on the chair by the bath. "You are not going to your brother's house today."

My blood heated with the first flames of my mounting rage. "So I'm your prisoner now?"

Ravik exhaled loudly while giving me an exasperated look. "Don't speak nonsense."

"Nonsense?" I spat, advancing two menacing steps towards him. "I'm trapped in your fucking fortress, miles away from my brother's house. You've blocked my access to my ship and hoverbike. You've gone so far as to forbid anyone from providing me any means of transportation. I can't even try to leave the compound without your guards herding me back in like a fucking sheep. What do *you* call that if not imprisonment?"

"It's called protection," he snapped.

"I didn't ask for your fucking protection!" I yelled. "Anton had already made arrangements for me with his father and his clan. *You* imposed yourself. If I'd known your offer meant putting a fucking leash on me, I'd have told you where to shove it."

"I'm the fucking Magnar, Ravena!" Ravik shouted, slapping his chest with both hands. "You are my woman. I'm already standing on shaky ground. If anything happens to you, instead of helping me rescue you, my detractors will come at me with everything they've got to seize power. If anyone is a prisoner here it's me, chained to my duty as ruler of Braxia." He sighed heavily, his gaze taking on a pleading edge. "I need you to stand with me, Ravena, not add to my burden."

I looked at him, disbelieving. "That's so unfair. So, it's not enough that I continue to lie by pretending to be something I'm not with those damn prosthetics to spare you having to deal with potential vultures that might come after me. Now, I'm supposed to remained locked up in here for the rest of my days like a fucking bedroom slave?"

Ravik closed his eyes and ran his fingers through his hair, gripping it in the back. He heaved a sigh, his broad, muscular shoulders drooping. When he reopened his eyes and looked at me, the helplessness I read within clawed at my heart. My anger slightly abated, as a sliver of guilt slipped in.

"Yes, Ravena. It *is* unfair to you. The mess on Braxia is not your burden to bear. Whatever you may think, I swear that I'm not trying to control, let alone enslave you. I respect you too much. But, right now, I need you to help me shoulder the weight just for a little while longer."

Arms crossed over my chest, I pinched my lips and looked away, moved more than I wanted to admit by the raw emotion on his face.

"Two days, Ravena," Ravik said, in a soft tone. My eyes snapped back to his. "Give me two more days for my men to finish sweeping the land. And then, on my honor, I promise to give you as big of an escort as you wish to go to your brother's house."

On his honor… The magic words.

Two more fucking days staring at the walls or being stared at for not fitting the Braxians' perception of females. I didn't relish the prospect, but I also couldn't ignore—nor was I indifferent to—his plight. Ravik was making a huge concession. He clearly wanted to prolong his 'protection' by more days than the two he'd requested.

Defeated, I gave him a baleful glare. "Fine. Now what am I supposed to be doing for the next two days?" I grumbled.

Ravik's expression softened, and a smile stretched his lips. "Actually, before you jumped on me when I arrived—"

He chuckled at my warning look.

"—I'd planned on asking if you wanted to come see the racers. We could even take them out for a ride. They're smaller than the battle karvelis, so you'd have no problem riding one of your own."

My jaw dropped, my eyes all but popping out of my head, all anger forgotten. "As in today?" I asked.

"More like as in right now," Ravik said, a playful spark in his dark eyes replacing his earlier upset one. "Well, after I'm done changing," he added, looking down at himself.

"Why aren't you done changing then?" I asked.

Ravik chuckled. "On it, Mistress."

I couldn't help the smile that blossomed on my lips.

Damn the man.

He shouldn't have such an easy time of bringing me down from my temper flares. That was way too much power over me. I feasted my eyes on the sea of rippling muscles in his back and the sexiest, round but firm globes of his ass as he stripped out of his pants and underwear. He opened the door to the bath to take a quick dip after his training. As he stepped through the doorway, he paused and looked at me over his shoulder. The softness, the tenderness of his expression—incredibly odd on his brutish face—made my stomach flip-flop.

"Thank you," he said with a gentle smile.

My stomach did another somersault, and my throat tightened at the heartfelt gratitude in his voice and in his eyes. Ravik turned around without another word and entered the water.

Damn that twice wretched man.

While inside the compound's walls, the racers' stables sat right next to a large set of reinforced doors, granting a side access to the fortress. It opened onto a wide, open field where a group of adult racers ran freely, loosely herded by four mounted Braxians. On each side of the doors, younger racers were being trained inside large corrals, their good actions rewarded with pieces of raw meat.

I approached the fence of one of the corrals, staring at the wondrous creatures in awe. Ravik had been right. Although completely scaled like the battle version of the karvelis, the racers' proportions resembled the Xelixian cavas. However, they were leaner, their lines more aerodynamic.

The perfect size for me to ride.

Well, not these foals, but definitely the adults.

"Ravik, they are magnificent," I whispered.

His arm wrapped around me, his hand resting on the side of my bum. "Thank you, little bird," he said before pressing a gentle kiss on my temple.

Leading me towards the open field, he raised a hand and waved at the men herding the beasts. One of them broke off, followed by a couple of the racers; a midnight-colored one and a dark, royal-purple one.

"Magnar," the man said, stopping his racer a couple of meters in front of him. He hopped off his mount and struck his chest with his fist in a sign of respect. The man cast a curious glance towards me and, almost imperceptibly, nodded his head, apparently uncertain how to address me, if at all.

"Cormak," Ravik said, nodding back at the man in greeting.

He raised a palm towards the black racer. The creature approached him, pressing the flat part of his snout against Ravik's hand.

"This is Sheeroh, the only racer that will tolerate me," Ravik said with a chuckle.

As if in response to that comment, Sheeroh whipped his scorpion tail over his head and tapped the rounded edge of the stinger against Ravik's forehead. My stomach dropped at the speed with which the deadly weapon had come at my mate. Yet, the touch had been gentle, controlled. I gaped at the creature, my heart skipping a beat.

"Isn't that stinger all kinds of lethally poisonous?" I asked, trying to downplay how much that had scared me.

"No more than the venom they can inflict with a bite," Ravik said, nonchalantly.

I blinked at him, my mind taking a second to process what he'd just said. "You mean, when we had put our hand in the battle karveli's mouth a few days ago…?"

He nodded, a broad grin on his face, and his obsidian eyes sparkling with mischief. "The trust isn't that the karveli won't chomp your arm off, but that he won't inject you with one of the most virulent poisons on Braxia."

I felt faint for how recklessly I'd shoved my hand in front of Voltar's face that day.

"Do not fret," Ravik said teasingly. "Sheeroh would never harm me. Her big brother would have her hide if she did."

"Her?" I asked, surprised. "She's a female?"

Ravik nodded. "They all are," he said, waving at the team of racers. "The females of the karvelis are called karvalas. The racers are only a subgroup of them, bred specifically for that purpose, or born showing great promise. This beauty," he said, raising his palm to the second racer that Cormak had brought, "is called Dajia. She's Voltar's mate."

My jaw dropped—again—as I watched the graceful female approach Ravik and press her snout to his palm. Her gaze, however, never strayed from me, assessing me with the same intense scrutiny Voltar had. I, too, examined her with new eyes. There was something regal about her that said 'don't fuck with me' and yet that also felt utterly enticing.

"Dajia, this is my female, Ravena Mercy Vrok."

For the second time, it struck me that Ravik had introduced me to the creatures using my full name. I wondered if there were any significance to that. But before I could ask, Dajia shoved her face in mine, sniffing at it as if to catch the scent of my breath. Her snout lowered to my neck then my breast, and then my stomach, each time pausing to inhale audibly. As expected, she concluded her exploration with a good sniff at my crotch, although it thankfully lasted a lot shorter than with her mate.

She backed up two steps. With a hiss, Dajia bared her needle-sharp teeth at me, her split, black, lizard tongue shooting out between them. Although fright-inducing, I perceived no menace in her stance. Shifting her head sideways, she slowly stretched her long, gracile neck, the sun reflecting on its lustrous scales. Tail whipping from side to side in an almost choreographed dance, the racer turned to expose her flank, lean, elegant, and strong. Even her long legs had something sexy to them, despite their vicious claws raking the ground like one would swat a bug.

How did I not immediately realize they were females?

It then struck me that Dajia was showing off. Had she been a single male, I would have called it courtship.

Maybe it is...

Was she seeking my approval just like I was hoping for hers so that I could ride on her back?

"You are truly magnificent, Dajia. I can see why Voltar would choose one as beautiful as you for his mate."

Dajia snorted and threw her head back in a sharp nod, her reptilian eye giving me a sideways glance. Lightning fast, her scorpion tail struck each of my horns with a dry 'tock-tock' sound. My startled yelp died in my throat, sounding like a single hiccup.

Eyes wide, I turned to Ravik, busy chuckling at my stunned expression.

"I guess that means she approves?" I asked.

"The first hit meant that she agreed with your compliment. The second meant that she thinks the same of you."

For some strange reason, that touched me. Looking back at the karvala, I gave her another appraising once over.

"Sassy female. I like you," I said, then blinked as Dajia double-knocked my horns again with her tail. Ravik and Cormak burst out laughing. I glared at them and then at the racer. "But I don't like this part so much."

Dajia snorted, her front clawed-hoof raking the ground.

"Is she laughing at me?" I asked, disbelieving.

"Yes," Ravik and Cormak replied in unison.

"Brat," I muttered under my breath, annoyed yet totally smitten by the karvala. A thought suddenly crossed my mind. "Wait a minute, if she's Voltar's mate, why is her stable at the other end of the city? Well, of the compound?"

Ravik smiled, his big, callused hand gently caressing my left horn. "Because the karvalas have no time and no use for males when outside of their mating heat."

My eyes bulged. "Seriously?"

Ravik nodded. "The females consider the males too needy. They represent too much work to keep around."

I raised an inquisitive eyebrow.

"The females are faster, which makes them better hunters. They usually catch smaller kills than the males can, but in larger quantity. Since they have a pack mentality, they feed everyone, not just themselves or their offspring. Problem is that the males tend to eat the largest portion while contributing the least, and then relentlessly pursue the females for sex. But they run too fast."

I snorted. "Sounds familiar."

Ravik playfully glared at me, which made me grin.

"Every time we've tried to keep males and females together, the karvalas eventually end up chasing the males from the pack, only allowing them back during their mating heat."

"Smart ladies," I said with a smirk.

Dajia and Sheeroh both snorted in agreement. I really liked these creatures. I made a mental note to speak to my sister about them. She loved riding the cavas but wouldn't be able to bring them to Haven, the new Veredian settlement our people were building. Unlike Xelix Prime that had no winter thanks to its two suns, Haven did. Such cold climates would kill the cavas. But Braxia had a similar climate to the new Veredian home world which the Tuureans had completed terraforming a few years ago. This would be one perfect trade opportunity between our peoples.

The introductions completed, Ravik offered to help me up onto the back of Dajia, but I insisted on doing it on my own. While staying with my mother and sisters on Xelix Prime, I'd ridden quite a few cavas without needing assistance. The racers were smaller still than those mounts; the perfect size for me. Although Voltar's horns and spurs had been bigger, Dajia's were more accessible—at least for me—and ideally positioned along the back of her neck to give me a good grip in a comfortable forward-leaning position during a race.

We started riding at a slow walk to give me time to adjust to my mount. Cormak returned to his duties with the running racers, but two bodyguards followed us from a respectable distance. They made their best effort to stay out of our line of sight and give us a semblance of privacy.

I sighed inwardly. When I first felt the Tuning in Anton's penthouse and realized that my soulmate was the Braxian ruler, my only real concern had been the misogynistic, overbearingly dominant, and controlling nature of his people. But the past few days, this morning's confrontation, and now this 'romantic' ride drove home the sad reality; a union with Ravik meant a union with Braxia. Whatever feelings he may develop for me over time, I already knew that Ravik would sacrifice his personal happiness to his duty.

To be by his side, I would need to give up on a great deal of the privacy that I cherished so much. My own wishes and personal aspirations would always have to take a backseat to the needs of his people.

'Our' people if I end up marrying him.

Ravik's words still echoed loud and clear in my mind.

"I need you to stand with me, Ravena, not add to my burden."

I stole a glance at him as he rode Sheeroh, possessive pride blooming in my heart. Ravik would never qualify as a handsome man, by any standard. And yet, he was the sexiest thing I had ever laid eyes on. I loved everything about him; from his fearsome face to his ridiculous strength that made me feel both vulnerable and utterly protected, those massive muscles on that giant body of his, and that humongous cock that always made me feel on the verge of being split in two, all the while making me sing with bliss.

But it wasn't just his body that had me falling hard and fast for the man. Despite his barbaric appearance and the savage ways of his people, Ravik was kingly. He rode his mount, back straight, chin up, with an ease of movement that exuded confidence, pride, and strength. His keen intelligence, the way he managed to accurately analyze a situation and promptly take action was the biggest turn on. Not to mention his unconditional devotion to the welfare of his people. However, it was his progressive mindset, and his respect for women—for me—that really got me. I somewhat hated that the events surrounding Lissy had put him on this path of change. Yet, I was grateful because I never could have been with the man he would have become under his father's rule.

Ravik had abolished slavery on his planet despite the violent outcry, freed his own slaves, paid them wages, and even went so far as to hire pleasure workers as permanent staff to not overly disrupt the *still* barbaric customs of his people. On Braxia, a slave was free-for-all. If a male wanted a female, he could simply bend her over the closest surface and have his way with her, even in public. While his men had behaved during the meal on the first night of our arrival, the following evening meals hadn't been so controlled.

There had been another erotic dance during the meal. As soon as it had ended, Hagan, one of the members of his council whom I fiercely disliked, had caught one of the dancers and ordered her to her knees to suck him off. I nearly lost my shit. Thank the Goddess for Ravik's prompt interference, explaining that the dancers were among thirty females of various species, including Braxian hybrids, to whom he guaranteed safe working conditions, free food and lodging, and decent wages to pleasure any man in his house that wanted them. It kept all other servants in his hall from being unduly pressured by unrequited advances.

A number of clans pushed back against so many rule changes, many because they couldn't afford it. With their sluggish economy, having to pay wages to slaves that only used to cost them minimal food and lodging was choking the already beleaguered Braxians. They needed to reinvent their economy, find new markets, educate their people, forge new alliances, and upgrade their technology; a colossal challenge, but one I could help with.

The question was whether I wanted to help shoulder such a burden, whether this was the future I wanted for myself. If I wished to be with my soulmate, I had to become his Dagna, his queen, with all the responsibilities that entailed.

Having no doubt sensed my gaze on him, Ravik turned his face towards me, looking more relaxed than I'd seen him in days, almost carefree.

"Ready to pick up the pace, little bird?" he asked.

"You better believe it, big boy."

He snorted and shook his head. "Remind me to spank that sexy bottom of yours when we return home."

His dark eyes smoldered, his expression filled with naughty promises. My stomach flip-flopped, and my pussy throbbed at the thought of that big hand smacking my behind the way he had on our first night here. I'd never admit it out loud, but I loved a good spanking.

Ravik's broad nose twitched, and a smug smile stretched his lips. The bastard knew he had me hot and bothered.

"Stop thinking of my cock, female, and follow. Do not try to pass me."

Before I could come up with a smart, sassy retort, he leaned over and set Sheeroh into a run, giving me a delectable view of his muscular butt.

Damn the man...

Leaning forward on Dajia, who snorted with impatience, I took hold of her horns. The karvala immediately gave chase. Wind whipped past us, my long braid flying behind me as my mount raced to catch up to our companions. I gave myself over to the pleasure of speed and the exhilarating sense of freedom and danger it always gave me. Dajia slowed to adjust her pace to Sheeroh's so they would run side by side. Looking towards him, my eyes connected with Ravik.

My mate...

In that instant, I knew I'd do everything in my power to always keep him this happy. I'd be his safe harbor in the storm that sought to engulf him.

Come what may, I would stand by him.

The next morning, Ravik left to visit various other clans all dealing with their own issues. Seeing how each of the main clans' compounds constituted a small city in its own right, this trip would be considered a series of state visits on other worlds. Some Elder Clans actually sheltered a number of smaller clans, so it was not a single bloodline dwelling under the same roof. Over multiple generations, the gap narrowed which often resulted in some of the smaller clans moving to a new Elder Clan's compound.

I wanted to ask Ravik to take me with him but resisted the urge. If I were to help him, getting firsthand account of his people's plight would take me a long way to understanding where I could be of assistance. However, it felt too bold this early into our relationship. In the short few days since my arrival, the Braxians had realized that something special was building between their ruler and me; something they eyed with caution and suspicion. I wasn't his Dagna—yet—and maybe I never would be, so I had to tread carefully not to overstep.

However, I didn't need to go to the other clans to get a first sense of what we had to work with. While I couldn't yet leave the walls of Ravik's compound, it would take me days to visit every nook and cranny if that's all I did from dusk 'til dawn. Wanting to remain inconspicuous considering the heavy scrutiny the Braxians subjected me to, I used a camera hidden in the gem of my necklace to record everything I encountered for screening later at my own leisure.

Males ran most of the establishments I visited, with females serving customers; as in the woman played fetch while the male owner ordered her around. When one of the owners asked a female, busy restocking shelves at the other end of the shop, to come bring him a tool less than three feet from where he currently stood, I had to bite my tongue not to tell him to just fucking get it himself. For all that, the female—and all the others I had encountered—didn't look miserable or abused. To them, this was normal.

A troubling thought crossed my mind as I passed from one establishment to the next. While I strongly believed these women needed to be given their rightful place in their society and be treated as equals, did I have the right to disrupt their way of life? To try to impose mine onto them? Granted, their ruler was already working towards that goal, but who was I to make waves? For one so used to speaking my mind, this would prove yet another challenge to add to my already long list of them.

To my relief, Braxia, or at least ruling Clan Xeldar's compound, rivaled most developed intergalactic cities I'd visited over the years. Granted, some of the technology in use or on display was a little dated, but nothing that couldn't be easily fixed with the right guidance and the right contacts provided, of course, by yours truly. What bothered me were all the other things that I didn't see. Walking through the streets of the Xeldar compound felt like one long trip through a giant quartermaster's storehouse. Everything was functional and provided for some kind of basic or essential need. The only place that offered any kind of fluff were food-related, be it restaurants, grocery stores, and especially bakeries.

But what of tourist-attraction types of businesses? Jewelry stores? Beauty parlors? Even the clothing stores offered a very limited inventory, with nothing extravagant or non-conformist. Where were the women's clothing and shoe stores? I'd only seen concubine outfits and discipline specific servant outfits. Yet, I distinctly remembered the wives and concubines at the side tables wearing some beautiful dresses and jewelry. Where did those come from?

When Ravik returned from his touring tonight, we would go to Councilor Fenton's home where we'd been invited for dinner. I liked the man. Although a little gruff, there was a great kindness in him and an unshakable loyalty towards Ravik. For that alone, I would have liked him. Until then, I hooked up my computer and started analyzing the footage I'd taken.

CHAPTER 11
RAVIK

I settled down in the shuttle as my two most trusted bodyguards took me to my next destination, Tagar at the helm and Nowik on the com. It had been a long, exhausting day. I just wanted to go home to my woman and lose myself in the softness of her embrace, not head to one of the Fifteen's compound. What a stupid idea to leave him for last in today's tour. I'd reasoned that seeing him first would have put me in a foul mood for the rest of the day. But after all the depressing visits I'd had thus far, every one of the clans struggling, and me helpless to provide any solution, I didn't trust myself not to lose it on Boros Grumar.

Clan Grumar's compound loomed ahead, sprawling at the foot of Mount Jyriak, its dark buildings cleverly erected and laid out in a way to give the illusion they blended in to the rocky face of the mountain. Once part of the elite, Clan Grumar had been renowned for the masterful craftsmanship of their blacksmiths, forging the best swords and weapons in the realm. But technology soon made their skills obsolete as it allowed anyone to achieve results of similar quality, faster. The only other sources of income for the clan stemmed from their stone quarries and duralium mining. But like Clan Caldes, Clan Grumar quickly found itself losing most of its clientele as better, stronger, more stable materials became available on the intergalactic markets. The limited local demand for stone and duralium no longer sufficed for the far too many clans that relied on the mining and selling of those products for their livelihood.

As we began our descent, Boros, his three sons, and elder council clansmen approached the landing pad to welcome me. I begrudgingly recognized he was showing me more courtesy than many of the clans, especially those whose situations had grown as dire as his. Stepping down the ramp after we landed, I let my gaze roam over the Clan Leader. Two years younger than I, Boros had aged well. As was often the case with non-warrior bloodlines, he stood noticeably smaller than I in both height and constitution. Still, by galactic standards, he'd be considered a very muscular giant. His shoulder-length dark-brown hair framed a proud, Braxian face where light-brown eyes peered at me, devoid of the fear mixed with hatred I usually received from the other Fifteen.

"Magnar Ravik," Boros said, hitting his chest with his fist. "Welcome to the Grumar compound. Health, strength, and prosperity to your clan. My home is yours."

His sons and council clansmen repeated the salutary gesture, although they remained silent.

"Thank you for your welcome, Clan Leader Boros," I said with a nod.

The heavy metal doors of Clan Grumar's Hall never ceased to impress me. The smithy work on them was exquisite with the clan's sigil carved on its face with laser precision, and filled with the opalescent nyrian stones abundantly found in this region. The doors parted to let us in. Within the large hall, with its maroon floors and light grey walls, a large stone sculpture of an anvil and hammer occupied the center of the room. Standing by the door, his clansmen on the left fisted their chest, heads bowed, the females and servants on the right getting on their knees, aside from his wife who remained standing, head and eyes down.

I gestured for all to rise, reflecting once again on how tired I had grown of these rituals, vestiges of an era long past. The last time I'd broached the subject of doing away with them, my close council had sternly warned me against it. However irritating it felt to me, it reminded people of my position and status. In these troubled times where some murmured about challenging my rule, removing symbols of my power could play against me.

Boros led me to his private chamber where he and his council clansmen spent the next forty minutes listing their woes and the hopeless situation their people drowned in.

"I cannot invent yet another civil project of no real use to the realm just to keep your men working," I said at last in exasperation.

"Nor are we asking you to," Boros countered, visibly stung. "The reality is that, come winter, my clan will starve. I do not challenge the new anti-slavery laws. However much it harms us right now, we agree that Braxia needs to change before we are further left behind. But I can no longer afford to pay their wages or even send them home. By month's end, I will release the majority of my servants, which includes all my former slaves, to seek their fortune elsewhere."

I barely repressed a flinch. For a clan to have no servants was the ultimate sign of degradation. Whatever my personal issues with Boros, I didn't want to see such an ancient house brought so low, not to mention how it would give my detractors more ammunition against me.

I heaved a sigh. "I will speak to my council about granting you another emergency fund—"

"No," Boros interrupted, before nervously rubbing his broad, flat nose. "It will be no more than using a glass of water to extinguish a forest fire."

True. But that's all there is.

"We have exhausted every avenue," Boros said in a tired tone. "Despite his efforts, Anton couldn't find buyers for the resources we produce. However, he found many primitive colonies that would love benefitting from our blacksmithing skills, since they are of no use here. But that means displacing and scattering my people. I will only resort to it as a last option."

I nodded, feeling for his pain in spite of everything. "So what would you have me do?" I asked.

He exchanged uncertain glances with his clansmen before turning his wary eyes back to me. I narrowed mine in suspicion.

"It has come to our attention…" Boros cleared his throat. "Well, the word is that your female is closely acquainted with the Tuurean leader."

My back stiffened, feeling instantly irritated as I did every time I heard mention of said relationship. Although Ravena had assured me there was nothing romantic between them, her vagueness as to the actual nature of their rapport set my teeth on edge.

"The Admiral is not their ruler. He only leads their military," I said, my voice colder than I wished it. It was petty of me, but pointing out that I outranked him—even if his power far exceeded mine—made me feel slightly better. "What of it?"

"The Tuureans are building a new home world for the Veredians on their planet, Tuur. They will need tons of basic resources and building materials," Boros said, shifting in his seat. His clansmen nodded, murmuring their approval. "If your female put in a good word, maybe they would consider procuring some from us."

I leaned back against my chair, my gaze roaming over the men assembled around the table. They stared back at me, faces strained by stress and worry, eyes full of hope.

"You would deign to let a female intercede on your behalf?" I asked, genuinely surprised.

"This is a matter of survival, Magnar," Boros said, his tone hardening. "Those who bark and yowl the loudest in your Hall are the wealthy who've grown fat, entitled, and lazy thanks to their fertile agricultural lands. Having to pay staff rather than enjoying free slave labor puts a dent in their already sizeable profits, and they don't like it. As for me, I don't care who mediates in our favor as long as it can result in us finding work so that my people will have food in their bellies come winter."

I nodded slowly. Anton had hinted something along the same lines, but I'd been reluctant to mix personal matters with business. I didn't want Ravena thinking my interest in her was due to her contacts and wealth. But my people were suffering, and I had a duty to uphold.

"I cannot promise you a positive outcome, but I will ask. Keep in mind that your materials are common," I said, cautiously.

"We are aware," Boros conceded, "and we are ready to undersell anyone… within reason."

"Very well," I said.

The conversation continued for a short while longer before I could finally take my leave.

"Magnar, if I may," Boros said as we rose to exit the chamber. "I would like a private word with you."

I narrowed my eyes at him, but nodded my assent. Boros' sons cast wary glances at him. He gestured with his head for them to go on, all would be fine. And it would be. The boys were foolish to fear I'd attack their father in his own home. As per Braxian law, you couldn't disrespect or harm a host after he had welcomed you within his house, extended the basic hospitalities to you, and you had accepted them. Magnar or not, such shameful action would result in banishment and even execution based on the gravity of the offense.

Once the door closed behind his youngest son, I raised an inquisitive brow at him.

"I will go straight to the point," Boros said, his voice firm but non-threatening. "As all the others, I'm aware you're eliminating the Fifteen, one by one."

My jaw clenched, and my eyes hardened. I couldn't believe he'd bring this up so bluntly. What did he have in mind?

"I do not dispute your right to seek vengeance. The day you issue your challenge, I will accept it, and fight." He lifted his chin proudly, holding my gaze without flinching. "Your quarrel is with me. When I fall—and we both know I will—I only request that you do not extend your wrath to my sons and my clan."

"Why the fuck should I care about your request?" I snarled.

"Because they are innocent!" Boros snapped. "They've done nothing to you."

"Lissy had done nothing to you. That didn't stop you!" I yelled.

My hands fisted, and I took two menacing steps towards him, forcing myself to go no further.

His light-brown eyes darkened as he leveled me with a hard glare. "*Your son* had done nothing to you. Did that stop you?"

Shock, disbelief, and a stabbing pain coursed through me at the cruel, but all too true, words. Blinded by rage, I rushed him. Grabbing him by the throat, I slammed him against the wall. Boros hissed but didn't resist or attempt to fight back. Arms hanging by his side, he held my furious gaze, unwavering. Did he have a death wish?

Is he trying to entrap me?

"Nice try, Grumar," I snarled in his face. "You will not have me executed for breaking hosting laws."

He recoiled. The genuine shock and outrage on his face threw me.

"I can have witnesses come in to confirm that I renounce my host privileges," Boros said in a voice hard enough to cut stone.

I released his neck with a brutal shove and took a few steps away from him. He straightened, stretched his neck, and rubbed the skin where a print of my hand had already started to appear.

"You think you're the only one who's been haunted ever since that wretched day?" Boros asked, his eyes filling with shame and sorrow. "Do you think I take pride in being counted among the Fifteen? Did it ever cross your mind that just like *you*, some of *us* also didn't want any part of what happened that day? That we'd been forced into acting against our will by order of our sires? I didn't want to go to your house to begin with. My father threatened to banish me. And when I tried to cut short, *your father* ordered me to go on longer because it wasn't enough. You were there!" he shouted, pointing an angry finger at me. "You saw it with your own eyes."

I blinked, my mind reluctantly going back to that day. The boys laughing, jeering, shouting encouragements at the one fucking my Lissy, some of them stroking their cocks in anticipation. And then Boros and Niklas, faces drawn, jaws clenched, and hands fisted.

Neither had wanted to be there.

Yes, I'd been there. And now that he'd brought it back to my attention, I distinctly remembered hearing my father asking Boros if he were a cock lover that he'd be done after three pumps; to get back in there and fuck her like a man. I'd been too lost in my own grief to acknowledge his.

But he'd still fucked her. Shouldn't Lissy be avenged of that?

And you let all of them fuck her, then killed your own son. Who will avenge them of you?

Head spinning, stomach churning, I turned away from him, staring at the trophies on his walls without seeing them. The silence stretched between us until Boros broke it with a soft voice.

"What we've done cannot be undone," he said. "We can only try to prevent it from ever happening again by changing the laws, as you have, and by raising our sons to be better than we were. I will not fight your right to vengeance, but please, do not bring more innocents into this."

My back still turned to him, I gave him a sharp nod and marched towards the closed door. I opened it to find his clan assembled outside, their expressions tense and fearful. Their gazes shifted over my shoulder, seeking their leader behind. When Boros walked out unscathed, a few of them sighed audibly while all faces lightened with relief.

As I neared my bodyguards standing by the front door, Boros' sons approached me with a medium-sized hovercart carrying a small crate.

"These are samples of our materials for your female," Boros said, "to give her a clear idea of what we have to offer."

"Very well," I said, my voice still filled with tension. "I will make sure to give them to her."

A soft—but not particularly natural—cough drew our attention. Boros' wife, Sorna, stared intently at her husband, her arm passed around the shoulders of their oldest daughter, Vela. The younger woman held a pretty, rectangular, flat box.

"Ah yes," Boros said, distracted. "My mate has prepared a present for your female, to thank her for assisting in the hunt and, in many ways, saving most of our men. We would be honored if you would accept it."

I stared at it, speechless for a moment. Females were not normally acknowledged in such a fashion, and least of all for battle prowess. The thought it might be a trap to hurt Ravena, and me through her, flashed through my mind, but I immediately dismissed the idea. The punishment for such a cowardly act would be too dire; his entire clan would be passed through the sword.

"You may approach," I said, softening my voice.

Sorna gave Boros another worried glance before leading her daughter towards me, their steps a little ungainly from nerves. They stopped before me, Sorna standing behind her daughter with both hands on her shoulders.

"My daughter is very talented with nyrian stones and made this for your female," Sorna said, nudging her daughter.

Vela stared at me, wide-eyed, her slender body shaking slightly. She looked unable to decide if she were awed or terrified to be in my presence. When she failed to react, a more forceful nudge from her mother snapped her out of her dazed trance. She lifted the lid of the box with a shaky hand to reveal a jewelry set; necklace, earrings, and bracelet. I didn't know much about jewelry but could immediately recognize the work as exquisite.

"Beautiful work," I said, genuinely impressed. "It is lovely. I'm sure Ravena will like it."

Vela's face heated with pleasure. She cast an uncertain look over her shoulder at her mother who smiled proudly and squeezed her shoulder, and then at her sire who nodded his approval. After I took the box from her hands, Vela and her mother bowed their heads before moving back to their place among the other females and servants.

With a final goodbye, I headed back to my shuttle, chest aching, head spinning, and wanting nothing more than the comfort of my little bird's presence.

～

Sitting at the breakfast table in my room, Ravena on my lap, I nuzzled her nape, while she scanned the stone and metal samples Boros had sent. She squirmed, mumbling for me to behave as my roaming hands cupped her breasts. I wanted her, again, despite having taken her twice since my return. Braxian males lived in an almost constant state of arousal. We could literally get hard on demand, even without being excited at all—which was a rare occurrence. However, getting soft without proper release actually proved far more complicated.

I'd never been so hungry for a female before. Yet, this hunger had grown stronger. Ravena's scent had started changing last night. Subtle at first, it had been growing steadily ever since. I initially wondered if she'd already conceived, but even if it were the case, the change of scent due to pregnancy didn't become noticeable before the first month, but usually closer to the second month. The aroma didn't match either. Ravena smelled like concentrated lust in its purest form. It took me a while to realize she was entering the early stages of her mating fever, which Veredians called *season*. I'd heard plenty of wild stories about how sexually voracious and aggressive they became then. I couldn't wait to see—and experience—it all.

Ravena sighed as she put down her scanner. I didn't need to ask why. I hadn't held much hope, but it still saddened me to have my suspicions confirmed.

"Useless, right?" I asked, my hand lifting the hem of her concubine dress to caress her inner thigh.

When I'd asked her to wear it, I'd expected her to tell me to fuck off. But she'd been willing to play along—as long as it remained within the privacy of our chamber. The diaphanous, sleeveless, white dress fell mid-thigh, transparent enough to show her curves but not details like her nipples.

"Hmmm, not useless, no," she said, spreading her legs ever so slightly. "But this stuff is available pretty much everywhere. Although, these stones have greater density and are sturdier. No wonder your buildings last forever."

"But that's not appealing enough to justify buying them over others?" I asked, my fingers venturing higher towards the apex of her legs.

"Technically, yes; it would be worth it if they were closer," Ravena said, turning slightly to the side. "But it's a long trip to the Western Quadrant. The transport costs alone will likely eat most of the profits they could possibly make. Assuming the Tuureans agree—which remains a big if—Clan Grumar will, at best, break even."

"That would still be a major improvement," I said, a sliver of hope taking root. "Break even means wages are paid, expenses are covered, and bellies are filled. As a temporary solution, it will keep them from starving until they find something else."

Ravena nodded. "True enough." Turning fully around, forcing my wandering fingers away from their target, she placed her legs on each side of me, and wrapped her arms around my neck. "Again, don't get your hopes up too high. It's still a long shot, but I'll do my best to convince the Admiral."

"That's all I can ask," I said before leaning down to kiss her.

My tongue demanded entry, which she promptly granted. Lifting the hem of her dress again, my palms rubbed over the naked globes of her bum. With the concubine dress, no underwear was allowed. One hand sliding up the silky skin of her back, the other slipped under and around her behind to tease her pussy. She gasped against my lips, trying to pull away from the kiss, but I didn't allow it. Holding her by the nape, my mouth plundered hers while my fingers explored her folds already getting wet for me.

I thanked the Ancestors that Ravena's sexual drive could keep up with mine, and that she was as wild and unleashed in her passion as I. She was truly made for me.

My woman moaned, her hardening nipples pressing against my chest. Proof of her arousal dripped over my fingers dipping in and out of her, the scent of her musk driving me insane with desire. Breaking the kiss, I lifted the dress off her, bending her backwards to suck on her taut nipples, my fingers still fucking her. I loved the sweet taste of her skin and her unique scent mixed with the spicy perfume she wore.

Ravena fisted my hair, pressing her breast to my face, then blindly fiddled with the clasp of my pant with her free hand.

"We're going to be late for dinner," she whispered between two moans.

"No, we won't," I grumbled against her chest, pulling my fingers from her slit to help her free my cock from its confines. "But I will have you scream my name once more before we leave."

I lifted her just enough to align the head of my cock with her opening before lowering her onto me. Her warmth engulfed me, the ridges of her inner walls greeting me with their now familiar squeezing and stroking.

"Ravena, you feel so fucking good," I hissed against her throat as I started pumping up into her. "I'm addicted to you."

"Mercy," she whispered, rocking her pelvis in counterpoint to my movements. "Call me Mercy when you fuck me."

What?

Pleasure made it hard for me to process her words.

"I can't call you Mercy during sex," I said, my words somewhat slurred as I picked up the pace. "It would sound like I'm begging you."

Her laughter choked into a strangled moan as my thumb caressed the Veredian markings on her nape. "I can make you," she panted.

"No, little bird, I don't beg for mercy, nor do I grant any," I said, slipping my arms behind her knees and holding her up as I rose to my feet. "Soon, you will be the one screaming my name."

Ravena hung onto my shoulders, her arms not quite long enough to wrap around my neck as I pounded into her. By the time she fell apart in my arms and her inner walls had clamped down on my cock, making me roar my release, I'd cried out Mercy three times.

CHAPTER 12
MERCY

Eyes lingering on my mountain of a mate, I closed the clasp of my stiletto sandals, a tender smile stretching my lips. I still throbbed with the most delicious soreness as I walked up to him and took from his hand the comb he'd been untangling his wavy, black hair with. I took his hand and led him to the edge of the bed where I made him sit. Ravik spread his legs for me to stand between them, his palms settling on the back of my thighs.

He closed his eyes and sighed with contentment as I ran the comb through the silky length of his hair. His hands slid up to my back. Leaning forward, he pressed his lips to my stomach then rested his head against me.

I chuckled and caressed the back of his head. "I can't comb your hair like that, silly man."

Ravik's arms tightened around me, and the mood in the room shifted.

"You bring me peace, Mercy," Ravik whispered, his voice thick with emotion that made me weak in the knees. "You are my safe haven in the constant torment that rages around me. I do not deserve you, but I thank the Ancestors who brought you to me."

My chest tightened at the rawness of the feelings seeping through me. Ravik saw himself as a monster. Sometimes, I wondered if his dedication to changing Braxia was driven more by the need to make amends than by deep conviction—not that it really mattered in the end.

Thoughts of my own dark past twisted my insides with shame. So many secrets and half-truths stood between us; *my* secrets, some of which weren't mine alone to reveal. When all of it came to the light of day, I feared the fallout.

Weaving my fingers through his hair, I pressed a kiss to the top of his head before resting my cheek on it.

"You more than deserve me, Ravik," I said softly. "Do not idealize me. I have plenty of shameful secrets of my own."

He snorted in disbelief. Pulling away from him, my eyes bore into his.

"Do you remember what I do for a living?" I asked, my eyes flicking between his.

"You're a tech consultant," Ravik said.

I smiled. "Not quite," I said, my fingers playing with the small hairs on his temple. "I own a series of advanced technology research and development facilities. My customers are mainly the military, intergalactic prisons, and first responders. I do not sell weapons, only safety, defense systems, and rescue apparatus."

"That sounds like commendable work," Ravik said, his thumbs caressing my sides.

"Yes, but it didn't start out that way."

Ravik watched me in silence, waiting for me to continue. My index finger traced his thick lips while I worked up the courage to confess part of my secrets.

"My father held tens of thousands of Veredian females imprisoned in his compounds. He forced my Veredian Sisters to breed with Korletheans in order to create more of us and unlock new psi powers that he could use or sell." Ravik nodded at my words, his gaze intense. I inhaled deeply then heaved a sigh. "Over the years, I created a lot of the technology that helped keep my Sisters and the Korletheans caged by dampening their powers with special gloves, bracelets, and necklaces."

Ravik stiffened but kept his expression neutral. I released him and walked away a few steps. Hugging my midsection, I turned to look through the giant window which offered a breathtaking view of the open field sprawling beyond the clan fortress' gates.

"Initially, I didn't know my father intended to use it on the Veredians. I was a curious child and loved taking on technological challenges." A shiver ran through me, and I absentmindedly rubbed my upper arms. "The day I found out, I lost my shit. My father and I had never had such a violent argument before. I refused to talk to him for over a month, feeling used and betrayed. Eventually, he brought Venya Solis to me, one of his Korlethean Oracle slaves."

I reached for my long braid and brought it over my shoulder, my fingers fiddling with it. It always gave me some kind of comfort. Funny thing was, Father said my niece Amalia—who he'd also considered his daughter—had a similar nervous tell, but with a lock of hair.

"I was wary of Oracles, especially enslaved ones. Why would they tell us the truth instead of deliberately sending us to our doom out of vengeance? But as much as she disliked us, Venya never lied. We had a mind-reading Veredian with us anyway to confirm the truth of her words."

I turned back to face Ravik, relieved that his gaze remained focused. Devoid of any disappointment or disgust, he stared at me full of curiosity.

"As always with Oracles, she gave me three possible outcomes to my no longer helping improve the technology used in my father's fortresses. In all cases, the Sisters and Korletheans would attempt to escape, one resulting with heavy casualties all around, one with failure and one with success. However, in all three cases, it would also result in the Veredian species becoming completely extinct within the next hundred years. But if I continued to help, every outcome resulted in the survival of our species. So I did."

Ravik looked at me with sympathy. Rising to his feet he closed the distance between us and took my hands in his.

"Then you did the right thing," Ravik said softly.

"Did I?" I asked, my eyes flicking between his. "I doubt my Sisters will feel the same the day they find out—and they will. My father enslaved and force bred them for nearly three generations, and then sold their daughters, partially with my help. Would you forgive that? Because of my last name, they took a major leap of faith welcoming me among them."

Ravik cupped my face in his hands, his thumbs caressing my cheeks. "They will be angry, and then they'll get over it once they realize you tried to save them… and did. You have already proven your loyalty.

I snorted. "Yeah, by betraying my baby brother and turning him over to be executed by the Xelixians."

"He was an evil man," Ravik argued.

"NO! He wasn't," I said, my throat tightening, and tears prickling my eyes. "He was a lost little boy, hurting and lashing out at the world because of his parents' abandonment. And Veredians—especially my mother—were to blame. His mother was Xelixian. She abandoned him when my father chose my mother over her. My father left Varrek on Guldar to be raised by nannies and tutors because he didn't want to upset my mother by flaunting his son from another woman before her. Varrek never fit in on Guldar with his grey skin and strange eyes inherited from his mother. But still, Guldar somewhat accepted him. That's why he dedicated his life to being the ultimate Guldan, and abusing Xelixians and Veredians."

"It was his choice, though," Ravik countered, gently. "His actions couldn't go unpunished."

"I know, but…" I heaved a sigh. "I got to know him on the journey back to Xelix Prime after I captured him. We'd never met before. He was the most brilliant mind I'd ever encountered. A true genius. Technology, science, medicine, nothing fazed him. Together, we could have accomplished amazing things. I actually considered freeing him before we landed. *He* told *me* to not even think about it. Things would be worse for all of us if I did."

"An Oracle had warned him?" Ravik rightly guessed.

I nodded. "I probably couldn't have gone through with it anyway.

Either way, I'd be betraying a sibling; my Veredian sister Aleina, or my Guldan brother Varrek. His final words to me were that he wished we'd met sooner. Things might have turned out quite differently. And I think so, too."

My throat tightened again with sorrow, remembering my brother's beautiful, exotic face. His final look towards me held no resentment or condemnation, only a calm acceptance and a sliver of regret.

Ravik kissed the tear forming at the corner of my eye, and I gave him a trembling smile. Inhaling deeply, I swallowed my growing sorrow, refusing to dwell on a past that couldn't be changed, and that I probably wouldn't even if I could.

"I didn't mean to turn into a weeping wreck," I said with self-derision. "There's actually a point to all this. Varrek did a lot of terrible things to Veredians and Xelixians, but in the end, they were key elements into finding the cure to Veredian infertility. What I did ensured the continuation of our species." I held on to his wrists, his hands still cupping my face. "And what you did set in motion the revolutionary changes you're bringing to Braxia. Terrible things must often be done before great things can happen. Forgive yourself, Ravik, like I'm trying to forgive myself, and focus on the battle ahead."

"My little bird," he whispered before pulling me into his arms.

His lips pressed between my horns, and I cuddled against him, feeling safe and cherished in the warmth of his strong body wrapped around me.

The door chime startled us. I couldn't tell whether seconds or minutes had passed.

"Open," Ravik said, releasing me.

The door swished sideways, revealing Tagar holding a pretty box.

"Ah yes," Ravik said, walking towards his loyal bodyguard. "Thank you."

I didn't miss his questioning look to Tagar, who responded to the unspoken question with a nod. Intrigued, I watched the door close behind the bodyguard as he left the room. Ravik approached me with a relaxed smile before handing over the box to me. Surprised, I raised an inquisitive eyebrow. My fingers caressed the delicate lattice work on the flat, rectangular, metal box.

"You got me a present?" I asked, disbelieving.

Ravik's stunned and then embarrassed look revealed that such an idea had never crossed his mind. Although feeling a slight disappointment, it didn't surprise me, nor had I expected such from a Braxian.

He cleared his throat. "Hmmm, no. It's a gift from Clan Leader Grumar's daughter, Vela." Ravik explained.

I slightly recoiled in surprise. "Clan Grumar? With the stones?" I asked.

He nodded.

"Why are you just giving it to me now?" I asked, confused. "And why was it in Tagar's possess..." My eyes widened in sudden understanding, a cold shiver running down my spine. "You feared foul play."

Ravik looked hesitant. "In truth, not really. Despite my differences with Boros, I didn't believe he would allow something so foolish from his house. But when it comes to your safety, I do not take chances."

I smiled and lifted my face towards him. Ravik leaned forward and gave me a gentle kiss. Looking back down at the box, I lifted the lid with undisguised curiosity. My breath caught in my throat as I gazed upon the magnificent jewelry set laid within on a velvety cushion. I gaped at Ravik, speechless. He seemed confused by my reaction.

"I can't accept that," I whispered, blown away.

Ravik frowned. "Why? Rejecting it would be considered an offense."

"But this is way too expensive a gift to accept from someone I don't know. I wouldn't even accept it from someone I know!"

It was Ravik's turn to look at me wide-eyed as if I'd grown a third eye. He laughed and shook his head.

"No, little bird, it's not expensive at all," Ravik said with an indulgent tone. "While I agree that the craftsmanship is beautiful, this material is cheap and commonplace. Nyrian crystal deposits are abundant in the Jyriak plateau and beneath Mount Jyriak. They're pretty but useless. The men often bring some back to the females to do… well, female stuff with it," he concluded with a shrug.

I stared at him, flabbergasted.

He truly has no idea…

The necklace had three rows of round gems, the first small, the middle one medium, and large, tear-shaped ones on the bottom row. Intricately interwoven silver-looking threads held them together. A matching pair of earrings and bracelet lay in the middle. I delicately picked up an earring and held it in the palm of my hand. Within seconds, the color of the gems darkened, slowly turning obsidian.

"What's happening?" I asked, feeling slightly worried.

"It's normal," Ravik said, reassuringly. "The gems always try to take on the eye-color of the wearer. There are ways to set a permanent color to the stones, but I couldn't tell you how that works other than it requires heat applied in a specific manner."

I nodded slowly, my wheels spinning. "What else do the females do?"

Ravik shrugged. "You will have to ask the females. Speaking of which, we need to get going. I'll have to tell Fenton how you made us late."

"Me?" I exclaimed, outraged.

"Come on, female," Ravik said, giving me a playful slap on the rear. "Let's go."

I hesitated for a second, tempted to wear the jewelry, but then decided to leave it for another time. After carefully placing the jewelry box on the dresser, I hurried back to Ravik. I took the hand he had extended towards me and let him lead me out of the room.

A thirty-minute shuttle flight took us to Clan Yagor's compound. It appeared half the size of Clan Xeldar's compound. However, smaller clan home clusters sprawled far and wide along the large body of water beyond it. Council Fenton had been Ravik's best friend since childhood and led one of the main fishing clans.

Fenton greeted us at the landing pad and escorted us into his hall. Although more humble than Ravik's, it boasted the same type of dark red floors and light grey walls, except for a clearly more nautical theme to the ornate carvings and lattice work of some of the wall panels. Where Clan Xeldar had giant warrior and karveli statues in the compound's plaza and in a few other strategic places in the streets, Clan Yagor had, in the center of their hall, a giant, polished skeleton of some terrifying aquatic creature I'd never seen before.

On the left side of the room, Fenton's clansmen and sons fisted their chests in greeting, while the females kneeled. It still bothered me to no end, but knowing that Ravik took no pleasure in the females' servile behavior alleviated some of my frustration.

An attractive Braxian female approached Fenton. Barefoot and wearing nothing more than a diaphanous concubine dress, she glanced at him for approval. When Fenton nodded, she proceeded to kneel before Ravik, head bowed. Ravik placed his palm on top of her head, granting her permission to rise. With a wave of his hand, he indicated for the other females and servants to do so as well.

"Magnar Ravik, welcome to my Hall," Fenton said. "My home and my concubine, Thala, are yours."

"I thank you and accept your hospitality." Ravik gave Thala an appreciative once over that made me want to claw his face. "Beautiful as ever, Thala," Ravik said, before caressing her bare forearm with his knuckles.

"Thank you, Magnar," she said, demurely.

"You may go," Ravik said.

Thala bowed her head, cast a furtive glance my way, and then returned to stand by Fenton.

Although I'd been warned of this custom ahead of time, it still twisted my insides and set my teeth on edge. Where wives were off limits under any circumstance, a host was expected to offer his concubine to the pleasure of a guest of similar or higher rank as a sign of respect. If the guest was entitled to take full benefit of that offer, fucking another man's concubine would express a lack of consideration for the host. It very rarely happened, unless the female was particularly beautiful or out of spite. However, the guest was expected to acknowledge the female's beauty, and honor the offer with a touch or a kiss, like Ravik had done by caressing her arm.

Fenton gestured for his people to take their leave before leading us to a private salon, with seating and dining areas. It contrasted sharply with the darker, more formal look of the entrance. While the walls remained a pale shade of grey, and the furniture a dark shade of brown, grey, or blue, a number of accent items brightened the place, with colorful carpets on the floor, throw pillows on the couch, and decorative artifacts on the shelves. When I complimented him on the décor, Fenton said it was all Thala's doing, which had her blushing with pride.

"I hope you are both hungry?" Fenton asked, inviting us to take our places at the table, which was big enough for eight. "Good!" he said when we responded in the affirmative. Turning to me, he continued, "I hope you do not mind the informal setting. But I figured you might enjoy not being the object of constant scrutiny, for once, and to have feminine company."

"Most certainly," I said smiling.

The females in Xeldar observed me with blatant curiosity but didn't dare approach me. The women avoided me, unless they were servants seeing to my comfort in one form or another. And even then, they kept those interactions to a strict minimum. I couldn't tell if they felt intimidated or had been warned against bothering me—probably a mixture of both.

Despite his imposing size and brutish features, Fenton's good-natured, gentle personality shone through, especially in the softness of his pale-green eyes.

We settled on one side of the table, Fenton and Thala sitting across the table from us. Under normal circumstances, Ravik should have been seated at the head of the table. However, he wasn't here as the Magnar, but as a man and his woman having dinner with friends.

Fenton waved a hand over a small plaque on the table I'd first assumed to be decoration. Moments later, two servants came in with drinks and appetizers. We launched into a light conversation, talking about everything from troubles Ravik and Fenton used to get into as boys, to epic hunts they took part in, endless questions about my travels, the Tuureans—which I dodged as best I could—the Veredians, my business in the tech industry, and more somber topics like Guldar and the reforms Ravik was instating.

Timid at first, Thala gradually opened up, proving to be quite charming, observant, and sharp-minded. For the first time, I could give a Braxian female a really good look without getting called out for staring. Like the males, they had prominent foreheads without the strong brows. Their noses, broad and flat, was narrower, and more refined. Maybe because of the softer line of their brows, their eyes appeared larger, with thick, long lashes. Thala's eyes were a pale shade of grey with blue accents. Where males had strong, square jaws, her full lips made her chin appear even pointier in her narrow face. Thala's face had a doll-like quality about it. Although smaller than the men, Braxian females averaged a height of 6'7 which made me look quite tiny when I didn't wear heels, and even then. Although sturdier, thanks to their thicker bone structure, their women were far smaller in general body mass, with delightfully feminine curves. They wouldn't qualify as classically beautiful by intergalactic standards, but they possessed an undeniable charm.

From what Ravik had told me, Thala had been Fenton's concubine, on and off, for years and had given him two of his four children; a male and a female. She wanted him to claim her as his wife but for some reason, he kept backing out. Seeing them together, the deep bond between them shone brightly. And yet, I could tell Fenton was keeping part of himself guarded off. Had he been hurt before? Had something gone wrong between them in the past that left a permanent scar?

I loved seeing Ravik so relaxed, his arm resting on the back of my chair, fiddling with my small hairs, or his hand on my lap, caressing my thigh, smiling, laughing, and making good fun of his friend. Good company, intelligent conversation, good wine, good food—although they could do with a bit less meat and a more balanced mix of vegetables and other sides—made for a thoroughly enjoyable evening. It almost felt like being in the 'normal' world.

Or rather, normal until we finished the meal. At that point, we fell back into ancient times where females had to leave the room while males had a strong drink and discussed manly matters. Under different circumstances, I might have bristled at that, but I actually wanted time alone with Thala.

She led me through a side door and up to her boudoir, located on the second floor of the building. Apparently, the Clan Leaders' bedroom and concubine suites were always located on the third floor, as with Ravik's fortress. I wondered if there was a concubine boudoir on the second floor of Xeldar's Hall. Thala's boudoir reflected the style of the décor in the private salon where we had just eaten, although far more feminine and even more colorful.

"This is where I receive and entertain the wives and other concubines," Thala said, her voice soft and musical.

She shadowed me as I walked around the room, perusing the plethora of decorative items on the shelves surrounding the seating area. Tall windows dominated the room with a breathtaking view of the river. Couches, chairs, cushioned stools and large poufs provided ample seating for at least two dozen people. Two giant screens hung on the wall by a long, rectangular stone table. An intricate mosaic of colorful, but dark, polished stones covered the table top.

"It's beautiful," I said with sincerity.

Thala smiled and lowered her eyes, her face heating again. She was adorable but I hoped, with time, she'd prove a bit more assertive, less timid. Based on my interactions with him, I had expected Fenton to be with someone a little less submissive. Could that be the source of his reluctance to marry her?

The room felt a bit more cluttered than I liked, yet I wouldn't change a thing. Each item told a unique story. However, the curtains by the double patio door were what retained my attention. They appeared to be embroidered with shimmering threads eerily identical in color to the nyrian gems of the necklace Grumar's daughter had given me.

"Did you make those?" I asked, pointing at the curtains.

"I wish," she said, making a face as we walked towards them. "I traded for them with Clan Leader Curik's wife. They live on the Jyriak Plateau, where the nyrian gems can be found."

"I thought Clan Grumar controlled that region?"

Thala smiled, her fingertips caressing the embroidery on the white curtains. "There are three clans sharing portions of the plateau—Curik, Grumar, and Hurwas," she explained. "Grumar is the biggest clan with the largest lands. Their females make lovely jewelry, especially the daughter, Vela. She's young but clever. Nobody really bothered with nyrian stones. It's a common material and too bright. As you've probably noticed by now, Braxians like dark and subdued colors. Having little to no access to the more appealing river stones," she said, pointing at the mosaic of polished stones covering the table, "Vela managed with what she had. We were reluctant to trade for them at first since there's no bragging to be had wearing a necklace made of common rocks. But her craftsmanship and her designs are just too beautiful to resist. Let me show you."

She headed toward a chest of drawers atop which sat a series of scented candles in beautifully sculpted holders.

Where had things such as these been in all the shops I visited in Xeldar?

Thala opened the top drawer and retrieved a datapad. Gesturing towards one of the dark grey couches, she invited me to take a seat, then settled next to me. She accessed a page with two dozen thumbnails of magnificent jewelry sets similar to the one I'd received earlier.

"This is Vela's latest collection," Thala said, pointing at the images. "Her first collection had been of comparable quality, although she does seem to get better and better every day. Many of us tried to convince her to recreate identical pieces with river stones instead. She refused. At first, I think it was because she had nothing to trade for the stones. But even when the wives of Clan Podek who have a near monopoly on the stones offered to provide them, she still declined insisting she only worked with nyrian gems."

Clever girl.

"So if you wanted her goods, you had no choice but to also take her gems," I said.

Thala nodded. "Over time, nyrian gems have grown on us, especially since Vela has mastered the art of setting the color of the gems to pretty much anything we want." She pointed at the curtains with her chin. "For the curtains, Keria, Clan Leader Curik's wife, has figured out a technique to crush the nyrian gems and spin them into threads that can be woven into pretty much any material and still retain their color setting properties."

I nodded, my mind reeling at the possibilities. "And what do the females of Clan Yagor do?" I asked.

Thala smiled, slightly puffing her chest. "We make perfumes, scented candles, poultices, and healing creams. Some scents can be pretty powerful to create a certain mood," she said, the naughty glimmer in her eyes making me laugh out loud. "You'd be surprised at the incredible properties hidden within some of the unusable and even toxic parts of fishes, crustaceans, and other aquatic creatures and plants."

No, I wouldn't be surprised by that, only by the women having acquired that knowledge.

"How did you learn all this?"

Thala shrugged. "The knowledge is passed from mother to daughter, each generation trying to add more to the art before passing it down to those who follow."

"So you have this whole underground market based on trade," I said, flabbergasted. "Why not open shops to freely buy and sell from each other?"

Thala frowned and shook her head. "Females do not own credits or earn wages. Our males wouldn't buy things they consider frivolous and pointless. And in our current economic situation, it would be even less likely to happen." She tucked a strand of her long, dark-brown hair behind her ear. "In truth, even if we could, I doubt any of us would want to, at least not here on Braxia. Sure, it would be flattering for off-worlders to want our products. But bartering is more than just getting pretty things that are indeed mostly useless, it's about the social interaction, bonding, and friendly rivalries between Braxian females. I would hate to see that go away."

"Are Braxian females happy?" I blurted out, instantly kicking myself for it.

She blinked, taken aback by the unexpected question. I was considering apologizing and withdrawing my question, but Thala didn't appear offended. Instead, she seriously pondered the question.

"Interesting question," she said at last. "Had you asked me that six or seven years ago, I would have said mostly not. But the Magnar has made some wonderful changes that have significantly improved the living conditions of females."

Her pale-grey eyes bore into mine with a strength and force of conviction I hadn't expected from someone, at least in appearance, as submissive as she.

"Braxia must appear strange, backwards, and even barbaric to you in its ways and customs. On some fronts, you would be right. On others, I would disagree. We do not feel diminished to not be 'allowed' at the main table in the Clan's Hall for evening meals. We do not wish to look at pleasure workers groping each other during our meal, or listen to the boasting and mostly idiotically belligerent conversations between the men to prove they have the bigger cock."

My eyes bulged at the unexpected crudeness, and Thala's face turned bright red. Seeing me burst out laughing reassured her I hadn't taken offense.

"Yes," I said, between giggles, "they indeed do a lot of that."

"Indeed," she echoed, rolling her eyes, no doubt reminiscing one of many such situations. "We do not mind not being allowed into the military or hunting parties. Our males are literally ten times stronger and faster than we are. We have heard of your prowess during the hunt but Braxian females do not have the speed you possess. In truth, we had no idea Guldan females could move as fast as you did seeing how you are the first any of us has ever encountered."

Guldan females can't. Veredian females of the Warrior breed can.

"Braxian females are naturally submissive and gladly yield the power to our males who thrive on wielding it, proving themselves worthy males, but doing so in a sensible manner." Thala shrugged. "Some may say it's because of our upbringing, but even the most liberal among us likes a dominant male. Even a female as strong and independent as *you* fell for the apex alpha of Braxia."

The way she said the last sentence held a challenge, daring me to speak to the contrary. But I couldn't. I loved being dominated by him, feeling fragile and vulnerable in his powerful embrace.

I smiled noncommittally, and she smiled back, knowingly.

Touché.

"But surely, some women aspire to greater power or control over their own lives, over government?" I asked.

"Yes," Thala conceded. "And we have it." She chuckled at my dubious expression. "Behind every great male in power, there is a strong female in his ear, giving him counsel. For generations, every good Magnar had an influential Dagna by his side. In some cases, *she* was the true ruler while he was merely her voice, her enforcer."

"Then why couldn't she be simply declared as such?" I challenged.

Thala laughed like I'd said something cute or naïve. "Look at me," she said, waving her hands at her body. "Even with your combat skills, neither I nor any other Braxian female before or after me, will ever be able to hang on to power. There's a reason that, despite his many detractors and those opposed to change, Ravik is still Magnar. No one, and I mean *no one*, has ever defeated him in single combat. You saw him carry out the sentence on Torvin Sedrak for his betrayal in the forest. Did the Magnar look even remotely in danger of losing?"

I shook my head. The battle had been almost insultingly easy for my man.

"Believe me, if anyone thought they had the slightest chance of winning, they would seek to depose him, but they can't. No female would survive a challenge," Thala said casually. "Like Guldar, Braxia's foundations rely on the survival of the fittest. We want the Magnar, our ruler and protector of the realm, to be the fiercest, wildest, most vicious beast of the land. When it comes to fighting for what we want, do not be fooled by our submissive dispositions. Never underestimate the power of words whispered on top of soft pillows."

CHAPTER 13
MERCY

Morning found Ravik in a foul mood. I didn't have to ask why. The closer we got to departure time to my brother's house, the fouler it became. Knowing concern for my well-being fueled it stirred a sliver of guilt within me. However, I initially came to Braxia with a specific goal in mind that had been derailed by the hunt and the Guldans' arrival.

I couldn't believe that only one week had gone by since Ravik and I first met at Anton's penthouse. My overprotective baby sister and my mother were certainly worrying about me… as always. I had hoped to delay a bit until I had good news for them the next time I sent them a com message but, with Clan Grumar's trade request, I'd have to send her a message tonight or tomorrow at the latest. The chances of finding my brother's clients list in my first day of search were slim to none. Still, stranger things had happened.

Casting a sideways glance at Ravik, I bit the inside of my cheeks not to laugh at the vicious way in which he glared at Gorav, Anton's youngest half-brother. It wasn't the poor man's fault that I insisted on going today.

"Stop giving my son the evil eye," Krygor said, slapping the back of Ravik's shoulder in a friendly way. "He and my clansmen will keep your female safe. Don't forget that Anton initially entrusted her protection to me," he teased.

"She has me," Ravik snarled, grumpier than ever.

Far from being intimidated, Krygor appeared amused by Ravik's tantrum. "Only because you snuck in before I could. We both know had she met me first, she'd have recognized me as the better man."

Ravik snorted, his mood reluctantly lighting a little. "You wish, old man."

"Hardly. I'm barely five years older than you," Krygor said in a dismissive tone. Turning towards me, he whispered in a conspiratorial voice. "Do not let a few grey hairs fool you. It is proof that I possess the wisdom he lacks. When you tire of him and want a real man, look me up."

I bit my bottom lip to keep from laughing, loving their banter. Looking at Anton's father, one would never guess at the humorous and rebellious persona behind the fearsome face. And he was right; had I not met Ravik first, I definitely would have been drawn to Krygor, especially knowing the hardships he had faced to protect his half-breed son.

"Do not make me crack your skull open, Krygor Aldriss," Ravik hissed, only half-joking.

Krygor waved a hand, unfazed. "Not today, you won't, unless you want to have one less voice for this morning's vote. Come on, pup, and kiss your woman goodbye. We have a council meeting to attend."

Ravik scrunched his face as if he'd bitten into something sour. Standing before him, I combed my fingers through his hair and lifted my face to look at him. His expression softened but the worry lingered in his eyes.

"Stop fretting, big boy," I said playfully. "You know they will keep me safe, and I'm not helpless."

He harrumphed but didn't resist when I drew his face towards mine. Rising to my tippy toes, I rubbed my nose against his before giving him a light kiss. His large hand on my nape, and his arm around my waist, prevented me from moving away as he deepened the kiss. Krygor cleared his throat behind us when that kiss stretched too long. Ravik growled in annoyance against my lips, making me chuckle.

Releasing me with obvious reluctance, Ravik gave me a stern stare. "You return to me tonight."

It wasn't a request. Far from annoying me, it made me want to smile again. "Yes, yes, Magnar, I will."

Not amused by my teasing tone, Ravik growled at me, but caressed my cheek gently. With a final warning glance at Gorav, he marched away with angry steps, shadowed by Krygor. Sighing, I hopped onto the shuttle with my security detail.

The forty-minute flight to Varrek's estate felt like an eternity. Even working on my portable computer failed to distract me from my impatience. Although I'd put my consulting services on hold, my research labs never stopped experimenting and developing new technology based on specs I'd provided them. Over the past week, I'd been negligent in keeping up to date with the latest reports and providing the required feedback for my staff so they could pursue their efforts.

As we approached our destination, I rolled my eyes at the sight of at least another dozen of Krygor's clansmen milling about the building. Talk about overkill. I clamped down on another wave of annoyance. This overprotectiveness was suffocating. I appreciated their intention and acknowledged that the Guldans represented a serious threat to me, not only because of my inheritance, but also as leverage against their Magnar. But this felt like a prison. I couldn't go anywhere without an escort and couldn't leave Ravik's fortress without permission. That wouldn't work in the long run.

Chasing away the somber thoughts, I turned my gaze to the one-story building made of dark stones and ash-colored wood. Tall, reinforced fences surrounded the property, including the landing pad. The drawn shutters on the tall windows all around it, the overgrown vegetation encroaching on the main path leading to the front door, and the covered solar panels on the roof offered ample indication that the place had been vacant for a while.

Interestingly enough, Varrek had refurbished an old hunter's lodge located on the unclaimed lands at almost equal distance between the compounds belonging to Clan Leaders Hagan Lorvis and Norbek Arthol, two of the Fifteen. Despite the bordering forest a stone's throw away from the house, Gorav assured me the place was safe. Only small prey dwelled in the vicinity; the larger creatures and predators roamed deeper in the thickest part of the forest which provided them with better camouflage.

The men watched us with undisguised curiosity as we walked up to the house. One of them approached us as we reached the staircase.

"We have secured the perimeter," the man said to Gorav. "However, none of the old hunter access codes work on the door. Unless you have another way to hack it, we have some armored men prepared to break down the door. However, if it comes to that, we will need you to take the female to a safe distance first as we do not know what traps the Guldan may have set up."

"That won't be necessary," I intervened. "I have broken through my brother's security before. This shouldn't be much different."

Ignoring his dubious look, I swiftly climbed the three steps to the front porch while activating a perimeter scan from the interface on my armband. As expected, the Braxians had missed the real threat, deactivating only the decoy detectors and alarm systems that my brother had set up to lure potential intruders into a false sense of security. Aside from the Tuureans and me, pretty much anyone else would have been fooled by it, too. Even then, I couldn't be certain I had detected everything. I pulled a wand-like device from the tool pouch hanging against my hip, the straps running across my chest. I calibrated it to the frequency of the security devices the Braxians had missed and sent a disruptor signal on that wavelength. Within seconds, each of them turned to inactive on my scanner.

They hadn't been a direct threat. But had they remained active, whatever defense mechanism Varrek had inside the house would have been armed upon our entrance. And *that* could have been lethal. I placed a magnetic descrambler on the door's lock panel. While it would break through it, my brother liked having little surprises that would set off through the process and mess things up. Resting my palm inconspicuously next to the descrambler, I opened my senses, seeking the sparks. As each trap triggered, I pushed a disable command. Less than two minutes later, the door unlocked.

Gorav insisted on going in first. I repressed the urge to roll my eyes and gestured for him to proceed. The four other men that had traveled with us squeezed in ahead of me. I ran another scan, this time for traps.

"Stay here while we secure the house," Gorav said.

"It's better if I come with you since I can see all the traps on this device," I argued, waving my forearm at him. "Like the one right over here in the wall lamp by the window."

Gorav stared at me, surprised. He looked at the lamp, down at his armband, then back up at the lamp. "It doesn't show on my scanner."

"Exactly," I said with a smirk.

He scrunched his face, somewhat disgruntled. It took nearly an hour going through the lodge, disabling traps. I didn't understand why Varrek had so many in this single-story building. The spacious rooms included a dormitory, which had been turned into a lab, and a cold room which contained a sickeningly large quantity of Bliss, a highly addictive—and extremely deadly—recreational drug. Varrek had unleashed it on the unsuspecting population before we'd managed to shut down his operation. He'd added a wall in one corner of the common room, creating an office and work area, and then turned the large equipment and trap storage room into his bedroom.

Once reassured that everything was secured, Gorav gave the clansmen outside leave to return to their compound. Along with my four other escorts, he settled in the common room to work on some tasks on the portable computers and datapads they had brought.

While I wanted to further explore the house, for now, his computer held my interest. It took little time to hack into it, thanks to my recent experience at our family home on Guldar. Unfortunately, I soon realized there would be no quick wins. Many of the files were encrypted, each using a different algorithm. It would take days, if not weeks to unlock all of them without setting off a trap that could destroy or corrupt the entire system.

With a heavy sigh, I set to work.

Over the next week, I hacked into hundreds of files but the clients list continued to elude me. I should have been further into my investigation but too often kept getting distracted by some brilliant analysis, research assumptions, or mind blowing schematics for a new concept or prototype. Each time, my chest ached that such a genius had gone to waste, partially with my aid.

To my surprise, I stumbled on a series of unexpected messages from a male named Rik who seemed infatuated with Varrek—actually more like obsessed and borderline stalker. I felt guilty reading those private conversations, but I assuaged my conscience by justifying it as a way to get to know my brother a bit more. From what juicy tidbits I'd found, my brother had had an affair with that male but put an end to it once he became too clingy. As I understood it, he'd also been a brilliant scientist who Varrek continued to work with on various projects for a while after ending their romantic involvement. But Rik's continued persistence to resume their affair eventually drove Varrek to put an end to their relationship, both professional and personal. I'd known my brother preferred men, but I wondered what other secrets I'd discover about him.

At last, my sister Aleina responded to the message I'd sent her on my first day at Varrek's house. Considering the great distance from here to Xelix Prime, we couldn't have a direct call but only recordings. My mother, my niece, and her children all made a token appearance on the video telling me how much they missed me and looked forward to my return. My throat tightened with emotion. I ached to hold them in my arms. Once more, I wondered at a life on Braxia, filled with duty, lack of privacy or freedom, in a culture utterly foreign to me, and located light years away from the family I had just been reunited with.

And yet, I was falling hard for my beast. The thought of parting with him was just as unbearable.

At least, there would be some good news to be announced. However, Ravik put a damper on my enthusiasm. Delivering good news without a concrete action plan would fall flat and open the door to too many questions we might not have answers for. Over the following week, I divided my time between hacking through Varrek's files and coordinating with Anton, Grace, and my sister to set up a solid plan that wouldn't fix all of the Braxians' problems, but would open the way to new opportunities while giving some clans more breathing room in the short-term. Ravik helped re-adjust a few things but mostly let me run with it.

He'd been busy successfully negotiating his own trade and service agreements with foreign dignitaries, a few of whom had come to Braxia. With no sign of further Guldan interference, and so many positive prospects for his people, Ravik's mood had greatly improved. He was more relaxed, but still as overbearingly protective. At least, he'd consented to reduce my number of 'babysitters' to two whenever I went to Varrek's house.

We'd settled into a comfortable routine; bath and breakfast together in the morning, off to our separate ways during the day, a couple of hours together—before or after last meal with the clan—where he'd make me discover the hidden beauties of Braxia, and of course, passionate nights of mind-blowing sex. Whenever possible, we'd have last meal at one of his close friends' compounds instead, like that night at Fenton's place. I loved those as they gave me great insights into the past that had shaped him into the man he'd become.

But not tonight.

For some silly reason, I felt nervous about revealing to the clans the various things we'd been working on to get some of them back on their feet. Tensions had further risen in some parts of Braxia as Ravik enforced the fines imposed on those caught pursuing slave labor. I wanted tonight to be a resounding success for him. All concerned clans, not usually in attendance in our Hall, would be present for last meal.

I turned to face the mirror for one final glance at myself. Over the past week, I'd taken to wearing Braxian 'underground' fashion, which I'd specifically commissioned from a few wives or had modified to fit my slender, less sturdy frame. Those sexy dresses were intended to retain the interest of their male or entice potential husbands. The dark colors preferred by the Braxians also matched my tastes. The females didn't get many opportunities to flaunt those dresses in public, aside from the quarterly fair which took place in the Keltrix Market.

Established in a central location near Braxia's space sport, it provided a one-stop shopping destination for the clans to buy and trade with each other rather than having to hop from clan to clan to explore their local markets.

The strapless, black, bandage cutout dress hugged my body like a second skin. Thigh-length, the cutouts on the sides exposed plenty of skin from the waist down. I donned the beautiful jewelry set that Vela had gifted me, the nyrian stones taking on an obsidian color to match my eyes. For a moment, I considered putting on my knee-length boots, but they made me look a little too hard, which wasn't the goal tonight. So I settled on black stilettos with heels tall enough to *almost* rival those Grace loved to wear.

Ravik approached me from behind, his muscular arm wrapping around my waist as he pressed his chest against my back.

"You look stunning, my mate," Ravik whispered.

My stomach flip-flopped at the title. This was his second time referring to me as such. I couldn't tell if it had been deliberate or a slip of the tongue. After only three weeks together, it was too early for me to expect that kind of commitment from him, not to mention I still needed to sort out my own feelings about life by his side and so far from my family.

Bending his head, Ravik nuzzled my ear and then his lips traced the curve from my neck to my shoulder. I purred, the pressure on my markings, even through the prosthetics, had delicious shivers running down my spine.

"Come on, little bird," Ravik said, leading me out of the room, his hand on my waist. "Our people await."

'Our' people...

This time, I no longer believe it to be a slip of the tongue. After all, this morning, he had inquired about my joining him in some of his official visits to the clans. He had justified it by saying the clans would benefit from fresh eyes with a good understanding of what appealed to foreign markets. Since I'd also expressed a great deal of curiosity about some of their natural resources for my personal research and development purposes, he figured it would be better for me to see it all firsthand. Although valid, I suspected his true motives lay elsewhere. When I argued that it might be misinterpreted, he'd shrugged and said that, when it came to me, he didn't give a shit what others thought.

I liked that.

We entered the dining hall under the heavy stares of the clansmen and in particular the Clan Leaders; Krygor's taunting, Fenton's amused, Pattel's unreadable, Raylor's subdued, Hagan's and Yorbek's —two of the five remaining Fifteen—full of venom, and a few such as Boros, Moktar, and Ferux—all from embattled clans—full of hope.

After the usual chest fisting greeting, Ravik indicated that the men take their seats, the females quietly slipping onto their chairs around the tables in the two side corners of the hall. I settled at my usual place at the head of the table next to him, his sons on each side of us. Ravik remained standing and gestured for the servants to fill everyone's glass. They burst into action, swift, efficient, and unobstrusive.

"I thank you all for joining my table under such short notice," Ravik said. "Times are difficult, more for some than others, and your constant efforts and sacrifices to provide for your clans have not gone unnoticed. Change never comes easily, but it is necessary for a greater benefit in the long term."

"But what if we don't survive to see that longer term?" Hagan intervened with barely disguised sarcasm.

"I haven't granted you leave to speak, Lorvis," Ravik said, his voice cold as ice.

Hagan flinched, properly put back in his place. Lips pinched, clearly seething, he leaned back against his chair, avoiding making eye contact with the other Clan Leaders sitting around the main table. Braxians didn't call each other by their last name. You only did so to indicate you didn't know them, they were of inferior rank to yours, or as a display of contempt. Ravik had intended to express the last two.

"As Lorvis so rudely pointed out," Ravik continued, adding insult to injury, "some clans are in a more dire situation, some even fearing not making it through winter. While we are still working on long-term solutions, in the short-term, my Ravena has come through for the Jyriak Plateau clans."

Ravik turned to me and caressed my right horn with his fingertips, pride and affection in his eyes. My cheeks heated, and my chest warmed for being thus publicly claimed and praised. He looked back towards the clan tables where Boros had perked up, looking as if he were holding his breath while waiting for Ravik to expand further.

"She has convinced the Tuureans to purchase three full cargos of stone and metals from each of the three clans of the Plateau at standard cost," Ravik continued.

A victorious roar rose from the three clans' tables, followed by thumping sounds as the other clansmen knocked their fists on the surface twice in quick succession in sign of approval. Although these shipments would only allow him to feed his people through the winter, Boros looked like a man who had the weight of the world lifted off his shoulders. The gratitude in his eyes as they connected with mine almost choked me.

"Thanks to our continued observance of their rules regarding people's rights and fair trade, the Galactic Council has lifted all embargo preventing its members from doing commerce with us. With the aid of Council Fenton, Council Krygor, Elder Pattel, and my heir Keran," Ravik said, waving at the four men all seated at the left side of the table, "I have signed agreements to reopen trade in meat, grains, and leather with three human colonies that used to do business with the clans of the Nemfor Plains."

The five clan leaders, including Hagan, expressed their satisfaction, although Hagan did so reluctantly.

"Other agreements are currently under discussion for the River Plains, the Woodlands Clearing, and the Dulman Range. I hope they will reach a positive conclusion in the upcoming weeks."

More nods of approval greeted his words, the mood in the room buzzing with energy and excitement.

"But if we want to prosper and reclaim our former glory, change needs to go further," Ravik said. A hush fell over the room as the clansmen eyed their ruler warily. "For generations, we have relied on the trade of traditional resources and the strength of our arms. It's no longer enough. We need to develop new markets, with new resources, and create demand for new things."

"Respectfully, Magnar," Clan Leader Ferux said, "we have tried. Boros, Moktar, and I have turned every stone, literally. You know this. We just have nothing else."

"Wrong," I intervened. All eyes turned to me. "You and the two other Jyriak Plateau clans are probably sitting on Braxia's greatest wealth."

Snorts and chuckles met my words, the men looking at me like I'd either lost my mind or was completely clueless—or a mixture of both.

"Do you have any idea of the value of your nyrian gems?" I asked, unfazed.

The room burst out laughing, and the glimmer of hope that had lurked in the eyes of the three Jyriak Plateau clan leaders died. I stood up, casting a glance at Ravik not to intervene. He gave me a subtle nod and sat.

"And this is what happens when you let females meddle in the affairs of men," Hagan shouted. "What do females know about business?"

"Clearly more than you," I said, with a hard voice. "Every single word that comes out of your mouth displays your ignorance and narrow-mindedness."

"You dare?" Hagan yelled. Jumping to his feet, face reddened with fury and muddy brown eyes throwing daggers, he looked on the verge of running towards me to bash my head in.

"I dare and double dare," I snapped back. "Sit down, you fool, and learn from your betters." Ignoring his gasp of outrage, I let my furious gaze roam over the attendance. "Your females are your greatest wealth, and you don't even know it. This necklace," I said, pointing at the one around my neck, "was created by the incredibly talented Vela Grumar. It's made of nyrian stones, trash according to Braxians. What would you say if I told you I was offered ten thousand credits for the necklace, earrings, and bracelet set?"

Shocked gasps resonated through the room. Eyes bulging, mouths agape, they stared at me disbelieving.

"Surprised? You haven't heard the best part yet," I said, making eye contact with as many people as possible. "I told the potential buyer that, while this particular set was not for sale, her ten thousand offer was offensive."

"Why would you do that?" Boros asked, flabbergasted. "That's an insane offer for those rocks!"

"No, Clan Leader Boros. It is not," I said, gently. "The beauty, purity, and especially the color shifting properties of the nyrian stones make them easily rival blue diamonds. I told the buyer any set she gets from Vela will be priced at a minimum of twenty-five thousand credits. She accepted."

The attendance reacted loudly to my statement, shocked and bewildered.

"She would like at least forty unique sets within a month," I continued, pressing my advantage. "That's a minimum of one million credits, more even considering some of the stones are bigger and will therefore cost the buyer more. The women of Clan Grumar already have over two hundred sets ready which they'd planned to trade with other clan females during the fair."

I gave the men a second to digest what I'd said before proceeding.

"I've sent samples of the craft work from your wives, concubines, and daughters to Grace Aldriss; you know, the wife of the hybrid so many of you show so much disdain towards," I said casting a meaningful glance towards a few of the culprits. "She presented them to businesses in the VIP section of Venus Hive. She's received large orders for the nyrian threads used for embroidering from Clan Curik, and the nyrian bejeweled decorations from Clan Hurwas. They want perfumes and beauty creams from Clan Yagor."

Pressing my palms on top of the table, I leaned forward to give more weight to my words.

"The fishing clans too are sitting on great wealth. Those non-consumable parts you've considered as waste contain the toxins which your females have been turning into healing creams and poultices that are as effective as Soltarin, but without the negative side effects caused by some of its ingredients to the Inugian people. They've placed an initial large order, and if further tests prove conclusive, they will want to instate a permanent, regular trade for it. I could go on for another twenty-minutes listing the unique resources you possess. Not all of them will make you rich, but every single one of them stacked together will make a huge difference."

Looking to the side at the set of tables where the females sat, their faces flushed with pride, excitement, and a bit of wariness, I waved a hand towards them.

"This is your future. Your females have been passing down a treasure trove of knowledge from mother to daughter for generations. As the humans say, one man's trash is another man's treasure. You have more wealth than you realize. Stop letting it go to waste."

I sat back down under the heavy silence as the guests still reeled from all this. Snapping out of it first, Boros thumped his fist twice on his table, imitated seconds later by a few others and then by most of the attendance. A tension I hadn't realized had been knotting the muscles between my shoulder blades suddenly loosened. I cast a sideways glance at Ravik who stared at me with open pride. He caressed my cheek with his knuckles then stood up.

"As my Ravena stated," Ravik said, "Braxia possesses greater wealth than we know. We need fresh eyes to be able to see it. For this reason, starting next week, Ravena will occasionally accompany me during my clan tours to help assess what unique assets you possess, if any."

Approving nods and mumbles welcomed his words.

"As for the orders Ravena received, Anton has rounded up a list of over thirty interested buyers who have consented to come to Braxia to review your merchandise and make offers. They will be here next week." More excited murmurs rose from the tables. "Anton has volunteered to review all your contracts for free before you enter into any agreements. I strongly suggest you take him up on his offer as he knows the fair prices and will spare you getting defrauded."

More nods ensued.

"Braxia was once one of the jewels of the Eastern Quadrant. We *will* endure through this hardship and rise again. The future is ours to seize, and seize it we will." Ravik raised his glass of wine. "To Braxia!"

Everyone in attendance stood up, raised their glasses, and shouted in unison.

"To Braxia!"

CHAPTER 14
RAVIK

Staring at Hagan's despicable face across the table from me in my private chambers, countless scenarios ran through my mind as to the multitude of ways in which I could demolish it, the oh-so-satisfying sound of his bones crushing beneath my fist, and his delightful screams of agony.

Soon, you son of a krillik. Soon, I will kill you.

In the week that followed our announcements regarding potential new trades using the women's crafts, he'd grown increasingly belligerent, going so far as to imply Mercy should be punished according to the old ways for her disrespect towards him. For that alone, I'd almost given in to the urge to kill him. Before I'd abolished that law, women were flogged if found guilty of showing disrespect to a male, or dishonoring him whether through her words or actions. The standard punishment consisted of twenty-five lashes, half of which were expected to break skin. The female would then be placed for three hours in a cage too small to stand in and too narrow to lie down or stretch. Only after that would she receive treatment for her wounds, which didn't guarantee painkillers, based on the gravity of her offense.

Despite our barbaric ways, such punishments didn't occur as often as one might think. Our males knew the extent of our strength compared to our females and how easily we could permanently damage or even kill them by losing control. Once was all it took. Our females also knew the severity of the punishments that would befall them for crossing certain lines and therefore trod carefully. But underlying this, no matter how dominant and superior men considered themselves to their women, they cared for their wives, concubines, and daughters, and inflicted punishments in keeping with one who loves well.

Still, too many acts of gratuitous violence condoned by our culture had been perpetrated against women. Even with the changes in law, such reprehensible acts continued to occur. Enforcing the law proved difficult with clans operating within the privacy of their own compounds which made reporting it less likely. Once more, it came down to laying the foundations and then working on changing mentalities.

But people such as Hagan couldn't change because they didn't want to. They enjoyed the power conferred to them by the old ways. And above all, they loved the easy profit from taking advantage of others. The success of the merchant meeting organized with Anton's help had left him more bitter than ever. The high demand for some of the goods—mainly the beauty products, and jewelry, and some of the nyrian woven fabric—had prompted Anton to offer to provide a prime real estate location on Venus Hive to run a Braxian shop, free of charge for two years. As a grain farmer, Hagan wouldn't benefit from the potentially insane profits the struggling clans could reap.

"I believe this is all moving too fast and creating unrealistic expectations," Hagan complained for the billionth time.

"The clansmen are well aware that there are no guarantees," Krygor said, dismissively. "Weren't you the one demanding we give the people hope? We've taken concrete steps and still you complain?"

"Your half-breed is once again trying to control the process with this shop idea," Hagan argued. "When he decides he no longer wants us there, what will happen?" he asked turning to Raylor Caldes for support.

Raylor hesitated, a troubled look crossing his features.

"Technically, he would be bound by the terms of the two-year contract he suggested. It is an extremely generous offer on his part and actually a loss."

I suspected my face reflected the same shock as everyone else's. Raylor had grown quite subdued since the whole debacle he had initiated by inviting the Guldans. But his hatred for Anton and the whole of Clan Aldriss had been legendary. We'd all expected him to jump at the opportunity to trash him.

"I know of the location he's proposing," Raylor explained in a somewhat defensive tone in light of our reactions. "It would rent for millions of credits per month. He's giving up a lot for nothing in return, while giving us access to the richest clientele in the Eastern Quadrant. Those who come to pleasure barges want to spend and be extravagant. With the store, we get to charge full price instead of the lower price we would normally get from trading with resellers."

"You're only defending him because you seek to profit from this," Hagan said, bitterly.

"Wouldn't you?" Raylor snapped back. "Duralium doesn't sell anymore. People want Titanium. My clan entirely depends on Anton's mercy in buying our metal sheets to expand and maintain his space stations. Unlike you with your farms, we had no other prospects until now. We don't have anything as fancy as nyrian turned out to be, but our females have been crafting beautiful decorative items using metal shavings with colorful resins. My wife has actually initiated talks with Boros' daughter for some jewelry concepts combining both our resources. Whatever my personal feelings, I have a duty to my clan, and I will see to it."

I was too shocked for words. Raylor had always been a practical man, but he was proving smarter and wiser than I'd expected. After the banishment of his son and his subsequent execution, Raylor had made one bad decision after another, and systematically associated with the wrong crowd. Maybe he could be redeemed after all.

"The topic isn't open for debate anyway," I said, ready to move on to another subject. "Anton will be reviewing with each clan the proposals submitted during yesterday's meeting with the merchants;

advising them as to which ones are worth pursuing or that require amending." Locking eyes with Hagan I smirked with undisguised malice. "If you fear losing your elite clan status, I suggest you stop fighting change and get onboard so that you're not left behind."

Hagan pinched his lips, looking for some snarky reply. A sudden commotion outside my chamber had my warning bells firing up.

"Ravena! No!" Tagar's muffled voice yelled from outside. "You can't go in there!"

My shoulders tensed at the sound of Ravena's angry growl seeping in through the closed door. My councilmen exchanged confused looks, while my eyes remained glued to the entrance. I rose to my feet just as the door burst open. Time appeared to stand still when she stepped inside. A feral expression on her face, a low, menacing growl rising from her throat in a constant flow, Ravena prowled towards the table like a predator, staring at me like prey.

And then it hit us: the potent scent of her arousal. This wasn't just my female being in the mood, this was her mating heat. It struck me like a punch in the gut, setting my blood on fire as it rushed to my groin. My councilmen's noses twitched, their nostrils flaring, and eyes widening. A few of them grabbed their crotches, pained expressions on their faces as Ravena's scent spurred their male instinct to sate the needs of the prime female.

"Mine," Ravena hissed, her eyes locked on me.

Moving so fast she blurred, Ravena closed the distance with three long steps, leapt between Krygor and Pattel onto the table, before throwing herself at me. Although I caught her, the force of the impact had me stumbling a couple of steps back, knocking my chair out of the way. Legs wrapped around my waist, she tore my shirt open with supernatural strength.

"Mine!" she hissed again. Still clawing at the remaining shreds of my shirt, she covered my neck and chest with hungry kisses.

"Ravena, stop!" I said, trying in vain to control her.

Slipping a hand between us, she ripped open the magnetic clasp of my pants and caught my cock in a vise-like grip. I grunted in pain and, hooking my hands under her armpits, I peeled her off me and slammed her back onto the top of the table. I clenched my teeth as she nearly tore off my cock, trying to hang onto it before it slipped out of her hand.

"Enough, woman!" I growled, as she used her legs to draw me closer and wiggled her hips to get some friction.

The short hem of her dress rode up, giving me a full view of her black thong, soaking wet with need. The scent of her musk slapped me hard. My stomach cramped painfully with burning desire. My exposed cocked jerked and throbbed. I felt dizzy, all rational thoughts fleeing. Ravena lifted her head, one hand stretching to get a hold of my shaft again. I caught her wrist, but lightning fast, she brought it to her face and brutally bit me. I yelped and, letting go, I wrapped my hand around her throat and slammed her back down on the table. She writhed and struggled against my hold, clawing my arm hard enough for angry welts to rise.

"I ache!" she cried out, unable to get free.

The pain, anguish, and desperation in her voice broke what resistance I had left. A lustful haze descended upon me, blurring my surroundings. Nothing mattered anymore but my mate's hot, willing body before me, the maddening scent of her desire, and the throbbing stiffness between my legs.

"Father, no! You'll kill her!"

I heard the words and vaguely recognized them as coming from my oldest son, but nothing mattered; only the searing heat of my woman's pussy engulfing me as I rammed myself home in one powerful thrust. Ravena's back arched off the table, her horns scraping against the hard surface with a raking sound. Her strangled cry of pain soon turned into a hungry moan.

"Yes! Yes!" she cried out as I pounded into her.

Her throaty moans, the rippling caress of her inner walls squeezing and massaging my shaft with each thrust had my stomach quivering from the waves of pleasure washing over me.

"Ancestors..." a voice whispered. "No Denax?"

A sliver of rational thinking pierced through the haze. "Get out!" I growled, my eyes never moving away from my beautiful female's face, her stunning features dissolved in an expression of pure bliss.

The scraping sound of chairs as my council rose to their feet was soon followed by the door closing behind them.

Releasing her neck, I wrapped my hands around both of her horns, lifting her head up. One of them resisted slightly, having gotten stuck in the surface of the table. Without slowing down my punishing pace, I crushed her mouth with a brutal, but brief kiss. Half-sitting at the edge of the table, Ravena wrapped her hands around my arms, near the elbow creases, as I held on to her horns. My thumbs rubbed their bases, pressing the specific points I knew to be most sensitive. Her head jerked backwards, and her eyes rolled as she unraveled with a guttural cry.

Arms falling to the side, Ravena's body shook from the spasms of her climax. One hand on her back, I held her up, and continued to pump in and out of her boneless body until she came down from her high. I wrested another orgasm from her before surrendering to my own release.

Panting, electric sparks of pleasure going off on every single one of my nerve endings, I laid Ravena back down on the table and leaned over her. She clung to me, nails digging into my back as if she feared I'd disappear or go away. Cock still buried balls deep inside my woman, I gently brushed aside the few locks of hair stuck to her forehead by a thin sheen of perspiration.

"You'll be the death of me, little bird."

Eyes smoldering, her dark gaze lowered to my lips but didn't seem to register the meaning of my words.

Her inner walls throbbed around me, and she lifted her pelvis.

"My beast," she whispered with a possessiveness that had my heart soaring with joy. "Again."

I snorted and shook my head.

"You'll be the death of me," I repeated, kissing her before resuming my most pleasurable duty.

❧

Ravena stirred against me as the morning light trickled into our bedroom. I couldn't tell which one of us was the sorest. I had heard of the Veredians' insane sexual appetite during their season, but this went above and beyond anything I could have ever imagined. I didn't look forward to facing my council again, having taken the coward's way out last night by having dinner with my woman in the privacy of our room.

My woman…

I'd fallen hard and fast for her. I never really questioned her saying we were soulmates, but now, no doubt lingered in my mind. And yet, the closer we grew together, the greater the gap that formed between us. Tossing the blanket to the side, I let my gaze roam over the perfection of my woman's golden body; her stunning face and slender neck, the soft curve of her shoulders covered in those lovely Veredian markings, her perky breasts with plump, dark-brown nipples, her flat stomach and narrow waist, which flared into beautifully rounded hips, and ended with long, shapely legs. My index finger circled the ring of her navel before my hand rested on her stomach, my thumb caressing it in a slow, tidal movement.

She could already be carrying my offspring. We'd been very active prior to her season beginning. But now, at the height of her fertility, and seeing how we'd been at each other almost non-stop, if my seed hadn't taken root yet, it would very soon. Despite the fear it inspired in me, thinking of all the ways that this child and my mate could be hurt, I wanted to sire Ravena's first child—and any other she would have. My fingers tightened protectively over her stomach.

Ravena stiffened.

Looking up at her face, I found her awake, observing me with a troubled expression. Eyes locked with hers, I slowly rubbed my palm over her belly, making clear the nature of the thoughts coursing through my mind. Her eyelashes fluttered, and then she averted her eyes. I frowned, a sinking feeling settling in the pit of my stomach. Slipping a hand behind Ravena's nape, I nudged her to look back at me. As my gaze bore into hers, searching, the sense of unease grew exponentially.

"Have you changed your mind then, Ravena?" I asked, relieved that my voice had remained neutral.

She huffed in frustration and shook her head.

"Ravena," she muttered under her breath, saying her name as if in disgust.

Heedless of her nudity, she rolled off the bed and took a few steps toward the patio, stopping halfway there. I stared at her back, confused.

"I'm sorry. I meant Mercy," I said, baffled by her strange behavior.

She sighed again and turned to look at me, her shoulders drooping. I got the distinct impression that, somehow, I'd completely missed the point.

"I don't understand why it's such a big deal," I said, at a total loss. "If you prefer to be called Mercy, why go by Ravena most of the time?"

"Because she's not me!" she said in a cry from the heart.

I blinked, my mind frozen for a moment. What did that even mean? Did she suffer from some kind of dual personality disorder? Her face constricted with such sorrow it tore at my heart. I straightened and sat at the edge of the bed.

"This," Ravena said, waving at her body. "This is me, Mercy, with my Veredian markings and my sass. The carefree, independent woman who knows what she wants and goes for it, the side of me that you met on Venus Hive—the woman that I can be when we're alone together. Ravena is a lie and Mercy is her prisoner!"

She ran her hands over her horns, gripping the tips like one would fist their hair in despair.

"I swore to myself I wouldn't do this anymore. And yet, here I am, sinking deeper and deeper into the same pattern, pretending to be someone I'm not, following rules I don't believe in so that you won't be embarrassed or challenged, and curbing my personality to avoid creating conflicts and to fit in your world. I'm a free woman, but in practice, I'm your prisoner. I can't do anything or go anywhere without first asking your permission."

I shot to my feet, offended. "That's not true!" I interjected. "You are free to come and go as you please."

"It. Is. True!" she shouted. "Your fortress is my jail. I'm free to walk around—with guards shadowing me—as long as I remain within its gates. I can't take Dajia out for a ride unless you accompany me. If I want to leave the compound for any reason other than going to my brother's house, the guards turn me around because you've not authorized it. I can't even get on my own fucking shuttle. So don't tell me I'm not your prisoner!"

I blinked, digesting her words. Yes, the guards would request my consent first as they would for any man's wife or concubine; by Braxian culture, women had no business outside the gates on their own.

"I will speak to them," I said, curtly.

"And tell them what?" she asked, hardly pacified. "Let her go where she will but stick a tail on her ass? Have them turn her around if they disapprove of her destination?"

"You don't know Braxia, and it isn't safe!" I snapped, starting to feel irritated. Granted, the loss of privacy was unpleasant, but why couldn't she understand that it was necessary and for her own protection?

"Would you treat me the same if I were a man?" she asked, crossing her arms over her chest.

"No, I would not," I answered honestly, without flinching. "A female roaming around all alone is considered worthless and therefore free-for-all. But even males do not travel alone, Mercy. They will always have at least one person with them. You think I'd allow less for you? Am I extra protective because you are *my* woman? Yes. But even had there been no personal relationship between us, you would have been treated the same. This is Braxia."

She huffed and shook her head.

"What of my career that takes me halfway across the galaxy on a regular basis to meet clients and assess their needs directly on their terrain? Sometimes I need to leave with minimal notice and be gone for weeks. Are you going to oppose that?"

I didn't speak, but my eyes expressed all that I felt at that prospect. To my shame, since her arrival in my life, I'd come to realize open-mindedness was easy to grant to others, but when it came to loved ones —to my woman—I still clung to a backwards and controlling mentality. I wasn't as evolved as I'd believed.

"So that's my future, here?" she asked, bitterly. "That's the future of my child if it is the Goddess' will that she should be unfortunate enough to be born female? And what of a boy? Will he also be kept under lock and key to prevent him from being hunted by those who would ignore your laws protecting hybrids? If our children are born with markings," she said, waving at the spotted pattern on her arm, "will they also be prisoners of their own bodies?"

I'm losing her.

I'd been sensing it for a while, but never so acutely as in this instant. Getting her pregnant and taking her on tours to the clans' compounds had been but a few of the ways my subconscious had tried to bind her to me, to Braxia. But deep in my heart, I'd always known this world had too little to offer and too many constraints for one such as her. Still, it felt like my blood had turned to acid.

"You want to leave me," I said, making no effort to hide the pain crushing me from within.

She recoiled and stared at me, stunned for a moment, and then her face crumpled into that earlier expression of pure sorrow. Ravena hugged herself, one hand rubbing her upper arm, as if seeking comfort.

"No," she said with a small voice, shaking her head.

I approached her and carefully drew her into my embrace. To my relief, she didn't fight, snuggling against me instead. One arm around her waist, I held the back of her head, her cheek resting on my chest. Her naked body trembled slightly against me, making my heart ache.

"I'm falling in love with you, Ravik. But I don't think I can do this, live like this," she whispered.

"And I'm falling in love with you, too, Mercy," I said against her hair. "Give me time. Things are already radically changing on Braxia, in large part thanks to you. I can't lose you. I won't. We can make this work. I just need you to give me a bit more time. Can you do that for me? For us?"

She looked up at me, her obsidian eyes overly bright and glistening, then nodded with a small, trembling smile. I smiled back and caressed her face, letting my fingers run over the markings along her neck and shoulder line.

"Mercy *will* get to come out of the shadows and live in the light," I pledged. "On my honor, I will personally see to it."

Her smile broadened slightly. Drawing my face to hers, she pressed her forehead against mine. We held each other in silence for a moment. I knew this was only a reprieve, but I needed to figure out a way to make her happy because I couldn't lose her—even if that meant renouncing Braxia.

CHAPTER 15
MERCY

Two days after my meltdown, I sat sipping on Rehmannia tea. I always carried loads of it with me wherever I traveled in case my season kicked in. It kept my hormonal imbalance in check, and prevented my aggressive and overly emotional behavior. It had taken me by surprise as I had not expected to go into heat for another few days. My cheeks still burned thinking of how I had all but given a free porn show to Ravik's council. But worse, I'd made a spectacle of myself the morning after when he'd asked if I no longer wanted a child with him.

Every word spoken remained valid, but I hadn't meant to dump them all on him like that. Guilt gnawed at me for having put more pressure on him with all the problems he already juggled on a daily basis. At the same time, I felt relieved to have it all out in the open. I couldn't deny that Ravik was going out of his way to please me. That same day, he'd lifted all movement restrictions on me—not that they had ever been instated to begin with. He had not told the guards not to let me out of the fortress or board my shuttle; they'd simply applied to me the same rules they applied to Braxian females.

However, while I could come and go as I pleased, a bodyguard would be assigned to me whenever I wanted to leave the fortress. An annoying, but acceptable compromise... for now.

Held up by other duties, Gorav informed me he would be a little over an hour late to take me to my brother's house. In between hacking into his computer, I'd taken to performing some experiments in his lab, not only on my personal stuff, but also on some of the ideas he'd been looking into that had me intrigued. Although eager to get back to it, I didn't mind the delay. It gave me an excuse to visit Dajia who I hadn't taken out riding in a few days. Gulping down the rest of my tea, I left Ravik's Hall on my way to the racers' stables. I'd barely exited the building when a familiar voice at my back called out to me.

"Good day, Ravena," Keran said.

Surprised, I stopped and looked over my shoulder as Ravik's oldest son approached me. His uncanny resemblance to his father never ceased to amaze me. If not for Ravik's bulkier muscle mass, slightly greater height, and twenty extra years of maturity to his features, father and son could have passed for twins. They certainly did from a distance.

Keran raising a slightly amused eyebrow made me realize I'd been ogling him.

"Like what you see?" he asked in a teasing tone.

"Yes," I said, unfazed. "I get to see in the flesh what my man looked like twenty years ago."

He chuckled, his eyes lit with an undefinable glimmer. "Good answer."

"I'm glad you approve," I replied in the same teasing tone.

Although still smiling, his gaze took on a speculative edge. "Would you walk with me, Ravena?"

Uh oh. This should be interesting.

He led me in the opposite direction from the stables towards the training grounds behind the Hall where the guards were sparring. Formerly used as a dueling pit and gladiator arena before a much larger one was built outside the compound's gates, four rows of elevated benches surrounded it on three sides. The Magnar's box occupied the top row of the central set of benches, with enough room to accommodate a dozen dignitaries. Keran and I strolled along the thick, waist-high, stone fence which enclosed the combat area.

I shamelessly enjoyed the eye candy. How could I not with over fifty bare-chested men straining and grunting as they clashed? I'd have to be dead to remain impervious to such an extensive display of muscular man-flesh glistening with sweat. It didn't arouse me, but I definitely didn't mind the view.

This location had been a smart choice. We walked in plain view so everyone could see that nothing unbecoming was happening, but far enough from indiscreet ears to ensure privacy, further aided by the noise of battle.

"What did you wish to talk about?" I asked Keran as we casually strolled alongside the fence.

"First, I guess I should thank you for the unusual way in which you liberated us from a particularly boring council meeting," he said with a smirk.

My cheeks heated at the reminder he'd seen me in such a primal, sex-hungry state.

"This is not the kind of incident you remind people of," I said with barely veiled disapproval.

"Why?" he asked, his voice devoid of sarcasm or malice. "There's no shame in having sex. You've been here long enough now to have witnessed it happening pretty much anywhere and anytime."

"Yes. With whores," I said, in a hardening tone.

Keran's eyes lost their taunting glint as he sobered. "First, you are not a whore, Ravena. No one here thinks it. Second, it happens with wives and concubines as well. Since Father changed the law, he's also been tempering this type of behavior, which is why you see so little of it in our Hall. If you spent more time in other clans' compounds, you would see the reality that still is Braxia."

His words lifted a weight off my shoulders I hadn't realized I'd been carrying around. I didn't care what people thought of me, personally, but I didn't want Ravik's people to think his female was trash.

"In order for us to draw more of the right kind of international partners to Braxia, and maybe even open its doors to tourism, we need to start behaving with more decorum. This would offend many dignitaries," Keran continued.

I nodded. Many worlds considered Braxia too barbaric and primitive in its ways to want any kind of interaction with them. In the time of the Great Wars, Braxians made the perfect hired soldiers to crush their enemies and die on the field on their behalf. But once the Galactic Council helped bring peace in the Eastern Quadrant, all those planets discarded Braxia, deeming them unfit for polite company.

"However, your little incident has raised quite a few questions," Keran said, the mocking spark returning in his dark eyes.

I gave him a 'are you serious?' look that he would return to that topic.

He ignored it.

"For a moment, the others and I feared Father would kill you, or at least cause you severe damage. After all, no non-Braxian female has ever managed to take one of us, least of all one of my father's girth, without thorough preparation."

I gaped at him, disbelieving. "Are we seriously having a conversation about the size of your father's cock?"

"Yes, because it's thrown a question mark in my theory about you," Keran said.

The intensity in his gaze made me uncomfortable. This wasn't some random chitchat to see how much he could embarrass me, but a carefully planned conversation.

"Theory?" I asked, my pace slowing down as we reached the halfway point of the training grounds.

"Well, seeing how Guldans keep their females even more strictly under lock and key than we do, we know very little about you. After all, you're the first one any of us has ever met in the flesh. Thing is, Guldan females do not go into heat. Very few species do."

My back stiffened, and my pulse picked up while I tried to maintain a neutral expression.

"So I can't decide if your ability to take my father without Denax is a Guldan trait or a Veredian one," Keran said, matter-of-factly.

I hadn't meant to give myself away but stopping dead in my tracks did exactly that. All humor left Keran's face as he stopped as well and turned to face me. Hands clasped behind his back, he lifted his chin, his eyes daring me to deny it. I considered it, but that had been too precise an answer for him to have taken a wild guess and correctly landed on Veredian. Had Ravik told him?

"Who?" I asked, my voice filled with tension.

"No one," Keran said. "I just did the math." He snorted at my disbelieving stare. "Of the three species that go into heat, only one goes almost feral like you did. Public records state you are the daughter of Gruuk Vrok and Maheva Vrok, formerly Maheva Fein, who happens to be a Veredian now living on Xelix Prime."

I swallowed hard, but kept quiet.

"She also happens to be the mother of Aleina Fein, now Aleina Delphin, the Veredian Ambassador on Xelix Prime. The same Ambassador who happened to have signed the resource trade agreements with the Tuureans. That would make her your baby sister. I'd wondered how you had managed to get her to sign this agreement so quickly and why, according to the word on the street, the Tuurean leader was so protective of you, a Guldan and the daughter of the greatest Veredian slaver in history."

"Well," I said, noncommittally, "someone has done a thorough investigation."

"As Father said, a good ruler knows everything that goes on in his realm, who walks within it, and what their intentions are."

"And what are my intentions?" I asked, crossing my arms over my chest with defiance.

"Now *that* is the real question."

"No theories about that one?" I asked with a bit of sarcasm.

"Of course, I do." Keran took in a deep breath, his gaze roaming over our surroundings. "Braxia is a harsh world, but not without beauty. It's blossoming a bit more everyday into what it is meant to be," he said wistfully before his eyes settled back on me. "In your short time among us, you have considerably contributed to that beauty. Father loves you. You love him. And you're planning a child together, which you may already have conceived since you're not drinking moon juice."

"Any child we could have would not be a threat to your reign," I said, defensively.

Keran waved a dismissive hand. "By the time any child you may have comes of age, Father will have long stepped down in my favor. So my other theory about you is that you're debating whether or not to break his heart."

My lips parted in shock, and a chill ran down my spine. I rubbed my upper arm, frazzled.

"I see the longing way in which you look at the sky sometimes, and the troubled look in your eyes at last meal, asking yourself what you're doing here, on this alien planet with customs so foreign to you."

I bit my lip, bewildered by his ability to see through me so clearly.

"What you are doing, Ravena, is showing us that a strong, independent female isn't a threat to us, but a blessing for our people. You are opening our eyes to the riches we possess but are too blind to see. You are helping my father get his reforms adopted years ahead of time. So, the question is: are you going to finish what you started, or is freedom and the call of the stars too great?"

I turned away from him and resumed walking, my head jumbled.

"It's not that simple, Keran."

"Nothing worthwhile is ever simple," he conceded. "But Braxia needs a Dagna that will lead by example. Braxia needs you. *I* need you."

I recoiled at those words. "What?"

"My father would abdicate his throne for you. I need him to continue to rule for a few more years," Keran said.

I looked at him, slightly confused. "Why? Usually, the heirs are dying to get their hands on power."

He chuckled. "No one is eager to deal with the headache of Braxia," he said, mockingly, although his words held a ring of truth. "You made me realize how little we know of the way other worlds are run and why it works. We've been too stuck in our ways. I intend to travel a lot over the upcoming years, as a Braxian Ambassador, to learn how the rest of the universe lives and functions, and to forge new alliances before my ascension. If my father steps down now, I will be bound to remain here."

"Goddess... You don't want to rule," I whispered at the sudden realization.

He shrugged. "I do not seek the trappings of power, but I love Braxia and have great plans for her that I can only accomplish as the Magnar. So yes, I do. Just not now."

His com beeped. Pulling it out of his pocket, he glanced at the display screen and slightly frowned.

"I'm afraid I must depart," Keran said. "Thanks for walking with me."

"I can see now why your father is so proud of you."

His harsh face softened with an affectionate smile as he thought of his father.

"As am I of him. Looking forward to seeing those Veredian markings, Dagna," Keran said mockingly.

Before I could answer, he struck his fist to his chest and then walked away. Damn the man; truly his father's son.

Once we arrived at Varrek's house, I spent what remained of the morning hacking a new batch of his files, allowing myself to get distracted by more of my brother's thwarted ex-lover's clingy messages. I shouldn't be reading this, least of all for entertainment, but it was just too juicy to pass up. And yet, part of me felt sorry for that man. Rik's obsessive love had clearly turned off my brother and driven him away, but he didn't seem to understand that. His relentless pursuit had only made matters worse as each message escalated in desperation. Guldan's despised weakness. How could he not see he was ruining things for himself? This last message had broken my heart.

"My dearest Varrek,

I have finally accepted that it is over, and that your affection for me has faded. No more will you hear pleas from me to resume the relationship that had taken me to the halls of the Goddess herself. I miss working with you, our conversations on science, and our revolutionary research. You are the most brilliant mind of our times, and I will never find another collaborator that can challenge me and push the boundaries the way only you can. Please, allow me to return to your side to pursue our work.

Your most loyal friend,

Rik"

How terrible it must have felt to have been so hungry for someone's presence as to resort to such manipulations to be with them again? I didn't doubt he had loved working with my brother. *I* would have given anything for a chance to work with such a genius, but even I could read between the lines that he had still hoped to rekindle their relationship.

With a sigh, I rubbed my eyes, then stretched as I stood from my chair. Gorav would be calling lunch break in less than thirty minutes, and I wanted to get the lab ready to work there in the afternoon. I'd brought some fresh plant samples on which I wanted to attempt some of the research Varrek had been performing. I'd concluded that Varrek's clients list wasn't on his computer, having already gone through all of the most likely folders. Therefore, I no longer plowed through the files with zealous determination but paced myself, alternating with more exciting tasks in between.

As I sorted the samples and pulled out the necessary equipment, a swishing sound made me look up. Although it sounded like a door opening, it had come from the back, left corner of the room, behind one of the cold storages. Before I could react, the Guldan Ambassador Lorik Zorak stepped out from the corner, and shot me with the dart gun in his hand.

I never got a chance to make a sound, instant numbness spreading from the sting at the base of my neck. I collapsed to the side, my vision blurring as he approached me with a cruel glint in his green eyes. Battling to remain conscious, I watched helplessly as he picked me up and carried me to the hidden lift my advanced scanners had never detected in the corner. As darkness engulfed me, the platform carried us into the bowels of the house.

~

My mouth felt dry and full of sand. I could think clearly, but my naked body tingled with dizziness from the lingering effects of the drug. I lay on my stomach on what appeared to be a short, spanking bench. Head dangling over the edge, arms folded and hands shackled by my sides, my feet rested on the floor, shackled as well at the base of the bench. I strained my ears in search of any presence in the room before moving, wishing to delay the time before my kidnapper realized I had regained consciousness. Silence reigned in the room but for the soft whistle of the ventilation system.

My eyes fluttered open. Grid-like, dark metal plates covered the floor. Turning my head to the side, I counted at least four, empty detention cells, although I suspected there were more beyond my line of sight. Various devices sat atop a long counter running the length of the wall in front of me. The right side of the room stood empty, but for a large, reinforced door. I didn't want to imagine what purpose this room had served for my brother. In spite of everything, he'd always provided his slaves with comfortable accommodations. This looked like a place you'd cage animals.

My hands were too big to slip out of the shackles, but I pulled on them anyway, trying to give my palms direct contact with the hard metal. I tried to push my psi power into the metal, hoping to infect it with an unravel command that would have the shackles crumbling within seconds. To my dismay, I didn't find a single nanite within to carry out my command. Pressing my palms to the side of the wooden bench, my heart sank at finding no nanites there either—not that I'd really expected any in that material.

Helpless, I struggled in vain against my restraints. The Goddess only knew how long I'd been unconscious. It could have been minutes or hours. Had Gorav noticed my disappearance? Had the Ambassador gotten him, too? I hadn't seen Gorav in the cells within my line of sight. But then, Lorik probably wouldn't have been able to carry such a massive Braxian on his own.

Oh Goddess, please let him be safe.

Over the past six weeks, I'd grown quite fond of Anton's youngest brother. I'd be devastated if anything had happened to him.

"Awake at last."

I yelped in surprise at hearing Lorik's voice behind me. Had he been in the room this whole time? I hadn't heard any door opening. Twisting my neck, I tried to look at him over my shoulder but he remained out of sight. My heart pounded into my throat when the sound of his footsteps stopped right behind me. Mind racing, I considered asking him what he wanted from me. Although I could think of at least a couple of reasons—like using me against Ravik or for my inheritance—I decided to keep my mouth shut until I had a better sense of his state of mind. I was in far too vulnerable a position to alienate him with no idea if any rescue was on the way.

His warm, oddly soft hand caressing my left butt cheek in a slow circle, startled me. I didn't want to think what this touch might lead to next. Whatever his intentions, he wouldn't kill me; I was too valuable alive. But that didn't mean he wouldn't entertain himself with me.

"You've caused a lot of people a lot of problems, Ravena Vrok. Derailed our plans of taking over this pathetic planet. Betrayed your own people for those savages."

With each word, his voice gradually lowered into a whisper—ominous and filled with growing anger. Lorik removing his hand from my ass had my stomach knotting with anxiety and my breath growing short. Seconds later, a whistling sound followed by a loud slapping sound echoed through the room. I cried out as pain exploded on my rear where he'd struck me with what I could only assume to be a wooden paddle.

"Betrayed your own brother."

Another blow followed the whistling sound, and a wave of agony radiate along my spine and down my legs.

"Captured him to be tortured."

WHACK!

"Abandoned him to be executed."

WHACK!

"You killed Varrek, you cunt!" Lorik yelled before raining blows on my ass and my legs.

Each strike resonated along my spine, making my stomach roil and churn. I felt like I was being flayed, the skin being ripped right off my flesh every time the paddle landed on me.

Goddess, he's going to kill me!

In a flash of lucidity before I lost consciousness again, I realized who he was.

Rik.

~

I couldn't tell which had brought me back out of the blessed darkness that had sheltered me from my tormentor; the tortured moans that rose from my throat in a constant flow or the excruciating pain from my waist down. I was parched, my throat raw from having screamed so much. The shackles binding me to the bench were the only reason I hadn't collapsed to the floor.

"Welcome back, Ravena," Lorik said, his voice almost cordial.

My head jerked up, and I shuddered at finding him seated nonchalantly in a chair a couple of meters in front of me. Fear coursed through me as his green eyes bore into mine, his fingers absentmindedly caressing the paddle resting on his lap. Like Doruk, Lorik was a very attractive man with his brown horns, long and curly dark-brown hair, a clean-shaven square jaw, and full lips. Surprisingly, the right side of his face didn't bear the tribal tattoos Guldans who shaved usually wore. But where Doruk's beauty had been marred by his underlying malice, Lorik's madness muddled his. He'd been so calm, quiet, and controlled that first night in Ravik's Hall. Who could have guessed this love-sick stalker lurked beneath the polished veneer?

"Under normal circumstances, I would beat you to death for what you've done. I'd break every single one of your bones and get off on your screams," Lorik said, his tone conversational. "But I have too many other purposes for you. Aside from ruining our plans, you've pissed off the wrong people who have requested the right to teach you proper respect. Those Braxian savages you've betrayed your people for don't like people talking back to them. And you, my dear, have quite a mouth on you."

He lifted the paddle and spun the handle. I stared in morbid fascination at the tool that had inflicted such horrible pain on me. That vermin, Hagan, had to be the person I'd pissed off. If he beat me with that paddle, he'd kill me. Deep-rooted hatred for me had burned in his eyes after I'd publicly humiliated him during last meal.

Paddle firmly in hand, Lorik rose to his feet and approached me. My stomach sank and my entire body stiffened, causing the throbbing pain in my abused flesh to flare up.

"You bruise beautifully, Ravena," Lorik said, his soft hand caressing my ass.

I swallowed a whimper as his touch, although gentle, hurt horribly.

"You have no idea how badly I want to beat you again."

His fingers dug into my left butt cheek, squeezing it savagely. I screamed in agony, the pain radiating up my back and down my right leg.

"Such a pretty scream," he whispered, releasing his brutal hold on me.

My eyes pricked, but I fought back the tears and the sob that wanted to rise from my throat. I'd never felt so weak, so helpless… so hopeless.

"But I won't beat you. At least, not for a while." His hand resumed caressing me, but thankfully moved away from the battered area, sliding up my back as he circled around the bench. He stopped next to my face and crouched so that we'd be eye to eye. His green eyes were devoid of emotion as he studied my face for a moment before peering up at my horns. "They're identical to his," Lorik said, his fingers tracing the patterns on my horns. "He loved when I held on to his horns when he fucked me. I never got to fuck him. He didn't take cock, only gave it. Before him, I'd never bottomed for anyone. But for Varrek…"

An odd mixture of wistfulness, longing, passion, and madness burned in his eyes. He stared at me, unseeing, his hand fisted around my horn and his thumb caressing the pattern. Heart pounding, I eyed him warily as he refocused on me. Lorik suddenly leaned forward, drawing my face towards him by my horn. Rubbing his cheek against mine, he inhaled deeply, and then pressed his lips to my ear.

"You smell like him, except for that stinky perfume you wear. Properly washed and with a touch of his Cologne, you'll smell *exactly* like him."

My eyes widened in horror. Surely, he didn't think…?

Lorik pulled away from me, his face inches from mine. "I have very nice, colored Xelixian lenses for your eyes; forest-green like Varrek's. After we're married, we'll have to make some modifications to your face. Some nice chevron-shaped bone implants in your forehead to recreate his crihnin. Did you know that he hated it? The silly man. His crihnin was as beautiful as everything else about him," Lorik said, caressing my forehead with his knuckles, the same wistful look on his face. "I've successfully completed the experimental phase of a new skin pigment. It's going to hurt a bit, but after a few injections, you will permanently have his beautiful silver color. You're going to be a masterpiece," he said, cupping my face in his hands before crushing my lips with a short, but brutal kiss.

"You're insane," I whispered, my mind refusing to accept he'd meant those words.

Lorik's expression went blank for a second, and then his features contorted with anger. He backhanded me with such violence, I feared my neck would break. Blood exploded from my mouth, and my teeth rattled in my head.

Dazed, my head hung down at the edge of the short spanking bench. Lorik's hand closed around my long braid and yanked back on it, forcing me to look at him. His features twisted in an angry grimace, his eyes promised a world of hurt.

"I am not insane, you cunt!" he spat. "But I can be. Disrespect me again, and you'll be reminded that Guldans know how to put whores in their place even better than Braxians."

Ignoring the throbbing on the right side of my face, I pressed my lips together to keep my stupid tongue from getting me into any more trouble.

"Here's what is going to happen," Lorik said, in a voice sharp enough to cut steel. "My Braxian partner is going to pay you a visit to settle that score with you; twenty-five lashes and the night in a cage."

I cast a horrified sideways glance at the empty animal cages.

"Oh no, sweetheart. Not those ones. Something a little more snug." The cruelty of the smile stretching his lips had my stomach in knots. "In the morning, fifteen Braxians will come say hello. They hope to bring along that animal you've been fucking, but he's a hard one to catch. Failing that, they'll prepare him a nice video of them making an intimate acquaintance with that cunt of yours for the day he does fall into their hands."

My body shook with an irrepressible trembling, each tremor sending new waves of agony along my tortured flesh.

"Now, now," Lorik said. His grip loosened on my braid, and his fingers gently massaged the sting in my scalp. "There's no need for this. I won't let them hurt you or damage you. Well... at least, not permanently," he amended. "By this time tomorrow afternoon, you and I will be on our way back to Guldar to celebrate our wedding. As you can guess, I'm not a fan of pussies. So I'll only fuck yours to impregnate you. The sooner you give me a couple of heirs to secure the Vrok estate for my bloodline, the sooner we'll both be free of such unpleasantness." The mad glint flashed through his eyes. "Your ass though... your ass I will fuck often, once we've fixed your appearance. Through you, I'll finally get to fuck my Varrek."

Leaning in again, Lorik kissed my lips with something akin to tenderness. He rose from his crouching position and walked away from me, towards the counter ahead. Too many emotions ran through me, mixed with lancing pain, preventing me from forming a rational plan. That man was stark, raving mad. If I didn't find a way to escape before the Fifteen arrived, I'd be dead or broken. And I didn't even want to think about what that would do to Ravik.

Oh Goddess, Ravik!

If they caught him, they would give him a slow, painful death.

Although I knew it to be hopeless, I tried to push my power into the metal shackles around my wrists again, in vain. My head jerked up as Lorik turned around and came back towards me, a large knife in his hand. Panicked, I pulled on my restraints, the hard edges scraping the skin from my wrists. I breathed loud and fast as he closed the distance.

"Relax, stupid female," Lorik snapped. "I already told you I'm not going to harm you."

On the verge of hyperventilating, I twisted my neck over my shoulder in a futile attempt to see what he intended to do with that blade. He picked up my braid and yanked my head back. For a split second, I thought he would slit my throat. Instead of the terror I'd expected, a cool blanket of peace and acceptance descended on me. Better death than what he'd planned for me. If my advanced scanners had failed to detect the hidden lift and the presence of an entire underground floor, Ravik and his men would never find me.

And then I felt pressure on my hair as the blade sawed through my braid.

"NOOOO!" I screamed.

With a soft snick, the pull on my scalp relented, and my head fell forward again, the short stump of my remaining braid brushing against my shoulder. Facing the metal plating on the floor, from the corner of my eyes, I watched Lorik walk back towards the counter. Something snapped inside of me at the sight of his hand casually holding my severed braid, its long tail dragging on the floor.

I wailed like my soul had been torn right out of me. What his beating hadn't achieved, losing the one symbol of my Veredian heritage that I'd never had to hide, even as Ravena, broke me. Like all my Sisters, I'd grown my hair since birth. Its purpose as a weapon had always been secondary. The spiritual beliefs of the Veredians dictated that the longer the hair, the stronger its roots, which symbolized the bond that tied all Veredians, the greater the wisdom of the bearer, and the more powerful their psionic ability.

The dam broke as I bawled with heart-wrenching sobs. I'd always considered myself a strong female, but I had nothing left. All the sorrows of my life came crashing down; the little girl I'd been who'd pined for a mother she wouldn't meet for decades, my lifetime of hiding in plain sight, the death of my father, the heartbreaking choice between my only brother and my Sisters, his untimely death by my fault, and my Ravik…

"Females… Always so much drama," Lorik mumbled with disgust.

Tears flowed freely down my cheeks, but I'd gone numb inside. I didn't react when Lorik came back to me, hands covered with surgical gloves. He loosened the knots of my remaining braid, then massaged some cream from a small container into my hair. A cold tingle spread through my scalp. His task done, he pinned my hair in a bun on top of my head. Taking a couple of steps back he admired his work with obvious satisfaction.

"You have very nice hair. It's responding well to the treatment," Lorik said, looking pleased. "We'll have it styled properly on our way back to Guldar. For now, I suggest you rest. I'm afraid tonight and tomorrow morning are not going to be much fun. Here, let me fix this for you," he said.

Lorik picked up a cushioned object from the counter and brought it over. Careful, almost gentle, he lifted my head and placed the headrest attachment to the spanking bench.

"There you go," he said, resting my head on the attachment, relieving the strain from my neck.

With one finger, he wiped the tears that continued to flow silently from my eyes, then caressed my hair almost reverently.

"Rest, my love. Soon it will be over."

His hand fell away from my face as he turned to leave, dragging with it a lock of my hair. It dangled in front of my eyes, its raven color having already paled to a light-grey which I knew would soon become the same silver-white my brother's had been.

CHAPTER 16
RAVIK

Walking back to my hoverbike, arms laden with gifts for Mercy, I glared at Tagar and Nowik. They made no effort to hide their amusement as I puzzled on how this would all fit in the storage compartment. The bastards had known the Clan Podek wives would have presents when they'd insisted earlier we travel by shuttle but omitted to specify the reason. I didn't care much for being cooped up in the small vessel, especially over such a short distance. Like my woman, I loved speed and never missed an opportunity to ride my bike.

Once again, I regretted not insisting that Ravena... Mercy, come with me on this clan visit. She'd become something of a role model for Braxian females, grateful for her helping them finally get their place in the sun and the recognition they deserved. But more than that, they were thankful for her bringing hope back to so many of the more desperate clans. They already considered her their Dagna, and an increasing number of clansmen had begun thinking of her on those terms as well. Two days ago, I would have been elated; now, not so much.

I had planned on asking her to become my wife at the next quarterly fair. After that difficult conversation, I feared she would think it a ploy to shackle her further to me, to Braxia. How could I get her to see that she was meant for this world? She'd been a free spirit her whole life, used to taking off on a whim to whatever destination called to her soul. As much as it hurt me to admit it, she'd fared just fine without my protection all these years. And, as much as I loved Braxia, no one would think of kidnapping its Dagna for ransom. Greater empires held far more appeal for pirates.

I couldn't leave Braxia right now, and my heir wasn't ready to take over my responsibilities. I loved Mercy and would do anything within my power to keep her happy. I'd been so busy trying to get everyone to move away from the old ways to realize that I, too, still clung to some of them. After our argument, I'd actually looked into foreign emperors and rulers. Many had spouses with political or other professional careers of their own which frequently took them off-world without their partner. That it had never been done on Braxia didn't mean it couldn't start now. I hated the thought of parting with my woman for any length of time. But if that was what it took not to lose her, I'd make the compromise.

Nowik finally took pity on me and relieved me of some of the gifts, which he tucked into his own storage compartment. We mounted our respective hoverbikes and, with me in the lead, we headed back to my fortress. Security protocols demanded that one of my bodyguards take the lead and the other the rear, with me in the middle, but we'd significantly relaxed some of these rules, especially now that things had been calming down, and the looming threat of civil unrest had abated.

The prospect of new trade opportunities, the surge of employment with so many of the men going back to work with a focus on new resources, had the clansmen in high spirits. A lot of the men struggled with the idea that their females had to work to help bring income to the household. It was their responsibility as men to be the providers. But, in their enthusiasm, the females had been reminding their consorts that to them, it was nothing more than pursuing the hobbies they already occupied their time with. And that, now, they'd be able to do bigger and better things thanks to the men providing them with more quality resources instead of them scraping for leftovers.

Clever females.

Lost in thoughts of Mercy, I gave myself over to the pleasure of the speed and the wind lashing at my face. As we approached Wincal Ridge, a spark flashed on the side of my bike with a clanking sound, startling me. I couldn't see anything that could have possibly caused a rock or some other hard debris to fly into the path of my hoverbike; especially not at that angle. When the second clank and spark struck my bike, close to the handles, I finally realized someone was shooting at me.

Heart pounding, I signaled for my men to speed up. We needed to get to safety but were already too far to turn back. I couldn't see any enemy, and my armband didn't detect anyone despite scanning on multiple frequencies. Yet, our foes were lurking in the shadows, launching their cowardly attack against us. Ravena had warned me that if the Guldans came back, they would have modified their cloaking shields from the previous setting to avoid detection.

Leaning forward on my hoverbike in a vain attempt to make myself smaller, I tapped my com.

"Magnar?" Krygor answered.

Before I could speak a word, something sharp embedded itself in my leg, the stinging sensation quickly replaced by a rapidly spreading numbness.

"We're under attack," I said, my words already slurring. "Protect Mercy and Keran."

"Protect who? Where are you?" Krygor shouted, his footsteps resonating through the com as he started running.

"Raven—"

Two more darts embedded themselves in my flesh: one in my neck, the other in my arm. My jaw immediately felt slack, and my vision blurred. The vague thought that I should slow down to lessen the impact when I fell crossed my mind. From the crashing sounds behind me, I knew my bodyguards had preceded me into unconsciousness. Seconds later, I joined them.

~

"Why isn't he awake yet?" a vaguely familiar voice asked with irritation.

"Relax, Braxian," a voice with a subtle Guldan accent said. "The shot takes a couple of minutes to neutralize the drug in his system, and then he'll need a couple more minutes to be functional."

The Braxian harrumphed, clearly displeased.

Throat dry, head pounding, I felt like I had the mother of all hangovers. Except, no revelry had put me in this state. Trying to remain inconspicuous, I quickly assessed my situation. My body felt somewhat battered, not from any beating but likely from the fall off my hoverbike.

At least, for now.

I was naked, kneeling on some kind of contraption, my face resting in the opening of a hollow headrest. My abductors had not strapped me to it. However, shackles and chains restrained my arms and legs, and a thick metal collar hung a little loose around my neck. The numbness in my limbs quickly faded and my mind cleared.

Mercy...

I prayed she was safe, that Gorav had protected her, and that Krygor had gotten to them in time. Yet a queasy feeling in the pit of my stomach, that had nothing to do with the aftermath of the drug, told me she wasn't.

My eyes opened to the sight of gridded, metal flooring, like those found at the back of a butcher's shop. Ideal to drain the blood of the slaughtered beasts: in this case, me. A hand suddenly fisted my hair and yanked back hard, forcing me to look up at a most hated face.

"Well, well, look who's awake at last," Hagan said, his dark-brown, almost black, eyes burning with malice. "I've waited a long time for this, you son of a krillik. I've waited a long fucking time."

I saw his fist come at my face as if in slow motion. With a loud clank, the chains on my shackles stopped my attempt to block the blow. It connected solidly with my face. Despite the sting, it barely fazed me.

Hagan had never amounted to much as a warrior. But he had me at his mercy. If a single blow from the weak bastard didn't bother me, the multiple ones he would definitely rain down on me would eventually take their toll. I bit back the snarky remark that burned my tongue. There was no point in further provoking his ire until I had figured out a plan to get myself out of this mess. I could only hope that Tagar and Nowik were okay.

"Your reign is over, *Magnar* Ravik," Hagan said, stating my title with contempt. "You never learned. And now you will die with the same shame and disgrace that you brought to your bloodline so many years ago."

My stomach dropped, and my back stiffened. The unspoken fear coursing through me must have shown on my face as Hagan's twisted smile broadened.

"Oh yeah," Hagan said with evil glee. "We've prepared a very special farewell celebration for you. And you will enjoy the front row seat."

Up until now, standing in front of me, Hagan had blocked my view of the room. Still holding my head up by the hair, the bastard took a step to the side, freeing my line of sight.

An animalistic roar rose from my throat as blind rage erupted through me at the horrible vision before me. I fought and strained against my restraints in a futile attempt to go to my woman. Shackled to a spanking bench sitting sideways in front of me so that I could see her profile, they had turned her face towards me and strapped her head to the headrest. She couldn't hide her pain from me, be it now or later when they would abuse her to hurt me. Her beautiful, long black hair had been desecrated. But what had me going feral were the large, black, purple, and yellow bruises covering her behind and the back of her thighs.

Hagan burst out laughing at my vain efforts. And yet, despite my seething rage, Mercy's eyes locking with mine brought me back to reason. With a subtle shake of her head, probably due in part to the strap holding her in place, she reminded me not to feed our enemy with my helpless anger.

My blood still boiling with fury, I forced a calm expression on my face but didn't hide the hatred in my eyes, as I turned to look at Hagan.

"When I get free, I will destroy you. Even Death will beg me to put an end to your agony."

His smile faltered, a glimmer of fear flashing through his eyes.

Coward.

Lifting his chin with bravado, but less confidence than moments before, Hagan shoved my head down as he released my hair. I stiffened my neck, keeping my head high and my defiant stare trained on him.

"You will *not* get free, Xeldar," Hagan said, thinking to insult me by using only my last name as one would for someone of inferior status. "After your death, your sons will step down or face challenges. The old order will be restored."

Movement at the edge of my vision drew my gaze to another presence.

I snorted. "Restored with Ambassador Zorak as your new master? He would make you his bitch."

Hagan backhanded me. The taste of iron filled my mouth. I laughed and licked the blood beading at the corner of my lips. It angered Hagan further as he struggled to find an appropriate comeback.

"Lorik has no interest in Braxia. He just wants that cunt," Hagan said, pointing a finger at Mercy. "But right now, it's time for *me* to make *her* my bitch. She will learn to respect her betters."

Looking over my shoulder, my stomach dropped, and cold sweat trickled down my back as Hagan reached for something on the large counter behind me. I could already guess what it would be, his comment on respect having given it away. The urge to fight against my restraints and plead for him not to harm her died in my throat as my eyes connected with Mercy's. The resolve within put me to shame.

"Be strong," she mouthed silently. "For me. For us."

But how? How could I be when the female who held my heart would be beaten bloody as I watched helplessly? And yet, for her, I would manage, somehow.

Teeth clenched, hands fisted, I held her gaze and silently mouthed back to her, "I love you."

Her eyes misted, and a watery smile stretched her lips. I tried to focus on the emotion they conveyed and not the swelling of her cheek where she'd been struck, or her split bottom lip where blood had coagulated.

"Let's see how proud you are now, little whore," Hagan said.

From the corner of my eyes, I saw him flick his wrist, unfolding the long whip in his hand. Refusing to look away from my woman, I swallowed hard and poured all the depth of my emotions for her into my gaze, lending her what strength I could.

The whip whistled, striking her back with a snapping sound. Mercy's body tensed, her eyes closing for a second as she winced in pain. Reopening them, she sought mine again, bracing for the second blow.

"That's for talking back to a man," Hagan said, striking again. "That's for calling me stupid." Another hit. "That's for humiliating me in public."

By the fifth lash, silent tears had begun trickling down her cheek. My stomach churned and roiled, each strike like so much acid in my veins. By the seventh lick, I'd tuned out Hagan's rambling. Despite her best efforts, pained whimpers escaped her each time the ropy leather made contact with her bare back, but especially on her already bruised legs. Bile rose in my throat when the thirteenth blow struck her. As per the old law, half the twenty-five lashings had to draw blood. Hagan would no longer hold back.

This time, I couldn't help glancing towards him. The maniacal hatred in his eyes filled me with dread as he brought down the whip with brute force. My heart skipped a beat as Mercy's body jerked over the spanking bench, a cry of agony tearing from her throat. Shaken with spasms, her eyes rolled in her head as she battled to retain consciousness.

Don't, my love. Don't fight it. Let go.

That way, even if for a short while, she wouldn't feel the pain.

"CAREFUL!" Lorik shouted, aiming a blaster at Hagan's face. "I have given you leave to punish her, not kill her. You will control yourself or forfeit the remaining lashes."

Hagan bared his teeth at him. For a desperate moment, I hoped he would push the Guldan into killing him, but my nemesis was too much of a coward to press his luck. With his superior strength, he could have easily overtaken Lorik. Why did he submit to him, anyway? Why not kill the Guldan and just do as he pleased with Mercy and me?

Although reluctant, Hagan obeyed, pulling back his blows. Still, each one broke skin, wresting a tortured cry from my woman, and stabbing at my heart. Rivulets of blood trickled down her sides. At last, thank the Ancestors, Mercy fainted from the pain with four lashes remaining. Hagan wanted to wait until she came back around. But Lorik, clearly eager to be done with this, told him to finish or relinquish.

"You've completed your punishment, now leave us," Lorik said.

Hagan stared at Mercy's abused body with obvious satisfaction, if not regret that it was already over.

"No. I still owe him his punishment," he said, pointing at me with his chin.

Lorik rolled his eyes in exasperation. "Make it quick."

I didn't care about a whipping. As a warrior, I'd been trained to endure extreme pain. But it was the Guldan preparing to inject Mercy with a strange syringe that had me worried.

"What are you doing to her?" I demanded.

Lorik paused and looked at me. "You mean this?" he asked, showing me the syringe.

"Oh, I'll tell him," Hagan said with a sadistic smile, absentmindedly spinning the handle of the whip. "Remember when I said you never learn? The Guldan says your female is three weeks pregnant. Since we can't wait for that abomination to be born to bash its head in at the second half of the party tomorrow, the contents of this syringe will flush it out."

"Sorry, but I can't have another man sire my future wife's heir," Lorik said before plunging the needle in her neck. "It's better like this. The pain from the abortion will mix with the one from the punishment. So, technically, she won't feel it."

My blood ran hot, and then immediately cold. Something broke inside of me.

I did this. I did this to her. To them.

When the first blow fell on my back, it didn't register. Or the second, or the third… I was numb, dead to the world. Mercy remained unconscious through my punishment and through the Guldan gently cleaning her wounds. When the pain from my lashings finally started seeping in, I welcomed it, embraced it—I deserved it.

My instincts had warned me to let her go. Keran had told me not to impregnate her. The Council had cautioned me about potential backlash. But I had wanted to bind her to me, to see her stomach swell with my child, to hold our offspring to my chest, and lift my baby high up for the world to see that never again would Ravik Xeldar fail the fruit of his loin. That I, too, had the courage of Krygor Aldriss to stand and defend my hybrid child.

I used her for my guilty conscience's need to make amends for Lissy and Goliath.

I gave myself over to Hagan's lashings. Although he didn't hold back, tearing my skin to shreds, I wished he'd strike even harder to cleanse me of my crimes, of my failure towards both of my hybrid offspring, and their foreign mothers I had loved.

"Are you fucking kidding me?" Lorik hissed, staring disbelieving at Mercy's unconscious form.

Intrigued, Hagan turned towards the Guldan. "What is it?"

Lorik took on a neutral expression. "You've done way more damage than you were entitled to. You've permanently scarred my woman."

He's deflecting.

That wasn't the reason he'd cussed. My eyes flicked to his hand pressing on Ravena's forearm before locking with his. He narrowed them at me.

Her Veredian markings! Her prosthetics must have been damaged by the lashing.

"Leave, now," Lorik said to Hagan in a tone that brooked no argument.

"But…"

"I fucking said LEAVE NOW!" Lorik yelled, pointing his blaster at Hagan again. "You've overstayed your welcome. I only tolerate your presence because a Guldan always honors his word. You've already got him half-dead. Either finish him or leave."

Hagan's broad nose twitched, a telltale sign that he felt offended or humiliated. Resentment burned in his eyes as he tossed the whip at my head. I turned just in time for it to strike my cheek before falling to the floor.

"See you at ten in the morning, *Magnar*," Hagan said with malice. "Rest your eyes well, for tomorrow, we're going to give you quite the show."

Pretending to be holding on to a pair of hips, he thrust his hips forward a few times. I knew all too well what it implied. With a final glare towards Lorik, he headed for the door.

"His guards are crawling all over the top floor," Lorik said. "See that you take the secret exit. Enter the same way in the morning. I will not delay the hour of my departure, so be on time."

Dismissing him, Lorik returned his focus to Mercy's wounds. With a hiss, Hagan turned around and left. As soon as he was gone, the Guldan went to the counter and rummaged through one of the cupboards above it from whence he retrieved a small bottle. It resembled the solvent Mercy used to loosen and remove her prosthetics. Our captor used it on her arms, nape, and legs, the disguise all but falling off on its own.

Dull at first, thanks to the mental numbness I'd been in, the lancing pain from my lacerated back gradually came to the forefront as I watched Lorik tend my woman.

"Full of secrets aren't you," Lorik whispered to a still unconscious Mercy. "If I'd known, I wouldn't have given you that shot. As the first ever Guldan-Braxian-Veredian hybrid, that baby would have been worth a fortune."

Daggers stabbed at my heart at the thought of our child. My only consolation was that Mercy didn't know of its existence and hopefully wouldn't realize what was happening because of her other injuries.

"He will betray you," I said, my voice as dead as I felt inside. "After they've defiled her in the morning, he will kill both you and me. And then, Hagan will return to the Council with your remains, claiming he stopped a would-be invader, unfortunately too late to save me, or her."

Lorik snorted. "Oh yes, he will try. But I will be ready for him. *This* changes everything," he said. His fingers caressing Mercy's Veredian markings made me want to break them off for touching my woman. "She's too valuable now to let those savages have at her."

Hope soared in my heart. If he absconded with her, at least she would survive. Whether or not I made it out alive, my close council, Anton, and the Tuureans would see to setting her free.

Mercy stirred with a pained moan as Lorik applied the last of the healing salve on her back and legs. He released the strap that had maintained her head facing me, then walked out of the room. Mercy's eyelids fluttered, her face grimacing with pain. Her bloodshot eyes settled on me. Despite the agony she was in, my woman's eyes filled with sorrow for me as she took in the damage Hagan had inflicted. Even though she couldn't see my back, the welts and torn skin on my arms, and the blood pooling at my feet, revealed everything.

She deserved so much better than me. I'd failed to protect her and sat here, helpless, while that twice damned son of a krillik beat her bloody. And still, she placed my pain above her own.

"It's okay, my love. I'm okay," I said, trying to hide the pain and shame from my voice. "Stay strong. They may currently have the upper hand, but we are not defeated yet. The battle is far from over."

Empty words in our current situation, but I meant every single one. A shaky smile stretched her lips, and she gave her assent with a subtle nod.

Lorik walking back in kept me from speaking further. He carried what I wrongly assumed to be a long white box until he walked past me, and I recognized it as a compacted inflatable mattress. He entered the cage next to the one at my back, and I winced while turning my head to look at him over my shoulder. He activated the inflate button and then dropped the foam-like box onto the floor. In seconds, it began to swell and expand, taking the shape of a thick and comfortable mattress. Warriors often used them on campaigns as they were as easy to unpack as they were to repack, took little storage space, and required little maintenance.

As Lorik strolled back towards my woman, I felt a begrudging sense of gratitude towards him that he would at least grant her that little comfort, and not put her in the Jenuvian Cage at the back of the room. Built too narrow and too short to allow the victim to stand or lie down, causing excruciating pain during long periods of incarceration, punished females used to spend many hours in them following a whipping like the one Mercy had received. I had no doubt her being Veredian brought about this sudden clemency.

Looming over Mercy, Lorik gently took her chin and forced her to look at him.

"What power do you have?" he asked.

Mercy blinked at him, her eyes glazing over.

"I asked you a question, female," Lorik said, his tone hardening. "What psi ability do you have?"

"N… None," she whispered. "Kor… Korlethean fathers give psi powers. My fa… father was Guldan."

My heart skipped a beat at her lie. It was clever. As the only Guldan-Veredian hybrid—as far as anyone knew—she could claim whatever she wanted without anyone being able to contradict her. However, that could backfire. Without psionic powers, although still worth a fortune, she wasn't anywhere near as valuable.

Lorik narrowed his eyes at her, torn between suspicion, disappointment and, oddly, relief.

"How do I know you're not lying?" he asked.

Mercy's sad laughter turned into a wince of pain. "W… Would I still be sha… shackled if I could free my… myself?"

"Fair point," he said. "I'm still not convinced you don't have any powers, but as long as you can't free yourself, we can get you gloves later. And if what you say is true, we'll just have to find you a Korlethean. For now, I'm not taking chances." He pulled a hypospray from his pocket. "Consider it a blessing. You get to sleep through the pain."

Lorik injected Mercy in the neck and freed her from the shackles only once she lost consciousness. Using great care not to reopen the wounds he'd just tended to, he carried her to the cell and laid her face-down on the mattress. He then proceeded to bind her wrists with shackles similar to mine, linked to a thick, long chain which he attached to the wall. The extra length of chain pooled loosely on the floor by the mattress. He didn't bother shackling her feet, and exited the cell, before locking it.

Our captor stopped in front of me. Examining my injuries, he whistled through his teeth.

"That Braxian sure had it in for you. I've got to give it to you, Magnar. A lesser man would have bled out by now, or would be writhing in agony. Too bad you proved so uncooperative." He glanced at the bloodied bench where Mercy had been tortured before looking back at me. "For your sake, I hope you die before morning. Your friends have terrible plans for you. If you still live come morning, maybe I'll be merciful and put you out of your misery before they arrive. Who knows?"

With a sadistic grin, he cast one last look at Mercy, thankfully lost in the oblivion of sleep, and then turned the lights off as he walked out of the room. Bound and kneeling in the darkness, guilt, pain, fear, and Mercy's shallow breathing my only company, I prayed to the Ancestors to guide me through this time of trial.

And then I started pulling on my restraints to try to rip them out of their moorings. Despite the slim odds, few men were as strong and as determined as I.

CHAPTER 17
MERCY

I emerged from a haunted dream only to reenter a nightmare. The softness of the mattress beneath me felt obscene compared to the lancing agony of my back and legs. My stomach still quivered from the aftershock of the terrible cramps that had woken me minutes or hours ago, I couldn't tell. With no windows, and the room drowned in darkness, who knew whether it was morning or still night.

The metallic stench of blood filled my nose. From the strength of the smell, it must have been spilled recently. Clenching my teeth through the pain, I shifted to the side to try and sit up. Alerted by the sticky wetness between my thighs, my head jerked towards them. Despite the darkness, my Veredian perfect night vision allowed me to see the mess of blood between my legs.

For a second, I thought I'd been violated while I'd been drugged and unconscious, but quickly dismissed that possibility. First, I didn't feel the kind of soreness linked to intercourse, and second, even if that had been the case, Guldan females didn't tear or bleed from that. As a Veredian, we also didn't have menstrual cycles. Only one thing could ever cause me to have vaginal bleeding.

Nooo!

A pain greater than the one raking my back clawed at my chest, and tears welled in my eyes. My child. My first child whose existence I'd not even been aware of. A keening sound rose from my throat. Heedless of my wounds, I curled up in a ball and wept.

"Mercy. Mercy. Do not cry, my love," Ravik's deep voice said in a gentle whisper. "We will get out of here and make them pay. We'll make them all pay a thousand-fold. Do not cry, my mate. In time, we shall have another, you and I, and as many more as you wish."

His voice seeped through the sea of sorrow I was drowning in.

He knows. He knows what we've lost.

Had his sensitive Braxian sense of smell told him? Had he already known I'd been pregnant?

But even as these questions fired in my head, my anguish and loss slowly shifted to anger and hatred for Lorik and the Fifteen. They had taken too much from my mate and me.

"Ravik," I whispered between two sniffles.

"I'm here, my love. I'm right here," he said, looking at me over his shoulder. He still kneeled on the restraining bench, hands and feet shackled, blood trickling from wounds that should have closed by now. "You must be strong for a little while longer. I need you. We can only make it out together."

He needed me like I needed him. And they needed to die. I embraced the rage and hatred filling my heart.

"They will pay," I said.

Ravik smiled, a savage glint in his eyes.

"They will pay," he repeated.

Muscles bunching and teeth clenching, Ravik pulled on his restraints. I realized then that he'd managed to tear the shackles free from the bench they'd been bolted into, for both his wrists and ankles. My lips parted in shock, awed by the incredible strength it must have required. Blood seeped from his wounds. No wonder they hadn't closed. From this angle, it looked like he could get up from the bench but needed to rip out the rivet that secured his chains to the floor, limiting the range of his movements. From the fissuring around the rivet on the right, he'd been working on it a while and would tear it out soon.

A pair of shackles bound my own wrists—different from the ones on the spanking bench I'd been tortured on. Heart pounding, I pressed my right palm over the metal ring on my left wrist and pushed my psionic power into it, seeking within any type of nanites that could be reprogrammed. I nearly wept when the white noise of their presence manifested itself in both the shackle and the chain. My initial impulse was to command them to unravel the metal, making it crumble but I chose a more discreet approach instead, setting the shackles' locks to open instead.

Slipping my wrists free, I clambered to my feet with a hiss of pain. What didn't hurt felt stiff, or numb. My stomach roiled, and more blood ran down my thighs. I shut it out, refusing to allow myself to sink into anguish. There would be a time to mourn. But first, we needed to survive.

"I can release us," I said.

With stiff steps, each movement pulling on wounds and bruises, I approached the cell's door, my eyes flicking this way and that in search of potential surveillance cameras. To my relief, I didn't see any. That didn't mean there were none, but at this point, we'd take our chances. Sadly, a quick look at the locking mechanism of the cell's door made my heart sink.

"Can you unlock it?" Ravik asked, his voice filled with hope.

I shook my head then realized he couldn't see me in the darkness.

"Not exactly," I said. "Technically, I can, but not without triggering an alarm. It would probably only take me seconds to disable the alarm, but the damage will be done by then." I looked at his restraints, an idea popping in my head. "Can you get your chain close enough for me to touch it?"

"Not yet," he said, shaking his head. "But I should be close to getting this one loose."

"Yes, you are. I can see the cracks all around it."

The look of relief on his face told me how worn out he was. I couldn't even begin to understand how he hadn't collapsed yet judging by the severe whipping he'd endured, the blood loss, and the amount of effort he had exerted so far to get free.

"I'll make this quick," he said, resuming his efforts. Grimacing from the strain, he stifled his grunts to avoid being heard outside the room.

"Let me see if I can make us some weapons," I said, returning to the chains lying near my bed.

I pushed my power into four of the big chain links, ordering the nanites to straighten. That done, I placed the metal sticks they had turned into end-to-end then ordered them to merge. Together, the four pieces had the length of a small dagger. Starting at one of the tips, I issued a command for the nanites to flatten the metal as much as possible. The number of nanites present in the chain being fairly low significantly slowed the process. I might as well have been watching grass grow. Putting it aside, I repeated the process with four more chain links.

Once again, I envied my sister Aleina's kinetic ability. She wouldn't have needed all these steps or suffered from such delays, simply visualizing the object she wanted to create and, in seconds, have her power reshape any inert material accordingly.

However, the ability to change the nature of the material—up to a certain extent—constituted a major upside of my power compared to hers. Once the 'blades' would be ready, we wouldn't be able to hold them for combat without hurting ourselves. The first one having sufficiently flattened, I pushed a 'stop' command so that the nanites wouldn't make it too flimsy. Handling it with care, I carved out a handle from the mattress, inserted the blade into it, and then ordered the nanites inside the handle to harden the material.

Just as I finished pushing the 'stop' command into the second blade, a clang, followed by the rattling sound of chains, startled me.

"You did it!" I breathed out, watching Ravik painfully get up on his feet.

Legs numb from so many hours in that position, weakened by his wounds and blood loss, Ravik put up a good front as he edged towards my cell dragging his chain. He advanced slowly, mostly blind in the darkness.

"Mercy," he whispered. "My beautiful mate."

The reverence and love in his voice brought tears to my eyes. His shackled hand slipped through the bars to caress my cheek. I leaned into his touch. My hand covering his, I pressed his palm even more against my face and closed my eyes, savoring a brief moment of tenderness. I kissed his palm and then pressed mine over the locking mechanism of his shackles. It quickly unlocked. My breath hitched, and my chest constricted, seeing the metal had chafed his skin raw no doubt during his effort to pull the shackles free.

"It's okay, my love. I'm fine," Ravik said.

But he wasn't fine. He had too many bleeding wounds that could be developing infections. If it came to that, he wouldn't be able to fight properly in this condition. I made quick work of unlocking his collar and the shackles around his other wrist and ankles.

"Check the counter to see if Lorik didn't leave the healing cream he used on me," I said, holding his hand, my thumb caressing his knuckles. "Look for painkillers, too."

Ravik nodded. He made as if to leave, hesitated, then drew my face to his for a brief kiss. Awkward though it was through the bars, it comforted me nonetheless. He rummaged for a few moments before finding a work light on the counter, and then returned to me with his hands full.

"There's the cream, but I'm not sure what those hyposprays are" Ravik said, showing them to me. "I can't read them."

Labeled in Guldanese, I had no problem reading them. "This one," I said, picking it up from his hand. "It's a good one, too, and has five shots left."

Raising it to his neck, I injected him with a dose. Ravik closed his eyes, a soft moan rumbling through his chest at the instant relief it gave him. Taking the hypospray from me, he shot a dose in my neck. I made no effort to stifle my own moan of pleasure as the excruciating pain that had been my constant companion immediately started fading.

I took the cream from him and asked him to turn around.

"Based on the clock on the counter, we should have approximately two hours before Lorik returns," Ravik said, complying with my request. "The Fifteen will be here at ten, but finding out you're a

Veredian hybrid has convinced Lorik to double-cross them. He'll come to take you away before then. I suspect it will be around nine, but we should be ready for him as of eight."

"Sounds good," I said, applying some of the cream on him.

He hissed but remained still. We quickly discussed our plan, deciding against him going out of the room to try to get the drop on Lorik. We didn't know if they had cameras outside, and we needed to recuperate as much as possible before the fight. When I finished with his back and arms, he applied a bit more cream on me, then returned everything to its place on the counter.

While I completed our weapons, he explored the room in search of anything else that could be of use. He found a hose, which was probably used to wash the animals formerly incarcerated here. I considered cleaning off the blood covering me but that would give us away when Lorik returned. With one last kiss, I gave Ravik one of the two weapons and we returned to our respective spots, putting back on the unlocked shackles, and rested while waiting for our prey.

The sound of the door opening startled me. Ravik had been wise to expect Lorik to come for me two hours before the Fifteen's agreed upon arrival. A little over thirty minutes ago, we'd both taken one last shot of painkillers before resuming our positions, lying in wait. It had to be only minutes after eight now. If all went well, we'd have plenty of time to escape before the others got here.

"Well, well," Lorik said, with undisguised admiration, "look who's still alive. You Braxians sure are made tough. No wonder you used to be such great warriors."

Turning my head to the side, I observed him through my cell's bars. My heart pounded when he stopped in front of Ravik, giving him a once over. I addressed a silent prayer to the Goddess that he wouldn't notice his shackles were no longer secured. Even if he did, Ravik would easily take him down, but we needed him to open my cell first to avoid triggering any alarm.

"When those idiots you call your people are done with their in-fighting, Guldar will swoop back in and put them all to good use. You were born too early, Magnar Ravik. They're too stupid to understand you were taking them on the right path," Lorik said, pensively. "You deserve better than what those animals have planned for you. When I'm done securing my future wife, if you wish it, I'll grant you mercy with a swift, honorable death."

It didn't surprise me. Guldans respected strength and despised weakness. Hagan's obvious lack of spine had earned him Lorik's contempt.

"I'm touched by your generosity," Ravik said in a growl.

"I aim to please," Lorik said with a smirk.

My pulse picked up further when he moved away from Ravik and towards my cell, but this time, due to anticipation and pre-battle adrenalin.

"I have a present for you, dear wife," Lorik said, waving a pair of gloves in front of him. "I'm still having a hard time believing you have no power, so I had to improvise."

Those weren't the gloves normally imposed on Veredians to stifle their psi ability, not that it would have made any difference. The nanites in the gloves acted as gatekeepers, and nanites were my bitches. No glove had ever worked on me. The only way to block my ability was to deprive me from nanites or any type of software.

I made to rise from the mattress, but he indicated for me to remain still until I had the gloves on. That suited me, reducing the risk of my shackles falling off by accident. At long last, he unlocked the door to my cell and opened it. Lorik took two steps inside and tossed the gloves at me.

"Put these on, quickly," he said.

I picked them up, examined them, and then looked up at him, pretending not to see Ravik's massive silhouette rising behind him.

"Hmm, I don't think so," I said with disdain. "They're not my style."

He recoiled, his eyes widening, first with shock, and then with dread as he finally sensed Ravik's presence behind him. Lorik only managed to turn halfway, his hand never reaching his blaster, before Ravik caught him by the throat. With the same frightening ease he'd shown in the forest, Ravik lifted Lorik with one hand and slammed him on the floor. Although he'd held back, the shock dazed his victim. He removed Lorik's blaster and tossed it at me but found no com device. He then placed the collar he'd worn around the Guldan's neck. He fought back but Ravik backhanded him hard enough to knock out a couple of teeth, and then punched him in the gut, winding him.

Lorik doubled over, gasping for breath, but Ravik yanked his head back so that I could slap my hand on the collar to lock it.

Pulling on the collar, Ravik drew Lorik's face to his, forcing him into a half-sitting position. "I hear you like paddling people. Let's see what's so fun about it."

Ravik dragged him by the collar to the center of the room. I rushed to the counter and picked up the remote to lower one of the chains hanging from the ceiling. He punched Lorik in the gut again when he tried to free himself, and then attached the chain to the collar's hook. I raised the chain back up so that Lorik would need to stand almost on the tip of his toes not to get strangled by the collar.

My mate picked up the paddle and gave it a twirl before looking at Lorik.

"You can't do this," the Guldan pleaded. "You need me to get out of here. This place only responds to digital prints and vocal commands."

I shrugged. "We'll just cut off your hand. Plus, you were right. Every Veredian has powers," I said, waving my own hands before him.

"This is for torturing my mate and killing my child," Ravik said, his voice giving me chills.

Although he *somewhat* held back so as not to instantly kill Lorik, each of Ravik's blows broke—or likely fractured—bones. I'd never considered myself a sadistic person, but in this instance, Lorik screeches of agony sounded like the sweetest music to me. My fingers instinctively reached for my braid, only to find the jagged edges of the short, silver locks brushing against my shoulders. Chest constricting, I forced the sorrow away, and placed my hand over my stomach, letting the hatred fill me again.

Yes, I enjoyed every single shred of his pain.

After fifteen blows or so—I'd lost count—Ravik stopped and tossed the paddle to the ground. He walked up to Lorik who was wheezing and gurgling, blood trickling from his mouth. From the sound, I assumed broken ribs had perforated his lungs. If his one 'good' leg didn't give out, sparing him from dying of suffocation, he'd still drown in his own blood long before the others arrived.

"I guess that was fun after all," Ravik affirmed, inches from Lorik's face. "I could kill you with the next blow, but that would be cruel considering you offered to grant me mercy earlier. While yours would have been to give me a swift death, mine will be to wish you a long life. Enjoy Ravik's mercy, Ambassador."

Equipped with the weapons I had made, Lorik's blaster, and Hagan's whip, we cautiously exited the room into a large hallway, followed by the rattling sound of our former captor's breathing. A series of empty shelves lined the open space right across from the cell room. In the corner, a lift sat with its door open.

"Oh Goddess!" I exclaimed, rushing for it.

It could only go up one floor. I tapped on the console without triggering any reaction.

"What's wrong?" Ravik asked, after I tried a few times in vain.

I placed my palm over it and pushed my power within. My heart sank as I realized Lorik had not just shut it down, he'd completely disabled it. It made sense with Ravik's men crawling all over the top floor. I could probably figure out how to get it going again, but it would take far more time than we could spare.

"It's dead," I said with a heavy sigh. "We need to find that secret exit."

He pinched his lips in frustration but gave me a stiff nod. We returned to the hallway. The left side closed on a dead end, with only a couple of doors on each side, whereas the right side stretched beyond the possible length of the hunter's lodge above.

Desperate for clothes and water, we checked the first couple of rooms on the left: a lab with small animals and animal parts floating in various liquids, and a storage room containing animal food and restraints. I nabbed the taser wand on one of the shelves. Moving to right left side of the hallway, we entered an old office that had been stripped of any equipment. I needed some kind of computer or com device to call for help. The next room turned out to be another empty detention area, this one clearly designed to receive people, with small cots, and shared hygiene rooms.

I thought of using the sink there to clean myself up but decided to keep going. There had to be a proper shower in here… I hoped. The next door opened on a small kitchen facing a large living area. I made a beeline for the replicator on the counter. Top of the line, it contained some of the fanciest recipes available and, thank the Goddess, it was still full. I selected a couple of meals for us and activated the machine, while Ravik rummaged through the cooling unit. He pulled out a couple of cold drinks for us, opened one and extended it to me.

Despite my thirst and hunger, I forced myself not to gulp down its contents. Without a word we headed out of the kitchen while finishing our drinks. Although the food would only take four minutes to prepare, before we settled down to eat, we first needed to make sure the place was secure and, if possible, send out a distress call. The next couple of rooms proved useless, the third one finally revealing a bedroom. Although reasonably spacious and comfortable, it didn't say Varrek to me. A lonely lab coat hung in the otherwise empty closet.

Ravik opened the door next to it, revealing a small hygiene room, complete with shower.

"Go ahead," Ravik said, indicating the room with his head. "Be quick. I'll go check the last couple of rooms in the meantime and come right back."

I hesitated for a second, wondering if it was wise to split up at all. Barely thirty minutes had elapsed since Lorik's arrival. Technically, we still had plenty of time ahead of us but we couldn't be sure. Still, I needed to get all this blood off me, especially between my thighs. Ravik could tell I ached to get clean, but I suspected seeing me in this state was also a painful reminder of what I had endured and of what we had lost.

"Okay," I whispered.

We exchanged a brief kiss, and I hurried into the shower. Even at the lowest setting, the raining water felt punishing on my lacerated back. Despite the pain, I welcomed the cleansing effect, both physical and mental, washing away a hurt that went beyond skin deep. As much as I wanted to linger, I quickly rinsed and stepped out of the shower, less than five minutes after I'd entered. If we survived this—*when* we survived this—I'd have plenty of time for leisure in Ravik's pool.

Halfway through drying myself, Ravik's voice called me out from beyond the door. Excitement, not fear, filled it. Intrigued, I stepped outside while still rubbing the towel over my hair. Fully dressed, a large grin on his face, he held up my Tuurean belt.

"Fuck yeah!"

I all but threw myself in his arms and crushed his lips with a grateful kiss. He grunted as I stupidly closed my arms around his wounded back, relieved that his own hand rested on my nape. Releasing him with a sheepish look, I stepped back and greedily took the belt from him.

"I found the rest of your clothes as well," Ravik said, pointing at them lying on the bed where he'd placed them. "Sadly, I didn't find any com or computer, or that secret exit Lorik talked about."

I reached for my clothes—black leggings and tank top that fit perfectly beneath my armor—my forehead creasing as I frowned at his words.

"It must be hidden," I said, stating the obvious. "If Lorik didn't tamper with it, my armor should be able to detect it. I'll get on it as soon as I'm dressed."

"Okay," Ravik said. "Let's get you fed while it scans. You need the energy."

I wanted to argue, but I did feel weak from hunger and blood loss. "Get started," I said, with a stiff nod. "I'll catch up in a minute. Don't argue," I said, sternly. "You've been bleeding through most of the night and overexerting yourself ripping out your restraints. We've got fifteen crazies coming after us. I'm relying on your strength to get us through this."

Yes, I was playing dirty, but we couldn't afford for him to play tough. From the look on his face, he knew I'd aimed at his sensitive protector chord. Not getting his body in optimal state by feeding it would be a form of neglect.

"Fine," he said with a growl and walked out of the room. I repressed a smile and hurried into my clothes. The thought of donning my armor over my naked body crossed my mind. The suit would automatically see my wounds and try to mend what it could. Being naked would facilitate healing and reduce the irritation of the fabric against my skin. But clothes offered an extra layer of protection if I had to remove my armor.

With my clothes and sandals on, I tied the belt around my waist and activated it. In seconds, the black, celesium suit wrapped around me. As I reached the bedroom door, the visor of my armor finished forming, the computer going online. The warning on the internal display of the visor indicated that Lorik had tried to mess with it but had been unsuccessful in hacking it open. Moments later, the nanites went to work on my wounds. I nearly moaned with relief. It couldn't fully heal me, but their job was to maintain the body in as functional and healthy a manner as possible, especially in a combat situation.

On my way to the kitchen, I performed a wide range scan. Once again, it didn't detect the presence of another floor. I would need to find out what technology was so efficiently fooling my scanner. Aside from Ravik, it also didn't detect the presence of any other lifeform in the vicinity.

I took from the replicator one of the two freshly prepared meals Ravik had made while waiting for me. He'd already wolfed down one of the now cold or lukewarm plates I'd prepared earlier and was starting on the second one. I didn't hide my smile this time. He'd been starving but would have endured through it. However, it made no sense not to fuel up considering we still hadn't found a way out and my suit would be doing the search for us while we ate.

I set the computer to scan every com frequency to try to reach one of our allies. But the same dampening field that prevented me from seeing the floor above us blocked my attempts to communicate with the outside world. At the same time, it analyzed the structure of the basement. After a few minutes, it revealed two flimsier sections that could correspond to doorways. One matched the location of the lift. The other matched the dead-end on the left side of the corridor, near the cell room.

"Got it," I said, breaking the silence otherwise only disturbed by us making quick work of our food.

"Let's go," Ravik said, swallowing his last mouthful.

I armed myself with my makeshift blade, secured Lorik's blaster to the right side of my belt and the taser wand to the left. Ravik held the other dagger I'd made, as well as the whip Hagan had used on us. As we reached the end wall of the corridor, I ran my palm over it, pushing in my power. It took mere moments to find the hidden switch. I didn't need my power to activate it, but without my suit to narrow down its general location, we probably never would have found it.

The entire back wall slid open, revealing a wide corridor which stretched far into the distance. My stomach knotted. I still couldn't see any incoming threat on my scan, but there would be no hiding if they entered the other end before we made it out.

We went in at a slow jog, my suit helping numb the pain from my wounds. I cast a furtive glance at Ravik, his face a pure mask of savage determination. Hurt or not, I felt sorry for any man who would face his wrath. After nearly fifteen minutes, I thanked the Goddess when my radar finally indicated a lift ahead. I couldn't believe they wouldn't have set up some kind of fast transportation to exit that tunnel, considering its length. We must have missed it on our way out.

As I still couldn't detect anything above us, we had no idea what we would be facing. From the distance we'd crossed, it had to be somewhere deep within the forest behind the hunter's lodge. I reached for the switch, but Ravik's massive hand on my wrist stopped me. Surprised, I looked up at him. The intensity of the emotion in his eyes melted my insides.

"I love you, Mercy," he said, drawing me into his arms. "If we survive this day, I would have you as my Dagna, if you would have me as your husband."

I wrapped my arms around him and looked at him with adoration. We still had our problems, but if this nightmare had taught me anything, it was that I'd fight Gharah himself to be with this man.

"I love you, too, Ravik. I am yours, and you are mine, now and always."

He smiled and kissed me, pouring all his feelings into the far too brief moment of intimacy. However, as soon as he released me, a severe expression took over any sign of tenderness. I braced, already knowing I wouldn't like his next words.

"If things go bad, promise me you will run for safety," Ravik said. "I need to know you will make it."

"You know I won't," I said, giving him the 'are you shitting me?' look. "Don't even waste your time arguing with me about this," I continued when he opened his mouth to insist. "You are my soulmate, Ravik. Do you expect me to go on living, knowing that I just ran off and left the other half of me to be massacred by our enemies? We stand or fall together, Ravik Xeldar. But if you want me to lie to you, I can."

"Mercy…" Ravik pleaded.

I covered his lips with my fingers. "There's no time for this. You know I won't leave, anyway. Your son asked me once if I would stand by you. The answer is yes."

"Keran?" he asked, stunned.

I nodded. "You raised a fine heir."

Without giving him time to respond, I pressed the button, and the platform lift took off. As soon as it began the short ride up, a panel opened above us, letting in the morning light of the sun. I set the long-range scan to run in a continuous loop. It showed nothing until we cleared the edges of the shaft. My com immediately went online and my radar, silent up to now, showed a couple of cloaked shuttles nearby and eighteen men closing in on our location.

"Incoming," I said as we both stepped off the platform.

It immediately flew back down the shaft, a thick metal panel closing over it and a second one with dirt and grass sliding seamlessly back on top.

As suspected, we had emerged in the middle of the forest. The thick trees could hide us from view, but if they ran a scanner, it would give away Ravik's presence. My suit's camouflage would keep me undetectable. While we ran for cover, I opened a com link to Krygor.

"Ravena?" he asked, answering within seconds of my system establishing the connection.

"We're in the woods, about one kilometer radius from the cabin, due north," I said without preamble. Typing frantically on the armband of my suit—that had also gone online once we'd cleared the shaft—I sent him the coordinates. "Hostiles incoming. Hagan is leading them."

"Krygor?" Ravik asked.

I nodded.

"Boros warned us something was going down with Hagan rallying the Fifteen," Krygor said through the com. "We're less than fifteen minutes away. Stay safe."

"Hurry." I ended the com then turned to Ravik. "Fifteen minutes max."

What a strangely coincidental number.

We exchanged a look, both coming down to the same conclusion: we could hold until help arrived. Their blood was ours.

Taking cover behind one of the giant trees, the trunk at least two meters in diameter, I activated my suit's disrupting field, which I hoped was strong enough to prevent any scanners they might use from detecting Ravik's presence.

Less than three minutes later, angry voices reached us. My hearing, enhanced by my suit, allowed me to distinguish their words clearly.

"For the hundredth time, Hagan, what is the meaning of this?" Raylor Caldes asked, his irritation unmistakable. "We have the Guldan spies. Let's just take them back to Ravik's Hall and end this."

"There's another. And I have a surprise for you all," Hagan said, sounding smug.

A few knowing laughs hailed his comment.

"And what surprise would that be that should interest the remaining

Fifteen and the Magnar's most vocal detractors?" Boros asked, blatant hostility in his voice.

Hidden by my armor's cloak, I leaned to the side to have a look at the men as they closed the distance to our location. Three Braxians I didn't know had blasters trained on three shackled Guldans who appeared to have been fairly roughed up.

"Something that will solve all of our problems, once and for all," Hagan snapped. "I will not sit by, idly waiting to be taken out by a madman!"

"Wait, what?" Raylor asked. "I thought we were here to capture the last Guldan spy. What's going on?"

Hagan stopped next to a dark rock and pressed his foot on the grass in a specific pattern. Seconds later, the ground parted, and the lift platform appeared.

"What is that? Where does it lead?" Raylor asked again, the tension steadily rising in his voice.

"The hunter's lodge," Hagan said, in a hard voice. "You know damn well what's going on."

"Oh no! No, no, no!" Raylor said, backing away. "Have you lost your mind? You touch that female, and you will bring civil war upon us. Do you have any idea what the Magnar will do to you and your clan?"

"You are a fool, Hagan," Boros said. "Take these Guldans to Ravik to earn his favor, and forget all this madness. Whatever your feelings towards him, both he and his female have done good for Braxia."

"How?" Hagan yelled. "By emasculating us and putting our females to work? He's making us weak. Braxians are warriors! That Guldan whore has him so enthralled he's only thinking with his cock. He learned nothing from the past and impregnated her. It is time we remind him of the ways of Braxia and end his reign."

"Ancestors!" Boros whispered, looking at the men around him. "Fifteen Braxians. You've brought us here to repeat that abomination from all those years ago. You are insane! I will have no part in this!"

"Nor I," said Niklas Colben, coming to stand by Boros.

"Nor I," said Raylor, joining them.

"He will kill you both!" Hagan shouted, pointing at Boros and Niklas. "You were part of the Fifteen. And you, Raylor, he's had your first born flayed over a fucking half-breed. Have you no pride? Have you no honor?"

"I lost a son because of his own stupidity!" Raylor yelled. "He almost brought down my entire clan with him. Whatever my personal feelings about the Magnar, I am no traitor to Braxia. This is treason!"

I cast a shocked glance towards Ravik who stared at the tree trunk as if he could see the men through it, seething rage on his face.

"It is too late to wimp out now," Yorbek said, one of the Fifteen, aiming a blaster at the three. "You're here now, and you're going to help us see this through. What his inner circle has hidden from everyone is that the Magnar and his whore are both our prisoners. Why do you think Pattel and Krygor suddenly cancelled all of his engagements?"

"She's all prepped and ready for our cocks," Hagan said in a sadistic tone. "And I can tell you firsthand that she doesn't need Denax to take a Braxian. So get down there now."

"I don't think so," Ravik said, stepping from behind the tree.

"I don't think so either," I said, deactivating my cloak.

"Impossible!" Hagan breathed out.

And then chaos reigned.

Yorbek turned his blaster towards us, but I shot him first with my own blaster, set to stun. He wouldn't get off that easy. He would suffer as he had intended for both Ravik and I to suffer—more even. Boros, Niklas, and Raylor threw themselves at three of the other Braxians. The Guldans tried to escape, causing the right diversion for me to stun their guards.

With a battle roar, Ravik charged our enemies. Fear kept a few of them paralyzed for a moment and then they jumped into action. Unlike the day of the hunt, they had not brought swords. While I had no qualms using the blaster and my makeshift blade, Ravik went in with his bare fists. The first man shifted his head to the right, avoiding the blow only for Ravik's other fist to land solidly in his gut. It hit him with such force he was lifted off his feet. He doubled over and Ravik brought down an elbow hard on the back of his neck, raising the other one to block an attack from another man. He kicked the second man hard in the chest, making him fly backwards. Turning back to the first man, he grabbed him by the neck, lifted him up with one hand, and slammed the back of his head on the ground. Dazed, he tried to get back up but never had a chance; Ravik's foot stomped down hard on his face. Even through the loud noise of battle, the sickening crunching sound resonated loud and clear. The man's body jerked violently before going still.

The second man charged Ravik again, who met his attack head on. Hagan tried to seize the opportunity to attack him from behind. Racing forward, I threw my makeshift dagger at him. It embedded itself in the meaty area below his shoulder. Hagan yelled and lost his momentum. He stumbled back away from Ravik while trying to remove the blade which remained out of his grasp. I reached him just as he started turning towards me. I backhanded him, my strength increased by the armor. His head jerked to the right, and then he screamed, his entire body seizing as I jammed the taser wand into his gut at maximum intensity. I pulled away the wand and yanked the blade from his shoulder. He cried out and swung his arm at me. I ducked and tased him again, but this time in the balls. Hagan started doubling over but I head-butted him, my horns cracking the bones of his prominent brows. He stumbled back and I slashed the blade across his stomach, enough to make him bleed, but not deep enough to kill.

An incoming Braxian forced me to step away from my prey. Unlike Hagan, this one was truly a warrior and put me on the defensive. Too fast for me to get a hit in, and too strong for me to sustain any of his blows without breaking, I kept dodging and backing away, seeking an opening that would give me the advantage. It came in the form of Ravik's whip wrapping around the man's neck and yanking him back. Or rather, my beast took over from there, bashing the man's face into a pulp, his victim's blows glancing off him seemingly without effect.

I turned back to see Hagan running off just as the sound of Krygor's approaching shuttle joined the chorus of battle.

"Ravik!" I yelled, extending a hand towards him.

Needing no more to guess I wanted the whip, he tossed it in my direction before resuming bashing on his helpless opponent. The wet spots on his back indicated his wounds had reopened, but it didn't seem to trouble him. I caught the whip mid-air and then chased after Hagan. The ground suddenly rushed towards me. Yorbek, having recovered from the stun, tripped me as I ran past him. I fell hard with an oomph. Rolling on my back, I raised the taser wand just in time to zap him as his massive hands reached for me. He shouted then slapped it out of my hand, hard enough that I feared for a second that he'd broken my fingers. Grabbing my dagger, I slashed at his face. He screamed and recoiled as the blade cut across his nose and cheek. Scrambling to my feet, I pushed a command inside the nanites of the makeshift weapon and threw it at him. He tried to avoid it but the improvised weapon found its mark, sinking into his side. Boros tackling him to the ground spared me from further delay in hunting down Hagan.

That son of Gharah was mine.

Ignoring Yorbek's tortured scream, I gave chase again. Boros would have no trouble with Yorbek as the blade would soon finish him anyway. The metal was reshaping itself to spread inside his body as tendrils the size of needles, piercing their way through organs and tissue.

From the corner of my eye, I saw Krygor's shuttle land, but didn't stop. Despite his significant head start, Hagan didn't have the speed of a Veredian. Arms and legs pumping, I quickly closed the distance between us, grateful for the painkiller and the healing nanites of my suit that kept me going. To my greatest pleasure, I sensed a large presence of basic nanites in the whip, a type often used to help soften leather or as part of the products used to treat it. An evil plan formed in my mind as I shot Hagan with the blaster adjusted to the lowest stun setting; I didn't want him unconscious, just slowed down a little, thanks to the stun setting of Guldan blasters being weak against Braxians.

Hagan stumbled, barely managing to keep himself from face-planting, then screeched when the whip licked his back. He turned around, his eyes wide with fear and pain. Anger descended upon his feature once he realized I—a female—was attacking him. He stepped towards me but I stunned him again, following up with three quick lashes which I didn't hold back, almost every blow tearing skin. He covered his face and tried to come at me, but I repeated the process of stun and whiplashes, counting his lashes out loud, until he fell to his knees.

By the thirtieth, Elder Pattel, Clan Leader Fenton, and a mix of their men surrounded us, none of them interfering. I no longer bothered with the blaster as I circled around Hagan, making sure every inch of his body felt my wrath. Ignoring the burn in my arm and the exhaustion seeping in, I carried out his punishment until it met fifty lashes. Breathing heavily, I stared with hatred at the back of the bloody mess kneeling before me.

With the battle clearly over, more men gathered around us, bearing witness in silence. My eyes locked with the beloved face of my beast. The same merciless flame that burned within me raged in his gaze.

Marching towards Hagan, I wrapped the whip around his waist and arms, letting the handle hang over his shoulder. Heedless of the confused looks of the Braxians, and the tortured whimpers from the traitor, I pushed a command into the nanites of the whip. Standing next to Hagan while the nanites tightened around him, I faced the men observing us.

Glad that I'd decided to wear my clothing beneath my armor after all, I deactivated the latter, revealing the wounds from the lashing I'd received as well as my Veredian markings. I lifted my chin in defiance at the surprised gasps.

"Yes. I am a Veredian-Guldan hybrid—a half breed as some of you like to say," I said, with a hard voice. "I will no longer hide my true nature for fear of narrow-minded people hunting me because of what the Goddess made me. I will no longer suffer being bullied or threatened for the right to live or to be free because of what I am—for the right to love my soulmate," I added, my gaze resting on Ravik.

The pride in his face further energized me.

"If you have a problem with my presence, learn to suck it up, because only one person has the power or the right to send me away, and that's him," I said, pointing a finger at my mate, who puffed his chest. "Don't fuck with a Veredian. We may look sweet and delicate, but when it comes to our survival, we don't play. The next one who thinks to come at me, this will be nothing in comparison to what will befall you," I said, waving at Hagan. "I have only one mercy, and that's my name."

Right on cue, his groans of pain turned to strangled screams as the whip tightening on him cut off his circulation and squeezed his bones to the verge of breaking point. Soon, they would cave in, and he would be crushed to death as the nanites continued, endlessly, their effort to close as much as possible. The men cast a horrified look as the bones of one of Hagan's arms broke, and then eyed me warily.

"Your Dagna has spoken," Ravik said, before approaching.

"Hail the Dagna!" Krygor shouted.

"Hail the Dagna," the men repeated, slapping their chests with their fist.

Taking me by the hand, Ravik led us back to the small clearing where the shuttles of our allies had landed, leaving Hagan to his agonizing death.

EPILOGUE
RAVIK

In the three weeks that followed, I sat in judgment of far more trials than I cared to. Only three of the fifteen men that had come to the secret entrance had refused to join this treason—three men I would have once labeled my enemies. Of the remaining twelve, nine of them had not even been part of the original Fifteen. Their greed and resentment against the changes I was making to Braxia had been their downfall. Only four of those twelve had survived the battle. For their swift and exemplary punishment, I'd personally flayed them alive before having them nailed to a pillar outside their respective clan compounds to meet a slow death. There they would remain to rot for a full month.

In the meantime, all twelve clans came groveling for mercy. But each had to prove they held no prior knowledge of their Clan Leader's intentions. Nine of the clans were spared. After I passed a judgement of Shunning on the remaining three, the clansmen from two of those clans banished the members that had been involved or been aware of the plot before pleading for leniency. Although I lifted the Shunning— which effectively meant the death of a clan with no one trading, dealing, or speaking with them—the stigma on their name would remain for a long while.

Mercy sat by my side throughout the trials and for every ruling. Some of the conservatives balked at a female's presence but kept their mumbling to a minimum. My woman had earned the respect and loyalty of my people. She'd first earned her place with those trade deals she'd negotiated for many of our clans in the direst need, and then cemented it with her display of strength, combat skill, and the ruthless savagery she'd dealt to those who crossed her. Hagan's mangled remains, his bones shattered by the shrinking whip, had been put on display at the entrance of his compound, a reminder to all who dared to cross her that retribution would be swift and unforgiving.

Mercy became Braxia's first new Dagna in nearly 150 years, my father and grandfather having both been content to sire their heir on concubines—as I had before meeting her. And she held the role with pride and dignity. As much as Braxians had rejected hybrids, finding out their Dagna was one of the rarest Veredians alive made them rally further behind her. She could have the world at her feet but chose us. My people now considered her a national treasure, the jewel of Braxia. Any attack or threat against her would be construed as an affront against all of us.

To think I had feared revealing her true nature.

To both Mercy's and my relief, Gorav and my bodyguards came out of this unscathed, aside from their wounded pride over their failure to keep us from getting kidnapped and tortured.

The three Guldans that had been held captive by Hagan were hobbled and dumped in the joarkal hunting territory for daring to aid Lorik in his attempted kidnapping of my mate. They'd merely been mercenaries hired by the Guldan Ambassador for his personal purpose. But while the Guldan Empire had no direct involvement in this, they had orchestrated the previous attack against us. We therefore sent a formal message to Emperor Ardrak that a full embargo had been set against any Guldan. No trade and no citizen of their home world would be allowed on Braxia. He tried to flex his muscles, threatening retaliation against us, only to have the Tuurean military leader, Admiral Lee, warn them that any attack on Braxia would be deemed an attack against them.

My Dagna had some powerful allies, and that, too, raised her prestige among our people. Granted, we didn't have a full alliance with the Tuureans as they would only intervene in the case of a war with Guldar. However, I intended to nurture that relationship until it equaled, or even rivaled, the one they entertained with the Xelixians.

It would take two more weeks after the trials before Mercy agreed for us to have our wedding. Despite my personal physician doing miracles healing both our wounds, leaving no scars on her, and barely noticeable ones on me, the loss of her braid had struck her hard. I didn't fully understand its importance, but her hair was growing back, and we had returned it to its original raven color. Yet, she felt bare and exposed without it, not to mention crippled in that it played an important defensive and offensive role in combat.

Mercy had taken to tying her hair in a bun to 'hide' how short it now was, refusing to wear a wig or extensions. But Braxian weddings, although expedited, required both mates to stand barefoot and naked except for a diaphanous robe, no jewelry or adornment, and no fancy hairdo. We'd exchanged our vows on the plaza before the Elders and the people, after which each Clan Leader took turns pledging loyalty and protection to the Dagna. A banquet followed with lots of drinking. To my dismay, Mercy warned me that she expected us to have a proper Veredian wedding the day we visited her family on Xelix Prime. It involved some extensive form of tribal dance to be performed by the bride and groom, as well as their guests.

I shuddered at the thought.

We held the fair two weeks after our wedding, Anton coming through for us above and beyond expectations. I didn't doubt that the news of the Veredian Dagna brought even more people, if only out of curiosity. Nevertheless, many more of our goods, previously perceived as useless by us, stirred the interest of buyers and new deals were struck. But Braxia's economy still had a long way to go, with many clans struggling. However, with more and more clans getting back on their feet thanks to these new trades, the burden on the Emergency Fund to support the others while they found their way, diminished significantly.

The first Braxian shop opened on Venus Hive. Despite its resounding success and the absurdly high prices people were willing to pay for our *useless* goods, it quickly became obvious that our males couldn't run that shop, not understanding the craft or the appeal of those pretty, luxury items or beauty products. To Mercy's dismay, Braxian fathers and mates refused to let their daughters go live and work on a pleasure barge. While I understood her anger, I would never admit that I, too, would have refused to let any daughter of mine go there without a full contingent to look after her.

Yeah, I still had a long way to go with this equality thing.

Finally, it was agreed to send Celia, Clan Leader Colpen's half-breed daughter. A pretty little thing, she'd been quite abused before I abolished the laws making slaves and half-breed females free-for-all. To his credit, Niklas had made his best efforts to send her away on various tasks whenever he had guests coming to his compound, but by law, even his clansmen could make use of her as they pleased. Now in her late thirties, although still beautiful, no man would take her as a concubine or wife, even with the changing mentalities, for she'd been too extensively used. Venus Hive gave her a chance at a new beginning, while still aiding the home world.

Mercy became a stout defender and protector of the hybrid females, providing them with employment in her new lab, and education to give them a chance at a better future. Although she struggled with the idea of being 'shackled' to Braxia, she decided to move the headquarters of her research center here, actually buying extensive lands near the Keltrix Market to build the facility, as well as a small residential area for the staff who would join. On top of a generous salary increase, as an added incentive, employees who relocated here would have a free home built and decorated to their specifications—although based on predetermined templates to respect Braxian architecture.

While Braxians eyed this sudden influx of foreigners with a certain amount of wariness, they welcomed the financial benefits with so much construction work to be done, from basic infrastructure, to roads, and everything else in-between. More importantly, some of the research projects Mercy intended to run were drawing the interest of some of the most brilliant minds in the galaxy. Right behind them, many investors wanted first dibs at the development licenses for some of her most revolutionary patents.

Sometimes, I almost felt ashamed by the tremendous help my mate had been. Without her, I doubted my reforms could have blossomed the way they currently were without bloodshed. Thanks to Mercy's wonderful insight about the women's craft, and now with her research center, she'd brought early proof to my people of the viability of my changes.

Still, we needed to pace ourselves. The men still struggled with their females working and contributing to their respective clan's income. Finding out Mercy was planning some basic combat training for the women proved too much for the men to handle. I walked into our bedroom, bracing for what I knew would be a heated conversation, only to find her already waiting for me, arms crossed, a mulish expression on her face. I groaned inwardly, and my shoulders slumped.

"Woman, don't…"

"Don't woman me!" Mercy said in a hard voice. "This is not open for debate."

"Mercy, you know I'm an advocate for change, but you can't just flip everything on its head overnight and not expect people to balk," I argued running my fingers through my hair. "The men have made plenty of concessions. Give them time to adjust before you demand more from them."

"It has nothing to do with them!" Mercy snapped back. "Why do men always have to make everything about themselves?"

"Because we are insecure idiots, and we need our females to coddle us otherwise we break. And when we do, it's excessive and ugly," I said, slowly approaching her.

She snorted. "THAT's your justification?"

"It's not a justification, merely facts," I said with a shrug. "Don't you think I deal with the same headache every time I—"

A subtle, unusual scent stopped me dead in my tracks. My nostrils flared as I inhaled deeply, parsing what struck me as an abnormal combination. Understanding finally dawned on me. My chest constricted at the same time my heart soared.

"What's wrong," Mercy asked, a look of confusion on her beautiful face.

"There will be no more fighting or training for you," I growled closing the distance between us. "I forbid it."

"You *forbid* it?" she exclaimed, outraged.

I didn't respond. Dropping to my knees before her, I pressed my nose to her stomach and inhaled deeply. Joy and wonder coursed through me as I received confirmation of my assumption.

Mercy gasped, her fingers slipping hesitantly through my hair. "Ravik?" she asked, her voice uncertain.

"My mate," I whispered rubbing my face against her flat stomach, before looking up at my woman. Her chin trembled as she gazed at me. "Twins," I said, in response to her unspoken question plainly written on her features.

Rising to my feet, I pulled her into my embrace. One hand still in my hair, Mercy slipped the other between us to lay her palm on her stomach.

"You... You can smell it?" she asked.

I nodded. "Yes. In the days following the first month of pregnancy, a pureblood is able to recognize the change in scent. You're at least four or five weeks in, and you're carrying a pair, boy and girl. That threw me off at first. Boys smell woodsy, while girls smell spicy. The mixed scent confused me. Braxians don't have twins."

"Twins," she whispered, rubbing her stomach with an air of wonder.

I kissed her. She returned it with fervor, full of love and tenderness, and then we rested our foreheads against each other's. Mercy wrapped both hands around my back, holding me tight. Moments later, I felt her mood shift.

"These twins, I will not fail. Promise me, we'll keep them safe," she said, looking back at me, a haunted look in her eyes.

"Nothing and no one will harm these children," I said with savage conviction. But just as I spoke those words, I realized she was thinking about more than what Lorik had done to our previous child. "You did not fail your sisters, my love. You may not have found your brother's clients list, but you *will* find your sisters. Your father promised your mother as much. In due time, when your Goddess wills it, you will be reunited." I caressed her horns before cupping her face in my hands. "The Fates never meant for you to find that list. They sent you here to find me, to save me, and to save Braxia."

"And for you to save me," she said, looking at me with adoration. "For Braxia to free me, and finally let me be Mercy."

I caressed her hair that had grown a few more inches in the three months since that terrible ordeal.

"I love you, Mercy," I said, my heart full to bursting.

"I love you, too, my beast," she said before burying her face in my neck.

"I mean it," I said after a beat. "No more fighting for you until they're born."

She stiffened and pulled back to glare at me. I smiled, a little smug. Mercy grimaced, the urge to do something unpleasant to me plain to see.

"I'm so going to kick your ass when it's done," she said.

"Bring it on, my love. Bring it on," I said before kissing her again.

MERCY

Ravik had not been kidding when he said Braxians could smell pregnancies. You would think a switch had been flicked on as that very morning, no one had paid me any mind. But that evening, for last meal, every Braxian who got a whiff of me first had the same confused expression plastered on their faces before it turned to shock and disbelief. Ravik preened and swaggered at having his superior virility thus confirmed by being the first Braxian to have planted twins in a woman's womb. I could have kicked him.

A few days later, I received a vidcom from my baby sister Aleina who had just delivered her first-born son. Naturally, she wanted to know when I'd be coming back to Xelix Prime to introduce my husband to the rest of the family and meet my new nephew. In my response, I revealed my own pregnancy. As expected, she demanded I return home at once so the Veredian healers could keep an eye on the health of the babies and me. When I politely declined, she threatened to get on one of her battlecruisers and bring me back kicking and screaming if needed.

So much for me being the oldest sibling…

Although I agreed with no more combat training for me, it annoyed me to no end that he would put his foot down about it. Anyway, the women took care of that, going into protective overdrive with me. They wouldn't allow me any type of exertion, strictly watched how many hours I worked, and ensured I ate properly. Even that damn racer Dajia wouldn't cut me some slack. Just like the Braxians, one whiff sufficed for her to know my condition. While she allowed me to ride her for the following four weeks, she refused to go at anything faster than a walk. Whenever I tried to urge her on, she'd knock on my horns with her tail.

At the end of those four weeks, the middle of my second month, she refused to let me ride her at all. I still visited her, though, or she'd throw hissy fits for being neglected.

By the third month, I stopped complaining about being mothered by all the females. My baby bump had swollen overnight. I couldn't see my toes anymore, even when stretching my neck to look over my stomach. My feet and ankles kept swelling, a discomfort only relieved by the wondrous creams made by the fishermen's wives of Clan Podek.

By the fourth month, regret at not obeying my sister's demands started settling in. My belly had grown to the size of a small moon. Working was no longer possible. Standing or even walking around for more than a few minutes proved too much for my back. I would never admit it, but as the fifth month creeped in on me, the underlying fear the Braxian females tried to hide from me echoed my own. Braxian babies were massive, thus the absence of multiple pregnancies. With my smaller frame, worry that I wouldn't carry them to term gnawed at me.

Despite his brave front, Ravik's face, too, showed concern for both the children and me when he thought I wasn't watching him. Thankfully, Veredian pregnancies only lasted six months. In the first week of the fifth one, a Tuurean ship landed on Braxia, bringing my mother and her mate, Dr. Minh. I blubbered all over her, relief and joy mixing in equal measure. I didn't know whether to kiss or punch my mate for keeping her impending arrival a secret from me. With her being one of the most powerful Veredian healers alive, and her mate being the top medical doctor from Xelix Prime who had helped solve the Veredian infertility issues, I no longer feared for the welfare of my babies, or myself.

The Tuurean presence further increased my prestige and, by extension, Ravik's standing. That Admiral Lee's second in command, Kamala, personally escorted my mother spoke volumes about the esteem the Tuureans held me in. Sexy as hell, covered from head to toe in her celesium armor, and her face covered by a shiny, black visor, Kamala was sex on legs. Despite her synthetic voice, she had every man drooling and speculating about her and the Tuurean race as a whole. I knew what hid beneath that armor, but it wasn't my secret to share… not even with my mate. I hated keeping things from him, but soon enough, all would be revealed.

Mother naturally freaked out at finding my hair so short. She berated me for being ashamed of it once I gave her the watered-down version of what had happened. And then, she berated me some more for not letting them know how serious things had gotten here, and for not asking the Tuureans and Xelixians for help.

Why did the whole world want to baby me?

Using her powers, she had my hair back to its original length in no time—which made me cry again—and then proceeded to fully heal the lingering scars that marred Ravik's back from the savage whipping Hagan had given him. This pregnancy had turned me into quite the crybaby. However, the awed expression on Mother's face every time she eyed the mountain of a man that was my husband always made me giggle.

In the three weeks leading up to me delivering the children, Minh took great interest in the healing creams and ointments the Braxian females were making, going so far as to spend time in my lab to perform some enhancements. His work served both his insatiable curiosity and passion for medical science, but also his paternal need to help me by aiding my new people. Although he wasn't my father, Minh had adopted me as his daughter—like he had my younger sister Aleina—the day he married my mother. While no one could ever take my real father's place in my heart, I liked Minh and was grateful Mother had found happiness again.

Or rather, real happiness.

When the babies finally decided the time had come, Mother, Kamala, and I lost our shit when Ravik thought to wait it out with his men in his Hall. Too bad I missed the proper dressing down Kamala gave him when she went to fetch him. The Braxian females screamed in outrage at the sight of a man entering a birthing chamber. If I hadn't been so busy pushing and screaming, I would have rolled my eyes.

I'd never seen my beast as distraught as he approached the birthing bed. He seemed at a complete loss and utterly anguished by my pain.

"I am helpless to aid you," he whispered when I stopped pushing, looking ashamed and vulnerable.

Holding on tightly to his hand, I peered at his beloved face. "We made these babies together, let's bring them into this world together. You can't take away my pain, but you can lend me your strength through it, like you've done once before."

An emotion I couldn't put a name to crossed his features, and then something seemed to fall into place for him. Ravik passed his strong arm behind my back, supporting me, and his other hand held mine. For the next eternity until our twins entered this world, through every push, through every pained scream, Ravik's warmth surrounded me, his rumbling voice whispering words of love and encouragement. Together, we delivered our twins.

I couldn't believe the gigantic size of the babies that came out of me. And yet, when Mother handed them over to their father after cleaning them, in his hands, they looked tiny. My firstborn was a gorgeous little girl, with a delicately-shaped Braxian nose, raven-colored hair like both of us, and Veredian markings. Unlike me, they didn't brand her as belonging to the Warrior breed but to the Scholars. She wouldn't have my physical skills for combat, but she would possess an innate ability to acquire knowledge in all its forms. Science, math, and technology would be child's play to her. To my chagrin, she didn't inherit my horns, therefore preventing her from ever claiming any Guldan heritage according to Guldar's current laws.

My second-born, a beautiful boy with silver white hair similar to my late brother Varrek's, thick, black horns like mine, a broad and flat Braxian nose, but no Veredian markings. Although, I didn't say it out loud, that broke my heart. Until that instant, I hadn't realized how strongly I identified as Veredian far more than as Guldan. As far as I knew, no Veredian had ever given birth to a child without markings. Did that mean he wouldn't have any powers either?

Still, my heart filled with love for my two little miracles.

After she was done cleaning me, Mother kissed my forehead, and then those of each of my children. Turning to Ravik, she caressed his cheek and then signaled for Thala—who had been assisting her—and Kamala to leave the room with her. Once alone, Ravik kissed my lips and then caressed the heads of our babies.

"Name your children, woman," Ravik said, his voice made even more gravelly by emotion.

He held our daughter to me, her obsidian eyes locked with mine as if she knew the importance of this moment.

"I name you Lissy, Lissy Xeldar," I said, caressing my daughter's markings. I smiled at Ravik's sharp intake of breath. "Your namesake set your father on the path to becoming a man I could love." I turned my gaze towards him. "A man I do love with all my heart." Facing my daughter again, I continued, "From this day forward, through you, the name Lissy will be a synonym for love, joy, new beginnings, and the ability to embrace change for the better."

"I love you," Ravik said, kissing me before I could answer.

Taking our daughter from me, he cradled her in his right arm, and gave me our son.

"I name you Garruk Vrok, after my father and brother," I said, caressing my son's horns.

Ravik recoiled, his strong brow creasing, making him look even more menacing than usual.

"Vrok?" Ravik said, his outrage unmistakable. "That's my son. His last name shall be Xeldar."

I shook my head, totally unfazed. "You already have your heir. This one is mine to continue my father's bloodline."

"He can still continue your father's bloodline with my name," Ravik said, his face taking on a mulish expression.

I rolled my eyes before looking at him. "Don't be silly, big boy. Anyway, everyone can see he's your blood, and females name children. The sire has no say."

"By Intergalactic Law, maybe, but not by ours. He must bear my name," Ravik said. "I insist."

Sighing in exasperation, I rolled my eyes again, itching to kick his butt. I'd known from the start he would push back—and couldn't actually blame him either. In his shoes, I'd probably feel the same. That didn't change the fact that my son would bear my father's name.

"Fine," I said, glaring at him with false anger before turning to our son. "Since your father is such a crybaby, I name you Garruk Xeldar Vrok, heir to the Vrok Empire."

"But—"

"No buts! He has your name, too. Push me on this, and I'll remove it altogether," I warned.

Ravik grimaced and muttered something about abusing gender rights, which only made me giggle.

"Stop your fussing, silly man. Give me more sons, and they can bear only your last name," I said before rubbing my nose against our son's. His yellowish-brown eyes, speckled with green, identical to my mother's, looked at me with wonder, and his lips stretched in a toothless smile.

"Rest assured that I will, woman," Ravik mumbled.

His massive hand gently caressed Garruk's head, his thumb running over the sharp little horns. Propping Lissy next to her brother, Ravik wrapped his arms around the three of us.

"On Venus Hive, you found a nearly broken man and made him and his failing world whole again," Ravik said. "As long as I draw breath, no one will ever harm our children or you, my Dagna, my love, my Mercy."

THE END.

ALSO BY REGINE ABEL

THE VEREDIAN CHRONICLES
Escaping Fate
Blind Fate
Raising Amalia
Twist of Fate
Hands of Fate
Defying Fate

BRAXIANS
Anton's Grace
Ravik's Mercy
Krygor's Hope

XIAN WARRIORS
Doom
Legion
Raven
Bane
Chaos
Varnog
Reaper
Wrath
Xenon
Nevrik
Rogue

PRIME MATING AGENCY
I Married A Lizardman
I Married A Naga
I Married A Birdman
I Married A Minotaur
I Married Wonjin

I Married A Merman
I Married A Dragon
I Married A Beast
I Married A Dryad

THE MIST
The Mistwalker
The Nightmare

DARK TALES
Bluebeard's Curse
The Hunchback

BLOOD MAIDENS OF KARTHIA
Claiming Thalia

VALOS OF SONHADRA
Unfrozen
Iced

EMPATHS OF LYRIA
An Alien For Christmas

THE SHADOW REALMS
Dark Swan

OTHER
True As Steel
Alien Awakening
Heart of Stone

ABOUT REGINE

USA Today bestselling author Regine Abel is a fantasy, paranormal and sci-fi junkie. Anything with a bit of magic, a touch of the unusual, and a lot of romance will have her jumping for joy. Hot alien warriors meeting no-nonsense, kick-ass heroines give her warm fuzzies.

Before devoting herself as a full-time writer, Regine had surrendered to the other passion in her life: video games! As a professional Game Designer and Creative Director, her previous career had led her from her home in Canada to the US and various countries in Europe and Asia.

Facebook
https://www.facebook.com/regine.abel.author/

Website
https://regineabel.com

Regine's Rebels Reader Group
https://www.facebook.com/groups/ReginesRebels/

Newsletter

http://smarturl.it/RA_Newsletter

Goodreads

http://smarturl.it/RA_Goodreads

Bookbub

https://www.bookbub.com/profile/regine-abel

Amazon

http://smarturl.it/AuthorAMS